Also by J. C. Pollock

GOERING'S LIST

LIST

J. C. Pollock

A DELL BOOK

Published by
Dell Publishing
a division of
Bantam Doubleday Dell Publishing Group, Inc.
1540 Broadway
New York, New York 10036

ISBN 0-440-20519-0

Reprinted by arrangement with Delacorte Press

Printed in the United States of America

Published simultaneously in Canada

December 1995

10 9 8 7 6 5 4 3 2

OPM

« 1 »

GERMANY—MAY 17, 1992

THE OLD MAN was tired. He had been traveling most of the day when he boarded the train from Munich to Berchtesgaden for the final leg of his journey. He was alone in the compartment, and as the train pulled out of the station he rested his head against the back of the seat and let the gentle rhythm of the rails ease the tension and weariness from his body.

Just a few more days was all he asked. And as though in response to his silent plea, the pain in his left arm subsided, and his breathing became less shallow and strained by the time the train skirted the dark blue waters of the Chiemsee and continued on toward Traunstein, where the rail route turned south, into the first foothills of the Bavarian Alps.

"La neige éternelle," the old man whispered at the sight of the distant peaks still glistening with snow, surprised that he recalled the poetic phrase from what little remained of his schoolboy French.

His face was a mask of quiet resignation as his hands rested on the worn and cracked leather portfolio he held in his lap. His fingers moved across a burr on the surface of the hide, just above the brass clasp, where he had long ago removed the SS runes embossed there and had rubbed in shoe polish to conceal the telltale scar. It was a tactile memory, and his thoughts

went even deeper into the past. In his mind's eye, he saw th
proud, young cadet at the SS officers' school at Flint Kasern
in Bad Tölz, when the portfolio, its fine leather then smoot
and glossy and new, carried his course work to class. He coul
almost feel again the velvety soft evening air after a warr
autumn day, and hear the chorus of young, strong voices r
peating the oath at the graduation ceremony in the quadrangl

> *I swear to you, Adolf Hitler, as Führer and Reich Char*
> *cellor, loyalty and bravery. I vow to you, and those yo*
> *have named to command me, obedience unto death. S*
> *help me God.*

It all seemed a lifetime ago, and it was. A life in which h
had been a twenty-eight-year-old major, *Sturmbannführer de*
Waffen SS, Heinz Dieter Strasser. A decorated war her
wounded in battle on the eastern front, and in deference to
shattered knee, assigned, for the duration of the war, to th
honor guard battalion hand-picked from the ranks of the S
Leibstandarte Adolf Hitler Panzer Division to provide securit
for the leaders of the Reich in their mountain retreat on th
Obersalzberg.

For the past forty-seven years he had lived in Erfurt, in wha
had been East Germany, never once traveling outside its bor
ders. He had led the simple, uncomplicated life of an electr
cian under yet another totalitarian regime, one with little us
for former Nazis; and he had managed to keep his SS past
secret, buried along with the uniform discarded at the war'
end, when he joined the tide of refugees that inundated th
German countryside as he made his way back to his wife.

His son, Jurgen, was born thirty-seven years ago, just whe
he and his wife had come to accept that it was not meant f
them to have children. The handsome child had been an unex
pected blessing, but a blessing that was somewhat diminishe

as he grew into a headstrong, disrespectful, and rebellious youth; but then he was of the new generation of Germans. After finishing his studies at the university, his son's visits home became sporadic and all too infrequent. A distance had grown between them, and in the past seven years Jurgen had not been home at all. There had been no telephone calls, not even an answer to a father's letter telling their only child that his mother had died, only a brief note when the East German government fell, giving a post office box in Frankfurt where he could now be contacted.

Strasser knew only that his son had been with the Ministry of State Security—the dreaded Stasi—but not exactly what he did. He often feared that something might have happened to him; perhaps he was doing dangerous work or had been arrested for his activities when the reunification came. But when the letter he sent three weeks ago, telling him of his illness and asking to see him for a brief, important reunion, was answered with another curt response and precise instructions, saying that he would do his best to be at the Obersalzberg on the chosen date, his worst fears were alleviated.

As the train clattered on through a narrow mountain pass, Strasser glanced down at the portfolio in his lap. For years, afraid that somehow he might place his family in danger, he'd never had the courage to put its contents to use, to test his theory of its importance and value. But perhaps it might still serve a purpose, to help his son establish himself with the intelligence service in the reunited Germany. It was all that he had to give him.

The compartment was suddenly cast into darkness as the train entered a tunnel, then once again filled with the late afternoon sun as it emerged and slowed to a stop at a station that brought another rush of memories. The small alpine village of Berchtesgaden was much as Strasser remembered it, a timeless place, enclosed on three sides by towering peaks that

rose sharply from deep pine forests covering the lower elevations. The village was more crowded and commercial than
when he had last seen it, but its essential character and unri-
valed natural beauty were still intact.

Each step took Strasser deeper into his past as he walked the
short distance from the train station to the post office and
boarded a tourist bus for the ride up a steep, winding mountain
road, a thousand feet above the valley floor, to the top of the
Obersalzberg. He got off the bus where the public access road
ended and left his fellow passengers, who would continue on
yet another bus, to the top of the Kehlstein over a hair-raising
road that was carved out of solid rock, and had taken two
thousand Czech and Italian laborers more than three years to
build. It was an engineering marvel that included three tunnels
and an elevator shaft, hewn out of the mountain itself, that
carried visitors the last four hundred feet to the summit and
the fortresslike teahouse built for Hitler, later called the Eagle's Nest by the American troops who first entered the area in
1945.

The memories became more intense as Strasser continued
on to his final destination, a few hundred yards back down the
mountain from where he had gotten off the bus. He was at first
disoriented—nothing was as he remembered it—but then it
had been forty-seven years since he had last been there. April
25, 1945, he thought, to be exact. He had vivid recollections of
that bright, sunny day when the air raid sirens sounded at 9:30
A.M., and he and the other SS guards had run from Goering's
luxurious chalet. They had escorted the reich marshal, now
under house arrest for treason by Hitler's order of the previous
day, down into the bowels of the underground system of tunnels and bunkers, equipped with iron doors, blast walls, and
gas locks, to escape the devastating barrage that followed.

The first of the one-thousand-pound bombs from the British
Lancaster bombers of 617 Squadron fell shortly after ten

o'clock. The second wave, using Tallboy bombs, began thirty minutes later. The raid lasted just over an hour, raining tons of high explosives onto the private mountain retreat of the Nazi hierarchy. Only six people had been killed and less than a dozen wounded out of the more than two thousand sheltered belowground. Goering, the only high-ranking Nazi in residence that day, had not been injured, but the devastating bombardment had reduced his home, and the rest of the buildings in the compound, to barely recognizable ruins.

The day after the bombing raid the SS commander made a decision not to defend the ruined compound. He released those of his men who wanted to fend for themselves and fled south with the remainder of his troops. The following day, with Goering and his family in custody, they crossed the nearby border into Austria. Strasser had stayed behind and remained in the area for another week, hiding in a small hut in the woods near Berchtesgaden while searching for the railroad cars containing part of Goering's looted art treasures. He found them, hidden safe from air raids, in the tunnel near the railroad station.

He finally left on the afternoon of May 4, upon sighting an advance element of the American Seventh Infantry Division as they entered the small mountain town. He was traveling on foot, and had no place to conceal the things he had taken from the looted treasures in the train cars. Fearing he would be shot if caught with them in his possession, he reluctantly left behind the heavy, cumbersome gold icons and jewel-encrusted daggers and chalices he had carefully selected. He kept only a few gold coins, concealed in the lining of his greatcoat, and, stuffed into his leather portfolio, the sheaf of documents that had piqued his interest.

The old man was now overwhelmed with memories vying for attention in his conscious thoughts. The simple act of remembering, of dwelling on the past, and his proximity to where these events had all occurred, caused a subconscious physical transformation in him as he walked slowly back down the mountain. The grade was steep, but he squared his shoulders and pulled himself to his full height. A slight spring even returned to his step, until his left knee, now painfully arthritic, reminded him that he was no longer the young man who had kept a brisk pace ten yards behind the Führer as he hiked the trails around the Obersalzberg.

He slowed to a more natural stride and kept to the edge of the road, pausing occasionally when he thought he recognized a particular part of the terrain. But he was only guessing. Gone were any traces of the chalets of Hitler, Bormann, Goebbels, and Goering. In 1952, the bombed-out ruins on the sites where the houses had once stood had been demolished under order of the Americans—symbolically blown up on the exact day that Hitler had committed suicide, even to the precise hour when his body had been burned seven years earlier in Berlin. The ground was then bulldozed and replanted to prevent the area from becoming a shrine to the defeated Nazis. All that remained of the once-grand mountain homes were scattered sections of foundation stone occasionally visible on the floor of the dense forest of larch and pine that now covered the area.

A few hundred yards from where he had gotten off the bus, Strasser stopped at the foot of a driveway leading to a small mountain inn, and another powerful wave of memories swept over him. The Gasthof Zum Turken—a smoldering ruin when he had last seen it, its walls still standing but the roof blown off and the inside gutted by fire—looked exactly as it did forty-seven years ago before the bombs had fallen, when it had served as Gestapo headquarters for the Obersalzberg area. He had not known what to expect when, to his surprise, he had seen it listed in the guidebook and had telephoned for reservations. But he had not expected to find it rebuilt to look precisely the way it had during the war.

As Strasser approached the front entrance, he noticed two

tour buses in the small parking lot, and a line of tourists near the rear of the inn. He walked over to where the people were queued and found that they were waiting to buy tickets to enter part of the remaining system of underground tunnels and bunkers that had once connected Gestapo headquarters at the Zum Turken to Hitler's chalet and the other principal buildings throughout the compound.

Returning to the front of the inn, Strasser found the door locked and a sign instructing visitors that entrance was barred to all but registered guests. The owner, Frau Graber, who answered the buzzer, apologized for the inconvenience and explained that it was a necessary precaution to deter the tourists visiting the tunnels from constantly asking to use the rest rooms.

"You are Herr Bauer?" the middle-aged woman said, as she stepped aside to let him in. "I hope your journey was pleasant."

"Yes, very pleasant," Strasser replied after a brief hesitation. He had almost forgotten that, as his son had instructed, he had made reservations for two rooms using his wife's maiden name. His son's note had been explicit: travel by train, register under mother's maiden name using a false home address, and pay in cash. Strasser had complied, not considering it an unusual request, in light of his son's profession.

The old man stood transfixed for a few moments, his eyes moving slowly over the interior of the inn. The reconstruction was remarkably faithful to the original building as he remembered it. The Gestapo had changed nothing during their occupancy, using the rooms much as they had served in their former capacity, and it was all hauntingly familiar to him.

Frau Graber studied her newly arrived guest closely. He was tall, unbent by age. A shock of once blond, now silver hair was combed straight back from a high forehead, and dark blue eyes set off strong features still handsome in spite of his advanced years. As the granddaughter of the original proprietor, who had built the inn in 1913 and was later forced to sell it to the Nazis, as were the other landowners on the Obersalzberg, Frau Graber had fought a legal battle with the Bavarian state government to regain possession of the property after the war. She now lived there during the tourist season and had personally managed the inn for the past twenty-five years. In that time, she had seen others like "Herr Bauer," all older men with the same distant look, come to pay homage to the past. A past they preferred not to acknowledge, she had observed on more than one occasion.

"This way, please," Frau Graber said, and led Strasser to a counter in the kitchen area that served as a registration desk, where he filled out a card in the name of Bauer, giving an address in Munich.

She handed him two keys. "One is for the front door, the other is your room key," she said. "Please lock the front door each time you leave and enter . . . the day tourists," she reminded him again, adding a disapproving frown.

"My son will be joining me sometime this evening," Strasser said.

"This early in the season, you will be our only guests. I have assigned him the room next to yours."

"Fine," Strasser said, as he peered into a small room off the kitchen area. He recalled that it had been the office of the Gestapo commandant—a squat stump of a man with a volatile temper and eyes like a pig. "I think I will unpack, then perhaps go for a walk."

"Would you like to purchase one of our tourist maps showing the historic sites nearby?"

"I believe I can find my way around."

"As you wish." The knowing smile appeared again. "We serve breakfast only, from seven until nine o'clock. When your son arrives I can direct you to a number of restaurants in town for lunch and dinner.''

"Thank you," Strasser said, and looked into the small dining room across the corridor as he turned to leave. He had once eaten lunch there, while meeting with the Gestapo to coordinate special security arrangements for Hitler's arrival for the Christmas holidays in 1943.

As Strasser walked down the hall and slowly took the steps to the second floor, Frau Graber noticed that his overnight bag was of a cheap synthetic fabric, probably East German in origin. The same was also true of his clothing, she thought, but not the worn leather portfolio he kept tucked under his arm.

STRASSER TRIED TO take a brief nap before the arrival of his son, but his physical presence in the old, historic inn had the discomfiting, almost mystical, effect of transporting him back in time. Once again he heard the echo of jackboots in the hallways and the shouting of sharp commands. A particularly unnerving memory sent a chill through him and drew him abruptly out of his half sleep: on one of his visits to the then Gestapo headquarters, he had heard a series of horrific screams arise from a basement room. He later learned that a Czech slave laborer was being tortured to find out who his accomplices were in a minor rebellion against the brutal working conditions suffered by those building the road to the teahouse. To clear his head of the unwelcome images, Strasser stepped outside onto the small balcony off his second-floor room, and stared out across the sloping forest to the distant mountain peaks, now edged in crimson from the setting sun.

It was early evening when he finally left his room. He walked down the hill and stopped after only fifty yards, where what had once been a driveway branched off the main mountain road and cut into the woods. Only a small section of the old blacktop surface remained. Pitted and crumbling, it ended in thick brush after ten or fifteen feet. But Strasser knew what it was—the former entrance drive to Hitler's Berghof. He had marched along it numerous times during his two years spent with the guard battalion. Earlier, while standing on the balcony, using the inn as a point of reference, he had little difficulty spotting the remnants of the driveway and orienting his memories of the area to the present-day lay of the land. He recalled that the Führer's house had been diagonally below the Zum Turken and approximately one hundred yards into what had once been alpine meadow, and was now dense woods.

He knew it was unwise to exert himself, better to return to the inn and rest until Jurgen arrived, but the old, familiar haunts drew him farther in search of the past. Ignoring a sign that warned of danger from sinkholes, Strasser climbed over a small brush pile and entered the forest, now deep in evening shadows, and followed a well-worn trail, used over the years by other curiosity seekers. The trail rose gently, but he began to perspire, and at the same time felt chilled by the evening air. A shortness of breath caused him to pause and rest, and he turned up the collar of his hiking parka against a cool mountain breeze that rattled the emerging leaves in a stand of larch trees.

He sat quietly on the forest floor, slowly scanning the surrounding area as a wave of dizziness came and went. His gaze stopped at what was clearly a section of a stone wall, something his old eyes had first missed in the failing light. The smooth stones were partially covered with moss and vines, but Strasser recognized them immediately as part of the garage wall, once located directly beneath the broad expanse of terrace at the front of Hitler's chalet.

Other long-forgotten memories came rushing back: exhaust fumes from the automobiles entering and leaving the huge garage often drifted up over the terrace and into the living room when the massive picture window overlooking the mountains was open. The design flaw was a constant sore point with the Führer, and countless attempts were made, unsuccessfully, to correct it.

As Strasser got to his feet to examine the wall closer, a brief vignette flashed through his mind: a crisp October morning when he and a squad of his men had reported to the Berghof to accompany the Führer on a hike. He had seen Eva Braun, dressed in shorts and a halter, practicing her gymnastics on a parallel bar set up on the terrace. She had smiled at him, and he had smiled back.

The pleasant image faded as Strasser reached the section of the garage wall and knelt to touch the damp, cold stones. He then stood and began to turn slowly in a circle, pausing briefly as he faced in various directions, until he determined precisely where the Berghof had been. Directly above him, on his left, was a large, unnatural mound covered with low brush and trees that he soon realized had been formed by the rubble from the demolished house.

A narrow footpath branched off the trail he had followed. It led up a steep embankment to the top of the mound. He started up the path, gripping branches to aid in the climb, when a sudden, sharp pain in his chest made him grunt forcefully and drop to his knees. He began to slide back down the path, and grabbed hold of a small sapling, which briefly slowed his descent before breaking. The terrible pain increased as he rolled onto his back and continued to slide, digging in the heels of his hiking boots in an effort to stop. And then the final, crushing blow struck with an excruciating pain that stunned and immobilized him. His heart, as the doctor had warned him it would, had failed.

In the few moments it took to slide the rest of the way down the embankment, Heinz Dieter Strasser died, only a few feet from where he had once proudly stood near the pinnacle of Nazi power.

* * *

THE AMERICAN ARMY sergeant and his wife of three days, taking
a break between passionate bouts of honeymoon lovemaking,
had left the General Walker Hotel on the Obersalzberg for an
evening run through the woods. His wife, who was setting the
pace, jogged ahead on the trail and almost tripped over
Strasser's body. The resulting scream brought her husband
immediately to her side.

The body was still warm when the sergeant knelt and placed
the fingertips of his right hand on the neck, feeling for a pulse.
He looked up at his young wife and slowly shook his head.

"Is he an American from the hotel?" she asked.

Her husband patted the outside cargo pockets of the old
man's parka and found the keys with the wooden identification
tags from the Zum Turken.

"Looks like he's staying at that place out on the main
road."

"Is there anything you can do for him?"

"I don't know. Run back to the hotel and call an ambulance. I'll try CPR on him," the sergeant said, "but I'm pretty
sure he's a goner."

« 2 »

JURGEN STRASSER TRUSTED no one, not even his own father. It was a mind-set that was an intrinsic part of his nature, reinforced by years of training and experience with the East German Stasi. The letter from his father had conveyed a sense of urgency, and Strasser's only concern was that it was in some way connected to a threat to his own security, perhaps the exposure of his past and his true identity. It would have never occurred to him, or even interested him, that his father simply wanted to meet with him for personal reasons—a dying man wishing to see his son one last time.

When he left Frankfurt that morning driving a gray Audi coupe, he conducted a thoroughly professional counter-surveillance effort that would have detected and evaded anyone long before his intended direction of travel became clear. He took a circuitous route, occasionally doubling back and making periodic stops, and outside of Stuttgart, he pulled into a restaurant just off the autobahn and changed clothes in a rest room stall. He also removed his expertly applied false beard and wig and horn-rimmed eyeglasses, and fifteen minutes later, bearing no resemblance to the man who had entered the restaurant, he left through the kitchen exit. He found the black BMW sedan where he had instructed a colleague to park it behind the building, and drove away, leaving the car in which he had arrived to be picked up later.

He avoided the autobahn, where it was relatively simple to position surveillance cars, well out of sight and in radio contact, both ahead of and behind a target vehicle. Instead, after heading south, he followed the scenic German Alpine Route east, through southern Bavaria. The arrow winding roads, with many secondary tracks branching off in all directions into remote mountain valleys and tiny villages, made it necessary for anyone tailing him to stay so close that even an amateur would have had no difficulty spotting them.

He reached Berchtesgaden two hours before the train from Munich was due, and parked in the lot at the rear of the station. The location he chose allowed him an unobstructed view of the platform where the passengers emerged, the departure point for the tourist buses to the Obersalzberg, and the parking lot's entrance and exit. He remained in the car, chain-smoking and studying the general rhythm of the place, and saw no increased activity and no one positioning themselves to conduct a surveillance prior to the train's arrival.

With no emotion other than vague suspicion, he had watched his father get off the train and walk to the adjacent post office where he boarded a bus. No one leaving the train had followed him or reacted in any discernible way to his arrival. There had been no disruption in the normal ebb and flow of the immediate area, nothing out of sync that would have alerted someone of Jurgen Strasser's background in covert operations that his visit had been compromised and his father was being used as a decoy to lure him into a trap.

The local cop, who used the train station parking lot as a turnaround on his routine rounds, had twice passed by the black BMW. Once, with a bored cop's disinterest, he had glanced in the direction of the man sitting behind the wheel, immediately dismissing him as someone waiting to pick up an incoming passenger. He had no way of knowing that the intense, watchful eyes—eyes that never left him until he drove out of sight—belonged to a man who, with the slightest real or imagined provocation, would have killed him in an instant. Nor did he have any reason to suspect that the man's hand was at that very moment resting on the grip of a submachine gun mounted under the dash of the BMW.

Any attempt to confront Jurgen Strasser by anything less than a trained counter-terrorist team would have ended in disaster. Someone approaching from the rear and off to the side of the vehicle, as experienced police officers always did, would have been in for yet another unpleasant and lethal surprise. Concealed inside the driver's-side door panel was a sawed-off, double-barreled twelve-gauge shotgun, the barrels flush with a hole cut into the trailing edge of the door. One end of a trip wire was attached under the dashboard and the other to the weapon's trigger, allowing the driver to open the door and, using the side-view mirror for sighting, accurately fire the shotgun without turning around or getting out of the car. Strasser had designed and installed the deadly device himself, and had found its use necessary on only one occasion. It had worked as intended, killing an American military policeman who had stopped him for a routine check as he made his escape from the Rhein-Main Air Force Base near Frankfurt, Germany, after planting a bomb in the post exchange.

The local cop in Berchtesgaden would have been even more astonished to learn that the man he had so readily dismissed as inconsequential was known to every counter-terrorist organization in the world as "Dieter." None of them knew his true name, or what he looked like, such were his ability to assume false identities and his chameleon-like powers of disguise and deception. They knew only that he was a capable, audacious, and violent adversary, infinitely more dangerous because of his ability to train people, plan operations, and select sensitive targets.

With seven years' experience in training terrorists for the East German Ministry of State Security, Jurgen Strasser had earned that sinister reputation. He had brought the latest technology to their arsenals while serving as the senior instructor at Massow, the Stasi's secret training camp twenty-five miles south of Berlin. Until it was abandoned, when the East German government fell, the thickly wooded, twelve-thousand-acre compound was without equal in teaching terrorists their lethal craft, and a perfect location for organizing and planning operations, then slipping into the West by passing through a then-divided Berlin.

Strasser had operated on his own since the demise of the Ministry of State Security, his efforts directed toward rebuilding the Red Army Faction, the once-feared and Stasi-supported West German terrorist organization. The ranks of the RAF had been decimated when an irate mob of East German citizens, in the early days of the revolution, had taken over the Stasi's East Berlin headquarters. The tentacles of the huge state security agency had been long and numerous, with eighty-five thousand full-time workers and over one hundred thousand paid informants keeping files on more than four million of their own citizens as well as two million West Germans. The files were of enormous interest to Western intelligence agencies, and consequently the mob that took over Stasi headquarters was infiltrated by West German and American agents in search of information that would expose Stasi officers and agents and their terrorist surrogates operating in the West. The Red Army Faction files had been among those that ended up in the hands of the American and West German counter-terrorist organizations.

Strasser had seen it coming, and two days before the headquarters was sacked, he had gone to East Berlin and taken steps to secure his future. In the confusion and chaos of rats fleeing a sinking ship, he had gained access to the archives and found and destroyed his hard-copy files. He then bullied one of the personnel clerks into erasing his entire computer file, including the backup disk, thereby effectively eliminating any bureaucratic traces of his ever having worked for the Stasi and of his assignment to Massow. His base of operations for the past two years had been a small farm in the German countryside, south of Baden-Baden. Purchased by a third party, an RAF supporter, it was isolated and remote, and filled his need for a planning and training site.

After leaving the train station parking lot, Strasser made a slow, careful sweep of the town. He had not eaten since breakfast, and stopped for an early dinner, sitting at a table where he could watch the street and the nearby central square. It was dark by the time he drove up the steep mountain road to the top of the Obersalzberg. Halfway there, he had to swerve onto the soft shoulder to avoid a police car that swung wide as it rounded a hairpin turn.

He slowed as he approached the driveway to the Zum Turken, noticing that only two cars were parked in the lot, near the rear of the building, probably belonging to the manager and an employee, he reasoned. Though the appearance of the police car could have been attributed to any number of innocuous reasons, it put him on edge. He drove past the small mountain inn without stopping, and continued on to the turnaround at the entrance to the private road leading to the Kehlstein. The area was completely deserted; the ticket office and the souvenir concession and snack bar were closed until morning. No one had followed him up the mountain, and no other cars appeared during the fifteen minutes he remained parked there in the night shadows, watching the road and smoking.

It was just before nine o'clock when he drove back down to the Zum Turken and rang the buzzer. The woman who an-

swered the door had a strange look on her face. A worrie
look. Strasser's instincts told him something wasn't right. Sh
held eye contact too long for a complete stranger. He unzippe
his leather jacket, letting it hang open, to allow him quic
access to the nine-millimeter Sig Sauer semiautomatic pistc
tucked into the waistband of his trousers at the small of hi
back.

Frau Graber had immediately noticed the family resem
blance in the man standing before her. He was tall and lanky
with an athletic build that suggested raw physical strength
The skin tone was different and the hair darker, thick an
wavy, and the features more finely boned, though he was jus
as strikingly handsome as his father must have been at tha
age. But it was the deep-set dark blue eyes, somewhat menac
ing and unfathomable, and the intensity that generated from
them that left no doubt in her mind.

"Herr Bauer?" she said, her voice filled with a genuin
sadness at having to inform a son of his father's death.

"Yes," Strasser said, his own voice deceptively calm as h
stepped farther into the dimly lit entrance hall. His eye
quickly scanned the dark corners and hallway shadows, watch
ing for any sudden movement and ready to respond to the firs
hint of a threat with an explosive violence that had served him
well throughout his career.

"I'm afraid something terrible has happened."

"What is it?"

"I'm sorry to have to tell you, but your father has suffered a
heart attack . . . he was pronounced dead when the ambu
lance arrived."

Frau Graber was puzzled by what she thought was an ex
pression of relief on the man's face, but dismissed it as a
manifestation of shock or grief.

Strasser remained silent for a few moments, fitting the police car into the picture. When he spoke his voice was devoid of emotion. ''Where are my father's belongings?''

''I believe they are in his room,'' Frau Graber said, taken aback by the indifferent response.

''Have the police gone through them?''

''No. They only asked who your father was, and I gave them his name and address from the registration card.''

''May I have the room key please.'' It was not a question.

''Of course.'' Frau Graber led him to the registration counter near the kitchen and gave him the key. ''The chief of police in Berchtesgaden has asked me to inform you on your arrival that he would appreciate it if you would contact him . . . to identify your father and make proper arrangements.''

Strasser simply nodded. ''Where is my father's room?''

''At the top of the stairs on the right, at the end of the hallway.''

Strasser turned and disappeared up the steps to the second floor, taking his carry-on flight bag with him. The upstairs hall was lit with only one small wall lamp that cast long shadows in the direction of the room. Still wary, his hand gripped the pistol at the small of his back as he walked the length of the darkened hallway and opened the door. A table lamp had been left on, and Strasser quickly determined that the room was empty before crossing to where an overnight bag and a leather portfolio lay on the bed.

He sat on the edge of the bed and opened the overnight bag, first removing his father's wallet and the East German identity papers that since reunification were no longer valid or necessary. He continued to search for any documents, personal papers, or receipts that could be used to establish his father's identity. He found only his return train ticket to Erfurt, and removed that, too, placing it with the others in his own bag.

When he dumped the contents of the leather portfolio on the bed, a light clinking of metal drew his attention. He picked up what appeared to be a military decoration, and upon close examination realized it was a Knight's Cross with oak leaves, one of the highest decorations for bravery given by Hitler's Germany. There were two other decorations emblazoned with the *Waffen SS* death's head insignia, one Strasser recognized as an SS medal for combating partisans who had infiltrated behind the German lines. His father had never spoken to him about what he had done during the war, always fending off any questions with some self-deprecating remark about how he was nothing more than an ordinary foot soldier. Now he knew why.

Strasser next turned his attention to a yellowed and dog-eared file folder. Inside, affixed with discolored and mildewed brass paper fasteners, was what appeared to be a series of reports on business transactions conducted in Switzerland during the war years on behalf of the Nazi Reich Marshal Hermann Goering. There were faint water stains on some of the documents and all of them bore the reich marshal's seal. Strasser skimmed the contents of the file, intrigued; but, unsure of what they were, he decided to study them later.

Eager to get away from the area without confronting an inquisitive local police chief, he slipped the file and the medals back into the portfolio, then placed it in his carry-on bag. He made a quick sweep of the room for anything else that could identify his father, and finding nothing, went back downstairs, where he found Frau Graber sitting in the small lounge off the entrance hall.

"I have a favor to ask of you," Strasser said.

"Yes, of course. If I can be of any help."

Strasser handed her an envelope into which he had placed ten thousand deutsche marks from the cache of five times that amount he always kept with him.

"This should provide for a proper burial for my father," he said. "Give it to a local undertaker of your choosing."

"You are not going to pay your last respects to your father?"

"My father is dead. A show of respect is a display for the living. I have neither the time nor the inclination."

Frau Graber was shocked by the callousness of Strasser's remarks. "But the police need you to identify the . . . body," she said delicately. "You should at least telephone them . . . and there is the matter of a final resting place for your father."

"Have him cremated."

Frau Graber's temper flared. "I must insist that you handle these matters yourself, Herr Bauer. It is not my place or my responsibility."

"Good evening," was all Strasser said in reply, and left before the stunned woman could say another word.

As he drove back down the mountain, Strasser's thoughts were of the father he had never known. He had never imagined him as anything other than an electrician, an ordinary man without aspirations. A lumpen proletariat. Someone who had led a dull, uneventful life, once caught up in a war he had wanted no part of. But recalling what he had read of the SS in his schoolbooks as a boy, there was little doubt left in Strasser's mind that his father had been anything but ordinary to have qualified for, and been decorated by, such an elite fighting unit.

Strasser looked down at the passenger seat, where he had placed the leather portfolio, and wondered what his father had in mind in bringing it with him. Did he know he was dying? Was he simply planning to reveal his past to his son? An old man's reconciliation. What was it his letter had said? "I have something important to give you," or was it "tell you"? He could not remember now. But what possible relevance could documents that were almost fifty years old have today? And why had his father kept them all these years?

It was just past ten o'clock when Strasser left the secondary road north of Bad Reichenhall and pulled onto the autobahn. He felt more secure on the main artery under the cover of darkness, and headed west, toward Munich. The traffic was light, but he kept to a comfortable speed and stayed in the far-right lane as he turned on the overhead map light. The mystery of the old documents had fired his imagination. He reached over and removed the file from the leather portfolio and began to read as he drove.

« 3 »

It HAD TAKEN Hans Becker, the Berchtesgaden chief of police, less than thirty minutes to learn that the Munich address the heart attack victim on the Obersalzberg had registered under at the Zum Turken was false. It turned out to be a tobacco shop just off the Marienplatz, run by a Moroccan immigrant. The actions of the son, as reported to Becker by Frau Graber an hour ago, had further intrigued him, and led him to suspect that the old man may have registered under a false name as well. He had subsequently sent one of his men to pick up the victim's possessions, and was informed that the contents of the overnight bag had been rifled and anything that could have established Heinz Bauer's true identity had been removed.

It was shortly before midnight and Becker was still in his office. He was usually at home no later than eight o'clock, drinking his self-imposed limit of three beers, then sitting down to dinner with his wife and teenage daughter, thoroughly bored after another day of minor traffic accidents, petty thefts, and an occasional disturbance of the peace. But today, the old man's death on the Obersalzberg had already provided him an opportunity to use the fax machine and the computer terminal that accessed the national criminal center data base, and appeared to be something that might require a thorough investigation.

Becker was sitting at his desk composing an inquiry to Interpol and the Bavarian State Police, a request for a name search for anyone using the alias of Heinz Bauer, when the telephone rang. It was one of the staff doctors at the local hospital, the same doctor, who was almost as old as the mysterious Herr Bauer, who had conducted the initial examination and concluded that there were no indications of foul play.

"One of our technicians in the morgue has found something I believe you should see," the doctor said. "It may help you in uncovering the true identity of the heart attack victim."

Becker had called the doctor earlier, after learning of the false registration at the Zum Turken. He had told him he was coming back to the hospital to get a full set of fingerprints to send along with his inquiries to Interpol and the state police. He took a fingerprinting kit with him and left the station immediately, feeling more enthusiastic about his profession than he had in months. He arrived at the town's small general hospital ten minutes later and went directly to the room in the basement that served as the morgue.

The doctor was waiting, and motioned for him to approach the stainless steel gurney against the wall at the far end of the room. He pulled the sheet covering the old man's body down to waist level and raised the left arm.

"Do you recognize this?" he asked Becker. He pointed to a faded and nearly illegible tattoo on the pale, withered skin on the under side of the upper arm.

Becker leaned in closer and squinted. He was able to make out what he thought were two jagged lines, vaguely resembling lightning bolts, followed by a six-digit number.

"No. What is it?"

"A relic from the past," the doctor said. "A revealing one. The two marks preceding the numbers are characters once used by the Germanic tribes of pre-Christian Europe. They are part of the runic alphabet.''

"I don't understand," Becker said. "Are you saying it has something to do with a religious cult?''

"Not in this case. These specific characters were known as the sieg rune and were symbolic of victory," he continued, pointing to the marks under the old man's arm. "Two sieg runes side by side were the insignia of Hitler's SS, usually the *Waffen SS*. You are familiar with the *Waffen SS*?''

"An elite fighting unit," Becker said, recalling what he had read about them. "Responsible for wartime atrocities.''

"Yes, but also a military brotherhood, as opposed to the political branch of the SS. And if memory serves, they were the only ones who had their service numbers tattooed on their bodies . . . on the inside of their upper left arms, as you see here.''

Becker took a notebook and pen from his uniform pocket and drew the SS insignia and copied down the six-digit number.

"I'll send this along to Interpol and the state police with his fingerprints.''

"I suggest you send the SS serial number to the Berlin Documents Center," the doctor said. "It is the central repository for Nazi records. They are the only ones who have an extensive archive of old SS military service files.''

THE COLD SPRING rain that started just south of Munich had changed to a fine mist by the time Jurgen Strasser pulled into a service plaza off the Munich-to-Nuremberg autobahn and stopped next to a telephone booth. He was excited by what he had read in the old file from his father's portfolio. Not only did he grasp its significance and potential value, but he was already formulating a rudimentary plan of action to put it to use.

The timing could not have been better. His funds were running low, and he was badly in need of money, a great deal of money, to support his existing network and to finance the ambitious operations he was planning. One month after the fall of East Germany, he had contacted the few remaining members of the Red Army Faction not compromised by the captured Stasi files, and easily assumed leadership of their fractured organization. He then recruited the best of his former instructors from Massow who had not fled to the terrorist training bases in Libya and Lebanon, and in less than a year had transformed what had once been a disorganized group of mindless murderers into a cohesive unit with a global reach. After severing their alliances with other European-based terrorist groups, for reasons of operational security, he set up a network of safe houses across the European continent, Great Britain, and the United States, using only new recruits as safe house keepers, preferably young female students with no history of involvement with the radical left or terrorists.

His financial problems were caused by the autonomy of his organization, and his adamant refusal to allow others to control his operations, an attitude that angered the Arab terrorist groups and those who sponsored them. His dire need of operating funds, however, did not alter his convictions about letting others dictate which targets he should hit, or about revealing details of his plans in advance—a stance that had caused the most recent rift between him and his Arab benefactors and the cutoff of what little funding they were still providing.

Upon realizing the magnitude of what the documents in his father's portfolio revealed had taken place between 1940 and 1945, came the further realization that having them in his possession could mean the end of his money problems. Those involved—Americans, Frenchmen, Englishmen, Italians, Spaniards, and Swiss, all wealthy, prominent families, he imagined—had had to be fully aware of what and with whom they were dealing. The evidence was undeniable. But were any of them still alive? Even if they weren't, he reminded himself again, they undoubtedly had families, children who were adults now, and possibly as vulnerable as their parents.

As Strasser closed the door to the telephone booth and dialed a number in Paris, he thought again of his father's having kept the file all those years. What had he initially had in mind? He felt a twinge of regret at not having made an effort to get to know the man, a man he had dismissed as inconsequential and uninformed. Where had he gotten the file? And what other secrets had he held? Whatever they were, they had died with him.

It was one-twenty in the morning when the telephone rang in the Paris apartment. It was answered on the fourth ring by a groggy-voiced man who grunted out a semblance of hello in thickly accented French.

"No names," Strasser said immediately.

"I have good news," the man said, now speaking German, his native language.

"Not now!" Strasser snapped. "Go to a public telephone and call me within fifteen minutes at this number." He read the number off the pay phone and then hung up.

« 4 »

THE MAN WHO had answered the telephone in the Paris apartment was Gunther Jost, one of the original and more virulent members of the Red Army Faction who was uncompromised by the Stasi files. He had been in Paris for a week, negotiating with an illegal arms dealer from whom he had purchased weapons and explosives in the past. He had concluded his bargaining for the specific items Strasser wanted, and all that remained was for them to come up with the money within thirty days, money that Strasser had assured him he would get.

The apartment was in the parish of Montmartre, on the Left Bank of the Seine at number 84 rue Lepic at the top of a steep and winding hill. It was one of two safe houses Strasser had established in Paris, and the one he always chose to use when in the city. Nestled among a tangle of narrow medieval streets with the charm and quiet of a French provincial village, it was only a short walk to the tourist area at the bottom of the hill, where it was easy to blend in with the crowds who, day and night, wandered the busy streets full of shops, nightclubs, cellar bars, and cafés. It was an excellent area for meetings; with a newspaper or a book propped against a cup or glass, one could sit on a café terrace and watch the interlocking dramas of Paris *quartier* life and, when necessary, become part of the crowd to disappear at will down impossibly narrow alleyways and streets.

Gunther Jost liked the location as well. He was short and wiry with close-set eyes and pinched, narrow features that had earned him the nickname "Rat" by the time he was seven years old. He had never had much success with women, unless he paid them or raped them, and his sexual tastes ran to the bizarre and deviant, often preferring voyeurism to actual participation. The proximity of the safe house to the infamous Pigalle district, with its sex shops, prostitutes, and transvestites, appealed to him, and he spent an inordinate amount of time frequenting the live sex-show clubs scattered throughout the area.

Strasser's precautions when using telephones were founded in well-established covert operations procedures. Jost, arrogant and careless, operated in a far less circumspect manner. Unknown to him, the brief conversation he had just had with Strasser had been overheard and recorded by two Israeli intelligence officers, Mossad agents under diplomatic cover at Israel's Paris embassy. They had placed the apartment under surveillance after receiving a tip from an informant, and the discovery of Jost had been an unexpected bonus. Their listening post was located diagonally across the street from the terrorists' safe house, through an arched entrance that created a keyhole effect, enhancing what was beyond: a courtyard full of plants surrounding a statue, and beyond that another arch and a farther courtyard where the glistening glass door of a two-story apartment reflected it all back again.

The second floor of the richly decorated and fastidiously maintained apartment was now littered with foam coffee cups, overflowing ashtrays, and empty takeout food containers—the debris and clutter of a typical stationary observation post. On a tabletop against one wall was a computer console, part of a sophisticated secure-communications system directly linked through a satellite relay to Mossad headquarters in Tel Aviv. On the wall opposite was a bank of audio and video monitors and recorders tuned to receive signals from electronic bugs that included microminiature transmitters and cameras with fiber optic lenses.

The bugs had been expertly concealed in each room of the terrorists' four-room safe house by another specialized Mossad team, who had gained access to the apartment when Josh left to wander the streets of Pigalle on the first night he arrived in Paris. The electronic bugs were state of the art, designed to collect information in digital form for fifteen seconds, then transmit it in an undetectable burst of one microsecond—their signals boosted by a radio-frequency repeater hidden beneath a piece of decorative masonry outside the window of the apartment. Installed in the Mossad listeners' apartment was a powerful, tripod-mounted night vision scope that was trained on the entrance to the terrorists' safe house, along with a video camera with an equally powerful zoom lens and night vision capabilities. Anyone arriving or dropping someone off was photographed along with the license numbers of their cars and motorcycles.

The apartment where the Mossad listeners kept their vigil, one of many available to them in Paris, had been hurriedly arranged through a *sayan*—one of the legion of volunteer Jewish helpers throughout the world who could be called on at a moment's notice to provide assistance. A deceptively small shadow organization, with less than twelve hundred employees, including secretaries and cleaning staff, with no reference to it in Israeli budgets, the Mossad had less than fifty case officers operating around the world at any one time, compared to the thousands fielded by the Americans and the Russians.

The unique *sayan* system allowed the Mossad to tap loyal supporters from the worldwide Jewish community outside of Israel, who provided them with assets far out of proportion to their actual organizational size. The assistance the *sayanim* rendered ranged from providing automobiles, apartments, and medical service for wounded operatives, to business addresses and telephone answering services. There were thousands of them around the world—in London alone there were two thousand active and another five thousand on file.

The two Mossad officers in the apartment across the street from Gunther Jost had been listening to and watching everything the terrorist said and did for the past week. They even had videotape of his perverse sexual practices with a prostitute he had hired for the night, and one particularly satisfying piece of tape of a young woman, a college student from the Sorbonne, recorded on the third night after his arrival. Jost had lured her to the apartment and made advances. When she rebuffed him, he had gotten physical. It soon became evident that the young woman had, at some point in her life, studied martial arts. The four lightning-fast kicks she delivered, three to Jost's head and another to his groin, had been perfectly executed and left him lying on the floor stunned and groaning in pain as she hurriedly exited the apartment.

To the Mossad's surprise, Jost's indiscretions on the telephone had revealed the name of the arms dealer with whom he was negotiating, along with their meeting place in a small park on the nearby Ile de la Cité. The arms dealer's name was immediately sent by computer to the Paris desk at Mossad headquarters in Tel Aviv, where the research department ran it through their extensive files—the same files that had identified Jost as old-line Red Army Faction and therefore a probable link to the infamous Dieter. Within the hour the listeners' computer terminal in the Paris apartment received a response from Tel Aviv, providing them with a complete background on the man with whom Jost was dealing. Another Mossad team was called in to cover the meetings, and using ultrasensitive parabolic microphones from a distance of thirty yards, they recorded a conversation that confirmed what Tel Aviv had suspected: Dieter was negotiating for a cache of chemical and biological warfare weapons stolen by a renegade Soviet army officer still stationed in eastern Germany and sold to the arms dealer.

The same team who had covered the meetings was now in position on the streets near the terrorists' safe house, ready to keep Jost under surveillance whenever he left the apartment. An effort had been made to discover which public telephone he used to make calls away from the apartment, and to bug it. But through no conscious design, Jost was as likely to use one public phone as another and the effort had failed. The listeners had quickly learned that the call-back number the late-night caller had given Jost was in Germany, somewhere between Munich and Nuremberg. But with no possibility of getting a team into position to locate the caller in such a short time period, they made no further attempt to narrow down the location. The man who had called was accustomed to giving orders, and Jost was accustomed to responding immediately, both indications that the caller could possibly be Dieter.

The listeners in the apartment used a portable radio to alert the surveillance team on the street to the incoming call, and they quickly moved into position to follow Jost when he appeared. For the first few days they had conducted a "motionless following"—a method designed to avoid any chance of detection. The technique involved watching a targeted person without actually tailing along behind. They had kept track of Jost in stages, with men in radio contact with each other, positioned at various locations around the immediate area. Once his schedule and normal route patterns were established, both for his daytime meetings and his nighttime activities, they then permanently positioned men along the way under various guises and cover that blended in with the local street life. On the rare occasions when Jost strayed from his established route, the stationary agents simply radioed a mobile team in nearby cars to take over. With the combined use of foot and auto surveillance, the followers were assured of immediate transportation in the event the target boarded a bus or train, or made contact with someone having his own vehicle.

The Mossad team of followers soon found that they need not have bothered with their elaborate precautions. Jost's carelessness in using the safe house telephone carried over to other areas as well. He seldom, if ever, bothered to take any actions to detect or evade a surveillance effort when making contacts or attending meetings. So flagrant were his violations of operational security that Mossad headquarters decided that he was not to be snatched off the street for interrogation as was originally intended. Instead they decided to keep him under close surveillance, but to let him operate without interference—a known entity whose actions could be counted on to compromise an entire operation and expose others in his organization whenever he turned up.

The Mossad team, however, had maintained their careful surveillance procedures, due to an unexpected complication that occurred soon after Jost's arrival in Paris. There was someone else watching him. One man, as far as they could determine, occasionally relieved by another man for short periods at unpredictable intervals. They suspected this surveillance was the work of the counter-terrorist branch of the *Direction Générale de Sécurité Extérieure*—DGSE—the French secret intelligence service. And they were certain the man they had spotted was unaware of Mossad's activities, but not wanting to chance their own operation's being compromised or exposed, they kept a watchful eye on him as well.

« 5 »

THE MAN THE Mossad team had discovered sat parked in an old
Renault sedan on a side street within sight of the entrance to
the terrorists' safe house. His name was Mike Semko, and he
had no official sanction for what he was doing. He was on his
own, out on a limb, and he didn't care. He had ceased to care
about political considerations and diplomatic subtleties years
ago. It was an attitude that occasionally placed him in the
category of a loose cannon; something that both frustrated and
angered his superiors at CIA headquarters. But he didn't care
about that either. He was good at what he did, very good, and
as long as he continued to get results, he knew they would
never pull him from the field, not when there were so few men
available to them with his qualifications and experience.

Semko's cover for his current assignment was as a civilian
consultant to the State Department's Regional Security Office
at the American embassy in Paris. At the age of forty-two, his
entire adult life from the age of twenty had centered on covert
special operations in one form or another. As a young Green
Beret buck sergeant in Vietnam, attached to the Special Operations Group, he had spent three years running top-secret reconnaissance missions into Laos and North Vietnam. Within
two years of the end of the war, he became one of the original

members of Delta Force, the U.S. Army's elite counter-terrorist unit, where he spent the remainder of his military career. Immediately upon retiring from the army as a sergeant major, after twenty years of service, he was recruited by the CIA as a contract employee, and for the past two years had been assigned to a highly secret unit within the Operations Directorate's counter-terrorist section.

Semko's unit, to be found nowhere on the CIA's organizational chart, was a tightly compartmented group of twelve men, all contract employees with Delta Force and SEAL Team Six experience, whose operations were known only to a handful of people within the CIA. Usually working alone in the initial intelligence-gathering phases of an operation, then as four- or six-man teams when the situation required it, they were America's final option in the fight against terrorism. Sanctioned to use whatever means necessary to bring to justice those terrorists who had wantonly killed American citizens, Semko and the other men worked under a very broad and secret charter.

If a terrorist was beyond the reach of the United States Justice Department, and the country harboring him refused to arrest and extradite him, it was Semko's unit who hunted him down and abducted him. A CIA aircraft was then dispatched to whisk the captured terrorist off to the United States, where he was interned in a top-secret interrogation center—a highly secure compound located within the confines of the CIA's training base, known as the Farm, at Camp Peary, Virginia. There, under the supervision of staff psychiatrists and professional interrogators, the terrorist would be kept in isolation and subjected to extended periods of sensory deprivation and the latest mind-altering chemicals, especially those that destroyed the will to resist, until every last detail of his terrorist organization and its members was revealed. Semko never knew what happened after that, nor did it matter to him, but none of the eight terrorists he and the others had kidnapped around the world and delivered to waiting aircraft in the past two years was ever heard from again.

Semko's current assignment was a preliminary intelligence-gathering mission to locate four members of the French terrorist group Direct Action. They had dropped from sight after claiming responsibility for blowing up a bus full of American senior citizens, tourists on a guided tour of the French château country. The blast had slaughtered twenty-three of them. Semko was given the task of determining if Direct Action was indeed responsible, and if so, to hunt down those involved and plan and execute an operation to abduct them. Even with the aid of the case officers at the CIA's Paris station, who had been instructed to give him full cooperation without being told of his true mission, he had come up empty. Every known member of the small but lethal terrorist group had disappeared from sight, and the few rumors and leads he had managed to garner from the station's local agents and assets had led him nowhere.

With his approved assignment finished for the immediate future, Semko had been recalled to Washington five days ago for debriefing and reassignment. He had ignored the order from headquarters upon receiving a tip from one of the CIA's Paris station case officers. Under diplomatic cover as a cultural affairs officer at the American embassy, the case officer had the usual spiderweb of contacts throughout the city. One of his contacts, a professor at the Sorbonne, whom he had run into at a cocktail party, told him of one of his students, a young woman who had been the victim of an attempted rape. The would-be rapist had bragged about being a terrorist, and had even taken her to his supposed safe house. Her proficiency in the martial arts had prevented the attack from going any further than the initial groping. The case officer passed the information on to Semko, along with a description of the professed terrorist, for what it was worth. It turned out to be of considerable worth. The description, and the reported behavior of the man, suggested to Semko that Gunther Jost had surfaced. While Jost was of little interest to him, his known ties to the Red Army Faction and to Dieter interested Semko a great deal.

Within thirty minutes of talking with the case officer, Semko had located the address the young woman had given the professor. He soon spotted Gunther Jost leaving the safe house, and immediately picked up on the man's complete lack of counter-surveillance measures. With the Paris station informed that his official assignment was over, Semko could expect no assistance from them, but Jost's carelessness meant that he could get by with the help of only one other man. Using his considerable powers of persuasion, he managed to enlist one of the embassy's Marine Corps guards, on his off-duty hours, to spell him periodically so he could get some sleep. The arrangement had worked perfectly.

Semko had been sitting in the parked car since tailing Jost back to the apartment two hours ago. He was settling in for the night watch when a figure appeared out of the shadows at the entrance to the safe house. He came fully alert at the sight of Jost skipping quickly down the steps and hurrying off at a pace far faster than he usually moved. It was the first time the terrorist had left the apartment after returning from his night prowling of the bars and clubs, and Semko suspected it had nothing to do with another sweep of Pigalle, or a late night meeting with the man he had earlier identified as an arms dealer known to him from his Delta Force days.

Again, Jost ignored even the rudiments of security procedures, and Semko, as before, simply got out of his car and began following on foot. The streets of the mostly residential section at the top of the hill were virtually deserted at the early morning hour, but Semko managed to stay close by using the deep shadows against the buildings, helped by the fact that

Jost never once bothered to look back. At the bottom of the hill, the tourist area was still alive with the late night crowd, and Semko had no difficulty following the terrorist to a crowded bar, where he went directly to a pay phone at the rear.

THE SERVICE PLAZA off the Munich-to-Nuremberg autobahn was deserted except for Strasser and the man in the booth on the center island working the graveyard shift, who paid no attention to him. The mist had changed back to a steady rain that streamed down the glass sides of the telephone booth where Strasser waited impatiently for his return call. He grabbed the receiver before the first ring fell silent.

"I want you to contact someone in Paris and arrange a meeting for tomorrow night," he said without preamble.

"Of course," Jost replied, still out of breath from his hurried pace after being awakened from a sound sleep.

"His name is Claude Drussard," Strasser said.

"Do you have his address?"

"No. But I believe he has a small art gallery on the rue de Seine. Bring him to the café where we last met; the one off Saint-Germain. Tomorrow night at eight o'clock. Do not use the telephone, find his shop and talk with him directly."

"What shall I tell him is the reason?"

"That I want to see him," Strasser snapped. "Identify me only as the man he dealt with four years ago in Berlin. He will understand."

"Yes, of course," Jost said, adding, "The meetings went well this week. Everything you want will be made available at the prices we discussed. There is of course the matter of payment. He has given us thirty days."

"Good," Strasser said, his mind no longer focused on the weapons deal, but on the file from his father's portfolio and its possibilities. "Make certain Drussard is there. On time," he said, and hung up.

As Strasser pulled out of the service plaza and entered the autobahn, he pressed the accelerator down firmly, taking full advantage of the BMW's powerful engine and the unrestricted speed limit. As he headed northwest toward Frankfurt through a steady rain, his mind again sorted through the various permutations of how he might handle what could well prove to be the most profitable operation of his life. He had to stop himself from speculating wildly and becoming too enthusiastic. There were no guarantees that any of the courses of action he was considering would in fact turn out to be possible. More than forty-five years had passed, he reminded himself again, and the information might well be worthless now, though somehow he doubted that. The initial answers he needed would be waiting in Paris. Drussard would know.

« 6 »

THE SMALL SQUARE off the boulevard Saint-Germain was once a gathering place for the legendary writers, philosophers, and painters of pre–World War II Paris. But word of their favorite haunts in the fashionable bohemian enclave spread quickly, and the sightseers and commercialism that flowed into the area soon drove them away.

The once-famous sidewalk café where Gunther Jost sat sipping his third glass of wine sparkled with lively chatter and the clink of glasses. Throughout the crowded square, greetings and mock protests and apologies and passes filled the air amid the soft music of a guitar duet played by two students who sat on the edge of the central fountain. Street wanderers, displaying none of the sullen irritability or malice the French are known to use to preserve their egos against the masses, strolled aimlessly about; while here and there young lovers, fallen under the magic spell of a warm spring evening in Paris, stood locked in embrace beneath the spreading trees that lined the sidewalks, enjoying the all-too-brief days of innocent love and youth that would never, however hard they tried, be quite the same again.

The café was lit only by tiny lights strung along the sculpted edge of the awning, and by the soft glow of flickering candles that dripped onto checkered tablecloths. The dim lighting and noisy conversations presented nearly insurmountable obstacles for the four Mossad agents in a nearby surveillance van. With no way of anticipating the meeting site, they were placed at a distinct disadvantage. Earlier in the day, they had fallen victim to a bad stroke of luck when Jost left the safe house to contact Claude Drussard.

Unsure of the precise location of Drussard's gallery, Jost had made a series of confused detours through narrow winding streets, and the Mossad's stationary surveillants soon lost sight of him. The mobile team, who were radioed to take over, experienced a similar misfortune when Jost walked up a one-way street, preventing the two men in the car from following without immediately being seen, even by someone as unobservant as Jost. By the time they got out of the car and continued on foot, their target had vanished. They had gone back to the safe house to wait for his return, and picked up the surveillance that evening when they followed him to the café.

The van was parked just off the square, a few yards into a side street that put the Mossad team at a bad angle and distance for both videotaping and audio recording. The square itself had proved an impossible location to conceal their activities from anyone who was alert to the possibility of surveillance, and they had to assume that whoever Jost was meeting would not be as incompetent and careless as he was. The side street became the Mossad's only option and unfortunately placed them near the limits of the optimum operating conditions for their equipment.

The Mossad agent wearing the headset in the back of the van shook his head in frustration. He had at first tried using a laser communications device to intercept the conversation, but the ultrasophisticated piece of equipment had proven useless in their present situation. There were too many errant sound vibrations that cluttered the intercept, and people moving about who blocked out the laser's direct path to the targets. He switched to his backup device, an omnidirectional parabolic microphone concealed in the open roof vent, and began to make a series of adjustments in an attempt to home in on Jost's table in a darkened corner of the café. This time he was more successful, but still unable to obtain the desired results. A group of teenagers stood at the edge of the sidewalk not far from where Jost sat talking to an unidentified subject who had just joined him. The teenagers were situated between the van and the targeted men, and their animated conversation, along with the ambient noise level from nearby tables and the street, still prevented the listener from locking on to Jost and his companion.

"I'm just getting bits and pieces," the audio operator said to the man next to him. "There's too much clutter."

The man operating the video camera at the one-way-glass window in the rear door of the van nodded in agreement. He was having similar difficulties. His angle of view was such that the milling crowd around the fountain in the center of the square at times all but obscured his line of sight to Jost's table. And when he did manage to focus on the subjects, the low illumination worked against him. He continued to manually adjust the camera lens, muttering in disgust as his efforts fell short.

"The light level is too low," he said to the audio operator. "We're not going to get anything but a grainy blur. Computer enhancement might bring out a recognizable image, but I wouldn't count on it."

He moved forward and spoke to the driver and the man in the front passenger seat.

"Get out and mix with the people in the square," he told them. "Get as close in as you can. If they split up when they move, we'll take Jost. You follow the man who just arrived. I'll do what I can to get him on tape.

''And keep an eye on the other guy who's been following Jost,'' he added as the two men slipped quietly out of the van and disappeared into the square.

MIKE SEMKO HAD also lost track of Jost in the warren of narrow streets and alleyways that morning, but after following him from the safe house to the café, his one-man surveillance was unhampered by the problems that plagued the Mossad team. The Israelis, aside from wanting to prevent the chemical and biological weapons sale for which Jost was negotiating, were charged with a standing Mossad order to find and abduct Dieter, and bring him back to Israel to stand trial for his bombing of an Amsterdam synagogue, which had resulted in the deaths of eighteen Jewish worshipers, four of them Israeli citizens. Semko simply wanted to kill the terrorist on sight.

Dieter was the primary reason Semko had accepted the CIA's offer of a job with their counter-terrorist section, rather than taking one of the many lucrative offers from international security companies in the private sector. There was nothing he would not do to get Dieter; with or without Agency approval, regardless of the personal consequences. Three years ago, an informer inside the PLO had told a CIA agent in Paris where the terrorist was holed up with a group of five Palestinians he had trained at Massow. He was preparing them for a ''graduation'' exercise—an attack on a nightclub frequented by American servicemen stationed at the air force base in Bitburg, Germany. Delta Force was called in, and Semko's team had stormed the apartment safe house in Düsseldorf, killing all five of the Palestinians. But Dieter had escaped, diving out a window after mortally wounding two Delta Force troopers.

There were sleepless nights when Semko was haunted by visions of the two men lying dead on the apartment floor—one of the men was a longtime friend with whom he had served in Vietnam and whose death had left a wife and two young children behind. Semko's shoulder had been shattered by two bullets that went wide of their mark as Dieter dived out the window, and there were times when he could, for an instant, feel the phantom pain of the old wound, and see the face of the man who had fired at him. Semko was the only outsider who had ever seen Dieter up close and lived, and despite the terrorist's efforts to disguise his appearance, there were things Semko would never forget about him.

The vendetta had grown and festered to the point of becoming an obsession. Once he found Dieter, he would retire, Semko had promised himself. Find a place in Montana or Wyoming so far removed from civilization, as he had half-jokingly told his superiors at the CIA, that he could take a piss off his back porch if he cared to. His army pension and the money he had saved would see him through; his needs were simple, and he had seen enough of the world to know that he no longer wanted to be a participant in it.

After following Jost to Saint-Germain, Semko had chosen an observation site at another sidewalk café, across the street from where the terrorist sat talking to a man who had just arrived. The location gave him a clear view of the subjects and anyone entering or leaving the small square. His eyes were fixed on the new arrival, whom he did not recognize as a major player from any of the files on known terrorists he had studied while with Delta Force or at the CIA. The man was much older than Jost, at least sixty, Semko estimated. He had pronounced Gallic features—heavy jowls and hooded eyes—and he looked nervous and uncomfortable in Jost's presence. The body language and gestures of the two men suggested they were waiting for someone else to join them; brief conversations, during which neither man leaned toward the other to indicate a guarded discussion, were followed by long periods of silence and expectant glances about the square.

Semko's gaze was suddenly drawn to a figure who appeared

in his peripheral vision. A tall, lanky man who had just entered the square was moving slowly toward the fountain, pausing, watching, then moving again, scanning the area. Semko felt a surge of adrenaline. There was something familiar about him. Nothing distinctly identifying, but subtleties that triggered a vague recognition. There was a professionalism and a feral intensity in the way the man very carefully observed his surroundings, alert for any sign of danger, coiled and ready to react. Semko recognized the behavior as part of his own demeanor when he sensed danger or was sniffing out a surveillance effort.

To the untrained eye the man blended perfectly with those around him. But beneath the surface his casual movements were full of purpose and intent. He sat briefly on the edge of the fountain and lit a cigarette, his attention ostensibly on the student guitarists. Semko tracked the line of his gaze; his eyes were fixed on the table where Jost sat with the older Frenchman, then moved in a slow arc across the café, until, through instincts and training, he dismissed the rest of the patrons as potential threats. He then turned his attention back to the square, watching for anything or anyone that seemed out of place or moved against the natural rhythm of the crowd.

Semko could not take his eyes off him. His mind searched for all the small nuances he had locked into memory during those brief moments in Dusseldorf three years ago, when he had seen Dieter enter the apartment before the Delta Force team assaulted, and then for a few seconds during the firefight before he dived out the window. He blocked out all other thoughts and stared hard at the hauntingly familiar figure, now up and moving around the fountain. The man's hair was dark blond, worn long at the ears and neck where it curled upward. His features were handsome and chiseled, his eyes were deep set, hard, and unyielding. He walked with a barely noticeable

limp, somewhat off balance and hunched over, which for an
instant made Semko doubt his initial suspicions.

Then he recalled the biographical data and character profile
he had read in the Agency's files, about how adept Dieter was
at totally changing his appearance. At times he was given to
the amateurish, the things every beginner thought of first: a
wig or a false mustache or beard, and horn-rimmed glasses.
Obvious disguises that in a few moments of privacy, in a telephone booth or a darkened doorway, could be brought into
play with little difficulty, but that in reality served only to draw
the attention of a competent observer.

But Dieter was also knowledgeable in the more esoteric and
effective aspects of tradecraft. Stick-on eyebrows, thick and
bushy, changed the face as much as a mustache or beard. A
lightweight raincoat and cap tightly folded and stuffed into the
pockets of a jacket provided a quick change in visual profile
and silhouette on a crowded street. A pair of shoes a size too
small that pinched the feet, or a stone in one shoe, could
change the gait and posture of the wearer, and could account
for the slight limp and awkward movement Semko had noticed
in the man who was now less than fifty feet away. A discussion
during the debriefing after the abortive assault on the Dusseldorf apartment came back to him: one of the Delta Force intelligence analysts had pointed out that the Dieter Semko had
seen, overweight, the top of his head shaved to appear bald, the
hair on the sides of his head dyed gray and thinned to further
age his appearance, was yet another manifestation of the ex-
tremes to which the master terrorist would go to conceal his
true identity.

But there were things that no man could conceal from a
keen observer, especially one who had burned into memory
every detail of a previous encounter. It was those details that
had risen from Semko's subconscious and drew his attention.
The shape of the man's head. The slope of his shoulders. The

deep chest that suggested upper body strength. And the way he carried himself, confident, capable. Things that were as much a part of him as his facial features, but were extremely difficult to conceal at will.

Semko continued to observe him, still not positive of his assessment. But he reacted immediately, in a practiced, casual manner, and angled his face away when he saw the man begin to turn in his direction and slowly, patiently, scan along the side of the square he had not yet scrutinized, missing nothing, studying everything.

If it was Dieter, Semko reasoned, it was highly unlikely the terrorist would recognize him from the few seconds of exposure during a hail of gunfire three years ago. But before he came under the man's probing gaze, he wanted to lower his profile. A young woman sat at the table to his left; he had earlier pegged her as a better-than-average-looking prostitute hoping to find an upscale client among the café patrons. He caught her eye, raised his coffee cup to her and smiled, then gestured for her to join him. She did so without hesitation, and sat opposite him just as Strasser's eyes swept past the table.

THE MOSSAD AGENTS in the van and on the street did not notice the tall, lanky man's presence until he completed his counter-surveillance effort and crossed to the café where he sat down unannounced at the table with Jost and his companion.

"Anybody recognize him?" the Mossad agent wearing the headset asked. He was speaking into a small portable radio, and the two men who had left the van to take up positions in the square heard him clearly through the tiny earpiece receivers they wore. Both men whispered a negative response into the microphones attached inside the lapels of their jackets.

The agent at the video camera in the van stopped adjusting the lens and again cursed under his breath. "I can't get him from this angle; just the back of his head."

He picked up the portable radio lying at his side. "If they split up when they leave," he said to the men in the square, "forget Jost, we know where to find him. We'll take the older one, you stay with the new arrival."

« 7 »

Jurgen Strasser didn't shake the hand Claude Drussard extended. He simply nodded to him and Jost as he sat down and poured himself a glass of wine from the carafe on the table.

"We'll talk later," he said to Jost, and motioned with his head for him to leave. Jost obediently got up from his chair and left without a word.

Strasser had recognized Drussard on sight from their meeting four years ago, when he had delivered four minor but valuable paintings and two gold chalices to him at a warehouse on the outskirts of West Berlin. Drussard had discreetly sold the items in a matter of days through his underground network, for far less than what they were worth, but more than Strasser had expected.

The paintings and chalices had been part of a treasure trove of artwork recovered over the years by the East German government from its citizens, who had been hoarding the looted and lost art since the end of World War II. A friend of Strasser's from his days at the Stasi training academy, and who at the time was with the counterintelligence section, had come to him with the scheme. He argued that the country they had served faithfully would soon no longer exist, and that it was the capitalists who would inherit their country's treasures, and it was from them they would be stealing. Strasser had agreed, and with information from a source who worked for his friend, they located a cache of minor art treasures hidden in an abandoned monastery near Weimar. They had taken four works by early twentieth-century German artists, and two twelfth-century chalices that were excellent examples of the work of medieval goldsmiths and had been looted from a Polish cathedral during the war. They deleted them from the inventory that was turned in to Stasi headquarters, then smuggled them into West Berlin, where they met with Drussard, whose name they had gotten from Stasi files.

"Do you remember me?" Strasser said. To put the Frenchman at ease he had not disguised his face, and he looked essentially the same as when they first met.

"Yes, yes of course," Drussard said. "I wasn't sure when your friend talked with me this afternoon. But now that I see you, you were one of the two men from the East German intelligence service for whom I . . . performed a service. You are Herr Koenig, if I remember correctly."

"Yes," Strasser said. "Are you still performing the same services?" His eyes began moving slowly around the café and the square as he spoke.

"But of course. For the right people, with the right merchandise."

Strasser reached into the inside pocket of his leather jacket and withdrew two sheets of paper on which he had copied information from the file in his father's portfolio. He handed one of the sheets to Drussard.

"Tell me if you consider this the right merchandise."

Drussard's eyes widened as he unfolded the paper and began to read. Halfway down the list he let out a barely audible gasp, but caught himself before he drew any attention from the nearby tables.

"Surely you are not suggesting that you have these in your possession?"

"No. But I have reason to believe they are within my reach. Are you interested?"

"Interested would hardly be the word," Drussard said, looking over the list again, this time reading carefully.

The names mesmerized him. They were some of the world's greatest artists: Monet, van Gogh, Raphael, Rembrandt, Botticelli, Goya, Degas, Dürer, Matisse, Cézanne, Renoir, Velázquez, and Pissarro. Two van Goghs, he noted, and continued to read. There was a Boucher from the eighteenth-century French school. A Rubens from the seventeenth-century Flemish school. A Cranach from the sixteenth-century German school. And a Ruysdael from the seventeenth-century Dutch school. He was not only familiar with the world-renowned artists, but with most of the individual paintings as they were described in a brief sentence after their names.

A failed artist and unsuccessful gallery owner, Drussard had spent the past thirty years in the world of stolen and forged art and antiques, rising to the top in a business that had reached such epidemic proportions that it was now second only to the drug trade as the world's largest illegal enterprise. The contacts he had developed—with thieves who stole to order, with dealers who ran fencing operations, and with customers who asked few, if any, questions—spanned the globe. His international theft network was capable of moving stolen art across oceans and continents in ways often too complex for police to trace, passing through four or five dealers' hands before ending up in the possession of a new breed of private collector in Venezuela, Japan, Saudi Arabia, or other sheikdoms where passionate buyers with enormous personal wealth hungered for status.

Drussard immediately realized the uniqueness of most of the paintings on the list he held in his hand. This was not recently stolen art that couldn't be easily moved because the notoriety of the theft would scare away any potential client no matter how greedy or covetous. These paintings were an answer to his most fervent prayers. They were plausibly deniable. They had been missing for more than forty-seven years, and, to the best of his knowledge, they did not appear on Interpol's "Most Wanted" list of stolen art, which dated back to 1938, and to which no statute of limitations applied. Though they could not be sold openly at auction houses or galleries without arousing suspicions, they could easily be sold to wealthy private collectors, especially in the Orient.

He suspected that all of the paintings were among the more than four thousand lost masterworks whose fate since World War II was still unknown. Some were believed to have been destroyed by American and British bombing raids; others were thought to have been stolen by the Nazis, then found and "liberated" by Allied soldiers, especially the Russians, and by the hordes of refugees and displaced persons who roamed the countryside in the midst of the chaos that swept through Germany in the spring of 1945.

The stories of the missing treasures were legend. A significant part of the Nazi program for conquest was to effect the impoverishment of the conquered nations and the enrichment of Germany through a deliberate and official process of looting works of art. In the Slavic countries the program called for pillaging the whole of the national cultural heritage. No collections—state, church, or private—were spared. In France, Belgium, and Holland, as well as in Austria and Germany itself, organized stealing was limited largely to private Jewish collections, which were systematically looted, or to cloak the transactions with a semblance of legality, the owners were forced to sell at ridiculously low prices, often just prior to being sent to the death camps.

It was Hitler's interest in art that spurred the wartime collecting frenzy; he considered the acquisitions of great importance for the cultural prestige of Germany. But Goering, and to a lesser extent Bormann and Goebbels, took an active part in the selection of works to be included in their personal collections purely for their own enrichment. The looting, thefts, and forced sales constituted one of history's most extensive and systematic plunders of art; but fortunately, the Germans, with their obsession for order, had recorded their activities with such thoroughness that it was possible to make considerable use of their records in restoring much of the stolen art to its rightful owners shortly after the end of the war. The major exceptions were the Jewish families whose property was forcibly taken from them. Most never survived the death camps, and despite the efforts of relatives in the years that followed, no accounting was ever given, and the majority of their treasured possessions were listed as whereabouts unknown. A few, in later years, appeared in auction houses from mysterious sources connected to the Soviet Union and were returned to the legitimate claimants, but most simply vanished, never to be seen again.

Drussard's own files would tell him more when he had a chance to check, but he further suspected that most of the paintings on the list Strasser had given him fell into the category of property confiscated from the Jews of Europe.

"Tell me more about their availability," the Frenchman said. "What is involved in obtaining them?"

Strasser handed him the second sheet of paper he had taken from his jacket. "The paintings on the list I gave you are numbered. The names with the corresponding numbers on the second list are the people who purchased them between 1941 and 1945."

"Purchased them?" Drussard's surprise was genuine.

"From a man by the name of Egon Hofer," Strasser said.

Drussard nodded knowingly. The name was familiar to him.

It was beginning to make sense. He had heard stories of paintings that were sold privately in Switzerland during the war, to raise hard currency for the Third Reich, or for the personal benefit of Nazi party and SS leaders who hid the proceeds in secret accounts.

"Hofer was Hermann Goering's personal representative in disposing of works of art the reich marshal did not want for his own collection," Drussard said. "He committed suicide shortly after the war ended."

"All of the transactions took place in Zurich, and as you can see from the list of names, some of the people who bought them were from countries who were at war with Germany at the time."

Drussard quickly skimmed the names on the list and recognized some of the more prominent families of Great Britain and America. Families known in the art world for their extensive collections.

"What I don't understand," Strasser said, "is why they would knowingly buy stolen art."

Drussard smiled. "*Knowingly* is the operative word, Herr Koenig. A work of art that is purchased with the knowledge that it has been stolen can be confiscated by the authorities, and the buyer has no legal recourse. However, in many countries, if the buyer has had the object in question in his possession for a period of two years, and he can reasonably argue that he had no idea it was stolen when he purchased it, he is then considered the legal owner."

"But these people had to know the source of the paintings," Strasser said. "How could they deny that they did not at least suspect they were part of the Nazis' loot?"

"I doubt that they ever considered the furor that would arise from the ashes of the war over the missing art. And if I am correct, none of these paintings have surfaced since the end of the war, which suggests that once they realized the repercussions if they displayed them openly, or tried to sell them, they simply became a permanent part of their collections, hidden from public view.''

''Why would anyone want a painting they can't openly display?''

''Art collectors are a strange breed. Especially those obsessed with possessing works by acknowledged masters. There are more than a few enormously wealthy people in the world who will buy certain paintings, regardless of their questionable provenance, and store them in bank vaults or hide them in their homes. I know of at least six such collectors who have specially constructed secret rooms for just that purpose. The legitimate art community, if in fact there is such a thing, the whores that they are, vehemently denies that these people exist. But I can assure you they do.''

''How marketable are the paintings on the list I gave you?''

''They are unique,'' Drussard said. ''At first glance, I would have to say that all of them were once the property of private collectors, probably wealthy Jews. Some perhaps even had supporting bills of sale, probably coerced from the original owners, but nonetheless, difficult to dispute if those owners died in the camps. That is probably the reason they were selected to be sold, and so readily purchased. But the outcome of the war, and the horrors that came to light in its aftermath, added another dimension: the new owners would have to admit they had dealt with the Nazis, which is undoubtedly why none of the paintings have ever been seen again.''

''You didn't answer my question,'' Strasser said, an edge to his voice. ''Will they be easy to sell?''

''Extremely so,'' Drussard said. ''It is a relatively simple matter to create expertly forged bills of sale, or auction receipts dating back to World War II. With those in hand, I have clients in Japan and Hong Kong who would purchase them immediately.''

"At what prices?"

"A fraction of their true value," Drussard said. "But in today's market that would still amount to a considerable sum. Perhaps three or four million dollars each for the more important pieces. Less my commission, of course."

"Which would be what?"

"May I suggest fifty percent?" The Frenchman's eyes sparkled, indicating the clarity and sharpness of his mind, despite the indolent look about him.

"You may suggest anything you like," Strasser said. "But you'll get forty percent."

Drussard shrugged in acquiescence. "Agreed. And now I have a question for you. How are you planning to obtain these paintings?"

"I'm going to steal them. And you're going to help me."

Drussard fell silent for a long moment, then a small ironic smile appeared at the corners of his mouth. "What a perfect example of pure poetic justice. Stealing stolen paintings. Thefts that can never be reported without admitting initial culpability."

"My thoughts exactly," Strasser said.

"But how do you expect me to help, outside of finding the right buyers?"

"Since the paintings have never been seen since the end of the war," Strasser said, "is it possible that they are still in the hands of the people who bought them from the Nazis?"

"Quite possible. I'm positive that none of them have been sold through the underground market in the last thirty years, or I would have known about it."

"Then I'll need to know if the original buyers are still alive, and if not, who inherited their legitimate collections. And I'll need their current addresses."

"That should not be difficult," Drussard said. "Most of these people, and their families, are well known in the art world." He glanced at the list of names again. "I can tell you now that three of them are still very much alive. They are in their late seventies or early eighties and live in New York City, and two of them hold positions on the board of directors of the Metropolitan Museum and the Museum of Modern Art."

Drussard hesitated, then saw an opening to suggest something that had excited him upon first seeing Strasser's list.

"I would like a special payment for my services in tracking down the present owners for you."

Strasser's eyes stopped moving over the café and the square and fixed hard on Drussard.

"With the exception of perhaps a Monet water lily," Drussard continued, tentatively, "there is no more desirable a commodity in the art world than a van Gogh iris, or one of his landscapes, earth colored and dark and bleak, with the sky hanging low over peat bogs and potato fields tended by mute, heavy-limbed peasants . . . such elemental power . . ." The Frenchman seemed to be in a trance as he spoke, enraptured by the thought of the painting he had in mind.

"Get to the point," Strasser said.

"I would like one of the van Goghs," Drussard said, pointing to the list. "This one. For myself."

Strasser considered the request for a moment, then nodded in agreement, adding his own conditions.

"You will select from the list the paintings that you consider most valuable, and we will agree on what the probable market value will be before I steal them. I will be paid my sixty percent for each painting based on the price we have agreed on. What you get for them is your business."

Strasser removed a notepad and pen from his jacket and scribbled down the name of a bank in Vaduz, Liechtenstein, along with his secret numbered account. "You will deposit my money directly into this account within seventy-two hours of delivery of the paintings."

"Agreed," Drussard said. "I have reliable contacts in New York, London, Rome, Geneva, Munich, Vienna, Mexico City, Tokyo, and Hong Kong. Once you have the paintings you can take them to my representative in the closest city. For the purposes of payment, it will be the same as delivering them to me."

Drussard made some comparative notes from the two lists Strasser had given him. Then, after some quick calculations, he wrote out a separate list for Strasser and handed it to him.

"According to your information, these eight paintings were originally purchased by the three men in New York City I mentioned earlier. If they are still in their possession, and assuming you can get them, I can guarantee you that your percentage will be approximately eighteen million dollars."

The thought of such an enormous sum of money, and the freedom it would give him to conduct and broaden his own terrorist operations, sent a rare shiver of eager anticipation through Strasser. "How soon can you get me the current addresses of the men in New York?"

"I should have the information you need by tomorrow afternoon. How will I contact you?"

"I'll call you," Strasser said. "And for your sake, I hope you are intelligent enough not even to consider cheating me."

The tone of Strasser's voice and the look in his eyes frightened Drussard, but he did not flinch. He had never cheated anyone in his thirty years in the business.

"I did not survive all these years by being stupid, Herr Koenig."

"Then here's to your continued good health," Strasser said, and raised his wineglass in a toast that seemed more like a threat to Drussard. "I will be in New York tomorrow night. I will call you from there. If all goes well you should have the paintings within a week."

"Excellent," Drussard said, and started to leave. He hesitated, adding, "If you don't mind my asking, whom do you represent . . . I mean, since your former employer no longer exists?"

"I represent a distinct threat to people who ask too many questions."

"Then until tomorrow," Drussard said, and got up from his chair.

Strasser lit a cigarette as the Frenchman left the café, and continued to follow his progress as he entered the square, watching to see if anyone showed the slightest interest in his departure.

« 8 »

THE TWO MOSSAD agents in the van were caught off guard by Strasser's staying behind and watching for surveillance on Drussard as he crossed the square. There hadn't been enough time or preparation to call in an additional team from the embassy, and now they were faced with the dilemma of whom to follow.

"He's waiting to see if anyone's tailing the old man," the agent at the video camera said. "We're not going to be able to get on him before he's out of sight without the guy at the table seeing us. It's one or the other, but not both of them."

"Forget the old man," the agent wearing the headset said. "From what little I got of the conversation, the one still at the café is in charge of whatever it is they're planning."

He picked up the portable radio and spoke to the two agents in the square. "Stay on the subject at the table," he told them. "We'll follow as close as we can for backup."

"Do you think it's Dieter?" the agent at the video camera said.

"He fits the profile, at least what we know about him. But then, what we know isn't much."

* * *

MIKE SEMKO HAD few doubts about the man's identity. The fragmented, but vivid, visual images he recalled from that day in Dusseldorf three years ago, and his gut instincts made him strongly suspect that he had found Dieter; enough so that he intended to confront the man and confirm it, one way or another. When the Frenchman got up to leave, Semko slipped the confused hooker fifty dollars and gave her a kiss on the cheek to affect the appearance of two friends parting.

He moved out into the square, his eyes never leaving Strasser as he slowly worked his way around the fountain toward the corner café. He paused behind a group of students giggling and sharing a joint, and reached inside his Windbreaker to flip the safety off the Browning High-Power nine-millimeter semiautomatic pistol in the shoulder holster beneath his left arm.

Strasser sat calmly watching the square and finishing his glass of wine. The focus of his attention had been on Drussard's departure, and although he had taken note of the lean, hard-looking man who had left the café on the opposite side of the square, he did not notice that he was now stalking him as he moved through the crowd around the fountain.

The two Mossad agents nearby did, however, see Semko, and held their positions to avoid compromising their own surveillance effort. The shorter of the two agents, a bull-like man and former Israeli paratrooper named Nathan Obert, had not missed Semko's right hand disappearing inside his jacket. He recognized the subtle movement for what it was, and whispered into his lapel microphone.

"The guy who's been following Jost is moving in on the subject in the café. He's armed, and I think he's got more than surveillance on his mind."

The agent in the van heard him clearly and issued instructions. "Back off and give him room."

Not knowing who or what they were dealing with, the Mossad team leader preferred to err on the side of caution rather than risk exposing their covert operation and creating a diplomatic incident if the man was with French intelligence.

The two agents in the square complied, and moved off in the middle distance between the fountain and the café.

Semko wedged his way through a small crowd who were watching a juggler of questionable talent performing on the far side of the fountain. He momentarily lost sight of Strasser, and when he emerged into the clear, he saw that he was gone. Quick, desperate glances finally found him as he walked along the sidewalk in the direction of a street leading off the square. Semko, being careful not to stand out in the slow-moving, meandering crowd, started after him.

Despite his caution, Strasser spotted him. Earlier, when he had noticed Semko leaving the café across the square, and had logged him into memory—gray Windbreaker, denim jeans, running shoes, approximately five feet eleven inches tall, wiry, with thick, dark brown hair, and fluid, agile movements—he had categorized him as a "possible." But when he failed to follow Drussard, Strasser lost interest. Upon seeing him again, while pausing to light a cigarette and looking over his shoulder, he was alerted to the threatening posture and the rhythm of his movement. Nothing about him fitted the detached, ambling manner of the rest of the people in the square. He was angling for position, for a field of view, and his head and eyes were fixed in one direction.

Strasser unzipped his leather jacket and discreetly withdrew the pistol tucked into his waistband at the small of his back, sliding it into the front of his trousers, just to the left of his belt buckle. He then paused for a moment at the entrance to a candy store and used the reflection in the windows to confirm that Semko was still there. He caught a fleeting glimpse of the gray Windbreaker as Semko stepped onto the sidewalk beneath a lamppost and fell in behind him, not twenty yards away. He left the doorway to the candy store and continued toward the side street, remaining composed and seemingly indifferent to his surroundings, and gave no indication that he was aware of Semko's surveillance.

Semko saw through the masquerade. He knew he had been made—the shopworn practices of using reflections in windows to spot a tail and the casual look over the shoulder while lighting a cigarette to check what was behind were some of the first tradecraft lessons taught. The realization freed him somewhat; there was no longer any need for stealth. He knew it would soon evolve into an all-out chase, and he picked up his pace. He crossed to the edge of the curb, getting ready to move past the people in front of him in the event Strasser made a break.

Strasser again looked over his shoulder, to gauge the distance and the time he had left to react, and to determine the factors in his favor. There was a rowdy group of four students, and an old couple between them, preventing Semko from getting a clear shot at him before he reached the corner, now only a few yards away. For some indistinct reason the circumstances made him feel far more uneasy then he usually did in tight situations. There was something vaguely familiar about the man following him, but in the excitement and tension of the moment, he could not recall what it was.

Strasser kept looking back until he caught a full view of Semko's face. He then stared directly at him, giving a subtle warning, to let him know he was aware and prepared, and if his intentions were strictly surveillance, he had better break it off before things got rough. It had worked before when an intelligence officer from one agency or another, unsure of whom he was following, and with no authorization to do anything other than observe, had ended the surveillance once he had been compromised.

But Semko didn't slow his pace at the overt acknowledgment of his presence. He kept coming, staring back at Strasser.

The direct eye contact removed the final doubts Semko had about the man's identity. It was Dieter, the same man he had seen diving out the window in Dusseldorf. The same look of supreme confidence, bordering on arrogance, combined with a grace under pressure that Semko had witnessed only a few times before in men who were under enormous stress—in the jungles of Vietnam, in battle-hardened combat veterans who had come to love the war, and to need it.

The two Mossad agents were now back in position to continue their surveillance. Thirty yards to the rear of Semko, behind a slow-moving young couple, they saw what was transpiring between the two men up ahead.

"This doesn't look good," the short, stocky Obert said to his partner. "These two guys are going to turn this into a gun battle at any moment."

Strasser reached the intersection where the narrow, crooked side street entered the square. He turned the corner and quickly surveyed the area in front of him. It was poorly lit, with deep shadows falling over an endless line of cars parked close together and half up on the curb to allow at least a semblance of a traffic lane. Numerous alleyways branched off the street, and his attention was drawn to an archway on his right that appeared to lead into a courtyard approximately fifty feet from where he stood.

Semko turned the corner just in time to see Strasser disappear through the archway. He broke into a run to close in before he got too far behind and lost him in the maze of blind alleys and passageways that seemed to lead in every direction. He stopped at the entrance to the courtyard and withdrew his weapon, and after a quick look from the protection of the stone arch, he crouched low and moved cautiously forward. His pistol was cocked and held firmly in a two-handed grip, and the barrel followed the track of his eyes as they swept the enclosed area.

A small statue and fountain filled the center of the court-yard, and all around, rising three stories above, the lights from apartment windows cast a soft glow on the scene below. A walkway led out the far side of the enclosure, and as Semko crossed and entered it, he saw Strasser reach the end and dis-appear around another corner. He ran after him, forgoing cau-tion, and emerged onto a one-way street to see Strasser look over his shoulder as he darted between two parked cars on the opposite side.

Strasser dropped to one knee behind the front end of a sta-tion wagon and drew his pistol. He fired three rounds in rapid succession. He had not attached the silencer, and the muzzle blasts resounded loudly off the walls of the surrounding build-ings as the bullets tore into the framework of the apartment doorway where Semko had taken cover, striking only inches from his head.

Semko returned the fire, shattering the windshield of the station wagon and showering Strasser with shards of glass. He saw him move toward the back of the car, and fired again, taking out a piece of the rear window.

The street was dark, and Semko lost sight of his target as Strasser stayed low behind a row of parked cars and worked his way toward another passageway between two apartment buildings directly behind him. Then Semko saw him again, for a brief moment, as he dashed from cover and sprinted down the opening between the two buildings.

Semko was about to give chase when the sound of heavy footsteps from the direction of the courtyard caught his atten-tion and caused him to pause and listen. Someone was follow-ing him, coming on fast. Without so much as a backward glance, Semko continued his pursuit and crossed the street, where he darted into the passageway after Strasser.

Nathan Obert had started running flat out at the sound of the gunshots. He had followed the two men through the courtyard, but had sent his partner around the corner at the next intersection to try to get ahead of them, where he could direct the two Mossad agents in the van into position. He was feeling very exposed and vulnerable as he ran, and the excess weight he carried was taking its toll. He was breathing heavily, gasping for breath as he crossed the one-way street and entered the passageway where he had last seen Semko. His eyes were fixed on the far end where it opened onto a broad, brightly lit avenue, and he did not notice the figure hiding in the darkened doorway on his right midway through the passage. The arm that swung out and caught him in the windpipe sent him sprawling on the damp concrete surface with a thud.

Semko dropped down beside the startled Mossad agent, driving a knee into his stomach as he pressed the barrel of his weapon firmly between his eyes. The pressure he held on the trigger was such that the slightest increase would have put a round through Obert's head and blown out the back of his skull.

"Who the hell are you?" Semko shouted.

"Consular office of the Israeli embassy!" Obert managed to blurt out in a half-choked, raspy voice. It was the way he always identified himself to outsiders, using his diplomatic cover and never admitting to being with Israeli intelligence.

"Mossad," Semko muttered, but kept the gun in place.

"Who are you?" Obert said, regaining a little of his composure. He had immediately recognized Semko's accent as American, and assumed he was CIA.

"Nobody you want to get to know too well. Just stay out of my way. Understand?"

Obert nodded rapidly, then lay motionless with the gun barrel still between his eyes. With his radio out of range of his partner and the agents in the van, he knew he was on his own, with no help on the way.

Semko quickly frisked the still shaken agent, whose eyes

kept staring at the tightly flexed finger on the trigger while he silently prayed that the man kneeling above him had some measure of control over his weapon.

Semko found a .38-caliber semiautomatic pistol in a holster on Obert's hip. He took it, shoved it into his pocket, and rose to a standing position.

Obert breathed a silent sigh of relief. At least Semko, in his haste to continue after his quarry, had stopped after finding the gun, and missed the small portable radio clipped to his belt on the opposite hip.

"You got fair warning," Semko said. "I see your face again, as far as I'm concerned, you're the enemy."

With that, Semko ran out the far end of the passageway, stopping abruptly as he reached the well-lighted quai de la Tournelle. He looked in both directions, straining to pick out a fast-moving subject among the pedestrians walking slowly along the sidewalk. Strasser was nowhere in sight.

Semko cursed under his breath, fearing he had lost him, when he heard a woman's scream coming from the opposite side of the street. He dashed across the broad, busy avenue, heedless of the oncoming traffic, and caused a near collision between two drivers who had slammed on their brakes and swerved to avoid hitting him.

He stopped at the top of a stone stairway that led down to the banks of the Seine. Near the bottom of the steps, he saw a woman picking herself up off the ground and shouting at someone who was walking along the quay above the river. Semko followed her gaze and saw the object of her anger. He was wearing a blue checked shirt that at first made Semko look past him, until he noticed the leather jacket the man was carrying under his arm, and the dark blond hair worn long at the neck and ears. He was trying to blend in with those around him, but his movements were charged and tense. When he

turned to look over his shoulder in the direction of the stairway, Semko knew that his luck was still with him.

He descended the stairs with reckless abandon, almost
knocking down the same woman as he reached the bottom and
took off in the direction he had seen Strasser go. The dark
waters of the Seine sparkled with the lights of the city, and the
pathway along the quay overlooking the river was cast in a
diffused golden light from the lampposts spaced at intervals
along the banks. Semko stopped for a moment and studied the
silhouetted pedestrian traffic. Young lovers walked arm in arm,
lost in their own intimate worlds, while prostitutes struck ste-
reotypical, almost comical, poses beneath the lampposts, and
winos sprawled in drunken indifference to their surroundings.

A sudden lateral movement ahead in the distance finally
caught Semko's attention. An old man walking his dog had
bent down to scoop the small animal up to avoid its being
trampled by someone who rushed past him. Semko broke into
a run, darting and weaving through the evening strollers while
trying to keep his eyes on the fleeing figure. He saw Strasser
slip on a loose paving stone and stumble over a wino who sat
slumped in his path. Regaining his balance, he veered toward
another stairway that led back up to the quai de la Tournelle.
He was at least seventy yards ahead and running fast.

Semko was now in an all-out sprint and gaining. He reached
the bottom of the stairway just as Strasser reached the top and
ran down the avenue out of sight. The sound of honking horns
and the screech of brakes told Semko that Strasser had crossed
the street against the traffic, and as he took the final steps two
at a time and emerged onto the sidewalk, he saw him run into
an alley on the opposite side of the street.

To the consternation of a man driving a delivery van, which
skidded sideways and bounced off the curb, Semko dashed
across the street and into the alley. Again, Strasser had disappeared. The alley was dark and empty. Semko could see to the

end, where it opened onto another street, but there was no one in front of him. He noticed a narrow cobbled lane that branched off to the right and he headed for it.

The dank, foul-smelling alley was silent, until the sound of a car engine broke the stillness. Semko ran into the cobbled lane to see a dark sedan pull out and speed off in the opposite direction. A small neon sign flickered and buzzed above the entrance to the neighborhood back-alley bar where Strasser had parked his car at the curb and walked to the meeting at the café. The light was bright enough for Semko to identify the departing sedan as a black BMW, and to see the driver throw a quick look over his shoulder as he pulled out. It was Dieter. Semko took aim with his pistol, but immediately realized that he didn't have a shot and lowered his weapon in disgust.

Strasser smiled to himself at the sight of Semko standing at the end of the lane with the pistol in his hand, and honked the horn twice in a defiant farewell.

Semko was about to accept defeat when he saw a man come out of the bar and stagger over to a primer-splotched Peugeot that had seen better days. He was fumbling with the keys in the door lock when Semko ran up to him, spun him around and punched him in the face. The drunken man reeled backward and collapsed into unconsciousness on the opposite curb, oblivious to what had just happened to him.

"Sorry," Semko said, and jumped into the car.

He pulled away with a grinding of gears and a howl of protest from the old engine as he skidded around the corner at the end of the lane. He saw the black BMW up ahead, two blocks away, turning right onto the rue d'Arcole. It was headed for the bridge that spanned the Seine and crossed the Ile de la Cité into the heart of Paris. Semko ran a red light and made up for some of the lost time.

Strasser, believing he was out of danger, and to avoid attracting attention, had slowed to the speed of the traffic flow.

He was looking through the rearview mirror when he saw the Peugeot run the light behind him and begin cutting wildly in and out of the one-way traffic across the bridge. He cursed and thumped the steering wheel with his fist, then floored the accelerator and began weaving through the slow-moving cars ahead.

Semko, caught up in the chase to the exclusion of all else, did not hear the wailing Klaxon, or see the flashing roof lights of the police car that had pulled out of an intersection two blocks back to join the high-speed pursuit. He was traveling at over seventy miles an hour, and the obstacle course of cars ahead demanded every bit of his concentration. He roared off the other side of the bridge having gained more than half the distance that separated him from the BMW, and took the dogleg turn to the left onto Victoria Avenue on two wheels.

The forces at work on the unbalanced and underengineered Peugeot were too much. Semko tried to finesse the skid when the wheels on the driver's side slammed back down onto the road, but he couldn't regain control of the car as it bounced, then lurched into a 360-degree spin, jumped the curb, and smashed into a streetlamp, shearing it off at the base before coming to an abrupt stop up on the sidewalk against a low stone wall that partially crumbled under the force of the impact. Semko tried in vain to continue the chase, but the car was damaged to the point where the engine only belched smoke, emitted a high-pitched whine, and gave no power to the rear wheels.

The police car screeched to a halt at the curb as Semko got out of the Peugeot to see the black BMW disappear in the distance. Now fully aware of the flashing lights, he turned to confront the two Parisian cops as they approached. His only hope was to come up with a believable story that at worst would get him off with a reckless driving charge, resulting in a stiff fine, if he was lucky. His cover assignment at the embassy's security section was a nonofficial cover (referred to at the Agency as NOC) and he did not have the diplomatic immunity that protected the permanent CIA station personnel.

The two young cops, accustomed to crazy drivers in a country that was widely believed to have given birth to them, seemed to be accepting the incident as routine. That was until they stopped in their tracks, their bodies tensing and their facial expressions changing as though a mask had been removed. They both remembered the radio call earlier, reporting that shots had been fired in the vicinity. They put the two incidents together as their eyes fixed on Semko's waistband, and they drew their weapons.

Semko was at first puzzled by their actions, then glanced down to see that his Windbreaker was open, and in plain sight, tucked into his waistband at the front of his jeans where he had placed it when he got in the car, was the Browning High-Power semiautomatic pistol.

"Ah, shit!" was all that he could say.

His knowledge of the French language was nonexistent, but he didn't need a phrase book to understand what the cops were shouting at him. He raised his hands above his head, then assumed the position over the trunk of the wrecked car.

THE TWO MOSSAD agents in the van had seen the Peugeot collide with the streetlamp and the wall from a distance. They drove slowly by the scene of the accident just as another police car arrived and the arresting officers were shoving Semko into the back of their patrol car, his hands cuffed behind his back.

"Did you get the license of the other car?" the audio man, who was now driving the van, asked.

"Never got the chance," the other agent said. "It looked like a Mercedes or a BMW, but I'm not sure. What now?"

"We'll go back to the safe house where Jost was hiding out. Maybe the tall guy with the blond hair will show up."

He stopped the van at a traffic light at the next intersection, just as the police car carrying Semko pulled up alongside in the left-turn lane. The intersection was well lit, and the agent driving the van inched forward until he had a clear view of Semko in the back. When Obert's radio transmission had finally reached them he had reported that the man who assaulted him was probably CIA, which meant he would probably have documents to support a false identity, making any information they could get on the arrest through contacts in the Parisian police department worthless.

With that in mind, the agent driving the van reached into a black nylon bag between the front seats and took out a camera equipped with automatic exposure and focus and a motor drive. All that was needed was to zoom in with the telephoto lens, which the Mossad agent did, snapping off a series of pictures.

"Maybe somebody back at headquarters can identify him," the driver said as he watched the patrol car swing left and head back across the river to the Saint-Germain precinct station house.

« 9 »

In Berlin's Zehlendorf district, at the edge of the idyllic Grunewald, passersby paid little attention to the few white, cottagelike buildings set inside a secure compound just off Wasserkafersteig Road. The scene is deceptively tranquil, revealing nothing of the appalling legacy that lies within. It is deep beneath the rich, dark brown earth, in a sprawling underground complex that was once an SS-controlled communications center, that a labyrinth of bleak, silent passageways and concrete bunkers holds the terrible secrets that still haunt the German nation.

Administered by the United States Army until 1953, then taken over by the U.S. State Department, the Berlin Documents Center is the central repository and archives for over thirty million official files from Nazi Germany, including the complete personnel records of the murderous SS. Access to the fenced-in compound is gained only through a gatehouse, and security guards screen all those who enter and leave the complex. Still, more than twenty thousand documents have disappeared over the years.

Paul Adamson, the American State Department official in charge of administering the center, knew, though he was unable to prove, that most of the missing documents had not been misplaced or lost as was claimed, but were smuggled out by some of the fifty German nationals who made up his staff of researchers and archivists. Many of those files, he eventually learned, turned up in the hands of dealers in Nazi memorabilia and were sold for thousands of dollars each to collectors around the world. Others were discovered in auction houses in Hamburg, Munich, and London and eventually returned, while still others were believed to have been used to blackmail former Nazis who had recast their lives, thinking their sordid pasts were long forgotten.

Werner Lindner was one of the German nationals working at the Berlin Documents Center. After falsifying his family background on his application form, he had taken the job upon graduating from the University of Munich fourteen years ago. It was a time when the specter of Nazi brutality had risen once again, in the form of the highly publicized trial of ten former SS officers, once guards at the Maidenak concentration camp in Poland where more than a quarter of a million Jews had perished. Lindner had his own private agenda for wanting the monotonous, low-paying job, and four months later, when he was assigned as an archivist in the SS personnel files section, he was finally in a position to accomplish what he had set out to do: to systematically destroy the files on his father and two of his father's friends, all of whom had served with the SS in the concentration camps during the war.

Over the years there had been other requests to expunge the records of frightened and desperate men, and in each case, Lindner sold his unique services to those in need. When not destroying or altering files, his performance as an archivist was otherwise exemplary, and he began work this morning as he had for the past two years, methodically sorting through and organizing the enormous number of documents in his section, in preparation for their transfer to microfilm. The request for a records search that had been routed to his small, cramped office space was slipped into his in basket shortly before noon.

The request had come from the chief of police in Berchtesgaden. The subject, Heinz Bauer, recently deceased, was believed to have been a member of the SS. The notation that the name *Bauer* was an alias made Lindner shake his head in amusement, until he saw that the SS service number was included. Without that, the task of determining who the man really was would have been impossible. The enclosed fingerprints were worthless to him. He had no way of expertly comparing them even if he did manage to stumble across the correct file. But he had long ago cross-indexed the personnel files with the SS service numbers that were available to him, and finding out who number 158-669 was would not take long.

Forty minutes later, Lindner took the elevator up to the first level and entered the anteroom to the administrator's office. The secretary announced his presence and opened the door to the inner office, where Paul Adamson rose from behind his desk and came around to greet his visitor with a warm handshake.

"Werner, what brings you up from the bowels of the earth?"

"I found something that I thought might be of interest to you, sir," Lindner said, handing Adamson the file and the letter from his in basket.

Adamson glanced at the request for information from the Berchtesgaden police, then opened the file and began paging through the attached documents, which were yellow with age.

"Heinz Dieter Strasser. Doesn't ring a bell. Should it?"

"May I," Lindner said, and reached over to indicate the last few pages of the file. "It seems *Sturmbannführer der Waffen SS* Strasser was the subject of an American OSS investigation in 1946, the forerunner of your Central Intelligence Agency, if I am not mistaken."

"That's correct," Adamson said, his interest piqued.

"The details of the investigation are noted as being classified top secret and are not included," Lindner continued. "And a further amendment shows that the file was again accessed in 1954, by the CIA, but there is no mention as to the purpose of that inquiry either."

Adamson skimmed the enclosed pages, frowning as he read. "Was he a war criminal, involved in the extermination programs?"

"No, sir. The years he served in the SS are all accounted for in his record. He was highly decorated, a Knight's Cross with oak leaves; he spent three years on the Russian front, and then was assigned to the security detachment at Obersalzberg until the end of the war."

Adamson shrugged. "Beats the hell out of me."

"Considering that the inquiry came from a police department," Lindner said, "I would normally comply with their request, but I thought you might want this handled differently, in light of the unusual history."

"Send them what they asked for," Adamson said. "But don't include any of the information from the supplementary documents on the investigation." A thought occurred to him, and he added, "I want to make a copy of the file. I'll send the original back down to you later today."

Lindner knew more about the machinations of intelligence agencies than he let on. Despite his anti-Semitic feelings, and a distorted view of history gained from a father who insisted that the Holocaust was a Jewish hoax, he was not above dealing with the very people he held in contempt. Four times in the past five years, he had provided copies of classified files for a man he was certain was an Israeli agent. The man had paid handsomely for the information, and it crossed Lindner's mind as he entered the elevator that the file on Heinz Strasser might interest him as well. He would make a copy for himself and contact the man at the number in Bonn he had been given for just such occasions.

Paul Adamson placed his own telephone call shortly after Lindner left. He used the scrambler-equipped line, provided for official State Department business, which was linked with the secure satellite communications network for other American government agencies throughout Europe.

The number he dialed rang in a second-floor office of the huge CIA base located in the old I. G. Farben Building adjacent to the Rhein-Main Air Force Base in Frankfurt. The man who answered the phone with a less-than-cheery announcement of his last name was Alex Tarkanian, an old friend with whom Adamson had served in Vietnam in an army intelligence unit. Tarkanian had been the Frankfurt chief of base for the past three years, an opportune time, what with the collapse of the Iron Curtain and the influx of defecting agents from throughout Eastern Europe who were providing a gold mine of intelligence information.

"How's everything in the land of smoke and mirrors?" Adamson said.

"Hey, Paul. How ya doin'? You in Frankfurt?"

"No, but I will be tomorrow."

"I'll look forward to it," Tarkanian said. "We'll toss a few back and lie about the old days. So what's up?"

"Something came across my desk this morning that I thought you might want to take a look at."

"What's that?"

"A file on a former SS officer, recently deceased. It seems your people had an interest in him back in '54. We got a request from the Berchtesgaden police for information; he was using an alias at the time of his death. Probably nothing to it, but since I'm coming down anyway, I thought I'd bring a copy of the file with me."

"Yeah, sure. Can't hurt. I'll pass it on to the research nerds at Langley, they like that kind of shit. Keeps them from dreaming up make-work for guys like me.''

"See you Friday," Adamson said, and hung up. He slipped the copies his secretary had made of the Strasser file and the police request into his briefcase, and thought no more about it.

AT 1:15 P.M., in the apartment across the street from the terror-ist safe house in the Montmartre section of Paris, the computer terminal at the communications console beeped three times. It was the reply from Mossad headquarters in Tel Aviv for which the agents manning the observation post had been waiting. Nathan Obert instructed the computer to decode and print out the encrypted message, then relayed the information to the three other men sitting around the front room overlooking the street.

"They want us to grab Gunther Jost."

"That doesn't make any sense," Moshe Harel said, getting up from his chair in front of the audio console. "As stupid as he is, he's extremely valuable to us; he's exposed every opera-tion he's been involved in."

"It isn't a request," Obert said to the team leader. "It's an order from the chief of operations."

Harel shook his head in disapproval. "What do they want us to do with him?"

"Take him to the safe house in the country and interrogate him," Obert said. "They want to know if the man we saw him with at the café was in fact Dieter, and what they are plan-ning."

"Any mention of the laboratory results on the things we sent them last night?" Harel asked. He had worked into the early morning hours preparing photographs to be faxed and using the satellite communications system to transmit the bits of conversation they had managed to pick up.

"They weren't able to do much with the recordings from

the meeting,'' Obert said. ''They did get enough to match the voice print of the tall blond subject at the café who spoke French with a German accent, to the voice of the man who called from Germany, but they have no recordings of Dieter to make a comparison.''

''What about the frames from the videotapes and the photographs I enlarged and faxed to them?''

''Nothing in the files on the guy the cops grabbed, or the Frenchman at the meeting, and the few frames we got of the one we suspected of being Dieter were too grainy and taken at a bad angle. Again there was nothing to compare them to.''

Harel was about to pick up his portable radio to inform the surveillance team down in the streets of their new orders when he saw a red light flash on one of the units at the audio console. The light indicated that Gunther Jost was receiving an incoming call. Harel sat back down in his chair and slipped on the headset, listening intently until the call was completed.

''Who was it?'' Obert asked.

Harel raised his hand for silence. He sorted through a stack of cassette tapes and found the one he wanted. He listened to a previously recorded call, then the call he had just intercepted, rewinding them both and playing them back again. He then removed the headset and immediately picked up the small portable radio and spoke to the agents in the streets.

''Jost will be coming out at any moment,'' he said. ''Get a car into position to grab him. Sedate him and take him directly to the safe house in Etampes.''

Harel then turned to the other men in the room. ''The caller just arranged for a meeting. I thought I recognized the voice, and I was right. It was the same man who called from Germany and told him to go to a pay phone the other night. And according to the message in your hand,'' he said to Obert, ''also the same man who spoke German-accented French at the café. Only this time he didn't bother enforcing operational security. He simply told Jost to meet him at the tobacconist shop at the bottom of the rue Lepic.''

"This doesn't feel right," Obert said. "Why speak openly on a phone he didn't consider secure only two days ago?"

Harel stared thoughtfully at Obert for a moment, then moved quickly to the tripod-mounted telescope at the window.

Down on the streets, the closest mobile surveillance unit that was part of the Mossad team was six blocks away, parked a short distance from the stationary agent at the outer perimeter of their coverage. The mobile team was working its way through the slow-moving traffic and the maze of one-way streets, back toward the terrorist safe house, when they heard Harel's voice come over the radio again.

"Mobile One, where are you?"

"Approximately four blocks from your location."

"Get into position fast. He just came out the door."

It HADN'T TAKEN Jurgen Strasser long to figure out who had compromised the meeting at the café, and he had no tolerance for carelessness and stupidity on the part of others, especially when they were in a position to endanger his life. He was parked two blocks down from the Israeli observation post, facing up the hill on the same side of the street as the safe house, when he saw Jost come out of the building and walk along the sidewalk toward him. There were no pedestrians within view, and Strasser slouched down in the seat and peered over the dashboard.

As Jost passed by, Strasser opened the car door and called out to him. "Gunther."

Jost turned to see Strasser staring at him from the driver's seat of the BMW. He smiled and walked back toward the car.

"You idiot!" was all Strasser said as he aligned the trailing edge of the car door with Jost's body and pulled the firing mechanism for the twelve-gauge shotgun concealed inside the panel.

A storm of steel pellets tore into Jost's chest and stomach. The force of the blast picked him up off his feet and threw him backward, slamming him against the wall of a building. The wide-eyed expression of horror and disbelief lasted only an instant as he slid to the pavement and slumped onto his side in a fast-forming pool of blood.

Strasser jumped out of the car and ran over to the motionless body. He drew his pistol and fired two shots into Jost's head for good measure. It was an unnecessary precaution; the shotgun blast had killed him before he hit the ground.

THE MUFFLED ROAR of the shotgun and the sharp report of the pistol shots were heard in the Mossad observation post and immediately recognized for what they were.

"Goddamnit!" Harel shouted, and spoke into the portable radio. "Jost has been hit!"

Harel heard the distant sound of tires squealing and the roar of an engine. He looked out the window to see a black BMW race by the safe house.

"Mobile One, where are you?"

"We have just turned off rue Tourlaque onto rue Lepic."

"The shooter is two blocks behind you, headed in your direction," Harel said. "He's driving a black BMW. Stop him! I want him alive. Wound him if you have to, but do not kill him unless absolutely unavoidable!"

The agent driving Mobile Unit One spun into a perfectly executed 180-degree turn, and came to a stop facing the wrong direction on the narrow one-way street. He positioned his car to block all but a small portion of the roadway and then, along with his partner, got out of the car and waited for the confrontation.

Back at the observation post, Harel glanced at the large-scale street map of Paris taped to the wall. "Mobile Two, what's your position?"

"We are on the rue Caulaincourt, just past the Montmartre cemetery."

"Continue north to the avenue Junot, follow it to where it intersects rue Lepic, and block the street on that end."

Harel looked at the map again. If the shooter managed to get past Mobile Unit One, the second unit was positioned to block the next intersection, giving them two chances to stop him.

STRASSER SMILED WITH an evil delight as he saw the white Opel sedan angled across the street ahead. It was the reckless, retributive side of his character that had led him to boldly confront his antagonists—to beard them in their own den, as he thought of it. The inclination to occasionally respond irrationally, out of anger and pride, was a flaw in his otherwise cold, calculating professional nature. A flaw that had, more than once in his adult life, caused him trouble that nearly ended in disaster; yet it was so inherent that it would not be denied. He knew that someone must have had Jost under surveillance, and assumed correctly that it was the Mossad, who had been trying to find him since the Amsterdam synagogue bombing. If they were foolish enough to believe that the man they knew as Dieter was an easy target, he would teach them a hard lesson.

The two Mossad agents from Mobile Unit One had opened the driver's and front passenger's doors and taken cover behind them. Their pistols were cocked and ready and braced between the doors and the body of the car.

Strasser reached beneath the dash of the BMW and pulled the H&K MP-5-SD nine-millimeter submachine gun from its mounting bracket and laid it across his lap. The deadly weapon was equipped with a sound suppressor and loaded with a thirty-round magazine of Teflon-coated full-jacketed ammunition. He waited until he was less than forty feet from the

Mossad car to come to a stop, then left the engine running, and sat staring at the two men with their weapons trained on him.

"Get out of the car and put your hands where I can see them!" the Mossad agent behind the driver's-side door shouted in French.

Strasser smiled as he clicked the safety off the short, compact submachine gun and braced it on the armrest and hand grip on the inside of the door. The weapon was out of sight, but within easy reach as he opened the door, raised both hands, and got slowly out of the car.

"Don't shoot!" he shouted back in French, keeping his hands low, only shoulder high.

"Put your hands behind your head and walk toward us," the same Mossad agent ordered. He kept his weapon aimed at Strasser's chest as he moved out into the open and cautiously approached.

Strasser, still standing partially behind the door, glanced to his left to see a small group of curious onlookers gathering at the edge of the sidewalk. One called out to him, asking if they were making a movie.

A few more people stopped to watch. One, an old man, announced in a loud, uneasy voice that there were no cameras. The distraction on the sidewalk drew the attention of the two Mossad agents. It was only a momentary lapse in their concentration, but a fatal one, and Strasser seized the opportunity.

With a swift, accomplished move that he had taught hundreds of his terrorist students, he snatched the submachine gun from the armrest and brought it smoothly into position at his shoulder. He fired instinctively and with a degree of accuracy of which few shooters are capable. His first three-round burst struck the agent moving toward him in the center of the chest, killing him instantly. The suppressor attached to the end of the barrel emitted nothing more than a low, muttering sound.

Shocked at the sight of his friend and partner dropping to

the ground, the second Mossad agent, still behind the car door, looked away for only a split second. But by the time he regained his sight picture and squeezed the trigger to fire, it was too late.

Amid the screams of the people on the sidewalk running for cover, Strasser fired off a second three-round burst, followed immediately by a third. The Teflon-coated ammunition ripped through the thin sheet metal on the car door and all six shots struck their target.

The second Mossad agent fired three shots wildly into the air and staggered backward, his body riddled with bullets as he collapsed on the street, mortally wounded.

Strasser wasted no time in getting away from the scene. A small space was open between the vehicle blocking his path and the cars parked at the curb on his right, but not enough for him to squeeze through. He pulled ahead until he made contact with the front bumper of the Mossad car, then pushed it back out of the way just enough to allow him to pass.

He sped north on the winding uphill grade, and three blocks later spotted the second Mossad car blocking the street just below the point where it intersected a broad avenue. It was parked in much the same manner as the first car, but the street was wider here and there was room to swerve up onto the sidewalk and break out.

The agents, positioned behind their car as the others had been, feared the worst after hearing the gunfire and being unable to raise the men in Mobile Unit One on the radio. Their fears were confirmed when they saw the black BMW appear around a bend and head toward them.

Strasser calmly evaluated his situation, and decided against pressing his luck twice in one day. He switched the lever on the submachine gun to full automatic instead of the three-round burst, and held it out the window in his left hand with the barrel resting between the side-view mirror and the car door. He slowed as he neared the intersection, to give the impression that he was about to stop. Then, fifty feet from where the Mossad agents were blocking the street, he floored the accelerator and opened fire.

The continuous hail of bullets that struck the car and ricocheted off the pavement caused the agents to duck down behind the doors and the panic-stricken pedestrians to scramble for safety. Strasser emptied the magazine just as he swerved up onto the sidewalk, sending a food vendor diving out of the way as the BMW rammed his cart and sent it crashing out into the avenue, where an oncoming car struck it again and sent it tumbling farther up the street.

The Mossad agents turned to fire at the fleeing vehicle, in hopes of shooting out the tires, but the terrified people on the sidewalk and the other traffic on the avenue Junot made it impossible. The agents watched helplessly as the black BMW bounced down off the curb, rounded the corner, and drove out of sight.

AIR FRANCE FLIGHT number 75 from Paris to New York City lifted off the runway at Charles de Gaulle Airport at 5:35 P.M. that evening. Strasser was seated in the first-class smoking section drinking a glass of champagne and smiling at the attractive flight attendant who refilled his glass after the plane finished its climb out. He bore only a passing resemblance to the man who two hours earlier had entered a room in the Sofitel Paris Hotel at the airport. He had trimmed and dyed his blond hair brown, and inserted soft contact lenses that turned his blue eyes a deep green. Dressed in an impeccably tailored dark gray business suit and crisp white shirt, with an Hermès print tie that added just the right touch of color, he looked the part of the well-to-do businessman.

He was traveling on one of four expertly forged passports from different countries that he had been issued by the Stasi for use in his terrorist operations. This time he had chosen to pass as a Canadian, Brian McConnell of Toronto. Perfected over the years, his unaccented English, with an occasional Canadian inflection added to the right words, would lead all but a trained linguist to believe that it was his first language.

Strasser's true expertise was in the areas of operational security and improvised demolitions. He was a meticulous planner and an innovative master at designing radio-controlled bombs, long-term digital timers, barometrically actuated firing devices, and other sophisticated techniques in the field of explosives. During his seven years at Massow, he had trained members of every major terrorist group, often accompanying them on actual missions as an adviser.

There had been five notable operations of his own planning and execution in the final year before the collapse of East Germany and the dissolution of the Stasi. Five horrifying acts in a seven-month period that had brought him to prominence in the world of international terrorism. All five had been contract operations accepted by the Stasi and instigated and paid for by the Iraqis and the Syrians, and all had been directed against American and Israeli targets on the European continent. All had been bloody massacres, and the counter-terrorist agencies around the world, frustrated in their attempts to learn anything about him, began calling him ''Dieter''—the code name he had used for the first of the five operations. He liked the uncompromising notoriety, and continued to use the name exclusively when leaving messages that claimed responsibility for the remaining terrorist acts he had planned and participated in that year.

Since the fall of East Germany, he had tested his newly reorganized Red Army Faction group only once—the bombing of the Amsterdam synagogue—and his team had functioned with clockwork execution and cold professionalism. Since then, primarily due to lack of funds, they had been operationally inactive, planning and training at the farmhouse south of Baden-Baden. But that, thanks to his father's legacy, was about to change.

As the plane leveled off at its cruising altitude for the long flight, Strasser adjusted the seat back and snapped open the clasps on his ostrich-skin briefcase. He removed the file his father had left him and placed it on the tray table. The embossed Nazi seal on the cover page, a swastika enclosed in a wreath and held in the talons of an eagle, caught the attention of the man seated beside him. Strasser gave the man—an American, he judged by his clothes and the magazine he was reading—a hard look that precluded any conversation or further violation of his privacy, then began to take notes as he opened the file and read.

« 10 »

THE COPY OF the file from the Berlin Documents Center that
Paul Adamson hand-delivered to Alex Tarkanian on Friday left
the Frankfurt base in the courier bag for CIA headquarters late
that same evening.

On Monday morning, the file was initially delivered to the
head of the German Branch in the European Division of the
Operations Directorate, who, with a full plate of current projects of his own to keep him busy, sent the obviously mislaid
and outdated documents on to the Intelligence Directorate's
Office of European Analysis, where, after a cursory inspection,
it was decided that whatever the file's significance, it was totally unrelated to anything in their bailiwick and was passed on
to the Office of Information Resources. From there, for some
unfathomable reason, it was routed to the Office of Resources,
Trade, and Technology, where someone with a more logical
train of thought finally directed it to the library's Historical
Intelligence Collection.

Had it not been for the fateful presence of Peter Barrett
Danning, the file on Heinz Strasser might have continued to be
ignored and eventually ended up in the library's stacks to be
forgotten. Every inch the Agency "Old Boy," Danning was a
remnant from the days when the OSS was referred to as "Oh

So Social," and most of its ranks were filled with young, dedicated men from America's Ivy League schools and its wealthiest and most socially prominent families. He had retired in 1988, after forty-five years of continuous service, and two years ago decided to write a definitive history of the Office of Strategic Services and the early years of the CIA. In deference to his years of service, he was provided an office at headquarters from which to do his research in the Agency's library, and was given access to the historical records for the time period related to his work.

Danning was in the midst of transcribing some personal notes from one of the volumes of a diary he had faithfully kept throughout his career when there was a knock at his office door. The young research assistant, who for the past two years had been generous with her time in helping him locate hard-to-find documents and files, came in with a steaming hot cup of coffee.

"Good morning, Mr. Danning. Fresh brewed. Thought you might like some."

"How thoughtful, my dear," Danning said, with his most charming smile, and took an appreciative sip before setting the cup down on his work table.

"How's the work going?"

"Fine. Moving right along."

"If you need anything, just let me know." She turned to leave, then remembered the envelopes tucked under her arm. "Oh, I almost forgot." She handed him the top envelope and said, "This just landed on my desk. Don't know if it's related to your work, but since it's the same era, I thought you might want to look through it before I filed it away."

Danning thanked her and took the envelope. He removed the enclosed file and glanced at the cover page. The name Heinz Strasser was strangely familiar, though he could not remember why. It was not until the young researcher left, and he flipped through the enclosed documents and reached the next-to-the-last page containing the brief acknowledgment of an OSS investigation in 1946, that it all came back to him.

AFTER THE LIBERATION of France, when Danning's work with the Resistance was over, he was assigned for a brief period to the OSS Art Looting Investigation Unit that had been rushed into Germany during the last days of the war to coordinate their efforts with the army's Monuments, Fine Arts, and Archives Unit. Nicknamed the Venus Fixers, their mission was to locate, recover, and return to their rightful owners the hundreds of millions of dollars in art treasures stolen by the Nazis, particularly the extensive collection that Reich Marshal Hermann Goering was believed to have in his possession.

Danning's specific assignment, at the direct order of Allen Dulles, chief of the OSS office in Switzerland, was to locate and confiscate any and all records involving Goering's art dealings in Switzerland during his years in power in the Third Reich, and to treat such records as top secret in expediting their shipment to Dulles's office in Bern. With the German empire crumbling all around them, Danning thought that placing such a high priority on documents dealing with business transactions a bit strange, but as a young OSS captain, he was in no position to question his orders.

The hunt for Hermann Goering did not take long. After fleeing Obersalzberg, the reich marshal had hidden out in a castle in Mauterndorf, Austria. Released from SS custody after Hitler's death, on the afternoon of May 8, 1945, Goering surrendered, with his family and Luftwaffe aides, to a detachment of thirty men from the reconnaissance company of the 636th Tank Destroyer Battalion under the personal command of Brig. Gen. Robert J. Stack, assistant commander of the 36th Infantry Division. General Stack's friendly handshake greeting of the famous Nazi earned him a stern reprimand from General Eisenhower when he learned of it, and from that point on Goering was treated as an ordinary prisoner of war. He was driven to the 36th Division headquarters in Kitzbühel, where the following day he was separated from his family and transferred to the Seventh Army Interrogation Center in Augsburg in southern Germany.

It was there that Danning found him. Stripped of his medals and jewel-encrusted reich marshal's baton, and forced to give up his elaborate uniforms, he was dressed in the plain, unadorned tunic and trousers of an ordinary Luftwaffe officer—a thoroughly defeated man, facing the additional humiliation of enforced withdrawal from the drugs to which he was addicted. But there was no sign of contrition in the egocentric personality, nor any indication that he had the slightest inkling of what fate had in store for him. (Within days, he would be indicted as a war criminal, subsequently put on trial in Nuremberg with the rest of the Nazi hierarchy, and found guilty, only to cheat the hangman by committing suicide by poison capsule in his cell minutes before his sentence was to be carried out.)

Danning spent the better part of a day conducting an indepth interview with the former reich marshal, and found him both charming and manipulative, and constantly had to remind himself that this man was one of the founding members of the National Socialist German Workers' Party. One of the *"Alte Kämpfer,"* the old fighters of the NSDAP movement. A man who had formed his liaison with Hitler in November of 1922; marched with him and was wounded at his side in November of 1923; and in 1939 was named Deputy Führer of the Third Reich, second only in power to Hitler. He had created the *Geheime Staatspolizei,* better known as the Gestapo; and was the impetus behind the building of the *Konzentrationslager,* the infamous concentration camp system, and consequently, a strong proponent of, and contributor to, the plan to exterminate the Jews.

Danning had listened with fascination to the stories of Goe-ring's last days in Berlin and the rush to his mountain chalet in Obersalzberg to save his own skin. Fully aware of the immi-nent collapse of the Third Reich, he had left the Führer's bunker on April 20, following Hitler's macabre birthday cele-bration: "Not for me a *Götterdämmerung* death beneath the streets of Berlin," he had told the young OSS captain.

Danning eventually established that the reich marshal's art treasures had preceded him to his mountain retreat. Nine train cars filled with the spoils of his twelve years in power: paint-ings, tapestries, oriental rugs, furniture, jewels, porcelains; and countless chalices, clocks, tankards, candelabra, and table or-naments, all of solid gold, estimated to be worth at least two hundred million dollars. Goering spoke of them lovingly, with great pride of possession, never once letting on that he had acquired them by less than legal means.

The vast collection, Goering said, had been removed from Karinhall, his country estate north of Berlin, and transported in his special train to Berchtesgaden. Some of it had not been evacuated in time, and had fallen into the hands of the advanc-ing Russians. But most of it, the last time Goering had seen it, was locked in the train cars that were parked inside a railroad tunnel on the outskirts of Berchtesgaden. With patient prod-ding, and without giving away the exact area of his interest, Danning determined that all of the reich marshal's records and files, including those of his art dealings, had been gathered by his administrative aide, Egon Hofer, and placed on board the train. To the best of Goering's knowledge, that was where they remained. Some duplicate records may have been captured by the Russians, but he could not be certain; they had packed and fled in such haste.

Danning lost no time in leaving Augsburg for Berchtesga-den. He drove the more than 130 miles into the heart of the Bavarian Alps at night in an open jeep, through an area that was far from secure and was reported to have isolated bands of SS troops, who had vowed to fight to the death, still roaming the countryside. In Berchtesgaden, he found the Goering collection in the hands of a battalion of the American 101st Airborne Division. The commander of the unit, after discovering the train and realizing the enormous value of its contents, had ordered everything moved to Unterstein, four miles outside of Berchtesgaden on the road to Königssee. There in a low rambling structure that had been a rest house for Luftwaffe pilots, Danning found a sight beyond belief. The Bavarian-peasant-style lodge appeared to have all of the finest artwork from all of Europe's museums crammed into every available space—an appearance, Danning realized after touring the building, that was not too far removed from reality.

The paintings alone, many of them recognized masterpieces, filled forty rooms, stacked ten or fifteen deep against the walls. Corridors were jammed with priceless sculpture. The entire length and width of the sixty-by-thirty-foot dining room overflowed with exquisite Italian Renaissance furniture piled carelessly to the ceiling. Other rooms were filled with tapestries and rugs. One room, with a guard posted outside, held Danning spellbound when he opened the door to see millions of dollars' worth of gold artifacts and precious jewels glistening in the shafts of morning sunlight streaming through the leaded glass windows.

The file cabinets containing the records of "purchases and sales of art," for which Danning was looking, were all stored in a small ground-floor room, and a careful search revealed that the file concerning all transactions made in Switzerland was missing.

At the suggestion of the American major in charge of securing the Goering collection, Danning's search took him to a local minor Nazi party official who owned a grocery store in Berchtesgaden. The man had been found with two paintings and a number of gold artifacts that he had taken from the train before the American troops arrived. After Danning threatened him with arrest as a war criminal, he admitted that, yes, he might know who had stolen some of the reich marshal's documents from the train. An SS major by the name of Heinz Strasser, whom he knew from the Obersalzberg security battalion, had hidden in a nearby mountain cabin after the bombing raid. He had come to him for food and had paid him with gold coins, and told him about the train and its treasures. The grocer had seen official documents with the reich marshal's seal in the leather portfolio Strasser carried, and had thought it quite odd, considering all of the intrinsically valuable things on the train, that the *Sturmbannführer* would bother with documents. No, he was no longer at the cabin, and he did not know where he was now.

Danning followed the next logical lead, and with the help of the OSS office in Munich, tracked Egon Hofer, Goering's administrative aide, to the home of his sister on the outskirts of Salzburg, Austria, where Hofer had gone into hiding after the reich marshal left Obersalzberg. Danning had no more than introduced himself as an OSS officer from the Art Looting Investigation Unit, than Hofer said, "First the Russians, now you," then walked calmly over to a desk in one corner of the large living room, removed a Luger pistol from the top drawer, and shot himself in the head without another word.

Danning continued his search for two more weeks, but with no trail, not even a scent to follow, he got no closer to Strasser or the documents on which his OSS superiors had placed such importance. With nothing else to be done, he submitted his written report to the OSS office in Bern, Switzerland, and was reassigned to more general work with the Art Looting Investigation Unit. He spent the next few months researching the claims of the nations conquered and ravaged by Hitler's armies, and helping to track down and return their looted treasures.

Ten months later, in March of 1946, when the captured service records of all SS personnel were gathered in what became the Berlin Documents Center, Danning was temporarily ordered to resume his search for the Goering file. He found that no fewer than twenty-three Heinz Strassers had been members of the SS, but only one, Heinz Dieter Strasser, had been assigned to the Obersalzberg security battalion when the war ended. The records showed his home to be in Elmshorn, in northern Germany. The trail ended abruptly when Danning visited the small, peaceful town in the countryside thirty-five miles northwest of Hamburg.

The house in which Heinz Strasser had spent his youth was now nothing but an empty lot filled with rubble; the result of an errant Royal Air Force bomber dropping its payload off target. According to the Strasser family's neighbors, the father, stationed on the Normandy coast, had been killed during the invasion, and the mother was killed in her sleep when the bomb hit the house. A younger brother, in the navy, died when the submarine he was aboard was sunk in the North Atlantic. The older brother, Heinz, they said, never came back after the war, and was presumed to be dead. It was a variation of a sad but not uncommon tale among the Germans in those days, and once more, with no leads to take him further, Danning's search ended.

AND NOW, FORTY-SIX years later, Heinz Strasser had cropped up again. In death as in life, elusive and mysterious, Danning thought as he read the copy of the request for information from the Berchtesgaden police and saw that Strasser had returned to the former symbol of Nazi power at Obersalzberg using an assumed name.

Danning turned to the last page in the file and noticed that a follow-up investigation of some sort had been conducted in 1954. There were no details, and he assumed that it was someone at the newly formed CIA attempting to clean up the unfinished business of its OSS predecessor.

The reemergence of Strasser intrigued Danning, and on a hunch, he switched on the Agency computer terminal on his work table and called up the Historical Intelligence Collection's data base. He instructed the computer to conduct a global search for the name *Heinz Dieter Strasser,* and to his surprise, a small window opened on the screen informing him that the CIA's file on Strasser was part of an operation code-named BACKLASH that was classified top secret. The identifiers preceding the code name attributed the operation's origin to the Counterintelligence Staff.

Danning thought it unusual that a highly classified file was openly listed as part of the library's data base, and out of curiosity, thinking that perhaps the classification had since been downgraded, attempted to call up the file. The screen flashed a warning that specific code-word access was required. Having no idea what the code word might be, and with confirmation that BACKLASH was still classified top secret, he made a note to ask his research assistant if she might know of any related unclassified information, then turned off the computer terminal to resume transcribing the notes from his diary.

FIVE FLOORS ABOVE Peter Danning's office, in a specially secured computer room in the Counterintelligence Center, Danning's interest in the Strasser file had set off a silent alarm. It was the first time since the operational file on BACKLASH was listed in the data base that that particular alarm had been tripped. The security officer on duty, not recognizing the alarm code, had to copy down the numbers indicated on the screen and consult his code book for instructions. Procedures called for immediate notification of the chief of the Counterintel-

ligence Staff. He was to be informed directly, bypassing the
normal chain of command.

IT TOOK THE security officers forty-five minutes to find the room
containing the computer terminal from which the request for
the BACKLASH file had originated.

Peter Danning was at first indignant, then angry, about the
conduct of the three brusque and overbearing young men who
entered without knocking. He didn't appreciate their disrespectful attitude at all, and found their behavior rude to say the
least. The officer in charge told him—not asked him, mind you
—to come with him immediately. Probably a lower-percentile
graduate of some obscure two-year community college, Danning told himself, typical of the quality of recruits the Agency
was getting these days.

"May I inquire as to the purpose of this intrusion?" Danning said, his voice well into its nasal range as he rose to his
feet and stood a head taller than the three men dressed in dark
blue suits and obviously carrying concealed weapons under
their jackets. His tone of voice and haughty downward gaze let
them know in no uncertain terms that he was not accustomed
to such treatment, nor would he tolerate it.

"I'm not at liberty to say," the officer in charge snapped
officiously, when in fact, he had no idea why he had been
dispatched, just that he was to bring whoever was responsible
to the office of the chief of the Counterintelligence Staff without delay.

"You are to come with me immediately," he repeated.

Danning, by now in high dudgeon, simply stood his ground
and fixed an icy stare on the officer, silently demanding an
explanation before he would budge.

Past experience in dealing with Agency heavyweights, and
the ability to recognize trouble when it was staring him in the
face, told the ranking security officer that the man standing

before him was in all probability somewhat more than a library staffer. Following his well-developed instincts for self-preservation, and his own personal maxim of "when in doubt, leave the man his balls," he diplomatically rephrased his demand in the form of an urgent request.

Danning, placated to some degree, exhaled a sharp huff of vindication and followed the three men out of the office and down the corridor to the elevator.

« 11 »

ALFRED PALMER WAS not a spy; he was a spycatcher. His primary responsibilities as chief of the Counterintelligence Staff were to prevent penetration of the CIA, and to expose and frustrate efforts to confuse and mislead the Agency with disinformation.

It was a profession that required Palmer to be suspicious of even his closest colleagues, and, by its very nature, a profession that was intensely isolating, with a flow and momentum that drove one deeper and deeper into that isolation and ultimately into a world of suspicion of betrayal and suspicion of conspiracy. To do the job successfully required a man of sophisticated intelligence, capable of analyzing and dissecting all aspects of the Agency's operations without falling into the abyss of paranoia that awaited those who became lost in the circular madness of plots and counterplots, double agents and provocations, and false defectors intrinsic to the work.

Counterintelligence was indeed the "wilderness of mirrors" that the brilliant dark prince and legendary former CI chief, James Angleton, had called it before a career that spanned three decades ended in ruins after he stepped irretrievably over the edge and was asked to resign by then–Director of Central Intelligence William E. Colby.

Palmer had been dancing on the edge for the past eight years, and had yet to lose his balance. His success was due largely to his ability to find the right thread to unravel the arcane and intricate operations launched against the CIA, and to his intuitive intelligence, which recognized where things logically ended, keeping him from getting caught up in a descending spiral of endless suspicions. He thrived on puzzles and enigmas, and enjoyed ferreting out the common denominator in disparate intelligence reports that seemed on the surface to bear no relation to one another, juggling all of the permutations until he found the hint of a pattern where others saw nothing but eclectic, meaningless bits and pieces. He was nothing if not dogged and persistent, a true professional who loved his work, and was comfortable only in that milieu. Cold and calculating by nature, he overcompensated for an innate shyness and social awkwardness with a forced geniality and charm, and sometimes stilted language and exaggerated manners, which led those who did not know him to misjudge the sharp, penetrating intelligence lurking just behind the thinly veiled facade. Those who underestimated him did so at their peril.

He greeted a still indignant Peter Danning with a handshake that Danning had always thought of as the exclusive province of Episcopalian ministers: as their right hands joined, Palmer folded his left hand over top, immobilizing the clasped hands. The variation of the traditional handshake was too smarmy and familiar for Danning's taste, and was, he had found, usually accompanied by steady eye contact and a relentlessly sincere monologue delivered two inches closer to one's face than was really necessary.

Releasing his grip, and breaking eye contact, Palmer flashed a cordial smile; then, with a subtle nod of his head, he commanded the three security officers to remain in the anteroom as he ushered Danning inside.

"So you're the culprit," he said, downplaying a matter that he had taken quite seriously until he saw the old cold warrior escorted into his office suite. He recalled that someone had told him Danning was working on a book about his OSS days, and immediately pieced together a plausible scenario for what might have happened.

"How've you been, Peter?"

"Quite well, until a few minutes ago. What's the meaning of this, Alfred?"

Danning had known the CI chief as a young case officer at the Prague station, when Danning was station chief there and Palmer had given a good account of himself during the tense atmosphere of the Warsaw Pact invasion of Czechoslovakia in August of 1968, when the Soviets had brutally crushed the popular uprising by the Czech people. He considered Palmer to be a competent, if not innovative and shrewd intelligence officer; about what one would expect from a fellow Princeton man from an old New England family who had been with the Agency for twenty-six years.

"I was curious about your interest in BACKLASH," Palmer said.

"Curious? I should think that sending three Neanderthals to abduct me went well beyond curious."

"An overreaction on their part, for which I apologize. Sit down, Peter," the CI chief said, and gestured to a grouping of two easy chairs and a sofa off to one side of his office. Danning took a chair opposite where Palmer sat on the sofa.

"Now, tell me, how's the book progressing? And how does BACKLASH fit into it?"

"The book is going well, and BACKLASH, whatever that might be, doesn't fit into it at all. The first I heard of it was when I tried to access the library file on a man by the name of Heinz Strasser."

"Strasser?" Palmer feigned ignorance while closely watch-

ing Danning's every expression for any hint that he was telling
less than the complete truth.

Danning told the CI chief about the file that had been given
to him earlier, and of how serendipitous he thought it was that
after all these years the name of the former SS officer should
crop up again.

Palmer listened patiently while Danning told him at length
of his investigation forty-six years ago. Halfway through the
old man's explicitly detailed recollection, he knew that his
initial supposition was correct. Danning was telling the truth;
it had been sheer coincidence that he had stumbled onto the
BACKLASH snare that Palmer had inherited from his predeces-
sors.

"I'm terribly sorry for the inconvenience," Palmer said,
when Danning had finished. "It's apparently a foul-up in the
data base. BACKLASH was declassified years ago."

"And that's why it's still programmed to trip an alarm
when someone attempts to access it?" Danning didn't believe
a word of the CI chief's disingenuous dismissal of the incident.

"Just an oversight," Palmer said. "Sorry to have troubled
you, Peter."

"Thought you caught a live one, didn't you, Alfred?" Danning winked mischievously as he got to his feet. "Well, I'll try
not to invade your domain again."

"That's very good of you," Palmer said as he escorted
Danning to the door. "And good luck with the book. I'm
looking forward to reading it.

"By the way," he added as nonchalantly as possible,
"would you mind if one of my security people accompanied
you back to your office to pick up the file on Strasser? I'd like
to take a look at it."

"Of course not. And I suppose it would be prudent of me in

my writing to gloss over the specifics of my old investigation of the man.''

"That might be best," Palmer said. "Even better if he weren't mentioned at all.''

"I'll bear that in mind. Even though the entire matter is of course declassified.''

The CI chief saw no humor in the patronizing taunt and did not rise to the bait.

"Thank you, Peter," he said as he opened the door. "You've been most helpful.''

Palmer nodded to the senior security officer standing by in the anteroom. "Mr. Danning has a file to give you to bring back to me.''

The man rose immediately to his feet and fell in alongside Danning, who cast a disapproving glance that suggested all thugs should walk three paces behind him to his left.

Palmer returned to his office and went directly to his desk. He unlocked the top center drawer and took out the file on BACKLASH that he had removed from his private vault and quickly reviewed before Danning had arrived. There had never been any danger of the top-secret case's being compromised; the entry in the library's computer data base index had been put there years ago to entrap anyone who showed the slightest interest in the file. Had Danning, through some glitch in the system, managed to bypass the specific code word required to access the file, he would have faced a blank screen. There was, in fact, no computer file on the case in existence, anywhere. It was Palmer's belief that no matter how secure the system, there was always the possibility of electronic penetration, and BACKLASH was considered far too sensitive to put into any computer.

Under normal circumstances, the Agency's hard copy files were kept in the file room on the ground floor at headquarters. Those with top-secret classifications were sealed with black tape, and the clerks were instructed that the files so designated were to be taken out only by officers on the approved list from the section where the operation had originated. But BACKLASH was compartmented well beyond even that secure procedure. From 1947, when the CIA was founded and BACKLASH was initiated, until the present, there had been only two copies of the file. The one Palmer held in his hand, and the one in the CIA director's possession—both were kept locked in highly secure office vaults.

The only people outside of Palmer and the director who knew even so much as the code word for BACKLASH were the President and his National Security Affairs adviser. The tight compartmentalization and strict micromanagement had been maintained over the forty-five-year span of the case, through nine consecutive administrations, with each succeeding president and his national security adviser being briefed in only the broadest possible terms upon taking office. The same rigid control remained in effect at the CIA, limiting knowledge to each newly appointed director of Central Intelligence and anyone replacing the chief of the Counterintelligence Staff. As a counterintelligence case, as opposed to a covert operation, there was no requirement to advise the Senate or House intelligence committees of BACKLASH's existence, let alone its significance, and consequently there had been no bothersome oversight or political interference.

The unusual vest-pocket nature of handling the case ensured that high-ranking CIA officials, powerful men, who far outranked Alfred Palmer and would have deeply resented the professional slight had they known, were shut out. They included the deputy director of the CIA, the executive director, the newly established deputy director for Planning and Coordination, and the deputy director for Operations—who, despite being the immediate superior of the chief of the Counterintelligence Staff, and therefore Palmer's boss, was still kept out of the loop. The strict application of the "need to know" principle was in keeping with what had become the longest-running counterintelligence case in the CIA's history.

Upon taking over as CI chief, Palmer had at first felt a personal triumph in the unique position in which BACKLASH placed him, like the newest member of an exclusive club or secret society, who took pleasure in closing the door behind him or knowing things that others did not. But the enormous responsibility that went with the case soon took its toll, and there were times, despite his supreme confidence in his ability to do his job, when he wished he could have called upon the experience and expertise of his superiors, especially the deputy director for Operations.

The security officer who had accompanied Danning back to his office returned shortly with the Berlin Documents Center file on Heinz Strasser. Palmer looked it over, and seeing that it was precisely the same as the duplicate included with the BACKLASH documents, his attention was drawn to the details of the inquiry from the Berchtesgaden police. His brow furrowed with concern at the mention of the former SS major using an alias. Perhaps it was nothing, but his intuition and experience told him differently.

After locking both the BACKLASH and Strasser files in his vault, he instructed his secretary to cancel his remaining appointments for that morning. The only matter of significance on his calendar for the rest of the day was a meeting with the heads of the area divisions' counterintelligence groups. Each area division had its own CI group, which concentrated on daily developments within the countries for which they were responsible. The CI Staff, which Palmer headed, reviewed and directed the collective counterintelligence cases from those divisions. With the more important matter of BACKLASH on the agenda, the weekly review could do without his presence, and Palmer placed a call on the in-house phone line to his operations chief, directing him to sit in on the eleven o'clock meeting, and to be prepared to brief him later that day. He then dialed the extension for the director's office, and spoke to the DCI's secretary.

"This is Alfred Palmer. Tell him I need to see him immediately. I'm on my way."

PALMER EXITED THE elevator on the seventh floor and walked briskly past the security guards posted outside the director's suite. He nodded to the secretary, who with a smile and a tilt of her head acknowledged that the director was expecting him and he should go right in.

George Sinclair looked up from the intelligence summary he was reading as Palmer knocked twice and opened the door. He motioned him toward a high-backed leather armchair off to one side of the huge mahogany desk positioned in front of a window overlooking the woods surrounding the headquarters complex.

Sinclair had been appointed DCI the previous year, over at least twenty men who were his senior and, in the view of the Old Guard, more qualified and experienced. His roots in the world of intelligence ran deep, but his thirty-three years of experience were with the Intelligence Directorate, the analytical side of the Agency, much to the displeasure of the operational side, who feared they would be doomed to the fate of a redheaded stepchild.

"What's got your adrenaline pumping, Al?"

"BACKLASH."

There was a momentary blank look in Sinclair's eyes as he searched through the hundreds of code names for cases and operations filed away in his prodigious memory, then the spark of recognition shone and his expression changed to one of rapt attention.

"A new development?"

"Perhaps. More like a voice from the past."

As Palmer recounted the incident with Peter Danning, the details of the initial OSS investigation came back to Sinclair. He had studied the file when he had first taken over as director, and had been fascinated by the origins of the case. He listened intently as Palmer gave his assessment of the reemergence of the long-lost Strasser.

"There's always the possibility that Strasser's copy of the Goering file no longer exists," Palmer said. "It's been over forty-six years, and it's never surfaced. But the use of an alias, for what ostensibly appears to be a dying man revisiting a part of his past, bothers me."

"Did the police inquiry to the Berlin Documents Center give any details of his death?"

"Just that he died of a heart attack. Maybe he's been living under an assumed name all these years," Palmer said, continuing with his original train of thought. "That would explain why we were never able to find him."

"What does Danning know beyond his original involvement?"

"Nothing. He was simply following orders at the end of the war; he never knew the significance of the Goering records. And he's been in this game longer than any of us; long enough to know not to look any further."

"If I know that old codger," Sinclair said, "he's probably got most of it pieced together by now anyway."

Sinclair smiled at the image of Danning rummaging around in his memories to come up with an answer for the CI chief's reaction to his inadvertent discovery of BACKLASH. Sinclair had met the old man a few years before he retired and, like most of his contemporaries, enjoyed listening to Danning's stories about the cold war and the early years of the Agency, to the point of occasionally inviting him to lunch in his private dining room in the hope of hearing more of them.

"I strongly suggest we follow up on this," Palmer said.

"I agree. What do you have in mind?"

"I'd like to send one of my people from the Munich base down to Berchtesgaden. Perhaps he can learn some of the details of Strasser's visit and his death."

The director nodded in agreement. "Keep me posted."

A SHORT DISTANCE down the seventh-floor corridor from the DCI's suite is the office of the DDO, the chief of the Operations Directorate. Also known as the clandestine services, it is the directorate that engages in espionage, counterintelligence, special operations, paramilitary actions, and covert activities that encompass the overthrowing of governments, bribery, kidnapping, counterfeiting, and a multitude of other "black" operations that seldom, if ever, see the light of day.

As the deputy director for Operations, Jack Brannigan was one of the least known, yet one of the most powerful men in the world. Broad shouldered and slim hipped, with a boyish face, he looked fifteen years younger than his fifty-nine years, the result of good genes and a rigid exercise program, which included running four miles each morning at dawn, followed by weight lifting every other day. He was a born leader with an easy Irish charm and sharp wit, and the ability to impress at will those he wanted to influence. But there was also a rough-hewn side to him, the legacy of a hardscrabble youth in a small steel town in western Pennsylvania. His conversations were often peppered with obscenities, and he had a mercurial temper that could explode into bullying displays of foulmouthed arrogance when he was forced to suffer fools. But such was his ability to instill confidence in others that any competent person who had ever worked with him had nothing but praise for the man, and would have, without question, followed him anywhere he cared to lead them.

Brannigan had spent his entire thirty-seven-year career in

the Operations Directorate, and had been considered a rising star since becoming the youngest station chief in Agency history—at the age of thirty-six, he had run the Saigon station during the height of the Vietnam War, then the CIA's largest and busiest station. Promoted to deputy director for Operations nine years ago, he was commonly believed to be next in line for the director's job.

An All-American linebacker and honors graduate from Penn State University, he had little use for those who had never been in the arena, often referring to them as narrowbacks and pencil necks. He had even less respect for the Agency's elitists: "goddamn privileged Ivy League pantywaists with last names for first names and unrealistic views of their own intelligence." If he were a religious man, which he was decidedly not, he would have thanked God that most of them were to be found on the analytical side of the Agency and not on his beloved operational side.

Brannigan was in the middle of reading the overnight cables that demanded his attention when his secretary announced that Steve Toland, the chief of the Operations Directorate's counter-terrorist section, was in the anteroom asking to see him.

"Send him in," Brannigan said.

Toland, a wiry, high-strung man who spoke in staccato bursts, at times reminded Brannigan of a parakeet on amphetamines, but his information was always free of conjecture, concise, and to the point. He began talking the moment he entered the office.

"You wanted an update on the status of Mike Semko. I just heard back from the Paris station."

Toland read off the list of charges the police had filed against Semko. As a member of a highly classified twelve-man unit within the counter-terrorist section, Semko was under the direct control of Toland, who reported only to Brannigan. So secret and sensitive were the extraterritorial kidnap missions the unit specialized in that Toland and Brannigan, who had hand-picked the twelve men himself, were the only ones, outside of the director and his deputy, with knowledge of the true purpose of the unit.

"That goddamn renegade," Brannigan mumbled after hearing the extent of the charges against Semko. There was a hint of amusement in his expression, but it vanished as quickly as it appeared.

"Who was he after? No. Let me guess. Dieter. He's fixated on that murderous bastard."

"The known facts seem to indicate that," Toland said. "One of the case officers at the Paris station gave Semko a lead on a terrorist by the name of Gunther Jost, believed to be connected to the Red Army Faction. Semko was tailing him at the time. Two incidents that occurred the following day suggest it probably was Dieter he was chasing. Jost was assassinated in broad daylight shortly after he left the safe house, and two Israelis carrying diplomatic passports, no doubt Mossad officers, were killed a few minutes later blocking the same street four blocks away in an attempt to snatch another man at gunpoint. Again, probably Dieter fleeing the scene."

"Where's Semko now?"

"In jail, where he's been for the past five days, awaiting arraignment. He wasn't carrying any identification on him when he was arrested, and he's refused to give them so much as his name."

"I'll take it from here," Brannigan said.

As Toland closed the door behind him Brannigan propped his feet up on the desk and stared at an engraved brass plaque on the wall to his right. Other than the photographs of his wife and daughter on his desk, it was the only personal adornment in the office. It read: THE EASIEST WAY TO ACHIEVE COMPLETE STRA- TEGIC SURPRISE IS TO COMMIT AN ACT THAT MAKES NO SENSE OR IS

EVEN SELF-DESTRUCTIVE. It was an aphorism that left no doubt in anyone's mind of the aggressive, unconventional attitude Brannigan had brought to the job. When people asked the origin of the quotation, he always said he couldn't recall, when in fact he remembered perfectly well where he had first heard it: from Mike Semko.

Brannigan had known Semko for twenty-three years. In 1969, when Semko was a young, highly decorated Green Beret buck sergeant on his second combat tour in Vietnam, Brannigan, then the Saigon station chief, had heard of his exploits and arranged through the commander of the Special Operations Group to pull him from the top-secret reconnaissance team he was running, and have him temporarily assigned to the CIA. Over the next six months, Semko ran a series of hair-raising suicide missions for Brannigan into North Vietnam. Missions for which there never were, and never would be, any records, and Semko had pulled them off in a manner that had astounded even Brannigan. He had made a point of keeping in touch with Semko after the war, and, when the need arose, took advantage of the Agency's hand-in-glove arrangements with the military's Special Operations forces, to borrow him from Delta Force for delicate missions. Upon Semko's retirement from the army, he had personally recruited him into the Agency to lead the elite, terrorist "snatch team" that had been Brannigan's brainchild.

There were few men Brannigan held in higher regard, and on a personal level he looked at Semko as the younger brother he never had; professionally he viewed him as his own personal samurai. With visions of him sitting in a French jail, he abruptly swung his feet off the desktop, picked up the secure telephone, and called the Paris station. The scrambled, satellite-relayed connection was completed in a matter of seconds.

"I want him out," Brannigan told the Paris station chief, Parker Britin Stevenson II.

"The French think he's a terrorist," Stevenson said. "They may not be so accommodating without getting an explanation we don't want to give, or more to the point, since I haven't been privy to the true purpose of this Semko's presence in Paris, a convincing explanation I am in no position to give."

It was a snide remark that laid bare Stevenson's resentment at being locked out of an operation on what was, after all, his turf. But he realized the moment he said it that it was the wrong response in the wrong tone of voice to a man who, for some inexplicable reason, invariably displayed an unstated, yet palpable personal animosity toward him.

"Fuck you, Parker!" Brannigan bellowed. "Get him out! Now! Call in some markers, finesse them, bullshit them, threaten them, whatever it takes, but get him out. And I want you to get your ass out from behind your desk and personally put him on a plane for Washington, and tell him to go directly to the safe house in Georgetown. He's to wait there until he hears from me."

« 12 »

IT WAS FOUR-THIRTY when the meeting of the board of trustees at New York's Metropolitan Museum of Art ended and Edward Winthrop Stewart, an elected trustee and one of the museum's most generous financial contributors, emerged from the massive building on Fifth Avenue. He walked south, along the sandstone wall that enclosed Central Park, tapping the tip of his cane rhythmically on the cobblestone pavement. He paused to breathe in the cool spring air, then walked a short distance into the park and sat on a bench overlooking a small playground. He was having one of his better days; the minor aches and pains and the stiffness in his joints—the indignities of being eighty-two years old, which he had learned to tolerate like annoying guests who had overstayed their welcome—were less persistent and bothersome.

The exclusive enclave of the Upper East Side, with its trappings of wealth and power, had been Stewart's domain since birth, and he moved easily in its luxurious circles. He was a man with an aura of dignity, and a bearing that hinted at the enormous wealth he possessed; in excess of seven hundred million dollars was a conservative estimate by those who were in a position to know.

Until a few years ago there were the yearly spring visits to old friends in England and Switzerland. But they were dead now; he had outlived them all, including his wife of fifty-one years, and their son, their only child. A terrible thing to outlive all those held dear, he thought. But his privileged life was peaceful and he was content, his routine set; and although he lived alone, with the exception of his housekeeper, he was not lonely. His life had been one of philanthropy and the pursuit of leisure, while reigning for four decades as the titular head, if not the actual administrator, of his far-flung financial interests. It was a life for which he had few regrets, and, if not examined too closely, would have been considered exemplary and well spent by any standards. The energy of youth was a dim, distant memory, but he was thankful for his good health; and thankful, too, that death, when it came, would probably be swift and sudden, not the drug-induced half-conscious ending to a prolonged and painful illness.

His one remaining passion was his art collection. He had inherited part of it from his father, and his grandfather—a wealthy industrialist from the days of the robber barons who had made the bulk of the family fortune. Stewart began adding to the collection soon after graduating from Harvard in 1931, when a sizable trust fund became his to use as he saw fit. Over the next sixty years, through shrewd and timely purchases, and an unerring eye for timeless quality and excellence, his private collection—especially of impressionist and postimpressionist paintings—had become recognized as one of the finest in the world.

When he died, and that was something he thought of more often these days, his vast fortune and control of the family philanthropic foundation would go to his grandchildren, but his art collection would go to the Metropolitan Museum. At least most of it would—there was the troublesome problem of what to do with his secret collection, his most cherished possessions. They could not go to the museum without eventually causing the venerable institution untold embarrassment, and tarnishing the rest of the collection that would bear his name. Nor could he bequeath them to his grandchildren without explaining their provenance, something he had no intention of doing. He knew that a decision had to be made soon, and the matter dealt with if he meant to keep the family's reputation intact. But for the moment, he would go on enjoying the tainted treasures as he had for nearly half a century.

He continued to sit quietly on the park bench, relaxing in the golden glow of a near perfect spring afternoon, and took no notice of the tall, lanky man with blond hair and deep-set dark blue eyes, who walked past him to where the path through the park branched off in the direction of the boathouse.

JURGEN STRASSER SAT on a bench within view of the impeccably dressed old man and lit a cigarette. He found none of the beauty or joy in the city that Stewart did. To him it was a foul, materialistic place, without redeeming features, overcrowded, filthy, and littered with the repulsive castoffs of a degenerate society who were reduced to begging for life's necessities.

Though Strasser's stated reasons for becoming a terrorist were to effect the downfall of capitalism and the corruption it engendered, his true reasons were not so lofty or politically motivated. A rabid anti-Semite, with a hatred of all things American, he was little more than a highly intelligent malignant sociopath. The strategist side of him enjoyed the challenge of intricate planning and precision execution required for a successful terrorist attack, but his true motivation was to be found in his darker, more ominous side: an anarchist and thrill seeker, he was wrapped up in the mystique of being a phantom figure, somewhere between myth and legend, with the power of life and death over people.

He had been following Stewart since early that morning, first to a doctor's appointment on Park Avenue, then to lunch at the Harvard Club, and finally to the museum. He had chosen him as his first target because he was in possession of four of the eight paintings Drussard wanted from the three men on the list who lived in the city.

The evening he arrived from Paris, Strasser decided to avoid the safe house he had set up eighteen months ago near the Columbia University campus—with what he had to do, he did not want the young untenured political science professor who took care of the place putting together his presence in the city and the events that were to follow. Using a valid credit card issued in the name of the alias he had assumed (the bills were paid through a cutout address in Toronto serviced by a Red Army Faction supporter living in Canada), he had checked into the Plaza Hotel, where he rinsed the temporary dye from his hair and removed the green-tinted contact lenses. He had called Drussard in Paris, and the following morning met with the Frenchman's colleague in New York City, the owner of a small art gallery on Madison Avenue near the corner of Sixty-third Street.

Photographs of the specific paintings the efficient Drussard had selected were waiting there for him, faxed from Paris along with the current addresses and brief background information on the three men who were his targets. After renting a minivan, using the same credit card and a Toronto driver's license (part of the full backup documentation provided with each of the forged passports issued by the Stasi), he spent the next three days reconnoitering the locations of the residences and getting the feel for the surrounding neighborhoods. The past two evenings were spent staking out Stewart's distinguished, five-story neo-Georgian town house on East Seventy-fourth Street just off Madison Avenue.

The street was quiet and tree-lined, and at night the dense foliage cast deep shadows over the front entrances of the rows of similar town houses crowded shoulder-to-shoulder the length of the block. Strasser had taken advantage of the common sight of the homeless throughout the city to provide cover for staking out the house. He had mussed his hair and disheveled his clothing before sitting on the sidewalk with his back against the wall of a building at the corner of Seventy-fourth Street and Madison Avenue. He remained there until late at night, occasionally sipping from a bottle of Evian water he had placed inside a paper bag as a prop. No one paid the slightest attention to him during the two evenings he had used the deception to study his quarry.

His initial concern of being confronted with an elaborate home-security system proved to be without merit. The windows on the first two floors were barred with decorative wrought iron, but the only active security was a cipher-lock for the front door, and a standard home alarm system with a control panel on the foyer wall that he had glimpsed as the old man came and went. The system presented a minor problem, but one Strasser felt he would have little difficulty getting around: a small closed-circuit video camera was mounted to one side of the entrance on the outside wall, allowing anyone inside to clearly see who was at the door, and an exterior speaker provided voice communication as well.

The only person, other than Stewart, he had seen enter and exit the home was a middle-aged, Spanish-looking woman, who wore a black-and-white maid's uniform. Strasser concluded that she was a live-in domestic, because he did not see her leave on the two evenings he watched the house—the time of day when he was most concerned with Stewart's routine activities. Her only function of concern to Strasser was her apparent duty of answering the door for deliveries or guests, and her negligent attitude was not lost on him. Of the three deliveries he had witnessed, Federal Express, United Parcel Service, and a bonded messenger from a bank, she had simply opened the door without questioning any of them.

As Strasser sat watching the old man in the park, he had not yet decided on his method of approach to getting inside the residence unobserved and without incident. One hour later his decision was made for him.

After leaving the park, Stewart stopped briefly at a drugstore on Madison Avenue to fill a prescription he had gotten from his doctor that morning. Before returning to his home, he made another stop, at a small gourmet delicatessen/grocery on Lexington Avenue, where he purchased two bags of groceries, leaving them for the store to deliver to his house only a few blocks away.

Strasser recognized the distinctive gray bags with the store logo; he had seen someone make a delivery from the same store the previous day to a house close to Stewart's. He watched a clerk at the checkout lane place a receipt with Stewart's address inside the bags, then set them aside on a counter near the entrance to the store that was full of other bags awaiting delivery.

Strasser immediately set his plan in motion. He hurriedly retrieved the rented van from a nearby parking garage, and squeezed it into a space a few doors down from Stewart's town house on the same side of the street. Returning to watch the store, he waited until one of the delivery boys left, then followed him to where he dropped off the groceries with a doorman at an apartment house on East Seventy-second Street. On the way back, Strasser came astride of his victim at a spot he had noted en route to the delivery. With his semiautomatic pistol concealed beneath his leather jacket, he jammed the tip of the silencer into the young man's ribs while putting an arm around his shoulder.

Without hesitation, Strasser pulled the startled teenager a few yards into an alleyway and behind a Dumpster, out of sight of the busy rush-hour street. A sharp cry of protest had not drawn so much as a glance from the constant stream of pedestrians hurrying along the sidewalk, and the single shot from the nine-millimeter pistol made no more noise than a finger snap as it entered the base of the boy's skull on an upward trajectory into his brain. Strasser quickly stripped the lifeless body of the gray smock bearing the store's logo on the chest pocket, and pulled it on over his jacket. So accustomed was he to taking a human life, killing without emotion or remorse when it suited his purpose or cause, that as he stepped back out onto the sidewalk, had someone checked his blood pressure and pulse rate they would have found them to be the same as before he had brutally murdered the young man he left lying in the alley.

The small gourmet grocery store was crowded with after-work shoppers buying last-minute items for the evening meal or prepared deli items to eat at home in front of the television. The confusion and bustle at the glass display cases of the delicatessen section near the front of the store worked to Strasser's advantage. He averted his face from the man working the single checkout lane as he entered the store and walked purposefully over to the deliveries counter. With Stewart's two bags of groceries held high to shield his features, he left the store unnoticed. Although it was just after six o'clock and still light, he correctly reasoned that he would attract no attention from Stewart's neighbors, who were accustomed to the familiar sight.

MARIA ALONZO WAS running late. After preparing a light snack consisting of a selection of cheeses and a fruit salad for Stewart, his usual dinner taken in his fifth-floor study while watching the local news, she changed clothes for an evening out. She planned to see a movie with a friend, but compulsive about a neat and orderly kitchen, she waited until Stewart was finished eating, then quickly attended to the unwashed dishes before leaving. It took her less than ten minutes to put things in order, but they were ten minutes that would cost her her life.

The front doorbell chimed as she reached the foyer and slipped into a light cotton sweater. She glanced at the closed-circuit television monitor set into the wall above the door and recognized the familiar gray smock worn by the man carrying the groceries. Muttering an impatient oath in Spanish under her breath, she tapped out the code on the key pad that disengaged the cipher lock, then turned the double dead bolts open and slipped the heavy chain from the door.

The tall, lanky man held the grocery bags high, concealing his face as he spoke. "Delivery for Mr. Stewart."

"Just put them over there," Maria said, indicating a red lacquer table set against the far wall beneath an ornate mirror.

Strasser stepped inside and placed the bags on the intricately carved antique pedestal table. He caught the scent of fresh flowers from an arrangement on a nearby stand as his eyes moved quickly around the spacious foyer and into the adjoining reception hall. Beyond that he caught a glimpse of a small sitting room and more flower arrangements, but there was no one in sight.

"Thank you," Maria said, and pulled open a drawer in a credenza on the opposite wall where she kept the money Stewart allotted for tips to service people. For one terrifying moment she felt the tremendous strength in the arms that gripped her, then a swift, violent twisting motion snapped her neck, killing her instantly.

Her body went limp in the powerful arms and her head slumped to her chest, flopping disjointedly from side to side as Strasser lowered her into a sitting position in a corner beside the credenza. Acting deliberately, but unhurried, he closed and locked the door, then drew his pistol and again screwed on the silencer as he moved cautiously into the reception hall, where he paused to listen for any sounds that might tell him what room Stewart was in. He had observed, on the two previous evenings, that shortly after six o'clock a light went on in a third-floor room fronting on the street. Strasser decided to go directly there, and crossed the highly polished marble surface, treading softly until he reached the carpeted stairs that led off the reception hall to the upper floors.

To the left of the circular staircase was an elevator, and Strasser noticed that it served all five floors of the town house. He was about to start up the stairs when a noise from the elevator caused him to stop and freeze in position. He stared at the illuminated panel above the elevator door as the hum of the motor filled the room. The panel indicated that someone was coming down from the fifth floor, and Strasser watched as the small circle of light descended and stopped at the number 3. A creature of habit, he thought, then began making his way slowly up the stairs.

Strasser had never seen such an elaborately decorated and elegant house. Every square inch seemed to overflow with art and antiques that he, even with his limited frame of reference, knew were extremely valuable. There were huge porcelain vases and ancient terra cotta statuary, some dating back to 200 B.C., in the corners of the landings; even the ceilings were works of art, graced with ornate plasterwork and moldings. The walls of the staircase and the landings, covered with hand-painted Chinese export wallpaper, were hung with tapestries and paintings that caused Strasser to pause on two occasions to consult the photographs Drussard had faxed him from Paris. His lack of knowledge would have been a severe drawback to identifying the right paintings had it not been for the Frenchman's foresight. Both paintings he thought he recognized were not the ones he was looking for, and he continued on, silently admonishing himself for being naive enough to think that the paintings on his list would be displayed openly.

As he reached the third-floor landing, he heard the faint

sounds of a Mozart symphony. To his right, at the end of a parquet hallway covered with rare silk Persian rugs, he could see part of a paneled library. In the center of the room, seated in a leather chair at an inlaid desk with his back to him, was Stewart.

Strasser moved cautiously down the hallway, glancing into the rooms on either side as he passed by the open doors. He paused at the entrance to the library and quickly scanned the spacious, high-ceilinged room. The old man was the only one there, sitting at the desk paging through a large book on Renaissance paintings.

Stewart was totally unaware of Strasser's presence until he stepped from behind the chair and smiled at him.

"Good evening, Mr. Stewart."

Stewart looked up from his reading and stared blankly into the unfamiliar face. The soft-spoken, even tone of the man standing over him at first caused no alarm. He thought perhaps he had forgotten an appointment he had made. His expression changed to one of concern when he noticed the gray smock the man was wearing.

"Who are you?" Stewart demanded. "And how did you get in here?"

"You may call me Dieter," Strasser said pleasantly. "And your housekeeper let me in."

Stewart pressed a button on the intercom on his desk. "Maria!" he called out, and started to rise from the chair. It was then that he saw the silenced pistol the stranger held at his side.

Strasser placed a firm hand on the old man's shoulder and gently forced him back down. "I'm afraid Maria is . . . indisposed."

"What is the meaning of this?" The first sign of fear manifested itself in a tightness in Stewart's voice. "Are you here to rob me?"

"That is a matter of viewpoint," Strasser said as he rested one hip on the arm of a Chesterfield sofa opposite the desk. "I prefer to think of it as a reclamation."

"I keep very little money in the house. But I'll give you what I have. There is no need for violence. I'll cooperate fully." Stewart's face showed the strain of what he now realized was a dangerous situation.

"It's not money I'm after."

"Then what? My paintings? My antiques?

"Some very special paintings," Strasser said, and glanced at the artwork on the library walls. He saw nothing that resembled the photographs in his jacket pocket.

Stewart slowly began to regain his equilibrium. The man's calm and unthreatening manner made him think that perhaps he could be dealt with and the situation defused.

"Take the Braque," Stewart said, indicating one of six paintings on the library walls. "It's the most valuable painting in the room." It was in fact the least valuable, but the foolish and dangerous ploy was intended to do more than test Strasser's knowledge of art.

Strasser smiled again, and keeping an eye on the old man, crossed to the fireplace where the Braque was hung above the mantel. He leaned his head against the paneling and peered behind the painting. The expertly installed motion detector affixed to the back of the frame was wired to send a silent alarm over the telephone lines to the central station of a security company, where a flashing light would indicate that the painting had been removed from the wall. A quick check revealed that the other five paintings in the room were similarly wired, as was every painting in the house, Strasser suspected.

"Shame on you, Mr. Stewart," Strasser said, returning to stand beside the desk. "You underestimate me. Perhaps we should get directly to the point."

Stewart's confidence waned. A slight tremor shook his

hands when Strasser's expression changed to one more menacing as he removed the four photographs from the inside pocket of his leather jacket and spread them out on the desk top.

"These are the paintings I'm interested in," Strasser said. "And please, do not insult my intelligence again, or I will raise the level of this encounter to a degree you will not find at all amusing."

Stewart looked at the photographs, and then at Strasser. "I'm sorry, but I'm not familiar with these paintings. I mean, I am vaguely familiar with them and the artists who painted them, but they are certainly not part of my collection. You may look for yourself, they are nowhere in this house."

"And they have never been in your possession?"

"No, of course not, I—"

The vicious backhanded slap caught Stewart flush on the side of the face, sending his reading glasses flying across the room. Tears formed in his eyes from the sting of the blow, and a small trickle of blood ran from the corner of his mouth.

"Do not lie to me again."

"Yes, all right! I once owned them, but they were sold, years ago."

"Another lie, Mr. Stewart. You disappoint me. What is your American baseball expression? Three strikes and you are out?" The calm, even voice was back again.

Stewart's gaze was fixed on Strasser's hands as he slipped the silenced pistol inside his waistband and withdrew a thin leather case from his jacket pocket. His eyes widened as Strasser zipped the case open and withdrew what appeared to be a large hat pin, approximately three inches in length, with a round stainless steel head on one end.

"What is that? What are you going to do?"

"I'm going to get the truth from you, Mr. Stewart," Strasser said as he placed the ominous-looking instrument on the desk top. "Or I'm going to subject you to a very slow and painful death. Or perhaps I'll do both. It depends on just how difficult you make this."

The old man stiffened at the sight of the thin leather straps Strasser next removed from his jacket. He offered no resistance as one wrist, then the other was tied securely to the arms of his desk chair.

"Please. You may have anything you want. I'll disarm the alarm system for the paintings. Take them all, I don't care."

"Of course you don't. They're insured. But I'm quite sure the paintings I want are not. Now once again, Mr. Stewart, where are they?"

"I can't give you what I do not have," Stewart argued. Despite the raw fear that now gripped him, he was determined not to give up his most prized possessions. There might still be some way of bargaining with this man, of convincing him of the lie. The movable section of built-in bookcases that concealed the cipher-locked steel door barring entrance to the hidden room would be impossible to find without knowledge of its existence.

Strasser simply smiled and walked over to the floor-to-ceiling windows overlooking the street. He cut a length of cord after drawing the draperies and returned to tie it tightly across Stewart's chest, effectively pinning the now terrified old man's arms to his sides as he knotted it at the back of the chair.

"And now, the moment of truth," Strasser said. "And you will, eventually, tell me the truth." With that, he forced open Stewart's mouth and stuffed a handkerchief into it, stifling a brief cry of alarm and ensuring that the shrieks of pain and low guttural moans that were to come would not be heard outside the room.

His expression became cold and sinister as he picked up the hat pin and rolled it between his thumb and forefinger. "You may not believe this, but I really do not enjoy this part of my profession. Although I have been told, by experts, that I do have a certain knack for it."

Strasser pushed back the leather chair, allowing him to sit on the edge of the desk directly in front of his subject. He leaned forward and took one of Stewart's thumbs in his hand, holding it steady as he brought the slender, steel hat pin into position.

The old man's eyes were wide with dreadful anticipation as he struggled in vain against the leather restraints that bound his wrists securely to the arms of the chair.

"We'll start slowly," Strasser said. "Be sure to let me know when your memory has improved."

« **13** »

MIKE SEMKO HAD been fingerprinted and booked at the Sixth Arrondissement police station in the Saint-Germain section of Paris as prisoner number 47238, and shortly thereafter was transported to the Fresnes provincial jail in the countryside fifteen miles outside of Paris. There, he made one telephone call, to an unlisted and virtually untraceable number that rang in the CIA's code room—a separate inner sanctum within the highly secure Communications Program Unit (CPU) in the United States embassy in Paris. Semko's request to speak with a nonexistent Tim Johnson was all that was necessary to identify him to the code clerk receiving the call, and to ensure that the message Semko left about his arrest and where he was being held would be passed on to the CIA's station chief for direct transmission to the chief of the counter-terrorist section at Langley.

After Semko repeatedly refused to give the authorities even his name, and with Interpol unable to identify him from his fingerprints and mug shots, it was decided that no court date for a hearing on the charges filed against him would be set until he agreed to cooperate, or until his identity could be established by a more extensive search of the international criminal records.

Semko had spent the past three days in solitary confinement, after hospitalizing two French intelligence officers who had taken him to an interrogation room and attempted to beat information out of him. On the morning of his sixth day at Fresnes, the prison warden received a telephone call from his immediate superior. All charges had been dropped against the mysterious and uncooperative prisoner. With a Gallic shrug, and a certain amount of relief at getting rid of him, the warden ordered his release. Forty-five minutes later Mike Semko walked through the front gate of the Fresnes prison to see the CIA's Paris station chief, Parker Stevenson, leaning against the fender of an embassy car in the parking lot.

"Get in the car, Semko."

"And a good morning to you, too, Parker."

"Get in the goddamn car."

Semko climbed into the front passenger seat and grinned at Stevenson as he slid behind the wheel.

"I fail to find any humor in this."

"Just drop me at my hotel. I've got things to do."

"You've got orders from the deputy director for Operations, that's what you've got, you arrogant son of a bitch." Stevenson reached into the pocket of his suit coat and removed an airline ticket, tossing it into Semko's lap. "You're to return immediately to Washington, go directly to the safe house, and stay there until you hear otherwise. Your flight leaves in two hours and I'm staying with you until I see it take off with you on it."

"I'll need to pick up my things."

"I had your passport, wallet, and personal belongings removed from that fleabag hotel you were staying in. They're in your luggage in the trunk."

Stevenson's anger again rose to full force. "Just who the hell do you think you are, running unauthorized ops on my turf?"

"Don't take it so personal, Parker."

"The hell I won't! I had to kiss Frog ass to tidy up your goddamn mess. A running gun battle through the streets of Paris, for Christ's sake! Assaulting a French citizen and stealing his car, then demolishing it, along with a section of a six-hundred-year-old wall. And you can't even clean up your act in prison; two DGSE people in the hospital, one with a broken jaw and nose, and the other with a possible ruptured spleen and a gouged eye that may be permanently damaged."

"They started it."

"You're a trouble junkie, Semko. You've been living on the edge so long, you can't function any other way."

"Yeah, well, I guess I'm just a little behind the curve on agency thinking about proper spook conduct."

"You're a little behind the curve on human behavior," Stevenson said, shaking his head in disgust. "I have no use for people like you, Semko. No right-thinking person does."

"Oh, yes you do. It's people like me who do your dirty work, make you look good, and give you somebody to deny and leave twisting in the wind when you screw up."

"Your kind never does get the big picture."

"Fuck your big picture. And fuck you, Parker."

The two men fell silent for the rest of the drive to Charles de Gaulle Airport. Stevenson sullenly recalled that it was the second time in as many days that someone had cursed him with those exact words. The DDO and now this reprobate. He wondered what it was about him that brought things like that out in people. Perhaps feelings of inadequacy or inferiority on their part. The strong-arm types always resorted to name calling and bullying tactics when they ran out of intellectual gas. Over the years he had met others like the man sitting beside him: tough, hard men with light trigger pulls, the covert operators, paramilitary cowboys, to whom everything looked like a nail when they had a hammer in their hand.

As Semko swung his garment bag over his shoulder and headed for the boarding ramp, Stevenson gripped his upper arm and said, ''The next time you run a rogue operation on my turf, I'll come down on you with both feet.''

Semko reached over and bent the station chief's fingers back almost to the point of breaking as he removed the offending hand from his arm. He spoke softly, but in a voice that made Stevenson take a precautionary step backward.

''I've been known to be a very bad boy, and more than a little bit dangerous. Don't press your luck with me, Parker.'' With a mischievous wink and a less-than-friendly slap on the shoulder, Semko turned and walked away.

As the huge jumbo jet lifted off the runway and gained altitude over the French countryside, Semko's thoughts were of Dieter and how he might again pick up the international terrorist's trail. He would have to cool his heels in Washington for a while, but whatever his next assignment, as long as Dieter was still out there, he was his primary objective, no matter how long it took, no matter what the personal costs. When the plane leveled off at thirty thousand feet for the long transatlantic flight, Semko reclined his seat and instructed the cabin attendant not to disturb him for the remainder of the journey. He closed his eyes and concentrated on the images of the events prior to his arrest, of the nighttime chase through the alleyways and streets of Paris, burning every detail of the encounter and every feature of the hated man's face into his memory.

As MIKE SEMKO'S flight streamed westward over the North Atlantic, Jonathan Westcott was in the office of his Madison Avenue art gallery, staring longingly at the four canvases propped against the wall opposite his desk. Never had he had anything quite so exquisite in his possession, however temporary that would prove to be. All four were acknowledged masterpieces. A Renoir, a Monet, and one of Cézanne's finest images of Mont Sainte-Victoire, the Provençal peak he painted more than fifty times.

But it was the fourth painting that held the gallery owner's attention. A van Gogh that Drussard had forewarned him was earmarked for his private collection, and for which he had been instructed to make special shipping arrangements. After locking the door leading out into the gallery, Westcott removed a painting from his office wall and replaced it with the van Gogh, then stepped back to admire it from the proper distance and angle. He was familiar with its history: lost to the world for nearly fifty years, as were the others, it was last known to have been owned by a wealthy Jewish banker from Berlin, who, along with his entire family, had perished in a Nazi death camp.

Titled *Waiter at the Pavement Café,* the direct portrait, a 25½" by 21¾" oil on canvas, had been painted in 1888, in Arles, and was signed and dated on the lower right. It was reminiscent of the artist's work during his early years, when people generally refused to pose for him and he had to rely on the tradespeople of Arles as his subjects. It was painted in the same location as another of his masterpieces, *Pavement Café at Night,* which now hung in the Rijksmuseum in Amsterdam. Westcott stood transfixed by the skillful techniques of the great painter: crisscrosses of yellow and green were built up in tufted confections of thick oil paint that peaked in little ridges to delineate the wallpaper behind the waiter; the waiter's white apron showed reflections of the yellow light of the terrace lanterns, and collections of tiny mounds of oil paint outlined the solemn subject's small, dark mustache, eyebrows, and ruddy flesh. Its value in today's market, with an unsullied provenance, would have been in excess of twenty million dollars; to Drussard's clients it would still bring a small fortune. Westcott would have sold his soul to possess it.

Strasser had brought the four paintings in through the back door of the gallery—wrapped in filthy moving blankets and tied together with rope, to Westcott's horror—and unceremoniously dropped them on top of the corner desk. Pearls to swine, Westcott thought, but dared say nothing to Strasser, whose mere presence had frightened him when they first met, and now made him even more uneasy: he had shot a delivery boy and broken a woman's neck with his bare hands, the news reports said, and it was unclear how the old man had died.

Strasser sat with his feet propped up on the desk, reading the newspaper accounts of the theft and the murders he had committed the night before. He was surprised by the fact that the bodies had been discovered so soon. An old friend of Stewart's, in the city for the day from Oyster Bay, Long Island, had stopped by less than an hour after Strasser left the town house. The friend, who had called earlier in the day and been assured by the housekeeper that Stewart would be home that evening, had become worried, fearing a medical emergency when no one answered the door or the telephone call his chauffeur placed from the car.

"When will the paintings leave the country?" Strasser asked, after finishing the article in the *Times* and glancing at the sensationalistic headline in one of the tabloids.

"With the exception of the van Gogh, they will be on their way to Mexico City tonight."

Something Westcott had been curious about since reading the articles in the papers got the best of him. "The *Times* said there were six other valuable paintings in that sealed room, and that they had all been missing since World War II. If you don't mind my asking, why did you leave them behind?"

"I mind," Strasser said. "Call Paris now, and tell Drussard I've delivered the first four." As Westcott picked up the telephone and began to dial, Strasser added, "And tell him you will have the next two by this time tomorrow." With that, he left by the rear door to where he had parked the rented minivan in the alleyway behind the gallery.

Deciding to keep the luxury apartment building overlooking the East River, in which another of the men on Drussard's list lived, until last, Strasser drove south through the tangled, frenetic traffic of Fifth Avenue toward the Gramercy Park area and the residence of his next victim.

« 14 »

AT THAT SAME moment, five thousand miles away and seven hours ahead of New York City, Rachel Sidrane, just back from her evening run, stepped from the shower and pulled on a white terry cloth robe before going out onto the terrace with a glass of wine and her newspaper. From her hilltop apartment the city of Tel Aviv loomed silent and miragelike in the distance across the bay. The high-rise beachfront hotels and square office towers, with their absence of history and shade, gave the impression of a place that had been built overnight, as if its founders had rushed to claim the once-shifting sand dunes, which still seeped up through the sidewalks to merge with the dust from the endless new construction projects.

The four-thousand-year-old port city of Jaffa stood in marked contrast to the modern and densely populated center of Israeli commerce. The ancient suburb, rich in biblical history, was only a leisurely thirty-minute walk along the seafront promenade from the downtown bustle of Tel Aviv, but gave one the feeling of entering an entirely different world, a venerable place of squat, stucco buildings with arched doorways and windows and graceful minarets towering above its mosques. According to Jewish tradition, after the great flood, Noah's youngest son, Japheth, founded the city on a hill overlooking the bay. And it was here that Saint Peter raised Tabitha from the dead, and Andromeda, of Greek mythology, was chained to a rock in the harbor to be rescued by Perseus on his winged white horse.

Forsaken and ignored by the founders of Tel Aviv at the turn of the century, Jaffa's timeworn buildings and stone ramparts were left to crumble in the sea air. Recently restored, it had been transformed from a neglected slum into a luxury quarter of restaurants, boutiques, and nightclubs, all nestled throughout an intricate web of shady paths and winding cobbled streets once roamed by Phoenician merchants and now filled with shoppers and diners from Tel Aviv seeking the old and picturesque.

Rachel's apartment sat high on a rock promontory at the end of a half-finished meandering pathway. Her small, stone terrace, with its commanding view of Jaffa Harbor, was her favorite place to relax and think. A fresh sea breeze, carrying the scent of the ocean, gently tossed her still-damp hair as she sat sipping her wine and squinting against the reflection of the setting sun off a broad expanse of dark blue water that stretched to the western horizon. Her eyes settled on the harbor scene directly below, where only faint echoes remained of a time when Jaffa, more than a century ago, was the busiest trading port in the eastern Mediterranean. Now private yachts and pleasure boats swayed with the gentle swells that rolled across the bay, while sea gulls swooped and glided along the shore, eyeing the fishermen who leaned against the parapet wall beside their rods, or sat in small boats, tending their nets.

The *New York Times* Rachel unfolded had been left at her door that day, as it was every day, by a friend with El Al Airlines. The paper was her way of keeping in touch with a city she had called home for twenty-six years, a still unsevered cord to her past, and to a life she had left behind eight years ago. Little remained of the naive, idealistic academic, fresh out of Vassar with a degree in art history, who, uncertain of what she wanted to do with her life, had taken her grandmother's advice and come to Israel to spend a year as a volunteer on a kibbutz north of Haifa. She had picked avocados and citrus fruit, and tended chickens, and taught children, and found the hard work and sense of community and extended family strangely gratifying after her self-involved and privileged life as the only child of a successful Wall Street investment banker. Her youth had been one of private boarding schools and summer camps, and the sharing and caring for others was new to her, but in the end she counted the time spent there as the most rewarding of her young life.

It was after leaving the kibbutz to do postdoctoral studies at Tel Aviv University that she met and fell madly in love with Aaron Sontag, a handsome former Israeli commando. They made plans for a future full of promise and purpose: Aaron would continue to carry on the fight against Israel's enemies, but this time in a more subtle way, as a case officer with Israeli intelligence; and she would teach at the university. Later, there would be children, two, they decided.

Then one month before they were to be married, on a hot August afternoon, a continent away from where she sat studying at the university library, her hopes and dreams for the future were torn from her by a senseless act of violence on a London street. Aaron, by then a graduate of the Mossad training academy, was operating under diplomatic cover in England. His airline ticket for his flight to Tel Aviv the next day was in his pocket, and his thoughts were of Rachel as he returned from a meeting with an agent he had just recruited. He was only a block from the Israeli embassy when he was gunned down by a Palestinian assassin, and Rachel's life was changed forever.

David Ben-David, Aaron's uncle and legal guardian after his parents were killed in a terrorist bombing in Jerusalem when he was seven years old, comforted Rachel and consoled her. He, more than anyone, convinced her to stay on in Israel, to make the Promised Land her home. There was much to be done and her contributions could make a difference, he told her, and so she began the process of becoming a naturalized citizen of her adopted country. Ben-David had invited her to his home for dinners and special occasions, and over the ensuing months made her a part of his family. And during one of her darkest hours of grief, he had quoted Yeats to her: "Now that my ladder's gone, I must lie down where all the ladders start, in the foul rag-and-bone shop of the heart."

Ben-David was then a high-ranking member of Israel's foreign intelligence service, officially *Ha Mossad, le Modiyn ve le Tafkidim Mayuhadim* (the Institute for Intelligence and Special Operations), but more commonly known as the Mossad or, by those who served in it, as the Institute. Within the year he would be appointed its chief, and ever the professional intelligence officer, he had recognized the potential in the self-confident and tough-minded young woman he had taken under his wing and into his heart, and guided her along a path that she could never have imagined her life would take. And months after Aaron's death, Rachel accepted the Mossad chief's offer to join the Institute, first as a researcher doing operational analysis; then, when Ben-David believed she was ready, he approached her with what he had in mind from the beginning, and her training at the academy as an operational intelligence officer began in earnest.

There were moments when Rachel missed the energy and vitality of the city in which she had grown up. For her, even with all of New York City's problems, there was still no other like it in the world. And as she sat on the terrace reading the *Times,* she felt another brief ache of nostalgia, accompanied by a twinge of guilt, and made a mental note to call her parents that evening. It had been two years since she had seen them, and the last visit had been uncomfortable. They knew nothing of her work with the Mossad, but disapproved of her becoming an Israeli citizen and rejecting her own country, as they so pointedly put it, to live in such a dangerous and troubled land. Sooner or later, the subject always came up, followed by the inevitable arguments, and so Rachel did what she always did with the conflict of emotions and pushed the thoughts of her parents to the back of her mind, where she knew they would stay until she began to feel guilty again. She continued reading the paper and turned to the Metropolitan News section, where a headline across the top of the first page drew her attention:

WORLD WAR II LOST ART FOUND IN MURDERED PHILANTHROPIST'S HOME

Rachel's doctoral dissertation had been titled "Lost Treasures of Europe," and dealt in depth with the art destroyed and lost during the Second World War. Over the years, through her advanced studies, she had kept current in her field, and as she continued to read the *Times* article, she was amazed that the thief in New York City had left behind paintings of enormous value, while, according to the reporter, it was established from the empty hooks on the wall that only four paintings, their identities a mystery, had been selectively taken.

Upon finishing the article, Rachel glanced at the accompanying photograph and drew a sharp breath, nearly knocking her wineglass from the table as she angled the paper to get the full benefit of the failing light. Her interest was more than scholastic as she stared long and hard at the image of a small painting inside what the reporter referred to as a "secret room."

The painting hung on a wall behind a New York City homicide detective who stood in the foreground of the photograph talking with another man identified as being from the police department's Stolen Art Squad. Rachel jumped up from the table and rushed inside to get a magnifying glass from her desk in the living room. She returned to the terrace and held the glass over the paper, slowly moving it in and out until she found the exact distance that gave her as clear an image as was possible from the grainy photograph.

"My God!" she said aloud.

The painting, an oil on canvas signed *Rembrandt f.* and dated 1651, was a romantic, rather than a realistic, interpretation of the ruins of a tower set at the bend of a river. Below the tower was a rustic cottage with several sheep grazing nearby. Although Rembrandt's drawings and etchings of landscapes were numerous, this was one of only eighteen the artist had done in oil. Rachel knew its history well. It had gone undiscovered and unrecorded until 1938, after which it was named *Landscape with a Square Tower,* and was said to be in the possession of a private collector in Vienna. The painting disappeared shortly thereafter, along with its alleged owner, and led to speculations by the art experts of the time that it was either a clever forgery hastily hidden away to prevent the embarrassment of those who had authenticated it, or, as was put forth by art historians at the end of the war, that it never really existed in the first place.

But Rachel knew the truth. Even though she had never seen the actual painting, or even a photograph of it until now, she could describe it in exacting detail: the white sky streaked with yellow, the umbers and dark greens of the foliage, the yellow ocher of the tower, the reflections of the sky in the river, and the overall warmth and solid massing of shadows that added depth and mystery to the scene.

The painting, more precisely its very personal history, had been the impetus for Rachel's becoming an art historian. And at that moment, as she sat on the terrace mesmerized by its image, a rare wave of uncontrollable emotion swept over her and tears welled in her eyes. The discovery of the painting had so dominated her thoughts that the significance of what she had read in the article did not at first occur to her. It was only after regaining her composure and reviewing the text, to make certain she had missed none of the pertinent facts, that she made the connection. The reporter had quoted the Stolen Art Squad detective as saying; "Art thieves aren't usually associated with this type of violence."

But terrorists are, Rachel thought, and her mind raced back to a top-secret meeting at Mossad headquarters early the previous week. Ben-David had called the members of her unit together for a special briefing. Two Mossad case officers had been killed in Paris. The man responsible was believed to be the international terrorist known only as Dieter, and Rachel's unit was instructed to begin gleaning every known fact about Dieter and his associates from the Mossad's extensive research department as the worldwide search began.

However, it was the briefing on the Mossad surveillance in Paris and the incidents prior to the death of the two intelligence officers that now resonated in Rachel's thoughts. She recalled that the "take" from the conversation between Dieter and his still unidentified companion at the café in Saint-Germain had been spotty at best. Only bits and pieces of occasional sentences were picked up and recorded. But she remembered that art had been one of the topics discussed, and a reference to stolen art was heard at least once.

Rachel left the terrace and, taking the *Times* with her, returned to the desk in her living room where she cut the article and the photograph from the newspaper and placed them in a manila envelope. Five minutes later, wearing hastily thrown on jeans, sweat shirt, and running shoes, her hair still damp, she drove out of her apartment driveway and sped north along the coast road.

« 15 »

As RACHEL SIDRANE worked her way through Tel Aviv's evening rush-hour traffic toward Mossad headquarters, Lt. Col. Nikolai Leonov was preparing to leave his office inside the tightly guarded, restricted compound that houses the headquarters of the *Sluzhba Vneshnei Razvedki* (SVR), the newly created Russian External Intelligence Service.

Formerly the First Chief Directorate of the KGB, the SVR is separate and apart from the reorganized internal security and police organizations and is analogous to the CIA in that it is solely responsible for all foreign intelligence. Located at Yasenevo, in a wooded area just outside the ring road southwest of Moscow, the main building bears a strong resemblance to CIA headquarters in Langley, Virginia; and as with CIA officers, who refer to their agency by a variety of nicknames of which "the Company" is best known, the SVR headquarters is commonly referred to as *"les"* (the forest) or *"Kontora"* (the office).

Leonov was in the process of locking some classified documents he had been reading in his desk safe when Capt. Yuri Sobchak, one of four assistants who made up his staff, entered the office with a concerned look on his face.

"Colonel Leonov, I believe this may be of some importance,'' he said, and handed him a report that had arrived with the latest cables from the Russian United Nations mission in New York City.

The report was a synopsis of overt intelligence information routinely sent on a daily basis to all sections of the SVR's First Department—the department responsible for intelligence operations against the United States and Americans anywhere in the world. The information in the report, and others like it gathered by the Russian embassy in Washington and missions and consulates throughout the country, contained daily summaries on matters of interest in politics, business, and technology, along with prominent news stories from major cities. Leonov's office received copies of the reports from every country covered by all SVR departments, which meant he received them from every country in the world.

As Leonov skimmed the neatly typed, single-spaced text, he shrugged and gave Sobchak a questioning look. ''And why do you bring this to my attention?''

''The fifth paragraph of the third page, please.''

Leonov turned to the paragraph Sobchak had indicated. His eyes narrowed and he leaned forward in his chair as he began reading a concise summary of a *New York Times* story concerning the death of Edward Winthrop Stewart, wealthy philanthropist and noted art collector.

''I recognized the name, and entered it in the computer,'' Sobchak said. ''Stewart has never been operational, but he is on our schedule for periodic reviews subject to your orders.''

Stewart's review status was something of which Leonov was well aware; a major part of his job was constantly updating every conceivable facet of the man's life, as well as the lives of others in the files of his tightly compartmented operations. The original file had consisted of eleven names, all prominent and wealthy men from five Western countries. Many of them were now retired or no longer active, but over the years most had been directed and coerced into recruiting a second generation (and in two cases a third), and the list now stood at twenty-nine.

Leonov looked up from the report after reading it a second time, his brow knit with concern. "Leave the office," he said abruptly to the young captain.

Sobchak responded immediately, with Leonov following him to the door and locking it behind him. Leonov then crossed to the far wall and entered the code for the cipher lock on the door of a ten-inch-thick steel security vault that took up the entire space of an adjoining room built specifically to house it.

Once inside the cold, cryptlike room, Leonov used a key, hidden inside the vault, to open a locked drawer, from which he removed a file folder before returning to his desk. The file was stamped across the top in bold black letters: EDWARD WINTHROP STEWART—USA—INACTIVE, and directly below it in parentheses (GENESIS: HERMANN GOERING—REICH MARSHAL).

The operations that had stemmed from the information in the series of files collectively known as the Goering File were the sole reason for the existence of Leonov's department, and the only operations with which he had been involved since joining the KGB twenty-five years ago. His four-man staff served under the same restrictions. Once assigned to the office, they would spend their entire careers there.

Leonov's department appeared on the SVR organizational chart as the Special Projects Office, ostensibly a small study-and-research group attached to an obscure subsection of Service R, a section that dealt with planning and analysis. Its operations, even knowledge of its existence, were born classified top secret under the NKVD in 1945, then passed on to its successor agencies, the NKGB, MGB, MVD, the KGB and finally to the SVR. Since the coup of 1991, only one of Leonov's superiors, the head of the SVR, who had the only other copy of the file locked in an equally secure vault, knew of the department's true purpose and the enormous amount of vital intelligence it had provided over the past forty-six years.

Consequently, to the puzzlement of the men who would ordinarily have been Leonov's immediate superiors, he bypassed the normal chain of command and dealt directly with the head of the SVR in all matters relating to the Goering File operations. The explanation given was that Leonov occasionally conducted highly sensitive research with a severely restricted access list. None of his superiors knew, or even suspected, that the soft-spoken and scholarly colonel orchestrated and conducted an operation that had managed to burrow deep within the American defense, intelligence, diplomatic, and scientific establishments, as well as those of France, Great Britain, Germany, and, to a lesser extent due to its relative insignificance, Spain.

With the recent upheaval in what had once been the Soviet Union, Leonov's work had taken on an even greater significance. Intelligence operations required support through local facilities and agent networks, and with Russian credibility as a world power shattered, the SVR's attempts to recruit new agents, even to hang on to those already in place, were seriously hampered. A necessary part of any intelligence officer's efforts to recruit spies was the promise, and ability, to protect them from exposure, and to be there for them when necessary; and there were few, if any, who would believe those promises from the Russians in the postcoup days.

It soon became apparent that the upheaval had left the SVR gravely wounded and temporarily eliminated from the game, and drastic measures were required to repair the damage. Entire agent networks needed to be rebuilt and security restored, and budget cuts had necessitated the reduction by half of their current overseas intelligence officers, making it necessary in the interim to place greater reliance on Line N agents, "illegals,'' who operated under deep cover outside the diplomatic community—a course of action that held the danger of exposing some of the SVR's most highly prized, long-in-place secret operatives. A new department was being formed, comprised of ''students'' who, taking advantage of the rapidly expanding student-exchange programs, would operate abroad under academic cover, away from the local *Rezidenturas* and the scrutiny of the host country's counterintelligence services. But such operations were not established overnight, and it would be at least another year before they were in place and producing results.

The new Russian government had made agreements with the West, pledging cooperation in the areas of drug trafficking and terrorism. And ''active measures''—aggressive covert acts of espionage—directed against the United States and the European Community were severely curtailed to prevent any incidents that might interfere with the continuation of vital financial and humanitarian aid. But the age-old paranoia and siege mentality rooted deep in the xenophobic Russian soul still worked its insidious way into the decisions of those responsible for the new nation's security. The policymakers were acutely aware of the domestic pressure to reduce military spending and improve the standard of living for the average person, and, with limited funds available, espionage was still the most effective and expedient way of squaring the circle, leaving the practitioners of the second-oldest profession with little choice but to continue the game as best they could.

Given the current situation, Leonov's operations, by far the most productive in garnering much-needed technological information and accessing the policies and intentions of the West, were considered one of the SVR's few remaining ''nuggets.'' His servicing and controlling of his longtime agents-in-place involved no new covert operations, and were so tightly controlled that there was virtually no risk of exposure. The unnerving incident involving Edward Winthrop Stewart was the first tear in the tightly woven fabric of an operation that had run flawlessly for the past forty-six years.

After reviewing the information in Stewart's file, and returning it to the vault, Leonov used the intercom to summon Sobchak back into the office.

"Send a priority cable to the *rezident* at the United Nations mission in New York City. I want complete details of the theft and the murder of Stewart, including any and all police reports available through our contacts."

As an afterthought, upon realizing that the *rezident,* the highest-ranking SVR officer at the mission, would not be motivated by a request from an obscure lieutenant colonel, Leonov added, "Make certain he understands the order is on the authority of the head of the External Intelligence Service. And I want to be notified immediately when the report comes in, regardless of the time.

"That will be all," he told the young captain, who had already turned on his heel and was on his way out of the office to compose and encrypt the cable on a one-time pad.

Leonov sat at his desk, smoking a cigarette and staring at a painting of a Ukrainian landscape on the wall where a portrait of Lenin had once hung. Stewart had never been an important cog in the wheel. In 1946, when MVD psychiatrists had done psychological profiles on the original eleven men on the list, Stewart, an arrogant man of supreme self-confidence, was judged to be the least likely to be susceptible to their overtures, and if coerced too ruthlessly, would be difficult to handle and a potential problem. The psychiatrists further suggested that, due to his enormous wealth, rather than allow himself to lose control over his life, he would most likely report any contact, and try to buy his way out of any difficulty the threatened exposure of his dealings with the Nazis might cause him.

Still, a soft, tentative approach was made, and rebuffed,

serving to prove the psychiatrists right. It was then decided that, since Stewart had no connections to the intelligence community, held no government office, and his business interests did not include any defense- or high-technology-related industries, he would be kept on file as a secondary opportunity and not approached again unless things changed and he could be put to use through other means. He remained one of only two men out of the original eleven whom the state security agency had been unable to bring into their fold. The second was a French count, a friend of de Gaulle, who had spent the war years in Switzerland and in 1946 was appointed to an important post in France's defense ministry. He committed suicide only hours after the threat of exposure was presented as his only option if he did not comply with the MVD demands. From that point on, the fledgling operation proceeded in the manner that had been hoped for, eventually to exceed all expectations.

Promoted to chief of the Special Projects Office twelve years ago, Leonov had run the Goering File operations to perfection. He controlled his agents-in-place with a steady and firm hand, and directed the occasional new recruitments into ever more productive areas as intelligence needs and emphasis changed. A large, bulky man, over six feet tall and carrying just under 220 pounds that ran mostly to fat, he gave the appearance of an out-of-shape, uninspired clerk. But as with most things in life, appearances were deceiving, and Leonov was anything but uninspired. He was a perceptive and intelligent man, who had learned early in his career never to accept coincidences as such. An accomplished lateral thinker, he inevitably found pathways through problems where others saw only an impenetrable maze.

The incident involving Stewart left him feeling uneasy. Perhaps the robbery/murder was a coincidence, and Stewart a victim of chance. But according to the newspaper article, there had been a selectivity to the theft. A selectivity that to Leonov suggested an unnerving design to what had taken place, and was quite possibly a harbinger of a much bigger problem.

He lit another cigarette, unaware that the first still burned in the ashtray, and picked up the receiver of his in-house phone with a direct line to the head of the SVR. Thus began a process that would eventually test Leonov's considerable skills as an intelligence officer to an extent never before required, in ways to which he was unaccustomed, and for reasons he would never have thought possible.

« 16 »

SEVEN TIME ZONES west of Lt. Col. Nikolai Leonov's office at SVR headquarters, Jurgen Strasser was finishing his reconnoitering of the immediate area around Arthur Cabot's residence on Gramercy Park West. Cabot, a retired career diplomat only a year younger than Stewart, according to the background information provided by Drussard, was equally careless about his personal security, from what Strasser had observed.

The only other resident of the elegant red-brick neoclassic town house was a much younger woman, in her mid-forties, whom Strasser correctly assumed to be Cabot's wife. An earlier surveillance had revealed that there was no live-in help; two female domestics arrived at eight in the morning and left shortly after five in the evening. As Strasser made a final sweep of the area looking for an unobtrusive place to park near the tree-lined square, a chance encounter yielded unexpected results. As he drove by the home, he saw Cabot's wife coming out the front door, and watched as she got into a limousine while a chauffeur placed three pieces of luggage in the trunk.

The license plates spelled out the name of the limousine service, and after parking the van, Strasser made a call to the dispatcher, pretending to be Cabot inquiring as to why the car had not yet arrived. He was assured that the driver had just picked up Mrs. Cabot, and that she was en route to the airport as they spoke. Strasser smiled to himself at learning the invaluable piece of information. Things were falling into place quite well; Cabot would be home alone.

The immediate area around the small, private park in the center of the square, with its locked gates for which only the residents had keys, was an exclusive enclave for some of the city's wealthiest citizens, old-monied and socially prominent. With its ornate streetlamps and historic town houses adorned with outside staircases and cast iron banisters and balconies, it was a part of New York that most recalled the past, and as such was one of the points of interest noted in the guidebooks. The surrounding neighborhood, however, deteriorated rapidly into a diverse cultural and economic mix where even the most bizarre behavior was not likely to attract attention.

It was late in the afternoon when Strasser spotted a small group of Japanese tourists, escorted by a guide, wandering about the square and snapping pictures at every turn. Their presence provided him with the cover he needed. He returned to where he had parked the minivan on a side street a short distance away, and got his camera from the glove box, then walked back to the square where he followed just behind the guided tour until they passed Cabot's town house. He stopped and feigned interest in the architectural merits of the turn-of-the-century structure and began taking pictures while stealing occasional glances down a narrow passageway between Cabot's home and that of an adjacent neighbor's.

With the guided tour's attention now on a statue in the park, Strasser held the camera to his eye as he casually slipped into the passageway playing the part of the intrusive tourist. He paused halfway to the rear of the house to point the camera up and focus on the neighbor's windows that had a view toward Cabot's home. He noted that the draperies were drawn and that the windows on the first two floors of both houses were barred in much the same manner as the Stewart home was. The passageway ended at the rear of the town houses, where locked wrought iron gates barred entrance to private gardens set behind seven-foot-high brick walls.

Strasser peered through the gate into Cabot's garden and carefully studied the enclosed area. He immediately dismissed the possibility of the security system's including exterior infrared beams; the arrangement of the shrubbery scattered throughout the well-tended garden precluded a line of sight that could detect an intruder approaching the rear of the house from the gate. He also ruled out microwave beams, capable of penetrating the shrubs, as impractical. His presence at the gate, with the beams passing through its evenly spaced bars, would have already tripped the alarm.

He allowed for the possibility of seismic sensor cables implanted in the ground, but they were of little concern to him; he knew how to defeat them for the distance of less than ten feet he would have to cover to reach the outside wall of the house. The sensors required several walking or running steps to produce the alternating vibrations necessary to violate the system. By slipping over the wall and lowering himself gently to the ground, then lying prone and slowly rolling toward the house in one continuous movement, he would distribute his weight over a large area, and avoid creating the unique vibrations caused by walking or running.

As Strasser turned his attention to the rear door and windows, his eyes swept past, then returned and fixed on, a small basement window below and to the left of the steps leading from the door into the garden. Partially hidden from view by shrubs and rosebushes, the window drew Strasser's close scrutiny. It had no bars, but the frame was different from those on the windows on the floors above. A heavy wire mesh was embedded in the frame and covered with glass, and behind the mesh, he could just make out four evenly spaced rows of plastic-coated wire. Strasser recognized it as an alarm screen, and it told him something else about the security system; it had been installed years ago by someone not very knowledgeable or conscientious about his work, and it was far from state of the art.

The windows on the first two floors at the rear of the four-story structure were barred like those at the side and front. As Strasser's eyes moved slowly across each of the windows, the movement of a large, gray-blue Persian cat, stretched out on a sill inside the first-floor window closest to him, caught his attention. The cat leaped out of sight as Strasser stared at it, and in doing so, gave him another vital piece of information about the security system: if there were infrared beams covering the interior rooms and hallways, they would be raised high enough off the floor so that the cat's movements would not break the beam, and therefore would provide Strasser with enough space to crawl under them if necessary.

He returned his attention to the single basement window, and decided on his approach to entering the house. He placed the lens of his camera through the bars of the gate and focused on the wire mesh screen. He took a quick series of pictures, then, for appearances' sake in the event someone was watching him, he turned the lens on the garden before leaving the passageway.

After eating an early dinner at a nearby restaurant, and studying the photos of the screened window, developed at a one-hour service center, he returned to the square shortly before seven o'clock. The last of the evening light was fading as he walked along the park side of the street and looked for interior lights that might tell him where Cabot was in the house. As he was about to cross over to the passageway, he saw the old man come out the front door and walk to the corner where he headed north, away from the square.

Strasser acted immediately, scanning the near-deserted

street as he crossed to the passageway and slipped unnoticed between the two buildings. If he could find the paintings and escape without a confrontation, so much the better. In a strong, agile move, he pulled himself up and swung easily over the brick wall next to the gate and lowered himself to the ground. He lay flat on the grass, with his arms stretched out in front of him, and rolled the ten feet to the rear wall of the town house, where he quickly rose to his knees next to the basement window but behind a large shrub that concealed him from the view of anyone looking into the garden.

The small waist pack he wore held all the equipment he would need. He used a small pair of wire cutters to cut the edge of the screen on both ends, then carefully pulled it away from the frame, giving him access to the alarm wires behind it. With the self-confidence of expert training and years of experience, he then performed the most delicate part of the task. He used a stainless steel folding knife with a razor-sharp blade, rather than wire strippers, which might inadvertently cut too deep, and gradually shaved away just enough of the plastic shield that coated the alarm wires to expose them without making contact. Within fifteen minutes he had shaved and exposed both ends of the four wires that ran the length of the frame. He next removed four jumper wires from his waist pack, each five feet long and fitted with alligator clips on both ends. Carefully, with precise timing, he attached them to the exposed ends of the alarm wires to complete a bypass circuit that allowed him to cut out the original wires and remove the screen without tripping the alarm.

The window had not been opened in years, but a solid blow to the frame, after using the knife to work the edges, allowed Strasser to force it open far enough for him to crawl inside and drop to the floor of a room that seemed inordinately cool. Using a shielded penlight, he saw that he was in a large wine

cellar with humidity and temperature controls that kept the
well-stocked room at a constant fifty-eight degrees.

He felt certain that the house was empty, but remained
crouched on the floor beneath the window, listening for any
indication that his entrance had been detected. After five minutes of silence, he crossed to a door that opened to a walnut-
paneled basement recreation room dominated by a billiard table. His penlight revealed a staircase leading to the upper
floors, and Strasser took it, pausing at the landing to again
listen before opening the door and entering the kitchen. He
leaned against the heavy oak door as he closed it, and stood
motionless once more as his eyes swept the walls and base-
boards for infrared beams. He saw none, and began to move
along a hallway toward the front of the house. He reached a
small sitting room and reception area off the entrance foyer
and was shining the penlight on the paintings hung about the
ornately decorated room when the sound of a dead bolt's turning caused him to dart into a corner behind a high-backed,
overstuffed chair.

Arthur Cabot's hands were shaking as he tucked the newspapers and a container of imported pipe tobacco under his arm
and fumbled with his keys. He stepped quickly into the foyer
and closed and locked the door, then tried to calm himself
with slow, deep breaths as he entered the code on the alarm
panel three times before getting the numbers correct and dis-
arming the system. He had spent the morning gardening, and
the rest of the day helping his wife prepare for her trip to
Boston, and had not watched the news shows, nor had he taken
his daily morning walk, when he usually picked up the *Times*
to read over breakfast. The tabloid headlines on the newsstand
in the tobacco shop had shocked him; he had known Edward
Winthrop Stewart socially. But it was not the man's death that
so disturbed him, rather the revelation of the secret collection
of missing works of art. All these years, Cabot had thought to

himself as he hurried home, and never imagining that they had both fallen victim to the same weakness a half century ago.

Eager to read the articles in the three papers he had purchased, especially the *Times* version, which at least wasn't trumpeted in grisly banner headlines, but at a glance appeared to be covered in more depth, he hurried from the foyer into the reception area and placed the papers on an end table while reaching to turn on a lamp. He stopped, frozen in fear with his hand extended, when in his peripheral vision he saw a shadowy figure appear from the darkened corner behind him.

Eight days before the American declaration of war against Nazi Germany on December 11, 1941, Cabot's good judgment and sense of human decency were temporarily overruled by greed and avarice when he purchased two paintings of questionable lineage from an art broker in Zurich, Switzerland. It was an act that had compromised the rest of his life, and for which he had paid a terrible price in personal torment. But, as he was about to learn when Jurgen Strasser reached over and switched on the table lamp, the final payment was yet to be exacted.

« 17 »

ARTHUR CABOT DIED of a massive cerebral hemorrhage caused by a fractured skull suffered in a fall as he tried to escape the man who had tortured him for what seemed an eternity. In reality, it was less than fifteen minutes before he could no longer tolerate the excruciating pain and gave Strasser the information he wanted. By the time the maids discovered the body, at eight o'clock the following morning, it was stiff from rigor mortis and locked in the grotesque position in which Cabot had landed at the bottom of the stairs: legs and arms askew, with the neck and head twisted at an impossible angle.

One hour after the homicide detective who caught the case arrived at the scene, with the news media close on his heels, all hell had broken loose. First in the mayor's office, then, within minutes, in the police commissioner's office on the fourteenth floor of One Police Plaza, and, shortly thereafter, in the chief of detectives' office on the floor below.

IT WAS THE smell of the place that got to him: the faint, sickening-sweet smell of death that hung in the air and permeated the entire building. Lt. Mike Kelly had been a homicide detective with the New York City Police Department for fourteen years, and had been to the morgue more times than he could remember, or cared to remember, and he had never gotten used to it.

His work day had started with a telephone call as he entered the detective squad room at the seventieth precinct in Brooklyn. The call was from a sergeant, the lead clerical in the chief of detectives' office at police headquarters. Kelly was to report there, forthwith.

Four years ago, as a sergeant, Kelly had served on another task force, and his innovative and brilliant work had caught the attention of the chief of detectives. That, and Kelly's reputation as a meticulous and dogged investigator, as well as his excellent record of success with high-profile cases over the past five years at the seventieth precinct, resulted in his being appointed the whip for the special task force formed to solve the homicides of two of the city's more prominent and wealthier citizens.

Empowered to select his own men, within the hour Kelly pulled in two detectives from his Brooklyn squad, and three more from other precincts, men he had worked with before and held in high regard. With the suspected connection between the two victims being their art collections, Kelly requested and was granted a sixth detective from the Stolen Art Squad, a small, two-man unit within the much larger Safe, Loft, and Truck Squad. Additionally, the chief of detectives had assured Kelly that Detective Borough Command would provide further manpower as needed. Such was the political pressure the two homicides had generated.

It was just before noon when Kelly entered the squat, gray-green building at Thirteenth Street and First Avenue that housed the New York City Medical Examiner's Office. The familiar thin odor of death greeted him at the door and grew stronger as he went down to the morgue where Richard Roth, the chief medical examiner and a forensic pathologist for over thirty years, was expecting him.

One of Roth's lab attendants stood off to the side, leaning against the pale-green ceramic tile that covered all four walls of the depressing room. Roth was standing between a stainless steel table and a gurney, his half-glasses resting on the tip of his nose as he pulled his surgical gloves up over the sleeves of his lab coat. The gurney contained the body of Edward Winthrop Stewart, covered by a white sheet. Stewart's autopsy had been completed the previous day, and his corpse had been brought out of the temperature-controlled lockers down the hall for the purpose of comparison. The steel table on the right held the body of Arthur Cabot, whose autopsy was scheduled to begin when Kelly arrived.

"What is it about this city, Lieutenant?" Roth said with a cheerful smile. "We never seem to run out of bodies, do we?"

"Must be something in the water," Kelly said. He hoped that the usually grumpy ME's good mood was related to his case.

Kelly had already learned from his telephone call to Roth earlier that morning that the cause of Stewart's death had been a massive heart attack, but questions remained as to what had brought it on. Roth believed it was a severe shock, or series of them, to the victim's central nervous system. The cause of Cabot's death from a cerebral hemorrhage due to a fractured skull was readily apparent from the start: a fall, or a shove, down a long flight of steep stairs to a marble floor in the entrance hall.

"Move in closer," Roth said. "There's something I want you to take a look at."

Kelly stepped forward and stood just behind Roth's left shoulder in the pool of bright light cast over Cabot's fully clothed body by a double bank of fluorescent ceiling lights. A perforated steel sheet ran the length of the autopsy table, with a double sink and taps at one end, to drain off blood and bodily fluids, Kelly knew. Suspended above the table were a microphone for recording the ME's remarks during the procedure, a high-intensity lamp on an articulated arm that provided a more direct illumination for close-up work, and a large scale to weigh the victim's organs. Kelly noticed that the rigor mortis, which under normal conditions would have remained in Cabot's body for another twenty-four hours, had been "broken"—the contracted muscles of the twisted limbs stretched back into their natural positions.

"This is Tony Morino," Roth said, and motioned for his attendant to join them. "If you had any doubts about whether or not these two homicides are related, Tony's sharp eyes and insights from his rather curious background are going to relieve you of them."

Roth raised Cabot's left hand, and brought the high-intensity lamp down to shine directly on it.

"If you look closely, you can see a small puncture wound under the left thumbnail."

Kelly bent at the waist and examined the barely visible mark.

"I missed it," Roth said. "My eyes aren't what they used to be. But Tony here, quite by accident, spotted it. As it turns out, the first victim, Stewart, has an identical mark in precisely the same location."

Roth turned to face the gurney and pulled back one side of the sheet to raise Stewart's left hand. He swung the high-intensity lamp around until the pinprick beneath the thumbnail was visible in the bright light.

"What caused them?" Kelly asked, and leaned in for a closer look at Stewart's thumb.

"Tell the lieutenant what you told me," Roth said to his attendant.

Morino, a short, muscular man with an abundance of nervous energy and a facial tic that caused his left eye to blink repeatedly, spoke in a soft, somewhat detached voice.

"About twenty-three years ago, I was with the Phoenix Program in Vietnam. Among other things, we conducted interrogations on prisoners . . . people suspected of being Vietcong infrastructure, mainly. Sometimes we tortured them for information. One of the methods used was somethin' I'll never forget. Never failed. This North Vietnamese captain, a defector the CIA put to use as an interrogator, used it all the time; the psychotic little son of a bitch really enjoyed it."

Morino's tic got worse as he continued. "He used a hat pin, maybe three inches long, and he'd stick it under the guy's thumbnail. Just a half inch or so at first, no big deal. Guy would tough it out, flinch, maybe grunt, suck some air between his teeth. He was tied in a chair, his wrists strapped to the arms so he couldn't move. Anyway, every time the guy refused to answer, the captain would use the butt of his pistol to tap the pin in a little farther, till it was down inside the first joint. Some guys could take it to that point, but nobody, and I mean nobody, took what came next."

Kelly had a vivid imagination, and had no trouble envisioning the pain connected with what Morino was describing. He shuddered involuntarily and flexed his thumb at the thought.

Morino's tic became a rapid eye flutter as he continued. Kelly suspected the morgue attendant might be reliving the experience of what he had witnessed years ago.

"The nasty little bastard would take the head of the pin and shake it, real hard, the needle part stuck in the joint, like I said. And I'm here to tell you, after two or three shakes, guys on the receiving end told them everything they knew, even stuff they didn't know; just made it up, whatever they wanted to hear. You had to stand back when it got to that point. They screamed and puked all over the place. Christ, they even fingered innocent people. Anything to stop the pain."

"More than enough to cause a heart attack in an old man,"

Roth said to Kelly. "Wouldn't you agree? And the strap marks on both victims' wrists coincide with what Tony just described."

"Did that particular interrogation method originate with the Vietnamese?" Kelly asked Morino, thinking that perhaps he had found some small insight into the killer. Maybe a Vietnam veteran once assigned to an intelligence unit that had specialized in interrogations.

"No," Morino said. "I asked him one day where he learned that evil shit. He said he got it from an East German adviser in Hanoi who told him the Nazis thought it up in World War II. I think he said the Gestapo used it. Figures."

So both victims had been tortured until they gave up the paintings the killer had been after, Kelly thought. Stewart until he revealed the location of his secret room, and Cabot until he disclosed their location in a small, private study off his bedroom. At least there appeared to be two paintings missing from the walls in Cabot's study, but it was kept locked so the maids never cleaned in there and couldn't confirm it. Mrs. Cabot, whom Kelly was eager to interview, was not expected back for another two days. She was staying with friends in Boston, and so far they had been unable to contact her.

One thing in particular, evident in both cases, bothered Kelly. The detective from the Art Squad had told him that the paintings left untouched in Cabot's home were worth millions; the same was true with the Stewart theft. That the paintings stolen from Stewart were kept in a secret room, with other stolen art that no one seemed to know the man had, meant that the killer had prior, and specific, knowledge of things few people knew. If the same proved true for Cabot, there was much more to the case than art thefts complicated by murder.

"Let's get on with it," Roth said, interrupting Kelly's thoughts. "Any preference for music today, Lieutenant?"

Kelly shook his head. The music helped some, but not

much. It was his job to witness the autopsy for purposes of the evidential chain, and the only part of being a homicide detective he hated.

The strains of Vivaldi's *Four Seasons* played softly in the background as Roth adjusted the overhead microphone and began his litany.

"This is Richard Roth, forensic pathologist for the city of New York, office of the medical examiner. We are conducting a postmortem examination on the body of . . ."

Kelly steeled himself for what was to come as Morino assisted in carefully removing the outer layer of clothing from Cabot's body.

Fifty blocks north of where the autopsy was being performed, Jurgen Strasser sat on a bench in Central Park overlooking a large grassy field known as the Sheep Meadow. He was finishing his lunch, a hot dog and a cup of coffee from a vendor's cart, and studying a large-scale street map of the Upper East Side, particularly the Sutton Place section of the city.

He had dropped off the Cabot paintings at Westcott's gallery that morning, then telephoned his bank in Liechtenstein and confirmed that payment for the first four paintings had been received and credited to his account. The thought of nine million dollars brought a broad smile to his usually stoic face. A subsequent call to Drussard in Paris after leaving the gallery assured him that an additional five million would be transferred to his account within the next twenty-four hours.

Not bad, he thought, fourteen million for a few hours' work, if the time for planning and preparation weren't factored in. He already had enough money to pay in full, many times over, for the stolen Russian chemical and biological weapons being held for him by the arms dealer in Paris, with more than enough left to allow him to operate independently for years to come. And there were still two more paintings in New York, worth four million dollars to him, and a total of nine paintings in London, Madrid, and Rome; less valuable works than the ones he had just stolen, Drussard had told him, but they would still bring him another eleven million dollars. If all went well, he would have almost thirty million dollars by the time he was finished.

Strasser stopped his mental calculations and daydreaming and forced himself to concentrate on his third victim, Philip Bancroft, and the two remaining paintings on his New York list. Bancroft's residence in a building of luxury condominiums overlooking the East River presented its own special security problems, problems that Strasser had not yet worked out. His primary concern was all the publicity the Stewart murder was getting, and Cabot, too, from what he had seen of the early television newscasts in Westcott's office.

He had telephoned the Bancroft home, posing as a dispatcher for Federal Express and inquiring if he had the correct address and when Philip Bancroft would be available to sign for a package that required his personal signature. A woman he assumed to be a maid had told him that Bancroft was out of the country and not expected home until the following day. The delay bothered Strasser. If Bancroft learned of the murders and thefts and drew the logical conclusion about his own vulnerability—and there was no reason to assume he would not—he might well go into hiding, or surround himself with security, making a one-man operation next to impossible. But the challenge held a strange appeal for Strasser, and even if it took an extremely forceful and violent approach to get to his objective, he believed he could somehow pull it off. In light of the publicity, he would have to be ready to act as soon as Bancroft returned, that same night, or perhaps during the day if the opportunity presented itself.

Strasser finished his lunch and tossed the napkin and foam cup into a nearby receptacle, then lit a cigarette and let it dangle from the corner of his mouth as he cupped his hands behind his head and tilted his face skyward, enjoying the warm spring sun on his face before leaving the park to study the building where Bancroft lived.

PHILIP BANCROFT WAS also basking in the sun. The Caribbean sun. He was stretched out on deck in the entertainment cockpit of his seventy-foot sailboat, the *Invincible,* anchored in a secluded cove on the island of Anguilla in the British West Indies. This was the private time he allowed himself each year: a full month of sailing among the islands. No telephone, newspapers, or television, and all corporate responsibilities delegated to his chief executive officer, who had explicit orders not to bother him no matter what the crisis.

Early tomorrow morning, his captain would sail the *Invincible* the short distance to Marigot Harbor on the island of Saint Martin. There Bancroft would board the Gulf Stream III corporate jet owned by Bancroft Industries, a major defense and space contractor, and a company he had founded and for which he still served as chairman of the board. Whisked away in luxurious comfort and privacy, he would be back in New York City no later than noon.

« **18** »

A TRANSCRIBED SUMMARY of the findings from Arthur Cabot's autopsy was completed by 1:15 that afternoon. One hour later, a copy of that summary, along with the related findings involving Stewart, was faxed directly to Alfred Palmer, chief of the Counterintelligence Staff at CIA headquarters in Langley, Virginia.

The information had been acquired through a CIA contact in the New York City Police Department's Intelligence Division. Palmer had made the initial request of the Agency's New York office for any information about the death of Stewart after seeing a CNN news report on the murder and the discovery of stolen art from World War II. It didn't take any great leap of imagination for the CI chief to connect what had happened in New York with the incident two days ago involving the BACKLASH file. And if any questions did remain, they were answered in a timely fashion fifteen minutes later, when he received a lengthy report cabled from the Munich base by the case officer who had sent a local agent to Berchtesgaden to look into the death of Heinz Strasser. The discovery that morning of Arthur Cabot's body only confirmed what Palmer already knew: there was potentially disastrous activity involving the BACKLASH case.

After a hurried meeting with George Sinclair, the CIA director, a decision was made to call in Jack Brannigan, the deputy director for Operations. What now seemed to have all the ingredients of a problem of major proportions, the DCI had argued, would require the expertise and assets of the DDO, and might prove impossible to run without his help. Palmer objected to including Brannigan, out of ego and territorial imperative he later admitted to himself, but the director's logic prevailed: "We don't want to end-run him now only to find out we need him later."

THE TOP-SECRET MEETING of three of the Agency's most powerful men took place at an estate owned by the CIA in the rolling countryside of northern Virginia, just outside the small town of Middleburg and only a short drive from Langley. The basement of the red-brick Georgian mansion had been reconstructed at a cost of over one million dollars, and housed an acoustically secure conference room, much like the "bubble" that served the same purpose at headquarters, and in American embassies around the world. The secluded one-hundred-acre estate was complete with tennis courts, swimming pool, and stables, and an array of sophisticated antennas carefully concealed throughout the grounds that were part of a secure satellite communications system capable of reaching anywhere in the world. The estate was used mostly to debrief high-level defectors, but occasionally served to provide a quiet, out-of-the-way place where nonattributable and officially unacknowledged courses of action that often swayed the fate of nations could be weighed and decided.

The purpose of the meeting was to bring Jack Brannigan into the loop, but only, the DCI had emphasized, to the extent necessary to allow him to function efficiently for what they had in mind. It was a few minutes before three o'clock in the afternoon when the three men entered the bubble and sat down at one end of a long, highly polished oak conference table with the DCI at the head.

Brannigan was not taken aback by what he heard in the director's opening remarks. He had been with the Agency long enough to know there were any number of close-held operations to which he was not privy. It was the nature of the profession, and he didn't take it personally. He was glancing over the reports of the murders in New York City that Alfred Palmer had handed him, when something in the concluding remarks in the autopsy summaries caused him to raise an eyebrow. The director interrupted his train of thought when he spoke.

"The origins of BACKLASH go back to 1944," Sinclair said. "When Allen Dulles ran the OSS office in Switzerland. He had heard rumors about the clandestine sale of looted Nazi art. Dulles was nothing if not farsighted, and he called in Jim Angleton, who was then a promising young OSS counterintelligence operative. He told him to look into what appeared to hold the potential for a postwar intelligence problem if the rumors involving prominent American families were true."

Brannigan smiled inwardly as he listened to Sinclair. He was not surprised that the fine hand of the renowned former chief of counterintelligence had once been at the helm. The legacy of more than a few of his operations still haunted the Agency. Angleton had been brilliant, but known to consider the shortest distance between two points to be a tunnel—the key to both his success and his fall from grace.

"It was Angleton who discovered the damning truth," the DCI continued. "From that point on, for almost thirty years, he controlled every facet of the case until his resignation. The narrow parameters for compartmentalization he established are still in effect today."

"Where did the stolen art come from?" Brannigan asked.

"Most of it was purchased, and I use that word advisedly,"

the DCI said, "when the Jewish Laws went into effect and the persecution of the Jews began in earnest, before America entered the war. The resales were handled by a man by the name of Hofer, through Swiss lawyers and bankers acting on behalf of their clients. The paintings were then smuggled out of the country and into the hands of the new owners. We tried to find out who the lawyers and bankers were, but thanks to the Swiss penchant for secrecy, we never did."

"How many Americans were involved?"

"We don't know."

"And what exactly is BACKLASH?"

"Patience, Jack. I'm getting to that," the DCI replied. "The stolen art that was sold was part of Hermann Goering's collection, and he, like all good Germans, kept meticulous records. Three copies of the file existed that contained the names of the people who purchased the art he put up for sale in Switzerland. From what we do know of those transactions, and that isn't much, there were approximately a dozen people, all from prominent and wealthy families in England, the United States, and Western Europe. We learned of the files after the capture of Goering. His man Hofer committed suicide before we got anything out of him, and Goering ended up under a sentence of death at Nuremberg and wasn't in the mood to cooperate. If he knew any of the names on the list, he took them to the grave with him. To make a long story short, we went after the files. We didn't get them. The Russians did."

Brannigan had no difficulty piecing the rest of the story together. "And the Russians have been blackmailing those involved ever since, and you've been trying to find out who they are for just as long."

"In 1946," Palmer said, "a man by the name of Edward Winthrop Stewart, the same man in the reports I just gave you, contacted an old friend from his days at Harvard who was with the OSS. His friend put him in touch with Dulles. He told

Dulles that he had been approached by the Russians. They wanted his help in reaching certain members of Congress, particularly the senator from New York to whose campaign Stewart had contributed heavily. They mentioned that his purchases of certain works of art could prove embarrassing if uncovered. Stewart told them to go to hell. He told Dulles that he had considered purchasing some of the Goering art, but had never gone through with the deal. Dulles didn't care whether he was telling the truth about the art or not, but the approach by the MVD confirmed what he had believed from the outset would be the inevitable result of the files falling into Soviet hands.''

"How do two murders in New York City forty-six years later tie into all this?" Brannigan asked, keeping what he had discovered in the autopsy summaries to himself.

Palmer told him about the death of Heinz Strasser and his connection to the Goering files, his use of a false name at the Zum Turken, and the subsequent discovery of his true identity through the archives at the Berlin Documents Center.

"We believe that the man committing the murders has the copy once in the possession of Heinz Strasser."

"Why?" Brannigan asked. For his own reasons, he was particularly interested in knowing more about the mysterious former SS major's visit to Berchtesgaden.

"We sent a local agent to Berchtesgaden, to the Zum Turken Inn, where Strasser was staying when he died. The owner, a Frau Graber," Palmer said, consulting his notes, "said the old man was there to meet his son. She believed he was from eastern Germany, something about his clothes and overnight bag. Which, as it turned out, went a long way toward explaining why we were never able to locate him after the war. The son arrived a short time after his father died. And left just as quickly, taking a leather portfolio his father had brought with him.''

"That's it?" Brannigan said.

"Not quite. Our local agent checked with the German federal police and established that a Heinz Dieter Strasser, who matched the father's description perfectly, lived in Erfurt with his wife, Emmi, now deceased, and a son Jurgen, thirty-seven, whereabouts and background unknown. Our people are still checking on him."

"Did the woman at the inn describe the son?" Brannigan asked.

"Tall, over six feet," Palmer said, again consulting his notes. "Dark blond hair, blue eyes."

"Anything else?"

"Nothing revealing. As I said, he left soon after he arrived. He didn't even stay long enough to make funeral arrangements."

"What kind of man doesn't even have the decency to see that his own father is properly buried?" the DCI interjected indignantly.

"A man who doesn't want any attention from the authorities," Brannigan said. "A man living outside the law. A terrorist."

"Why a terrorist?" the counterintelligence chief said, alarmed at the implications.

"Because that's what you're dealing with," Brannigan said. "And not just any terrorist. If I'm right, this one goes by the name of Dieter; and until a few minutes ago, neither I, nor anyone else in the international counter-terrorist community, knew his real name was Jurgen Strasser."

"Just how on earth did you reach that conclusion?" Palmer asked.

"The information in the autopsy findings," Brannigan said. "Dieter has one trademark we've never seen anyone else in his profession use. The same method of torture used to extract information described in these reports. And also one of the few facts known about his background: he was connected to the Stasi's terrorist training camp in East Germany.''

"Get your people in the counter-terrorist section to do an immediate biographical intelligence work-up on him,'' the director said. "Develop a personal profile we can put to use: his habits, idiosyncrasies, motivations, strengths and weaknesses, modus operandi. Anything that can help us predict his future moves.''

"We've been trying to do just that for the past five years,'' Brannigan said, "and we still don't have enough on him to fill a three-by-five card. But I can tell you this much, with a great deal of conviction: If Dieter is Jurgen Strasser, and right now I'm inclined to believe he is, and he's the man you're after, and he has the file, you've got a major problem on your hands.''

"Judging from the murders of Stewart and Cabot, he only sees the monetary possibilities,'' Palmer said, defensively. "A way to get his hands on valuable works of art that are going to be easy to move in the illegal market. And I've heard you say on any number of occasions that most terrorists these days, when you strip them of their phony political and ideological ranting, are nothing more than criminal organizations whose sole motivation is money. And so far there's no reason to believe Strasser knows, or even suspects, the file's intelligence value.''

"So far,'' Brannigan said, his implication clear. "You said Stewart was never recruited by the Russians. What about Cabot?''

"We have to assume that he was,'' Palmer said.

"And what was his profession?''

"A thirty-five-year career diplomat. Once the ambassador to West Germany, among other things.''

"Jesus!'' Brannigan said.

"As you can see, we're not talking about low-level recruitment, considering that everyone on that list had to be wealthy and well connected to deal in those circles,'' the CI chief said, ''and wealth brings influence and access to the corridors of power. I don't have to tell you how it works. Blackmail is the oldest and most certain way of agent recruitment. Choose the ones with the most to lose. Those with corporations or government careers dependent on public trust. Get them to do something insignificant that carries no risk. Nothing classified, something innocent as hell at first, while threatening to expose their dealings with the Nazis. Once you get your hooks into them, they're yours for the rest of their lives. It's no longer a question of embarrassing art purchases, once they're on record as having cooperated with the Russians; it's treason.

''And it's not just those initially involved,'' the director added. ''As they got older there's no doubt the Russians worked them for everything they could. Forced them to recruit their replacements before they retired or died. Probably even within their own families. Especially if the children were going into the same careers or taking over the family business; a son or a daughter not wanting to refuse a father and be responsible for disgracing the family name if the Russians leaked their activities when they were through with them as an example to the others. Forty-six goddamn years. Can you imagine how far they've penetrated? It's like a stone hitting a windshield and spiderwebbing out in a thousand directions.''

''As we all know,'' Palmer said, ''the spy game goes on whether there's a cold war or a cool peace. And I can assure you, when the Russians find out what this Dieter—or Strasser —is up to, and I'm certain they will, if they haven't already, they're going to pull out all the stops to get that file, especially if they even think we're on to it.''

All three men in the room had a healthy mistrust of the Russians, and knew full well what the new Russia was up against. With monumental internal problems and seriously diminished power and influence throughout the world, they were little more than a bankrupt, humiliated, unstable third world nation with thousands of nuclear warheads, who couldn't even properly feed or clothe their own people—not a reassuring scenario for anyone with a sense of history.

The world had changed drastically, and in a remarkably short period of time. And the conclusion of all the Agency's analysts came down to one inescapable fact: For at least the next decade, the world would be driven by economics, and the force behind that drive would be technology. The United States would not only need to protect its high technology from its old enemies, but also from its old friends as well, like the French, who had already been caught in the act. Without the talent or the scientific infrastructure to compete on the same level as the West, espionage was the only hope the Russians had of narrowing the gap; and, as the three men sitting at the table understood only too well, espionage was, and always had been, the Russians' strong suit. And despite the profound changes in the East-West arena, there were some things that would never change: the desire for secrets and knowledge that made clandestine manipulation possible was a basic, immutable obsession of men and governments that did not end with the cold war.

The signs were already there to indicate the Russians were becoming more aggressive in their pursuit of Western technology, and from what Brannigan had just heard from the DCI and the CI chief, he knew Palmer was right: the long-running penetration operation was one the Russians could ill afford to lose and would undoubtedly take whatever measures were necessary to keep it intact.

In Brannigan's mind, there was no question as to why the Agency had kept the Russian penetration operation a tightly held secret. Widespread knowledge of a potential threat from highly placed moles burrowing deep within America's secret gardens would have destroyed careers and paralyzed the intelligence community with innuendo and rumor. It occurred to him that Angleton had done that very thing twenty years ago, and probably because of this same Russian operation.

"I take it I'm being briefed on this for the obvious reason," Brannigan said.

"We want you to run the operation," the director said. "As quietly as possible. But the bottom line is, we want that file. I don't have to tell you what it means if we get it."

"You might have another problem," Brannigan said. "The Israelis, or more to the point, the Mossad."

"Why the Mossad?" Sinclair asked.

"Dieter . . . or Strasser killed two of their people in Paris last week. If they follow their usual pattern when someone kills their own, they're in the process of putting together a full-blown effort to find him. They won't back off, and it's best not to underestimate them."

"What are you suggesting?" Sinclair said.

"Bring them in on it."

"Brief them on BACKLASH?" Palmer said. "Not on your life. We can't request outside help, it would alert every intelligence agency that something big is happening. And the last thing we want is someone else getting to the file first."

"I'm only talking about the Israelis. We brief them on a hunt for an international terrorist, whom we have a common interest in finding," Brannigan said. "They're the most likely to get in our way, and I'd rather have them where I can see them. Because if *they* get their hands on that file we'll end up paying through the nose for the next twenty years just to get a look at part of it."

"We'll be defeating the purpose of keeping this low profile," Palmer said.

"With what I have in mind," Brannigan said, "we can still keep it very low profile."

"I'm sorry," Palmer argued. "I can't subscribe to that."

"What do you have in mind?" the director said, raising a hand-to silence any further objections from Palmer.

"One man from my counter-terrorist section. A contract employee by the name of Mike Semko. He's head of our 'snatch team,' and he knows more about Dieter than anyone. He can take the point."

Brannigan let the suggestion hang in the air, watching the director's eyes as his mind considered all the ramifications of using a member of the top-secret team only he and Brannigan and the deputy director knew about.

"Snatch team?" Palmer said.

"I'll brief you later," Sinclair told his CI chief. "I like it," he said to Brannigan. "Good sound covert operations principles. The fewer people involved, the better. If we have to go after this Strasser out of the country, your station chiefs can support Semko, knowing only that it's a counter-terrorist operation. As a contract employee, Semko is unknown to the intelligence community; used to working by himself with no official cover, he's experienced in the right areas, and he only needs to know he's going after a terrorist. Which is what he's paid to do. A perfect cover. When he finds Strasser, he can call in his team if necessary, and you can be there to grab the file. It all works. Contract employees, deniable, and expendable."

"Deniable," Brannigan said, a sharp edge to his voice, "but not expendable. I'll go along with keeping Semko in the dark about the true nature of his mission, but under no circumstances will I hang him out to dry."

"Agreed," Sinclair said.

"And how do we handle the Israelis?" Palmer asked, forgoing his objections in light of the director's enthusiasm.

"We tell them we'll work this as a joint operation," Brannigan said. "Offer to let them assign one of their people to work

alongside Semko. They can be there at the end, without ever
having any knowledge of what we're really after."

"What about the New York cops?" Brannigan said, the list
of details requiring immediate attention forming in his mind.

"We have a line into them," Palmer said. "We'll keep you
informed of everything they're doing."

"And the FBI counterintelligence people? New York is their
turf."

"Fuck the Feebs," the CI chief blurted out in a rare display
of vulgarity that indicated his intense dislike of the FBI's
counterintelligence division; he considered them nothing more
than rank amateurs who had fouled up a number of his operations in the past. "They've got the investigative abilities of a
group of children on an Easter egg hunt," he added with an
indignant huff.

"The authority for the operation?" Brannigan asked, wanting to hear it straight from the director.

"The line of authority goes all the way to the President,"
Sinclair said. "I spoke with him less than an hour ago. We
have his full and unequivocal support to run with this as the
situation demands, outside of normal channels."

"After all," Palmer added, having regained his composure,
"on the surface, this isn't about us and the Russians. If anything blows up in our faces, as far as the congressional oversight committees are concerned, we weren't running an illegal
covert operation, we were after a terrorist; the rest is plausibly
deniable . . . if it ever comes to that."

"How soon can you bring Semko into the equation?" the
DCI asked.

"Within the hour," Brannigan said.

IT WAS RAINING when Palmer turned onto the entrance ramp and
headed east on Route 66 on his way back to Langley. Sinclair
had called David Ben-David, the Mossad chief, from a secure

line at the estate, and reached him at ten-thirty at night, Tel
Aviv time, just as he was about to leave his office.

Palmer had hoped that Ben-David would decline the offer of
a joint operation, but to his disappointment, he had agreed.
Palmer's doubts were eased somewhat when Sinclair told him
that the Mossad chief, upon hearing about the "art murders,"
had suggested sending one of his researchers, an art historian,
to work with Semko in tracking down Strasser. At least it
would not be one of their combatants, who would be difficult
to control in the final phase of the operation.

There was something else bothering Palmer as he drove
slowly through the rush-hour traffic, made worse by the driving rain. Shutting the DDO out of an operation was one thing
—there were precedents and sound operational principles to
warrant that—but lying to him, even if only by omission, was
quite another. The director's argument about motives mitigat-
ing methods did little to convince the CI chief otherwise. As
much as Palmer had initially disapproved of Brannigan's being
brought into the loop, he felt just as strongly that once it had
been done, they should have leveled with him. The DDO was a
powerful and resourceful man, with influential friends outside
the Agency, and it was not in anyone's best interest to cross
him.

Palmer did not approve of in-house conspiracies; it had been
a conspiracy of silence that, in the end, brought Angleton
down. The CI chief believed that at some point in everyone's
life, one inevitably sat down to a banquet of consequences, and
at that moment, there was little doubt in his mind that there
would be serious consequences when Brannigan learned he
had not been told the whole truth.

« **19** »

MIKE SEMKO HAD never set foot inside the CIA's Langley headquarters. The briefings and planning sessions for his team's operations always took place at safe houses scattered throughout Washington and the surrounding Virginia and Maryland countryside. The safe house where he had spent the past two days was in the heart of Georgetown, hemmed in by similar elegant row houses and stately Federal-style homes halfway down a narrow, tree-shaded cobblestone street with brick sidewalks.

Semko sat drinking a can of beer on a small, overstuffed sofa in the cozy, book-filled study on the lower level, which opened onto a walled-in garden and terrace at the rear of the house. He was wearing jeans and a T-shirt, and his feet, clad in running shoes that had seen better days, were propped up on the coffee table. The rain was over and he had opened the french doors to the scent of the garden and the fresh, cool breeze of a late-spring afternoon.

He was watching the CNN Early Prime News with the volume down low, and he was bored and restless and needed to get out and move around, anything to break the tedious routine of the past few days. The inactivity had done what it always did to him: drove his thoughts into the past, dredging up mem-

ories and old dreams that were best left alone. It was just past
five o'clock when he heard the front door open on the floor
above, and he instinctively reached for the weapon in the
shoulder holster he had taken off and placed on the table. He
lowered the barrel of the nine-millimeter semiautomatic pistol
as he looked up to see Jack Brannigan come down the stairs.

Brannigan paused at the bottom of the steps. The sight of
Semko sitting there with a pistol in his hand and a deadly look
in his eyes reminded him of an earlier time, more than twenty
years ago, when the two men had first met. He was as tough a
warrior as the DDO had ever known, and they soon found
themselves to be kindred spirits, their similar backgrounds
helping to form a friendship that had only strengthened over
the years. Semko was a coal-cracker from northeastern Pennsylvania who had come up the hard way, as had Brannigan. An
All-State tailback on his high school team, Semko had attended Syracuse University on a football scholarship. After
setting a record for yards rushed by a freshman, he abruptly
left college, without explanation, in the beginning of his soph-
omore year.

Brannigan was one of the few people to whom the intensely
private man had confided the reason for his giving up a future
that almost certainly assured a lucrative career in professional
football. During the first week of September in 1967, Semko
learned of, and was deeply affected by, the deaths of two of his
high school friends, both killed in Vietnam. Unable to recon-
cile his sheltered campus life and self-centered commitment to
what was, after all, a game, with the sacrifices of his friends,
he made a decision to share the burden that hundreds of thousands of young Americans were about to bear. Two days later,
he enlisted in the army and never looked back, nor did anyone
ever hear him speak in wistful terms of opportunities lost.

That single act of character and conscience was only one of
the reasons why Brannigan respected and admired the man. It

took a firm hand to control him, evidenced by the recent episode in Paris, but whenever there was a highly sensitive "black" operation that required a cool, totally dependable operative, it was always Mike Semko he thought of first.

"You've been a bad boy, Mike," Brannigan said in the manner of a tolerant teacher scolding an errant schoolboy.

"Yeah, well, what else is new?" Semko said, and pulled a can of beer from the six-pack on the coffee table and tossed it to Brannigan.

The DDO made a one-handed catch and popped the top as he went to the french doors and shut them, then drew the drapes closed, casting the small study into a soft light filtered through the curtains on the window behind the sofa.

"What am I going to do with you?" Brannigan said as he crossed to where Semko sat slouched in front of the television. He placed a fraternal hand on his shoulder before lowering himself into a chair and angling it to face him. The long years of friendship and the powerful bond of shared experiences were evident in the absence of formalities and the ease each man felt in the other's presence. There was no need for role playing or posturing between them, such was the depth and strength of their relationship.

"Parker Stevenson, the Paris station chief, said you were disrespectful to him, even arrogant . . . and I think he added thoroughly unprofessional and dangerous."

"If Stevenson ever had an original thought he'd go into convulsions."

"Now, Michael me lad," Brannigan said in his best Irish brogue, "that's no way to be talkin' about your superiors."

"I hope you mean in rank."

Brannigan simply grinned and shook his head in amusement.

"Look," Semko continued, "before you say whatever it is

you came to tell me, I just want you to know I'm sorry if I put you in a bad position, but I'm not sorry for what I did.''

''Where have I heard that before?''

''If I'd have waited to get official sanction from a tight-assed desk jockey like Stevenson, Dieter would have been long gone. I only had one thing in mind: to get that son of a bitch.''

''You're making this too personal, Mike. You let him get inside. You're losing your perspective, and that can be fatal.''

''What I'm losing is the belief that any of this makes a difference anymore,'' Semko said. ''I screwed up in Paris, and if you want me out, I'll understand. I've put you on the spot any number of times, I know that. And I know I'm becoming a liability. So if you want to cut your losses before I destroy your career completely, just say the word. No hard feelings. If it wasn't for unfinished business with Dieter I wouldn't be here now. I've had enough of this crap to last two lifetimes.''

''Paris wasn't any worse than some of the other things you've done,'' Brannigan said. ''Your methods have always been a little unorthodox, to say the least, but you always get the desired results. And besides, your liabilities just might prove to be assets for what I've got in mind.''

Semko stared hard at his old friend. ''You're not here to give me my walking papers?''

Brannigan smiled. ''As it turns out, I'm here to give you your dream come true.''

''Why am I not smiling?''

''Because you don't know what I know,'' Brannigan said, and gestured toward the television. ''You heard anything on the news about the murders in New York City?''

''Murders in New York City are news?''

''These are. Two wealthy old men were tortured and murdered, and some of their art was stolen.''

''What does that have to do with us?''

''I want you to look into it, find the guy who did it.''

"That's a case for the New York cops. Besides, what the hell do I know about art? I wouldn't know a masterpiece from an Etch-A-Sketch."

"This isn't about art, it's about Jurgen Strasser raising funds for his terrorist ops."

"Strasser? Name doesn't ring any bells."

"You know him as Dieter."

The expression on Semko's face went from one of surprise to menace, the light of action in his eyes again. "That's his name? Jurgen Strasser?"

"That's the way it stacks up."

"How'd you find that out?"

Brannigan told him about the old man's death in Berchtesgaden and all that had happened since, including the telltale torture method used on the victims in New York, and how it all tied into Semko's seeing Strasser in Paris. He left out any mention of BACKLASH, and the possibility of Russian involvement, telling Semko only what would be required to recognize the file he was to get: memoranda concerning the sale of art in Switzerland during the early years of World War II.

"What's the big deal about fifty-year-old records?"

"Need to know, Mike. You know how it works." Brannigan had expected the question. "And all you need to know is the DCI doesn't want them falling into the wrong hands. So you get to go after Dieter, no holds barred, and the Agency gets what it wants."

"You want him alive or dead?"

"That's optional," Brannigan said. "But dead would be better, as long as you get the file first. The thinking is that it would be best if he's not around to reveal what he learned from it."

"And no holds barred in the way I go after him?"

"With one caveat," Brannigan said. "As far as anyone outside this room is concerned, this is a counter-terrorist operation. You're after Dieter. No mention of the file, and you cannot go outside the Company for any help.''

''And when I find him?''

''It's your call. Bring in your team if you feel the need, but the primary objective is to retrieve the file. Understood?''

''Oh, yeah,'' Semko said. ''Is he still in New York?''

''Palmer, the CI chief, thinks he might be. It makes sense that he's using someone in the underground art world to move the stuff he's been stealing. As soon as you get in the city, one of our people from the New York office will fill you in on what the local cops are up to, and get you a list of galleries suspected of dealing in stolen and forged art. You can start there. Any questions?''

''Yeah. When do I leave?''

Brannigan looked at his watch. It was five forty-five. ''There's a Delta shuttle flight from National Airport in about an hour.''

''I'll be on it,'' Semko said.

''We have a safe house on West Sixty-eighth street you can use. I'll have someone meet your flight and set you up.''

Brannigan paused, having saved what he knew would be a bone of contention until last, then added, ''There is one hitch you're not going to like. You're going to be working with someone else.''

''Who? Someone from my team?''

''No. Non-Agency.''

Semko bristled. ''Tell me you're not going to saddle me with one of the FBI's by-the-book counter-terrorist 'experts.' ''

''Okay. I can tell you that.''

''Then who?''

''A Mossad officer.''

''Ah, Jesus, Jack. Those people are impossible to work

with, they don't cooperate with anybody. And I goddamn near killed one of them in Paris."

"Sorry, but it's a done deal. Strasser killed two of their case officers in Paris and they've got a full-court press on for him. If we didn't bring them in they'd only end up stepping all over our operation."

"How much do they know?"

"That it's a counter-terrorist op to get Strasser."

"They know nothing about the file?"

"Nothing. And make damn sure they don't get their hands on it before you do."

"And just who am I going to be working with?"

"Don't know. You'll make contact in New York tomorrow. My Mossad counterpart will let me know where and when sometime tonight. I'll call you at the safe house as soon as I hear.

"One more thing," Brannigan said. "You're working for me, and only me. Report directly. No cut-outs. And I do mean report, Mike. None of your usual out-of-touch-for-days shit; not on this one."

Semko nodded his understanding. "And if I need up-to-date intel, weapons, equipment?"

"You'll have my full support, and through me, the support of the station and base chiefs wherever you go. Any questions or problems from any of my people, refer them to me. I'll handle things at this end. The operations center will have orders to patch you through to me anytime, day or night."

Semko got up from the sofa and started from the room, then stopped at the foot of the stairs and turned to Brannigan. "Thanks, Jack. I won't let you down."

"The thought never entered my mind."

SEMKO, AT AGE forty-two and with the life he had led, sometimes felt old and worn, but he was feeling alive and vital that evening as he walked down the boarding ramp to Delta's Washington-to-New York shuttle. He had an operation, and not just any operation, but Agency sanction to go after Dieter and bring him down in any way he saw fit. This was it, he told himself as took his seat in the half-empty plane. His last operation.

As with most men who spent their adult lives in the shadowed places of special operations, Semko was a loner at heart, cloistered in the world of his work. Due to his near-constant overseas assignments, he had no home to speak of, just a sparsely furnished apartment in the Washington area that served as little more than a place to sleep occasionally and a mail drop for his bills. His telephone answering unit summed up his personal life outside the Agency as well as anything: upon returning home from an operation that had led him back and forth across Europe for six weeks, he found not one message on the unit.

Semko had never come to see himself as others did: as a capable, fearless, sometimes brilliant covert operator, who could survive anything. As far as he was concerned, he was just Michael Thaddeus Semko, a hunky kid from the Pennsylvania hard-coal regions. A kid who had spent the first seventeen years of his life trying to turn himself into something his father, a foul-tempered coal miner with a hate-filled heart, would pay the least bit of attention to, only to realize, just before the old man died, that in the end, it wasn't worth the effort.

Semko had lived with fear most of his life. And he had told Brannigan, and anyone else who asked, that courage wasn't the absence of fear, it was doing what had to be done in spite of it. He had never seen the glory in war; he had too many friends whose remains could have been sent home in sandwich bags, and others who would spend the rest of their lives in wheelchairs with stumps where there used to be legs and arms.

And he hated the word *hero;* all the heroes he had ever known were either dead or in jail. He had simply done what he had been trained to do, enduring the terrible risks, the pain and the bloodshed, and the constant threat of death that were a part of it. And now he had to do it one last time, and the fear again gripped him, knotting his stomach and making him queasy. But he knew it would pass, as it always did, once he was back in the thick of it.

For years he had struggled to attain the self-discipline necessary to be a man of ideas and logic and not of emotions. But the victory was tenuous at best, and as the plane taxied for takeoff his thoughts were of Walt Shumate, who had died in his arms in that apartment in Dusseldorf three years ago, and how now, finally, he could make the son of a bitch who did it pay with his own worthless life.

« 20 »

ON HERZEL ROAD in West Jerusalem there is a place filled with terrible, heart-wrenching images of unimaginable acts of brutality and genocide, a place of pilgrimage for not only Israelis, but for Jews the world over. It is the Yad Vashem Museum, the memorial to the victims of the Holocaust, where tens of thousands make solemn journeys each year to view its exhibits in stunned and reverent silence.

A short distance from the museum a winding road leads down a hill past the village of Ein Keren and on into the Jerusalem forest with its light green stands of pine trees not native to this ancient land. The forest itself is a memorial, with cool, shaded groves where granite plaques in both English and Hebrew commemorate Israeli heroes who died in the struggle for her statehood and in all of her wars since. A few miles farther on and to the north, where the evergreen forest begins to thin out, there is a plaque that stands alone. The inscription is also in English and Hebrew, and it reads: JAMES JESUS ANGLETON. 1917–1987. IN MEMORY OF A FRIEND.

It is a tribute to a man and a time when the relationship between the intelligence agencies of the United States and Israel was one of friendship and cautious trust despite their political and ideological differences. During the early years of the cold war, the fledgling Jewish state was in dire need of powerful friends and found one in James Angleton, then the CIA counterintelligence chief. Israel had little in the way of natural resources with which to barter for desperately needed military and financial aid, but did have a network of Jews loyal to the Zionist cause living throughout Eastern Europe and the Soviet Union, who could be put at the disposal of the CIA to gather intelligence information in places where the Agency did not or could not have a direct presence. Thus began a secret liaison that was mutually beneficial to both countries, at least until Angleton's resignation from the CIA in 1974.

The present condition of the memorial to Angleton from his friends in the Mossad is indicative of what has become of that earlier relationship. Unlike the inscriptions carved in granite in the well-tended groves honoring Israel's fallen heroes, the words honoring Angleton are not etched in stone, but rather inscribed on a thick sheet of plastic screwed onto the face of the granite. The plastic is now yellowed and clouded from exposure; most of the evergreens are dead or dying and the area itself is neglected and littered with trash.

THE HADAR DAFNA Building in the heart of downtown Tel Aviv is a gray, featureless concrete structure set among other modern high-rise office towers with glass-fronted lobbies and broad plazas. The lower floors of the building contain private businesses including shops, boutiques, a bank, and a public cafeteria. The upper floors, and inner central portion of the building, house the headquarters of Israeli intelligence. By design, it is a building within a building and access is gained through an office on the second floor, just down from the cafeteria, where authorized personnel can enter and take a private elevator to the Mossad's inner sanctum.

Rachel Sidrane arrived at the Mossad chief's tenth-floor office shortly after 11:00 P.M. Earlier that evening, after spending the better part of the day accessing the computer files of known terrorist associates of Dieter, she had returned to her apartment in Jaffa. She had just finished preparing her dinner when the call came to report back to headquarters.

Ben-David had summoned her following his telephone call from the CIA director, and as Rachel entered the office, he greeted her with a warm, friendly smile and rose from his chair to embrace her. Six years ago they had quietly suffered the pain and sorrow of Aaron Sontag's death, his adopted son and Rachel's fiancé, a tragedy that in the end had bound them inextricably together.

He had never regretted his decision to recruit Rachel into the Mossad, nor of convincing her to join the special unit he had in mind for her from the beginning. Her quiet, haunting beauty was an attribute that eventually proved an invaluable asset in her work. Her classic features, framed in shoulder-length, raven black hair, were strong, yet feminine and sensuous; and beneath softly arched eyebrows a sense of sadness reached out from eyes that appeared dark and opaque from a distance, but on closer inspection proved chestnut brown and gold flecked and hinted at the intelligence behind the steady, self-confident gaze.

Her physical beauty, along with her practical intelligence and mental toughness, were what had at first made Ben-David consider her for the Mossad's most secret unit, the *Kidon,* a Hebrew word meaning bayonet. Quietly referred to, by the select few in a position to know of its existence, as "the long arm of Israeli justice," the *Kidon* is hidden within a much larger department that is in charge of infiltrating agents under deep cover into Arab countries. Personally chosen by the Mossad chief, the *Kidon*'s numbers are small, consisting of three dedicated and highly trained teams of twelve whose areas of expertise are assassination and kidnapping.

Rachel brought all the advantages that a woman can bring to

the deadliest of professions. And there were profound and distinct advantages. A woman can get closer to a man than another man can. They can go unnoticed, except for their physical attractiveness, at parties or in crowds, and are generally taken for granted by even the most professional of bodyguards. They can get a man drunk, or with promises of sexual favors take him to where he is most vulnerable—to a hotel room or a quiet, remote spot—without arousing his suspicions. They can meet their target in a public or private place and anyone observing will see nothing that appears unusual and assume they know what is going on. By nature, women are more disciplined and discerning, and seldom, if ever, are they suspected of being hardened killers, which accounts for an astonishing statistic unknown outside the international intelligence community: fully 65 percent of the world's top assassins are women. And Rachel Sidrane had proved herself to be one of the best.

The details of her discussion the previous evening with her unit commander concerning the murder of Stewart in New York City had already reached Ben-David by the time she returned to headquarters.

"Your suspicions about Dieter and the murder in New York were correct," Ben-David told her as she sat in the chair in front of his desk. "We've had further confirmation from the Americans."

"They're positive it's Dieter?"

"Yes, and there's been a second murder. Another art collector."

"Involving stolen art from World War II?"

"That hasn't been established yet," Ben-David said. "But our CIA friends have learned Dieter's true identity. It seems he is one Jurgen Strasser, a former East German."

"Do we have any information on him?"

"So far we haven't found anything. But our research people re still checking."

"Are you sending a team to New York?"

"I'm sending you," Ben-David said.

"Alone?"

"As far as the Americans are concerned, yes," Ben-David aid. "You are to coordinate our efforts with the CIA's opera-on to get Strasser. You will be working with a man by the ame of Michael Semko. You were the logical choice, I ought; an American by birth, raised in New York City, and our art history background may prove to be a valuable asset. lso, your being a fellow American should have the psycho-gical effect of putting him somewhat at ease."

"What do we know about him?"

"My CIA counterpart tells me he is an intelligence special-t with their counter-terrorist section. Somehow I think he is uch more than that."

Ben-David removed a series of photographs from a file older and slid them across the desktop for Rachel to see. They ere the pictures taken of Semko in the Parisian police car fter his arrest.

"If my hunch is right, these are photographs of Michael emko."

"The man who was following Dieter in Paris?" Rachel aid, having seen the same photos during the briefing after the eath of the two Mossad officers at the hands of Strasser. "I elieve there was also some videotape of him stalking Dieter s he left the café."

"There was," Ben-David said.

"Why are we conducting a joint operation with the CIA?"

"Because they requested it. And because at this point I elieve they know more about Strasser than they are telling s."

"What were they told about me?"

"That you are one of our research analysts with a PhD in a history. Nothing else."

Rachel sat silently for a few moments, then asked, "David can you assure me this is not an operation against the United States?"

"Absolutely. It is not," Ben-David said with conviction well aware of the one promise Rachel had asked of him befor joining the Mossad: that she would never be asked to partici pate in any operations directed against her native country.

"What support will I have?" Rachel asked.

"Six members of your unit will be arriving separately. Yo will meet them at one of our operational apartments in New York and work out the details of how you want to conduct ou side of the operation. They will stay in the background, but i position to help you when necessary."

"How are we to handle Dieter . . . Strasser, when we fin him?"

"The committee has placed his name at the top of the exe cution list since the Paris murders," Ben-David answered, no needing to say more.

The committee the Mossad chief had referred to was one o the most tightly held secrets in the Israeli government. A official execution list exists, and at times can number as man as seventy or eighty names, depending on the number of peo ple identified as active anti-Israeli terrorists. The orders fo government-sanctioned assassinations and abductions are no given lightly. The process is quasi-legal and one of thoughtfu deliberation by a special judicial committee who holds trials i absentia, weighs the evidence, and decides the fate of the per son the Mossad chief has submitted by way of the prime min ister.

"You are to keep your team fully informed of your ever move," Ben-David said, his tone now more one of a con cerned friend than a superior. "If it was Semko we saw i

Paris, he is a man at home with violence and prone to acting on impulse. And I don't have to tell you how dangerous Strasser is. Take no unnecessary risks with either of these men.''

Rachel nodded her understanding. ''What is the CIA's objective in finding Strasser?''

''I'm not sure,'' Ben-David said. ''The call came from Sinclair, the CIA director, bypassing his local station chief, who would have normally made such a request. It may be that their sole interest in Strasser is to prevent him from acquiring the stolen Russian biological and chemical weapons, and this is the simple joint counter-terrorist effort they are representing it to be. But my instincts, and past experience with our American friends, tell me they are being less than completely honest about the reason for inviting us to work with them.''

Rachel recalled a private conversation with Ben-David shortly after she graduated from the Mossad academy. He had warned her about trusting anyone outside of her Mossad colleagues, telling her that in liaison relationships with members of allied intelligence agencies, especially the CIA, it was to her benefit to accept their overtures of friendship, but she must never forget one cardinal rule: ''When you are sitting with your friend, he is not sitting with *his* friend.''

Ben-David tore a slip of paper from his desk notepad and handed it to Rachel. ''Here is the address of the safe house you and your team will be using on East Fifty-second Street. You are booked on the El Al flight to New York City leaving at two-thirty A.M. and arriving at seven-thirty A.M. Plenty of time to sleep on the plane.''

''And the rest of my team?''

Ben-David glanced at his watch. ''They are already en route on an unscheduled flight. You will make your initial contact with Semko at the sea lion pool in the Central Park Zoo tomorrow at noon. I will inform the Americans of the meeting site.''

"Can we expect any help from the police?"

"I have been told we have a 'helper' on the task force formed by the New York City police to investigate the murders attributed to Strasser. He is a detective from the Stolen Art Squad, and his name and home telephone number are included with the safe house address.

"Be well, Rachel, and be careful," Ben-David said, and again rose to embrace her as she got up to leave.

As RACHEL LEFT the office, Ben-David used the in-house telephone to summon the head of his research department. The man who arrived minutes later was in his seventies, small and frail, with large, liquid brown eyes made to seem even larger by thick, rimless glasses. His presence at headquarters at that hour was not unusual—he generally worked late into the night —and it was said, only half in jest, that his legendary memory held more information than all of the computer data bases in his renowned department.

His name was Moshe Simon, and it was he who had made the connection between Ben-David's request for information on Jurgen Strasser after his call from the CIA, and the copy of a file from the Berlin Documents Center, including the request for information from the Berchtesgaden police, that had landed on his desk two days ago from a Mossad agent in Bonn, Germany. It was a piece of the puzzle the CIA director was unaware the Mossad had, and one Ben-David was trying to fit into place.

"Moshe," Ben-David said, "tell me what association there might be between the Nazis' mountain retreat on the Obersalzberg, and stolen works of art going back to the Second World War that have recently surfaced in New York City?"

The wizened old man paused for only a moment before answering. "The art treasures looted by Reich Marshal Hermann Goering were found at Obersalzberg by the Americans at the end of the war. In a number of railroad cars hidden inside a tunnel, if I am not mistaken.''

"And the file you brought to my attention earlier on the SS major, Strasser, didn't you tell me he was once stationed with the security battalion there?''

"At the end of the war. That is correct.''

"See what you can learn of the circumstances surrounding the late Major Strasser's death, why he would have used an alias, and his relationship to Jurgen Strasser.''

"Yes, sir,'' the old man said, then paused as he was about to leave. "I seem to recall that immediately after the war there was some Russian interest in Goering's art dealings. Something Kavalkov, the KGB defector the British shared with us, said . . . a top-secret section in what used to be their First Chief Directorate a drunken colleague told him of one night. I don't think there were any details, but it did stand out as an unusual preoccupation with something so dated. That was ten . . . or twelve years ago; I'll have to check the transcripts of the debriefings.''

"Thank you, Moshe; as always, you never fail me.''

The old man's stern, sallow face allowed a small smile as he turned and left the office.

BEFORE LEAVING MOSSAD headquarters, Rachel stopped to check the in basket on her desk and found the manila envelope put there by a friend in the photographic analysis laboratory. The note taped to the outside read: This is the best I could do.

The enlarged and computer-enhanced image of the painting in the background of the photograph she had clipped from the newspaper the previous day was grainy and slightly blurred, but the eight-by-ten blowup of the Rembrandt landscape was clearly recognizable. It was the one part of her discovery in the *New York Times* article that she had not mentioned to her unit commander or to Ben-David, considering it a personal matter that she preferred to handle in her own way. After placing a telephone call, she left the headquarters building at eleven-thirty, allowing her three hours until her flight was due to leave, more than enough time to make the one stop she had in mind before going back to her apartment to pack for the trip to New York.

She drove east, to the outskirts of the city and the exclusive residential suburb of Savian, locally known as the Beverly Hills of Tel Aviv. Here, amid lush citrus groves, well-land-scaped estates with swimming pools and tennis courts contain some of the finest homes in all of Israel. Rachel's grand-mother's home, bought for her by Rachel's father when she moved to Israel at the age of seventy after deciding to spend her final years in the Jewish homeland, was just off a cul-de-sac in a quiet, peaceful spot surrounded on two sides by or-ange groves. The old woman, as was her custom before going to bed, had been reading on the small glass-enclosed terrace off her bedroom when Rachel called and told her she was stopping by to see her.

Born in Vienna in 1909, Esther Sidrane had lived what most people would consider two lifetimes. At the age of twenty-two, before the Nazis came to power, she married Eugen Sidrane, a wealthy businessman ten years her senior. Their son, David, Rachel's father, was born the following year, and their daugh-ter, Rachel (Rachel's namesake), five years later. They had chosen to remain in the land of their birth through the early years of Nazi doctrine that brought the boycott action against Jewish businesses and the exclusion of Jews from public ser-vice and cultural life, believing that it was only a stage and the Germans would soon come to their senses. But with the in-crease in Nazi power, the hateful doctrines only worsened. In 1935, the Nuremberg Laws removed citizenship and voting rights from Jews, and with the annexation of Austria in 1938,

Vienna felt the full force of what only German Jews had suffered previously.

Esther's husband was forced to sell his textile factories at far below market value, and David, as were all Jewish children, was excluded from Aryan schools. The family survived on the meager proceeds from the sale of Eugen's business, and by selling and trading personal possessions for the necessities of life, but still they clung to the belief that this would all soon pass. They continued to believe so even after October 20, 1941, when, as a result of the Nazis' attempts to alleviate the acute housing shortage in Vienna and hasten the deportation of the Jews, their home, as well as most of its contents, was confiscated by an SS colonel who forced them to sign a bill of sale at a ridiculously low price. By then it was too late to legally emigrate, and the next six months were spent living with other Jewish families in a series of crowded apartments in Vienna neighborhoods designated as Jewish areas. The list of restrictions was endless: Jews were prohibited from leaving their homes without police permits, forbidden to buy clothes, use public telephones, smoke tobacco, keep pets, or own electrical appliances, typewriters, or bicycles.

By autumn of 1942, now confined to a barracks camp outside of the city, any hope Esther and her husband once had of their lives returning to normal was gone forever. Too late they realized that what they had believed to be only a passing phase had become a way of life. They had managed to have David, then ten years old, smuggled into Switzerland to the safekeeping of the family of a former business associate of Eugen's, but Rachel, five years old and frail, was unable to make the difficult journey. In December of 1942, Esther and her family, along with more than 270 other Jews confined to the barracks camp, were transported to a nearby railroad junction. Told they were to be relocated to a place called Auschwitz that some had heard of only in whispered conversations, they were forced into grossly overcrowded cattle cars for a grueling journey that claimed the lives of most of the old and sick.

Esther Sidrane had never spoken to her granddaughter, or anyone else, about the horrors of her two and one-half years in the death camp. She had told Rachel only that, upon arrival at Auschwitz, she was separated from her husband, whom she would never see again, and that her five-year-old daughter, Rachel's namesake, terribly weakened by the horrible journey, was immediately taken from her and, she would later learn, killed in a gas chamber. She would sometimes speak of the death march that began during the second week of January in 1945, when she and the surviving inmates from Auschwitz were evacuated and moved westward to the interior of Germany, from one concentration camp to the next according to the various stages of the German retreat from the advancing Russian Army.

With all trucks and railroad cars filled with the fleeing Nazi army, the prisoners were marched on foot, columns, miles long, of starving and sick men and women dressed in little more than rags, struggling through deep snow. Stragglers were shot at the roadside by SS guards, and their route was marked every few hundred yards by the bodies of prisoners who had been executed or died of starvation and disease. They scavenged what they could from the villages they passed, at times going for days without food or water. They slept on the frozen forest floor or huddled together in open fields whipped by icy winds, often to find those beside them frozen to death in the morning. Dreading each new day, they lived with the constant fear of not being able to continue and being shot by the guards.

Esther's final destination had been the Buchenwald concentration camp, where, near death by starvation, she was liberated by American soldiers from Patton's Third Army in April of 1945. Taken to a displaced persons' camp near Vienna and nursed back to health, ten months later, with the help of the

Red Cross, she was finally reunited with her son, David, Rachel's father. The Swiss family who had cared for him since his escape from Austria in 1942 had been instrumental in helping Esther and her son emigrate to the United States the following year.

Upon reaching her grandmother's home in Savian, Rachel parked in the driveway and followed a stone pathway around to the glassed-in terrace at the rear of the house where she could see the old woman silhouetted in the soft glow of a table lamp beside her reading chair. Esther Sidrane looked up from her book and set it aside as Rachel entered. An unemotional woman, saddened by a life that others could barely imagine, Esther always brightened at the sight of her granddaughter. With the exception of her son, Rachel was the one remaining joy in her life. No photographs remained of her own daughter, only the images in her mind, and unknown to Rachel, her remarkable physical resemblance to her namesake often brought unbearable memories and tears to the old woman's eyes after being in her granddaughter's presence.

"It is so good to see you, Rachel, even at such a late hour," Esther said. She got up to embrace her, then held her at arm's length and looked into her eyes. "Something is troubling you?"

"I won't be able to have dinner with you tomorrow night," Rachel said. "I'm going to be away for a while."

"Is anything wrong?" The old woman lowered herself back into her chair and motioned Rachel to sit on the small settee opposite, holding her hand as she did.

"No, Grandmommie, nothing's wrong. I have to go to New York. It's related to my work at the university." Rachel had never told her grandmother of joining the Mossad, letting her believe the official cover story of her being an associate professor of art history at Tel Aviv University.

"There *is* something troubling you, Rachel. I can always tell."

Rachel smiled and squeezed her grandmother's hand. "Yes, you can, can't you?"

"What is it, my darling?"

Rachel opened the large manila envelope she held in her lap and removed the photograph of the Rembrandt landscape. "Something from your past, and I hope it isn't too disturbing, but I thought you would want to know."

Rachel handed the photograph to Esther and watched as she held it close to the reading lamp. At first there was no discernible reaction, then a slight tremor shook the old woman's hands and tears filled her eyes.

Rachel knew every detail of the significance of the painting in the photograph. Her grandmother's youthful passion had been art. She had studied at the University of Vienna and hoped one day to be a curator in the city's Kunsthistorisches Museum. She had forgone her dream to marry Eugen, but always maintained her passion for the works of the great masters, passing her love of art on to her granddaughter. The Rembrandt landscape had been a present from her husband upon the birth of their daughter. She had told Rachel of the joy she had felt when her husband gave it to her; he had hoped that in some small way it would make up for the career their marriage had denied her. She had described the painting in loving detail to Rachel, and how proud Eugen was of finding the previously unknown work. And of how he argued with the SS colonel who had taken their home, argued to the point of being pistol-whipped unconscious on the sidewalk in front of the house before giving up the painting he knew meant so much to his wife.

That fateful October day in 1942 was the last time Esther Sidrane had seen the treasured painting, and now, a half century later, in a land that came to be from the suffering she and others had endured, she sat silently staring at the blurred image from the past, her face streaked with tears, lost in the bittersweet memories it evoked.

"You remembered," the old woman said, her voice choked with emotion.

"Yes, Grandmommie, I remembered." Rachel moved closer to embrace her. It was the first time she had seen her grandmother cry, and her own eyes soon welled with tears. "And I'm going to do everything I can to get it back for you. I promise."

AT 4:30 A.M. Moscow time, two hours after Rachel's New York–bound flight took off from Tel Aviv, Lt. Col. Nikolai Leonov drove through the gates of the External Intelligence Service compound in Yasenevo en route to Moscow's Sheremetyevo Airport and a flight to the same destination.

Leonov sat in the rear of the chauffeur-driven car provided by the head of the SVR, his mind going over the details of the meeting that had just ended. The cabled report from the United Nations mission in New York City concerning the murder of Arthur Cabot had confirmed his worst fears. The chief of the SVR, awakened from a sound sleep at two-thirty that morning in his Moscow apartment, minutes after the cable was received, had agreed with Leonov's conclusion: a previously unknown copy of the Goering File had surfaced and their operations were in danger of being exposed. Important questions needed to be answered immediately. Into whose hands had the file fallen? Were the CIA's antennas raised by the murders and the common thread of stolen art from World War II? And if so, did they have any incidental or parallel pieces of intelligence information somewhere in their computer data bases that might cause them to look closer at what had happened?

The losses so far were negligible: Stewart had never been active, and Cabot was retired and inactive, with those he had recruited during his years with the State Department firmly in place and operational. Leonov believed, at this point, that those in immediate danger were limited to the original purchasers of the stolen Nazi art, and not the network of spies established through them. And so far what facts they had learned from the newspapers and the *rezident* in New York pointed to the art thefts as the primary motivation for the two murders, with no indication that the true value of the file had been discovered. But the time factor was critical. Whoever was responsible had to be found and stopped before the entire Goering File operation came unraveled. Undue media attention on the murders, and any future victims, could easily set off a chain reaction of panic among those recruited by Cabot causing them to take irrational actions that would draw attention to their activities. Leonov had already seen four lengthy news reports on CNN, coverage that would only increase with any new, unsolved murders.

The most logical approach was to anticipate the next victim, who Leonov believed, if for no other reason than proximity to where the first two murders had occurred, was likely to be Philip Bancroft. His active position as head of a huge corporation, a major defense contractor of high-technology weapons systems, made him an invaluable source of information, and a man who had made it possible through his recruitments to penetrate some of the most top-secret research facilities in the United States. Someone they could ill afford to lose in light of present intelligence requirements. Those with the knowledge and the authority to do so decided to warn Bancroft of the imminent danger, if he was not already aware of the deaths of Stewart and Cabot and the common denominator that linked him to them; to let him know that they, too, were aware and were taking steps to protect him, and were in no way responsible for what had happened.

Each of the remaining active spies from the original Goering File, along with those they had recruited over the years, had his own, "dedicated," Line N illegal intelligence officer assigned to him. Deployed abroad by the "S" Directorate (responsible for supporting and maintaining clandestine communications with illegals around the world) Line N illegals operated outside the diplomatic community under various covers for extended periods of time, the best often remaining in position for decades. Leonov's illegals were seconded to him, and him alone, by the head of the SVR, with no one outside of his office having knowledge of their assignments.

Leonov's first course of action was to contact the Line N illegal, operating under deep cover as a taxi driver in New York City, whose sole responsibility it was to service Bancroft by arranging the transfer of information and instructions through dead-letter drops, or, when necessary, through clandestine meetings, acting as a cutout between him and any legal Russian intelligence officer. Within an hour the coded reply had come back to Yasenevo from Bancroft's illegal, reporting that his subject was presently on his yacht in the Caribbean and incommunicado; he was expected back in the city the coming afternoon. A return cable from Leonov instructed the illegal to stand by for further orders, and to make himself available for a personal meeting at a time and place to be designated upon Leonov's arrival in New York.

With the SVR chief's approval, and with no explanation as to who Bancroft was, Leonov then sent a priority cable, along with photographs of Bancroft, to the *rezident* at the Russian United Nations mission in New York City, instructing him to assign his best operatives to him. They were to conduct a discreet surveillance of Bancroft's residence at One Sutton Place South for the purpose of personal security of which the subject was not to be aware. He further specified that no personal contact was to be made with Bancroft without explicit orders to do so, and anyone appearing to be conducting their own surveillance of the subject, or his residence, was to be forcibly abducted and taken, alive and unharmed, to an SVR safe house in the Russian emigré community in the Brighton Beach section of Brooklyn where he was to be restrained until arrangements could be made to interrogate him.

Leonov's blanket sanction from the SVR chief, to do whatever was necessary to protect his operation, was unprecedented: all *rezidents* (the SVR officers in charge of intelligence operations in Russian embassies and consulates throughout the world and the rough equivalent of a CIA station chief) and their assets were put at his disposal, and anyone reluctant to respond to his orders was to be referred directly to the head of the SVR. The unusual authority had not instilled in Leonov the confidence it should have. With the recent internal upheaval, from which Russian intelligence operations worldwide were still not fully recovered, their operational intelligence officers and assets had been greatly diminished. Immediately following the coup of August 1991, and throughout the formation of the new Russian commonwealth, defectors from the former KGB and GRU (Russian military intelligence) as well as estranged intelligence officers from the former secret police forces of Eastern Europe once under Moscow's control, had blown countless operations around the world. As a result, hundreds of agents had been exposed and "rolled up"; others had to be presumed compromised, while more than a few had simply turned themselves in to the governments they had betrayed rather than wait to become a Russian defector's meal ticket.

Transformed into a new Western-style intelligence agency, free from interference by politically appointed Communist party bureaucrats who had plagued its predecessor, the SVR had emerged stronger and more efficient than the First Chief Directorate had ever been. But many of the former KGB's best foreign operators had remained with the newly formed agency, making it necessary to curtail their activities until it could be established which of them had been exposed by defectors; a situation that called for those operating under diplomatic cover in the West to take excessive security precautions, which in themselves made matters worse—alerting opposing counter-intelligence officers to undiplomatic behavior. And now, given the events of the past few days in New York City, even Leonov's long-in-place illegals, once thought to be totally secure, had to be viewed with a jaundiced eye—a turn of events that was foremost in Leonov's mind as the chauffeur-driven car sped through the gray predawn light toward the airport on the outskirts of Moscow.

With the exception of a brief vacation in Prague with his wife and daughter twenty-six years ago, before joining the KGB, this was Leonov's only trip outside the borders of his country. Had he been an operational intelligence officer who had worked in the West and was on file with the world's intelligence agencies as such, it would have been necessary for him to travel under an alias, taking a circuitous route, changing destinations, flights, and identities at least three times along the way. But with no chance of his ever having been logged into CIA or FBI counterintelligence computers as a Russian intelligence officer, none of the standard precautions was necessary. He was booked on the Lufthansa Airlines Moscow-to-Frankfurt flight at 6:10 A.M., with a connection to New York City, arriving shortly after noon that same day. His diplomatic passport and documents identified him as a cultural affairs officer assigned to the United Nations mission.

The airport was virtually deserted at that early hour, and Leonov felt an unfamiliar sense of power as he moved through passport control. The officer at the divided partition pulled himself to a more erect posture as he gave Leonov's documents a cursory inspection before motioning him through with a respectful nod. It was with both anticipation and trepidation that Leonov boarded his flight: the anticipation of the chase and of his first field assignment, and the trepidation of the prospect of failure if he did not prove up to the task.

AFTER CARRYING LEONOV'S bags to the boarding gate, Misha Karpov waited until the flight bound for Frankfurt took off before returning to where he had parked the car in a space reserved for official vehicles. Karpov had once been a KGB officer with the now-abolished Fifth Directorate, the notorious department that dealt with internal dissent. He was among those who had voiced their support for the attempted coup, and within months of the demise of the Soviet Union and the breakup of the KGB his promising career was in ruins; stripped of his rank, he was relegated to the pool of chauffeurs and bodyguards assigned to the upper echelon of the External Intelligence Service.

The lowly position had unexpectedly opened new doors for him, doors that Karpov would never have considered stepping through before his demotion. The attractive American woman, claiming to be a consular affairs officer at the Moscow embassy, had approached him in Gorky Park. His reaction only a few short weeks prior to the obvious and clumsy attempt to recruit him would have been to rebuff the agent and report the incident, but that was before he was demoted and reassigned to such a demeaning job.

The Americans were keenly interested in the organizational structure and top personnel of the newly created External Intelligence Service, information that Karpov was in a unique position to provide. And they paid in cash, in dollars, although he had to argue long and hard for that concession—his handler warning that possessing American money would draw unwanted attention to him. "Fuck your mother," he had said, "I'll take my chances," and got the hard currency he demanded.

As Karpov pulled slowly away from the departures terminal

and onto the main road back to Moscow, he repeatedly checked his rearview mirror to make certain he wasn't being followed close enough that his activities inside the car could be observed. Once certain that he was not under surveillance, he removed the miniature recorder/transmitter/receiver from his jacket pocket and turned it on, talking into the built-in microphone as he drove.

> *"Awakened at two forty-five this morning to pick up Yevgeny Primakov, chief of SVR, and drive him to Yasenevo. Approximately two hours later Primakov personally instructed me to drive a man to the airport. This man was unknown to me, and is not one of the SVR hierarchy. I was able to establish his identity as Nikolai Leonov by seeing the diplomatic passport presented to the passport control officer at the airport. I also learned from the Lufthansa ticket counter at the boarding gate that Leonov had reservations on the flight to Frankfurt with a connecting flight to New York City."*

His report complete, Karpov clicked off the recorder and turned on the car radio. The SVR chief, a fan of Western music, had ordered the car equipped with a tape player. Karpov took advantage of the opportunity and, after rooting through the selection of cassettes in the glove compartment, put on a Billy Joel tape and turned up the volume, singing along out of key and in horribly accented English as he drove.

The miniature recorder/transmitter/receiver issued to Karpov by his CIA handler was state of the art in agent clandestine communications. The device contained an integral encoder and a burst transmitter that compressed lengthy recordings into split-second transmissions, sending them, by way of relay, to a highly secret CIA communications satellite that enabled Karpov's messages to reach Langley headquarters within seconds of being transmitted.

Code-named PYRAMIDER, the elaborate and costly operation was, in effect, a global push-button agent-communication system the Russians could only dream about one day equaling. Case officers in Langley could communicate directly with their assets in denied areas anywhere in the world without ever leaving their offices. Whether in a snow-swept Moscow alley or a darkened corner of a Beijing park, agents equipped with the same pocket-sized device Karpov had been issued could receive and send messages of varying lengths to their handlers. With one hundred separate, simultaneous channels, and frequency jumping, burst transmission, and encryption capabilities, contact was virtually instantaneous and without risk of interception.

In central Moscow, Karpov took a short detour from his route back to the garage and drove slowly past the American embassy. From inside the car, he pointed the small, esoteric device in his hand in the direction of the embassy and pressed the transmit button, sending his prerecorded message to the receiving-and-relay equipment in the CIA code and communications room in less time than it would take to snap his fingers. Just as quickly, that same message was relayed to a satellite orbiting high above the earth and back down to the CIA operations center in Langley, Virginia.

« 21 »

WITHIN ONE HOUR of his meeting with Mike Semko at the Georgetown safe house, Jack Brannigan ordered a separate room set up in the CIA's twenty-four-hour Operations Center at Langley to monitor and direct PRAIRIE FIRE, the code name he had given the operation to find Jurgen Strasser. Comfortable chairs and a conference table were brought in as technicians installed telephones, computers, and an elaborate array of sophisticated satellite communications equipment, plugging them into outlets beneath the raised floor of the soundproof room.

Shortly after 8:30 P.M. Washington time, communications intercept people at the National Security Agency reported unusual back-channel cable traffic from Yasenevo to the Russian mission in New York City, and the hunt was on. The cables were immediately followed by a series of encoded telephone calls from the *rezident's* private line to the Russian-owned estate at Glen Cove, Long Island, the living quarters for most of the legal intelligence officers assigned to the UN mission.

With the recent change in Russian codes, the NSA had little chance of deciphering the messages, but the fact that the cables had been sent during Moscow's predawn hours, when east-to-west traffic was usually light, if not nonexistent, and had subsequently caused a flurry of late evening activity in New York, alerted Brannigan and his counterintelligence chief, Alfred Palmer, that something was in the works. Misha Karpov's message was received at 11:55 P.M. (6:55 A.M. Moscow time), followed three hours later by a cabled message from one of Palmer's CI officers at the Agency's Frankfurt base, located only minutes from the Lufthansa airline terminal.

Palmer's man in Frankfurt verified the arrival of Nikolai Leonov on the flight from Moscow, and by having him paged to the information counter with a well-disguised ruse to confirm his connecting flight, the Frankfurt CI officer had taken a photograph of the unsuspecting Russian, which he had then faxed along with the message. Both Brannigan and Palmer worked on into the small hours of the night, and by 4:15 that morning in Langley, as Lufthansa flight number 400, with Leonov on board, reached altitude over the French countryside en route to New York City, they believed they were on to the man the Russians had sent to orchestrate their own hunt for Strasser.

The fact that no file existed anywhere on Leonov, or on anyone using that alias, and that he was also unknown to the Moscow station, only strengthened Brannigan's conviction that he had found the right man. At 4:30 A.M., Brannigan sent Palmer, with a copy of the photograph taken in Frankfurt, to a safe house in nearby Alexandria, Virginia, where Yuri Lysenko, a former high-level KGB defector, was sequestered while undergoing the final stages of his year-long debriefing. Lysenko had spent most of his career with the External Intelligence Service's predecessor, the First Chief Directorate, rising to the post of deputy chief before going into hiding after the aborted coup attempt in August of 1991—an action that he had supported, marking him for arrest by Yeltsin's people, along with dozens of other upper-echelon KGB who had chosen the wrong side. Ten days later, Lysenko escaped to Finland and into the waiting arms of the CIA.

Palmer's call from the Alexandria safe house provided what Brannigan considered to be the final piece of conclusive evidence linking the mysterious Leonov to the hunt for Strasser.

"Lysenko remembers Leonov as a lieutenant colonel who had exceptional clearances and bypassed the normal chain of command in his dealings with the head of the First Chief Directorate," Palmer said. "But he never knew what he did, only that his office was a sub-section of Service R, Special Projects, and that its function, supposedly research, had the highest security classification. He heard rumors that Leonov was in some way connected to the Illegals Directorate, but he emphasized they were only rumors."

"It fits," Brannigan said. "He's got to be our man. What time does his flight get into JFK?"

"Twelve thirty-five," Palmer said.

"I'll have him under surveillance as soon as he arrives."

MIKE SEMKO WAS jarred from a fitful sleep when the telephone rang in the third-floor bedroom of the three-story brownstone on Sixty-eighth Street just off Central Park West in New York City. He swung his legs over the edge of the bed and glanced at the bright green numbers on the clock radio, groaning his disapproval. Before picking up the receiver, he shook the cobwebs from his head and turned the small key at the base of the telephone to activate the scrambler.

"And the top of the mornin' to you too, Jack," Semko said, with no doubt it was the deputy director for Operations on the other end.

"Rise and shine, Michael, me lad; the chase is on."

"At five-thirty in the morning? What's up?"

"The Russians have entered the game."

"On whose side?"

"Their own."

"What are they doing in the middle of this? Hell, they supported Strasser and his Stasi buddies for forty-five years."

"Apparently they're on to the same thing we are," the DDO hedged.

"Fuck the Russians. Fuck them all."

"You're not a morning person, are you?" Brannigan said with a chuckle.

"A snake that sheds its skin is still a snake."

"Abide by the rules, Mike; no direct confrontations unless absolutely unavoidable. We don't want an international incident with our newfound friends."

"That's what makes us such a great nation, you know, Jack. We're so goddamn naive and optimistic. Part of our charm, to people who don't have to depend on us."

"Just give them a wide berth."

"Yeah, sure," Semko said in a less than convincing tone.

"The meeting with your Mossad sidekick is set for noon today at the sea lion pool in the Central Park Zoo. Carry a *Time* magazine folded in half lengthwise, front cover out, in your left hand."

"Jesus, those people watch too many movies."

"It's their call. They probably want to check out the area before they commit their man, and they don't trust our safe house and don't want to admit they have any of their own in New York."

"Another joint operation based on mutual trust and respect."

"Don't make the mistake of underestimating them, Mike. By the way, did you get the list of suspect art galleries?" Brannigan asked, referring to the information the CIA liaison to the New York City Police Department's Intelligence Division had managed to obtain.

"Yeah. Your man who picked me up at the airport gave it to me."

"Start there. Strasser has to be using someone in the business to handle the paintings he's been stealing."

"Anything else I should know?"

"You may run into some of the FBI's counterintelligence people. They'll start their own surveillance if they pick up on any unusual Russian activity out of the UN mission and Glen Cove."

"Great. With the New York cops, Mossad, the Russians, the FBI, and us all after the same person, this operation could turn into a Chinese fire drill real quick."

"If you start crossing paths with the FBI, let me know. I'll try to get them to back off."

"Can I shoot some of them if they get in the way?"

"That's not funny, Mike."

"It wasn't meant to be."

"Stay in touch."

NEW YORK IS the only American city where luxury apartments, as opposed to houses, are the preferred residences of the superrich. But only in what are known as the "Good Buildings." The forty-two acknowledged Good Buildings are all cooperative apartment houses located on the Upper East Side in what is known as the Triangle—an area that incorporates Fifty-seventh Street from Sutton Place to Fifth Avenue on the south, then north to Ninety-eighth Street, and diagonally back down to Sutton Place.

The Good Building designation has little or nothing to do with quality of construction or grandness (though all are well built and handsome structures); rather, the title is based on the social standing and personal wealth of those who live there. Entertainers and people with a high public profile are generally excluded from ownership, and most of the building's coop boards will not accept anyone unless he or she pays in cash, carries no mortgage, and can show a net worth of at least twenty-five million dollars. There are approximately five hundred apartments in the forty-two Good Buildings, at an average cost of four million dollars, with monthly maintenance fees—often in excess of ten thousand dollars—that cannot be dependent on the owner's professional or business income for the money to pay them; yet, in testament to their high desirability for the wealthy of the world, there is usually a waiting list for any apartment that comes on the market.

Number One Sutton Place South, located on the corner where Fifty-seventh Street ends at the East River, was one of Manhattan's Good Buildings. It was built, as were all of the Good Buildings, prior to World War II. Most of the eighth floor and part of the ninth floor of the venerable brick-and-limestone structure were taken up by Philip Bancroft's New York City residence. The elevator from the lobby opened onto a private eighth-floor vestibule that led to only one entrance: the three-inch-thick carved-oak door to Bancroft's apartment. A mansion by definition to all but the most jaded, its twenty-plus rooms, some with twenty-foot ceilings, included a two-story entry gallery with a curved staircase, a reception hall, guest salon, library, a large country kitchen, servants' wing, and a thirty-five-foot-long living room, with a dining room only a few feet smaller.

Security for the building, with doormen, elevator operators, and reception personnel in the entrance lobby, was adequate enough to give pause to any common criminal with thoughts of hitting the mother lode, but not enough to deter someone of Jurgen Strasser's abilities and experience. Strasser had walked the Sutton Place neighborhood the previous day and again late that same evening, and was now, at shortly after 7:00 A.M., back for a final reconnaissance before the expected arrival of Bancroft that afternoon.

Yesterday's surveillance of the building, beginning just before noon, had proved fortuitous; Strasser was there in time to see a four-man crew of interior painters use one of the service entrances as they left and returned from their lunch break. The service entrance fronted on the street at the north end of the building and had a glass door, covered with a steel grating, that was kept locked at all times. Strasser had watched as the painting crew rang the bell and were admitted by a maintenance man, who locked the door behind them.

Strasser returned to the location later that same afternoon to observe the painters when they left for the day, taking note of the contractor's name on the van—Unique Interiors—and the type of coveralls they wore and any equipment they took home with them. By the time they arrived for work at eight-thirty the following morning, Strasser was again positioned to observe the routine they followed to get into the building.

The painters parked their van just around the corner from the entrance, where Fifty-seventh Street ends in a forty-foot-square section of pavement, enclosed on one side by the north wall of One Sutton Place South and on the other by the south side of the elegant brick town house that is the official residence of the secretary general of the United Nations. The attractive tree-lined area serves primarily as a cul-de-sac, providing parking spaces for waiting limousines and vehicles belonging to those having business in One Sutton Place South.

Just behind the parking area, Sutton Place Park fronts on the East River. Little more than a large brick courtyard, the miniature park is lined with benches that offer a panoramic view of the East River and Roosevelt Island, partially framed by the Fifty-ninth Street Bridge, and is frequented by area residents, some of them elderly and in wheelchairs pushed by private nurses, who come to read or sit in the sun and eat their lunch from old-fashioned straw picnic baskets.

Strasser sat on a bench at the top of the entrance ramp

leading down to the small park, allowing him an unobstructed view of the painting contractor's van as it arrived. He observed the workmen unloading their equipment, and saw that they now wore clean coveralls that were a close match for those he had purchased from an industrial supply store the previous evening. He got up and strolled casually to the corner and continued to watch as the painters again rang the bell to gain admittance by the maintenance man—a squat, powerfully built Hispanic who looked more than capable of taking care of himself, Strasser noticed, this time getting a good look at him.

Strasser's attention was then drawn to the New York City Police officer from the nineteenth precinct, who sat in a small enclosed three-wheeled vehicle, called a scooter, that he had parked at the curb in front of the official residence of the secretary general of the United Nations. Strasser had established the cop's routine the previous day: he arrived shortly before the secretary general was due to return to his home (escorted by three plainclothes bodyguards from the United Nations security force, who left after dropping him off) and remained outside at the curb until the secretary general again left his residence. Additional protection was provided by an interior guard wearing the gray doormanlike uniform of UN security; a telltale bulge under the left arm of the gold-piped uniform jacket revealed that he carried a concealed weapon in a shoulder holster. He remained in the residence at all times, leaving only to open and close the door for the secretary general and escort him to his chauffeur-driven car at the curb and into the custody of his personal bodyguards.

As Strasser observed the morning routine at the official residence, he saw the plainclothes security team pull up and the secretary general escorted out to the waiting car to be driven to his office at the United Nations. Within minutes, the cop in the scooter left, and the uniformed guard was back inside. If Strasser's plan went smoothly, the intermittent activity and the presence of the cop would not present a problem, but he had learned long ago to leave nothing to chance, and always factored any unpredictable elements into his contingency plans.

Satisfied with what he had observed thus far, Strasser returned to the park and sat on a bench overlooking the river, where he made the decision to carry out his plan early that afternoon, providing Bancroft arrived home as expected. He remained sitting on the bench for a short time, studying the photographs (one full face and one profile) clipped from old art magazine articles by Drussard and sent overnight to the gallery owner on Madison Avenue. His concentration was broken by a recurring memory from the night at Arthur Cabot's town house. Something the old man had said, just after he had taken the leather straps from his wrists and forced him to disarm the alarm system for the small study where the paintings were kept. "You can tell your filthy Russian masters that in the end I had the last laugh," Cabot had whispered hoarsely through his pain and anguish. Then, when Strasser's attention was on the paintings, the badly shaken old man had turned and run unsteadily down the second-floor hallway, where he tripped on a Persian carpet and tumbled down the stairwell to his death.

His words still bothered Strasser. What was there to laugh about? And what had led the old man to think he was a Russian? Occasionally, when he was angry, a slight German accent slipped into his near-perfect English. Perhaps Cabot had mistaken it for a Russian accent. Perhaps. Strasser dismissed the nagging thought, once again concentrating on the task ahead as he got up and left the park to take one final walk around the immediate area.

Completely preoccupied with the details of his plan, Strasser didn't notice the man who was keeping pace with him from across the street as he walked south toward the intersec-

tion at East Fifty-sixth en route to the parking garage where he
had left his minivan.

ALTHOUGH THE COP who had just pulled away from the curb in
front of the secretary general's residence was of no immediate
concern to Strasser, his off-and-on presence had created a
problem for the Russian intelligence officer in charge of the
surveillance of One Sutton Place South. Three vehicles, each
with two men in them, parked for extended periods in the
relatively quiet, exclusive neighborhood, were bound to be noticed by the cop in the scooter, and, eventually, by the police
radio cars that routinely patrolled the area.

The Russian had solved the problem by keeping two of his
two-man teams in their vehicles as mobile response units one
block west on First Avenue, a much busier thoroughfare where
their presence was less likely to draw attention. The cars were
moved frequently and their occupants rotated every two hours,
with the third two-man team assigned to work the Sutton Place
South neighborhood on foot. In radio contact with the men in
the cars, the men on foot served as an immediate reaction team
in the event Bancroft was approached on his arrival, and to
summon help if a surveillance other than their own was spotted.

With each two-hour rotation, the men taking over the street
posts on Sutton Place South changed into a variety of jackets
and hats, kept in the cars, and periodically switched their assigned sectors so they did not walk the same route or take up
the same observation post for more than fifteen minutes at a
time. The well-conceived deception made it possible for them
to present a different and changing profile to the ubiquitous
doormen stationed at the entrances to the apartment houses
lining both sides of the street in the block-long area of the
surveillance. From midnight through dawn, only one man
worked the street; posing as one of the city's innumerable

homeless, he had wedged himself into a corner at the bottom of a town house stairwell on Fifty-seventh Street just off Sutton Place South within view of Bancroft's apartment building.

Due to the recent reduction in the number of intelligence officers assigned to the Russian UN mission, the officer in charge of the surveillance operation was limited to two six-man teams. He was working them twelve hours on and twelve hours off, and the nighttime team, who had initiated the surveillance at nine-thirty the previous evening, had been relieved just prior to Strasser's arrival that morning.

The Russian walking along the opposite side of the street from One Sutton Place South took notice of the tall, lanky man who came out of the park. Something about him jogged his memory: the dark blond hair, the expensive leather jacket, and the way he carried himself. He had seen him before, lingering about the park when he first came on duty, and again, at least twice, walking along the street. He was certain of it. He slowed his pace to stay even with the man's progress, and followed him to the East Fifty-sixth Street intersection, where he broke off his parallel surveillance when his quarry crossed to his side of the street.

The Russian continued heading south, past the intersection, then, after glancing over his shoulder, doubled back as soon as the tall blond man entered the side street. By the time he reached the corner and scanned the narrow one-way street, he had lost his man in the stream of pedestrians jostling along the crowded sidewalks. Uneasy about being out of position to observe the area around Bancroft's building, he shrugged off the encounter, attributing the man's presence to his living somewhere in the neighborhood, and quickly returned to his assigned sector.

« 22 »

Friendly nations spying on each other is far from an uncommon occurrence; the sin is in getting caught. The Israeli Mossad has repeatedly denied that it has ever conducted any covert operations against the United States, or that it has ever maintained operational apartments (the Mossad term for safe houses) on American soil. The truth, however, is quite different. The Mossad's foremost mission is to spy on Israel's enemies—the Arab world and their network of vehemently anti-Israeli terrorist groups. Of almost equal importance are its intelligence-gathering operations in the United States. With the help of American Jews both in and out of government, Mossad has always managed to get the information it needs, and in many areas has been far more successful than the Russians have ever been. Their success in suborning otherwise fiercely loyal Americans is based on a simple, yet emotionally powerful appeal: fifty years ago, when help was needed and no one responded, the result was the Holocaust.

The Mossad operations directed against the United States are not, however, so much anti-American as they are pro-Israeli. Mossad efforts in New York City are primarily aimed at the United Nations diplomatic community, gathering information on the Arab world and the PLO, with one of their more productive operations being the running of an escort service that provides high-class call girls, with rudimentary agent training, to diplomats and UN employees with access to sensitive information. In Washington, covert intelligence-gathering operations are carried out through contacts established with staffers on key Senate and House committees, and by Mossad officers within Israel's legitimate attaché community, who work the cocktail party circuit. They are constantly looking for any changes of policy or wavering of US support that could affect the vital military and financial aid on which they depend, and, when unavailable through official channels, technical intelligence information applicable to the defense of Israel that Washington is unwilling to give them. Their motivation for continuing to jeopardize the much-needed relationship with the United States is based on one compelling obsession present in every Israeli's life: their very survival as a nation and as a people.

The apartment on the fifth floor of 421 East Fifty-second Street was one of seven safe houses the Mossad had at its disposal in New York City, all made available to them by *sayanim,* the huge network of "helpers" in a city whose Jewish community is exceeded in numbers only by Tel Aviv. The six men sitting around the oval-shaped glass dining room table were all members of Rachel Sidrane's *Kidon* unit who had arrived early that morning on a private jet arranged for by the Mossad. They were studying detailed Park Service maps of the Central Park area, selecting observation sites for the meeting at the sea lion pool, when the doorbell rang twice, then, after a few seconds pause, three more times.

The Mossad officer who opened the door had gone through the training academy with Rachel, and after tucking his pistol back into his waistband and closing and locking the door behind her, greeted her warmly. The other men responded with equal displays of friendship and respect as she joined them at the table. Her acceptance by those with whom she now worked had not been easily won. She was at first considered little more than a highly desirable, but unattainable, bedroom conquest by the male-dominated Mossad.

That all changed with her first assignment, which came nine weeks after completing her training and being assigned to the *Kidon* unit. Fourteen months had passed since her fiancé, Aaron Sontag, was gunned down on a London street, but his murderer had finally been identified and located. Ben-David, with his own ideas of poetic justice, and being a firm believer in an-eye-for-an-eye retribution, provided Rachel the opportunity to avenge Aaron's death. She accepted without hesitation, and six days later, on a crisp autumn afternoon, on a busy street in Brussels, a twenty-nine-year-old woman, who had never purposely harmed another living thing, and whose idea of mortal combat only a short time ago was an impassioned academic debate over the merits of a colleague's opinion, found, and learned to live with, the darkness in her soul.

The short, burly Arab in his early thirties had returned Rachel's suggestive eye contact and pleasant smile as she approached and stood next to him at a bus stop just off Brussels's Grand Place Square. When Rachel smiled again, the Arab's eyes roamed in slow appraisal over her body, eagerly responding to what he believed were the flirtations of a remarkably beautiful woman. He never saw the .22-caliber semiautomatic Beretta pistol fitted with a sound suppressor come out of her shoulder bag, nor did he feel more than an instant of pain when the two bullets entered the back of his head. The dozen or so people waiting at the bus stop had watched in horror as the well-dressed young woman stood over her already dead victim and fired three more rounds directly into his heart.

Rachel had forgotten none of her training in the heat of the action. She had remained calm and collected under pressure and used precisely five shots as planned. The two rounds remaining in the magazine, and the one in the chamber, were intended for anyone who tried to stop her as she stepped off the curb and climbed into a "taxi" that had screeched to a halt and paused only long enough for her to get in before speeding away to disappear down a side street. The message was clear, and understood by those for whom it was intended: the Mossad had struck in their signature fashion, on a busy street, in broad daylight, leaving nothing behind but untraceable shell casings, a body, and the conflicting accounts and descriptions of the witnesses.

After the Brussels assignment the men in the *Kidon* began referring to Rachel as the "Avenging Angel," a name she detested, but came to understand was given out of respect, and was final confirmation that she had been accepted into their ranks. That was five years ago, and the respect of her peers had only grown with each successful assignment, and there had been many. She had been surprised, and relieved, to find that she was able to separate the professional from the personal, and had felt only a brief period of remorse and moral conflict after her initiation in Brussels; something Ben-David had assured her was a natural reaction for civilized human beings who were called upon to do things that were anathema to them in normal situations. It hadn't taken long—the bombing of a bus filled with schoolchildren on the West Bank was the primary catalyst—until Rachel had, without conscious effort, managed to depersonalize her victims, seeing them only as unconscionable, indiscriminate murderers of innocent people, mindless terrorists who had forfeited their right to exist in a decent society.

The six men now seated around the table with Rachel in the New York safe house were unaware that something unrelated to the operation at hand was bothering her. Just prior to arriving at the apartment, she had called the Mossad "helper" with the Stolen Art Squad who was assigned to the special task force to solve the murders of Stewart and Cabot. She had asked him about the current status of the paintings found in Stewart's apartment. The information the detective had given her was less than encouraging. Four of the paintings that were not subsequently identified as being stolen property, including the Rembrandt landscape, were, under the provisions of Edward Winthrop Stewart's will, being claimed by the Metropolitan Museum of Art as part of his legitimate collection. All of the paintings discovered in Stewart's hidden room were currently being held in the police property room at the nineteenth precinct until the rightful owners could be established by the courts. Rachel was disheartened at the realization that any attempt to obtain the painting that rightfully belonged to her grandmother would entail a long, drawn-out legal battle, with little hope of success without proper documentation, which no longer existed.

Focusing her attention on the discussion at the table, Rachel sat quietly listening to the briefing by the leader of her six-man support team, which included updated information from Tel Aviv headquarters related to the unsolved murder cases. Both the CIA and the Mossad had agreed not to inform the New York police of their identification of Jurgen Strasser as the murderer, or of their own efforts to find him. Ben-David did not want Strasser arrested in a state that would only sentence him to life imprisonment for his crimes, making it quite possible, given Strasser's skills, that at some point he would escape; and Brannigan was taking no chances that the file, of which the Mossad was unaware, would fall into the hands of the New York cops. Brannigan had not yet informed Ben-David of the Russian involvement, making a piece of intelligence information that had come to the attention of the support team that morning appear unrelated to their current operation.

A Mossad agent inside the Russian emigré community in

the Brighton Beach section of Brooklyn had informed his handler of an intelligence operation directed at an unknown subject at One Sutton Place South in the city. The surveillance operation, to avoid drawing the attention of the FBI's Foreign Counterintelligence Squads, was being run out of a Brighton Beach safe house rather than the Russian UN mission or their Glen Cove estate. Two six-man teams were being rotated on a twelve-hour basis. Rachel made a mental note of the information, and one hour after arriving at the apartment, after going over the loss-of-contact procedures and schedule of communications with her support team, and being issued a .38-caliber Walther PPKS pistol equipped with a sound suppressor, left for her meeting in the park.

MIKE SEMKO STOOD at the railing enclosing the sea lion pool in the Central Park Zoo surrounded by a cheerful and expectant group of grade school children on a chaperoned class outing. The children squealed and laughed with delight as the slick, powerful mammals honked noisily and swam at dizzying speeds around the circumference of the pool, swirling and leaping out of the water to be hand-fed fish by their caretakers.

Rachel Sidrane sat on a bench in a far corner of the zoo's central garden partially hidden by a bed of shrubs and perennial plants, studying the man in the midst of the children. Just under six feet tall with close-cropped brown hair and a trim athletic build, and dressed casually in khaki slacks, running shoes, and a gray Windbreaker, he had, immediately upon arrival, drawn her attention. The children, pressed close at his side, prevented her from seeing the magazine in his left hand, but the prearranged signal had proven unnecessary. Ben-David's hunch was correct; he was the man in the photographs and videotape taken in Paris. There was a stillness, a coiled sense of readiness about him as he stood at the railing, his weight resting on one hip, observing his surroundings. The only movement was in his intense, watchful eyes, devoid of emotion and reflecting the calm awareness of the supremely confident. Everything about him told of a man trained to live with and by violence, much as Ben-David had warned her he would be. Rachel had seen men like him before. Men she categorized as dangerously handsome, trouble for anyone foolish enough to get involved with them. If he had been on the opposing side, he would have been bad news.

It was a few minutes before noon when, in his peripheral vision, Semko caught a glimpse of an attractive woman leaving a bench behind him and to his left. He dismissed her as inconsequential as she continued to approach, edging her way through a cluster of gleeful children to stand next to him. Her raven black hair, iridescent in the bright sunlight, was pulled back, and her eyes were hidden behind mirrored, metal-rimmed sunglasses. She wore no makeup, and her nails, Semko noticed as she placed her hands on the railing, were short, square, and unpolished. She had on slacks and a tailored linen jacket and silk blouse that emphasized a shapely figure— someone with whom he would have definitely struck up a conversation under different circumstances, he thought, until she spoke to him.

"A wet bird flies at night," Rachel said, and flashed a playful smile.

"Excuse me?"

"A wet bird flies at night," Rachel repeated, and wiggled her eyebrows above the sunglasses.

Semko was usually quite adept at quickly distinguishing the deranged from the normal in a city that he felt was fast making such distinctions increasingly difficult, but this one didn't fit the mold. He looked hard at the obviously disturbed woman, then, without a word, backed away from his spot at the railing to walk slowly around the edge of the pool, only to find that she was following close behind. He stopped in his tracks and turned to face her.

"I don't have time for this lady; what is it you want?"

Rachel smiled and, making certain they were out of earshot of the milling crowd, reached over to take the *Time* magazine from his hand. "Relax, Semko. I thought you CIA types liked secret code words."

"Who the hell are you?"

"The person you're waiting for," Rachel said.

"Oh, yeah?" Semko's surprise was genuine. "You're not exactly what I was expecting."

"And I expected an Ivy League type wearing a blue blazer or tweed jacket with a rep tie and smoking a pipe. And maybe tassel loafers from Gucci."

"They only work the field in the movies. I'm what the boys in the suits call a paramilitary type, a knuckle dragger. They play by the rules; we don't, so we get the dirty work."

Taking Rachel's arm, he led her away from the crowd at the sea lion pool and up a small flight of steps to a covered colonnaded walkway adjacent to another, larger pool complete with rock promontories and waterfalls that was designed as a habitat for a colony of Japanese snow monkeys. He escorted her to a corner near the edge of the habitat that was quiet and out of the way except for the occasional passerby.

"You've been assigned to work with me?"

"Rachel Sidrane," she said, and extended her hand.

Semko ignored the outstretched hand and slowly shook his head. "I don't believe this."

Rachel bristled at recognizing an attitude she had encountered throughout her adult life and deeply resented. He had assessed her with a typical male bias; a misjudgment that fortunately would not cost him his life as it had others who made the mistake of underestimating her.

"Let me guess. A woman's place is in the kitchen, barefoot in the winter and pregnant in the summer."

"Something like that," Semko said, though it was far from a philosophy he embraced. "What are your qualifications for this operation?"

"I have a PhD in art history."

"Terrific! When we catch up to Strasser you can bore him to death?"

"What a delight you are, Semko. Why is it I get the feeling I could carve all of your admirable qualities on the head of a pin with a chisel and still have room for the unabridged *Oxford English Dictionary*?"

"In my world college degrees don't mean much, lady. I learned a long time ago not to confuse academic achievement with intelligence. Even pigeons can memorize simple repetitive tasks, if they're color coded."

Rachel took a slow deep breath to control her anger, but only partially succeeded. "I can see where the value of a formal education would be an alien concept to you, but trust me, in this case it will serve you well."

"Yeah? How?" Semko said, intrigued as Rachel removed her sunglasses and made direct and challenging eye contact. They were intelligent eyes, he thought, not the kind you find on the easy-to-surprise types, like a deer caught in headlights.

"The idea is to anticipate Strasser's next move. What do you know about the art underground, or art in general for that matter?"

"I've got a pretty good collection of Elvis on velvet."

"Somehow that doesn't surprise me."

"Look, lady—"

"It's Rachel."

"Look, Rachel, nothing personal, but I don't think a woman has any place in the field, and definitely not on an operation that can get real ugly, real fast, like this one."

"I was given this assignment the same as you were. Now if you want to call it off, that's your choice, but I suggest you put your petty prejudices aside and we concentrate on what's really important: finding Strasser before he kills again. Unless I'm mistaken, it's the first time he's stayed out in the open this long, and the best opportunity either one of us has ever had of getting him."

Semko had no doubt that any complaints to the DDO about working with a woman would fall on deaf ears, and at best only delay the operation and possibly blow any chance they had at finding Strasser quickly. He nodded in acquiescence and extended his hand. Rachel relaxed and shook it.

"Does this mean we can get to work and stop insulting each other?"

"Why not," Semko said. "You know you sound a lot more like an American than an Israeli."

"I'm a naturalized citizen of Israel, born and raised right here in New York City."

"That should prove helpful."

"Oh, golly gee, you mean I just might be of some use?"

Semko laughed, and with it melted away the last of the animosity. "Look, I'm sorry we got off on the wrong foot. My objection to you isn't that you're a woman, it's that you're an art history major. Strasser is a stone killer who'll blow your brains out as soon as look at you. Finding him is only one of the problems; bringing him down is going to be a nasty piece of business."

"I'll try to stay out of the way."

"Then let's set the ground rules right now. We work as a team, just the two of us. I don't want to be tripping over any of your friends."

"Agreed."

"Fine," Semko said, and gestured with his thumb in the direction of the sea lion pool and the central garden. "Tell the guy on the bench at ten o'clock pretending to read a newspaper, and the other one standing just to the left of the guy feeding the seals, to take a hike, permanently. I don't want to see their faces again. If I spotted them, so will Strasser, and then we've lost him.''

"Ah, you're more than just a pretty face," Rachel joked in an attempt to hide her embarrassment at having the two men from her unit discovered.

"You level with me on what you know and I'll do the same with you," Semko said, although he had no intention of telling her about the file that was the Agency's primary concern. "But I'll tell you up front, I've had some bad experiences with your organization. You don't trust anyone, and in this type of operation that can get people killed."

"History's taught us some hard lessons, Semko."

"We've all learned hard lessons. Now are you going to tell your friends to get lost or am I? If I do it, they aren't going like it much."

Rachel caught the eye of the Mossad man at the sea lion pool and made a barely noticeable gesture with her head. The man turned and walked over to his counterpart seated on the bench. Both men left, respecting Rachel's earlier request that if their surveillance was spotted they would return to the safe house to await further contact.

"From now on, as far as our support people are concerned, we check in with them for intel updates and that's it. Understood?"

With a nod, Rachel indicated that she did.

"Now," Semko said, "let's compare notes and get on with it."

Rachel told him what she knew and suspected about Strasser, and Semko reciprocated, telling her of their past history in Dusseldorf and his attempts to find Dieter since.

"And your orders are to call in your people to take him out when we find him?"

"Something like that."

"Well, I doubt they'll get the chance," Semko said. "I'm going to kill the son of a bitch on sight."

"Whichever comes first," was all Rachel said.

"How much money is there in the art he's stealing?"

"Millions, for the right paintings."

"Millions, huh? Think my Elvis paintings might be worth something?"

"Probably exactly what you paid for them, if you sell them at the right truck stop."

"Don't make fun of the King."

"There's something that doesn't quite jell here," Rachel said. "We've got two people dead in a matter of two days. According to the police reports neither of them knew the other very well, certainly not well enough to discuss the stolen art in their collections."

"What's your point?"

"How does a terrorist like Strasser find out they have it?"

"Maybe they were trying to sell it through the same crooked art dealer who had terrorist connections and decided to rip them off."

"Both men decided after almost fifty years to sell their stolen collections at the same time? No. That's too much of a stretch."

"Maybe someone found out they had it; Interpol might have had something on them and Strasser or an art dealer got hold of it."

"Before I left Tel Aviv, I ran a check with Interpol. They had never even had an inquiry about Stewart or Cabot, and none of the paintings were on file with their stolen art section. It was a curator at the Metropolitan Museum of Art who recognized some of them and informed the police they had been missing since World War II."

"We find the art dealer Strasser's using, maybe we'll find the answer," Semko said, eager to get off the subject before Rachel's reasoning led her any further. Her questions had triggered his own deductive logic, and he strongly suspected that the information she believed Strasser had managed to get his hands on was in the file that Brannigan, and now apparently the Russians, were after. "There is something else," he said, realizing it would be foolish, if not dangerous, to withhold the information. "The Russians have entered the picture."

"Why the Russians?"

"I don't know," Semko lied, "unless Strasser knows where too many bodies are buried from his Stasi days and they're afraid he's going to spill his guts if he gets caught."

"We just got a report of a Russian surveillance at One Sutton Place South."

"What's One Sutton Place South?"

"One of the best addresses in the city."

"Wealthy people who might have art collections live there?"

"Definitely."

"Let's check it out first, then we'll start on the galleries and see if we can find who's moving the stuff Strasser's stealing. You have any tradecraft training?"

"Some," Rachel said. "A basic course," admitting to only what a research analyst might be expected to know.

"Good. You're going to need it."

As they left the park in the direction of Fifth Avenue, Semko realized what it was about Rachel that was bothering him. She had some of the same qualities of his ex-wife, Janet; the same intuitive intelligence and directness, and eyes that spoke of an innately decent soul. The unsettling similarities brought a palpable momentary flashback to a time he tried never to think about: a late evening drive back to Fort Bragg at the end of a lazy, sunny weekend at Myrtle Beach. The top was down on his beat-up Pontiac GTO, spray-painted in woodland camouflage by a friend in the motor pool, and Janet, her chestnut hair tossed by the wind, was curled up beside him, sitting close enough to wear his smile. It was their first weekend together, and they had made love, long and often. She was a nurse's aide at the Cape Fear Hospital, and he was a young buck sergeant just out of Special Forces schools, as proud of his green beret as he was of anything he had accomplished in his young life. They were married within a month, and one week later his Special Forces A Team was sent to Vietnam.

She had suffered through the long, lonely absences inherent in the life of a career soldier. But she was always there for him; his anchor, his lover, and his friend, sharing his personal triumphs and tragedies throughout his tours of duty in Vietnam and his years with Delta Force. She had understood his commitment to serving his country, loving him and supporting him through it all, and he had repaid her by forgetting birthdays and anniversaries, and, one year, even forgetting to get her a Christmas present.

The final callous and selfish act was his not being at her side in the hospital when she almost died during a miscarriage of the only child they had tried to conceive. She was in her sixth month, and he had known she wasn't feeling well and that there might be complications with the baby. But rather than going straight home from the base that evening after a HALO training jump, he had gone drinking with his buddies at the Green Beret Club. A neighbor had found Janet unconscious on the kitchen floor, just in time to rush her to the hospital.

He had failed her when she needed him most, and it was the one thing she had been unable to forgive, and for which he had never forgiven himself. Their eleven-year marriage ended with a note beneath a smiley-face magnet on the refrigerator door, and it was at that moment when he realized how much he really loved and needed her, and, in the years since, how much heavier the burden had become for what he had left behind. Other than purely physical affairs with a long list of women he cared nothing about, there had been no one else, nothing meaningful in his life but his work.

Semko snapped out of his disturbing reverie as they reached Fifth Avenue and Rachel stepped to the curb. Placing two fingers in her mouth, she let out a loud, shrill whistle that caused a taxi in the far lane of the broad one-way street to cut across traffic and swerve to an abrupt halt at their feet.

"Yeah. You're a New Yorker all right," Semko said as he opened the cab door.

"You don't really have a collection of Elvis on velvet, do you?"

"No, but I have one of those prints of dogs playing poker hanging over the sofa in my apartment. Is that any better?"

"Not much."

« 23 »

NIKOLAI LEONOV'S BRIEF clandestine meeting at the Lincoln
Center Plaza with the Line N illegal assigned to Bancroft had
gone well. He was inordinately proud of himself for detecting
and evading the surveillance effort he had been warned to
expect. Twenty-five years had passed since his basic tradecraft
courses at the KGB schools, and never having had the opportunity to put the training to practical use, he was surprised at
how much of it had come back to him.

The *rezident,* the senior intelligence officer at the Russian
mission, in compliance with Leonov's instructions cabled
from Yasenevo, had ordered his operations officer to work out
a route and location for a meeting with an illegal who was to
be informed of the site and time prior to Leonov's arrival in
New York City. The information, delivered to Leonov at the
airport, allowed him to go directly to the meeting site. Following the operations officer's instructions to the letter, Leonov
had spotted and shaken the man he assumed to be CIA after
leaving his third change of taxis four blocks from his intended
destination to travel the rest of the way on foot.

An earlier call by the operations officer to the Bancroft Industries hangar at Butler Aviation in Newark, under the guise
of being a member of their corporate security staff, revealed

that the company's private jet from Saint Martin was due in at
1:10 P.M. Adding another forty-five minutes for the drive from
the Butler Aviation terminal, the operations officer had included Bancroft's expected time of arrival at his apartment
building in the instructions delivered to Leonov at the airport.
The immediacy and complicated nature of the situation precluded the use of a dead drop, the usual, and much safer,
method of contact between an illegal and his agent. And after
careful deliberation, Leonov decided, due to the time element,
to instruct the illegal to pass a message to Bancroft when he
returned to One Sutton Place South, rather than risk his not
making it to the Newark airport in time for the plane's arrival.
Leonov had personally crafted the note, wording the message
to convey the seriousness of the affair without causing alarm:
Bancroft was to meet with his illegal regarding a matter of
some urgency as soon as possible in the manner set forth in the
message.

At the Russian mission on East Sixty-seventh Street, Leonov took the elevator directly to the seventh floor *referentura*—
the code and communications room. Finding no cables from
the head of the External Intelligence Service, he took the stairwell to the eighth floor and entered the office the *rezident* had
allocated for him. After sitting quietly for a few minutes to
collect his thoughts, he used the secure telephone to contact
the Brighton Beach safe house and alert the officer in charge
of the surveillance at One Sutton Place South to Bancroft's
pending arrival. He further informed the ranking intelligence
officer that a message would be passed to Bancroft for the
purpose of arranging a clandestine meeting later that same
day, and that he, and his men, were to continue to provide
security during and after the clandestine contact until he was
instructed to stand down.

* * *

"YOU LOST HIM?" Brannigan bellowed at Alfred Palmer. "Your CI people goddamn lost him?"

"Two of our cars got tied up in a detour around a street construction site," Palmer said sheepishly. "One of the men jumped into a cab to follow, but Leonov spotted him when he got out to pursue on foot. He pretended to break off the surveillance and by the time he was back in position Leonov was gone."

"A man who's fucking never even worked the field, and he makes one of your people?" The DDO sent a chair crashing into the wall of the room inside the twenty-four-hour operations center, his foulmouthed outrage at full force. "The cocksucker was probably contacting one of his illegals; a direct lead to Strasser's next victim, and Strasser himself."

"There'll be a stern reprimand," Palmer offered calmly, regretting his choice of words almost as he said them.

"Reprimand? A fucking lot of good that'll do!"

"They have him back under surveillance now; he's at the Russian mission."

"You tell your people: They lose him again, they finish out their careers cleaning toilets at the goddamn Farm."

JURGEN STRASSER HAD learned Bancroft's expected arrival time in much the same manner as the Russian operations officer. He had first called Bancroft Industries headquarters in the city and represented himself as an FAA inspector to a secretary who told him where their corporate aircraft were based. A second call to the private hangar at the Newark airport, claiming to be an executive assistant with important papers to deliver to Bancroft as soon as his plane landed, got him the estimated arrival time.

Strasser pulled the rented minivan into the small cul-de-sac at One Sutton Place South only minutes before Philip Bancroft's black Mercedes limousine swung over to the curb at the

entrance to the building. Strasser had parked at the corner, in
front of the larger van belonging to the painting contractors,
placing the entrance within his view. He watched as the chauffeur released the trunk lid and got out to open the rear door for
a tall, elderly man elegantly dressed in gabardine slacks and a
silk shirt and sporting a deep, even tan. The chauffeur then
walked around to the rear of the limousine and delivered three
pieces of leather luggage into the eager arms of two doormen
who had appeared as soon as the black Mercedes with the
mirrored windows pulled up.

Strasser recognized Bancroft immediately and continued to
study him as he stood in the middle of the sidewalk and arched
his back in a slow stretch, surveying the broad avenue as
though he owned it and causing other pedestrians to walk
around him. Strasser's attention was momentarily diverted to
the driver of a taxi that pulled in behind the limousine. The
driver got out and stepped onto the sidewalk, jostling Bancroft
as he walked past him. He continued on without apology to
approach one of the doormen, whom he engaged in a brief
conversation before returning to his taxi and driving off. The
incident had all the earmarks of a well-trained agent executing
a perfect "brush contact," but Strasser cracked a small smile
at his professional paranoia and dismissed the incident as a
typical occurrence in a city known for the rudeness of its
inhabitants.

As Bancroft entered the building, the chauffeur pulled the
long, black Mercedes into a tight U-turn on the broad avenue
and swung into the cul-de-sac where he parked across from
Strasser. The chauffeur remained in the limousine, waiting at
Bancroft's instructions to drive him to his office within the
hour. He paid no attention to the minivan that now bore a
superficial resemblance to the painting contractor's van that
had been a permanent fixture in the area for the past week.

The previous evening, Strasser had gone to the Manhattan

Sign and Banner Company on Eighth Avenue, and paid extra to have his order ready by noon the following day. The two magnetic signs he had picked up an hour ago, one for each side of the minivan, did not have the elaborate hand-painted design of the contractor's van, but the "Unique Interiors" logo, with the company's address and telephone number below, were enough to lend credence to its presence in the cul-de-sac.

Strasser slipped out from behind the steering wheel and from the side of the van removed a canvas tarp and a can of paint. In the coveralls he had purchased at the industrial supplies store, and with a bandanna tied around his forehead, he looked the part he was about to play. As an added touch, he stuffed two paintbrushes into the loops at the waist of the coveralls before closing the door and turning the corner in the direction of the service entrance he had watched the painters use.

ERNESTO MARTINEZ, THE building superintendent in charge of maintenance, sat with his feet up on his desk in the tiny room that served as his office. He was finishing off the last of the ham-and-cheese sandwiches his wife had packed for his lunch when he heard the bell at the service entrance ring.

"You're late," he said, taking in at a glance the man's coveralls and painting equipment as he unlocked and opened the door. "The rest of your crew got back from lunch an hour ago."

A second, more careful, look made Martinez hesitate before admitting the man. He thought he recalled all of the painters returning at the same time. "I don't remember you."

"The boss said we were behind schedule here. I was transferred from another crew."

Martinez nodded knowingly, then moved his solid two hundred pounds aside to let Strasser through, closing and locking the door behind him. "Come on, I'll take you up," he said, and gestured with his head toward the service elevator on the wall opposite the doorway.

Strasser followed Martinez into the elevator and watched as the burly superintendent pressed the button for the tenth floor.

"Bancroft's on the tenth floor?" Strasser asked, hoping the question would prompt Martinez to give him the information he needed.

"No, Bancroft is on eight," Martinez said. "Your people are working on ten, the Andersons."

Strasser placed the paint can he was carrying on the floor and moved to one side of the large service elevator. Martinez looked over his shoulder to ask how the man knew Philip Bancroft and found himself staring at the tip of the sound suppressor threaded onto the barrel of the nine-millimeter pistol protruding from beneath the tarp draped over Strasser's right arm.

"What are you, crazy, man?" Martinez said. Having spent most of his teenage years in a street gang, it was not the first time the lifelong resident of Spanish Harlem had faced a gun. He was frightened, but not immobilized by the fear, and in a swift, forceful move, angled his body away from the barrel and grabbed Strasser's wrist with his left hand just as he fired, causing the shot to hit the elevator wall.

Strasser was surprised at the speed and agility of the stocky, powerful man. They were now face-to-face, with Martinez pinning him to the rear of the elevator, forcing his gun hand over his head. Strasser brought his left hand up and dug his fingers into Martinez's eyes, eliciting a cry of pain, but doing nothing to break the man's hold on his right wrist. He then delivered a solid hammer blow to Martinez's kidney, then another, and another, and he felt his attacker give ground and his grip begin to weaken. But Martinez did not quit, and Strasser was rocked by a beefy fist that smashed into his ear and momentarily stunned him.

With renewed strength, Martinez again tightened his grip and slammed Strasser back against the rear of the elevator. He threw another wild overhand right that Strasser slipped with a lateral movement of his head, causing Martinez's fist to hit the wall, breaking three of his knuckles. Ignoring the excruciating pain, Martinez threw another punch, this time connecting with Strasser's left temple. The blow buckled Strasser's knees and knocked him off balance. The struggle was at such close quarters that Martinez did not see Strasser's left hand reach through the vented side of his coveralls to the pocket of the slacks worn underneath, and too late he heard the unmistakable sound of a switchblade springing open.

Strasser drove the six-inch blade deep into Martinez's lower stomach, burying it to the hilt, twisting and pulling it upward. The valiant struggle ended as Martinez expelled a guttural cry of pain, then shuddered and slumped against Strasser before staggering backward to stare at the dark stain spreading over his trousers and the lower portion of his jacket. He dropped to his knees, both hands pressed against the massive wound in an attempt to keep his intestines from spilling out. His eyes rolled back into his head as he raised a blood-drenched hand to make the sign of the cross. "Holy Mary, mother of God, pray for—" was all he managed to whisper before he keeled over and died.

Strasser was more than a little shaken by the encounter. He was breathing heavily, and in addition to a red welt swelling at his temple, his ears still rang from the heavy blows to his head. He looked up at the indicator lights over the door to see the number seven illuminated, and quickly reached over to the control panel to press the button for the eighth floor. The slow-moving freight elevator came to a smooth stop and the doors rolled back to reveal the private paneled vestibule at the entrance to Philip Bancroft's apartment. Strasser locked the elevator doors open, and after wiping the knife blade clean on Martinez's trousers, folded it and slipped it back into his pocket. He then pulled the body to the rear of the elevator and stripped off the blood-soaked gray-blue jacket bearing the name of the building. He removed the bandanna from his forehead and stepped out of his coveralls before pulling the jacket on and holding the tarp to cover the large wet stain on the lower half as he entered the vestibule.

He heard a humming sound as he passed the residents' main elevator that serviced the lobby, and after waiting until he was certain it was not stopping on the eighth floor, continued to the far end of the vestibule and rang the buzzer for Bancroft's apartment.

GLYNIS EVANS WAS twenty-three years old and was employed by the Bancrofts as a housekeeper at their London town house when Bitsy Bancroft asked her to come to the States to work. She had eagerly accepted, hoping one day to become a permanent resident in a city that held an endless fascination for her. She had been in New York only a week, and the glow of her expectations had yet to wear off. Responding to the buzzer on the second ring, she looked up at the closed circuit monitor to see a man she did not recognize standing outside in the vestibule. She did, however, recognize the jacket worn by the building's maintenance personnel and assumed that the man was there to fix some problem she had not been told about.

She had no more than unlocked the door and turned the knob than she was thrown backward onto the floor. She was too startled to scream as she looked up to see Strasser burst into the apartment and point a gun at her head.

''Where is Bancroft?'' Strasser said, scanning the two-story entrance gallery as he switched gun hands and took off the bloody jacket and tossed it aside with the canvas tarp.

Glynis Evans's eyes were wide with fright and her lower lip quivered. "Mr. Bancroft is away," she said, fully aware that he was at the opposite end of the apartment, and equally aware that due to Mrs. Bancroft's being in Palm Beach, and Mr. Bancroft's having just returned, the full staff was off until the following morning. With the exception of an elderly cook who was nearly deaf and some ten rooms away napping in the servants' wing, the young housekeeper was the only one on duty.

Strasser moved forward and stood over the terrified girl, pressing the tip of the sound suppressor into the center of her forehead. "Lie to me again and I'll kill you," he said, and yanked her to her feet. "Who else is in the apartment?"

Glynis told him the truth, her courage dissolved by the menacing look on the face of the man now twisting her arm at the elbow.

"Take me to Bancroft."

"I will! I will! Please don't hurt me!"

The sprawling apartment seemed to go on forever as Strasser followed her through a series of large, high-ceilinged rooms filled with expensive furnishings. The three-foot-thick outside walls kept out the sounds of the city, making Strasser feel as though he were in an English country manor house rather than an apartment eight floors above the streets of Manhattan.

The young girl kept looking over her shoulder, frightened by the gun and the man gripping her arm so tightly that the pain traveled throughout her body. At the end of a long carpeted hallway, she paused at the double doors leading into the master bedroom suite.

"I believe he's in here," she said, her voice barely audible.

"Inside," Strasser ordered, throwing the doors open and shoving her ahead of him.

Philip Bancroft was standing on a small balcony off the

master bedroom that overlooked the East River. At the sound
of the commotion, he stepped back inside to see the hysterical
housekeeper stumble into the room and cry out.

"I'm sorry, sir. I truly am," she sobbed. "He said he'd kill
me."

Bancroft's gaze fell on the pistol now pointed at his chest.
"What do you want?" he demanded, his composure betraying
none of the icy fear that gripped him.

Bancroft had little doubt that the note he found in the pocket
of his slacks when reaching for his apartment key was directly
related to what was unfolding before his eyes. The lacy black
ashes were still warm in the ashtray where he had burned the
message after memorizing the instructions.

Without a word, Strasser turned the pistol on the young
housekeeper and fired one shot into the back of her head.
Glynis Evans's life was over before she collapsed to the floor
at Bancroft's feet.

"Just thought I'd set the tone for our little tête-à-tête,"
Strasser said.

Bancroft stared in horror at the fallen girl, then stepped
back to drop heavily into a chair behind him.

THE RUSSIAN INTELLIGENCE officer stationed at an observation
point across the street from the entrance to One Sutton Place
South had also seen the taxi driver bump into Bancroft, and,
forewarned by his team leader, recognized the brush contact
for what it was. He had also noticed the tall, lanky man who
got out of the minivan. At first the white coveralls and the
bandanna had fooled him, but when he saw the dark blond hair
and the sharp features and the way he carried himself, he soon
realized it was the same man he had seen in the area, and
briefly followed, earlier that morning.

The Russian had reacted after watching Strasser approach
the service entrance and ring the bell to be admitted by the

maintenance man. Whispering into a miniature sleeve micro-phone wired to a small portable radio attached to his belt, he alerted the leader of his six-man team to what he had just witnessed. From his car on First Avenue, the team leader used a hand-held radio with a greater range to relay the information to the Brighton Beach safe house. His orders came back im-mediately. He was to take three men with him into the build-ing using the service entrance and determine where the sus-pect had gone. The remaining two men were to stay outside to watch the main entrance in the event Bancroft came out.

It had taken a full fifteen minutes for the two men circling the block in their car to find a parking place, get back to join the other men on First Avenue, and walk over to Sutton Place South. The Russian who had seen Strasser had waited in place until all of his teammates arrived, and was relieved to see the doorman, who had been standing beneath the portico in full view of the service entrance, go back inside to the lobby. Instead of approaching the building together, the men sepa-rated, with the team leader making the initial attempt to gain entrance. He found the door locked, and after getting no re-sponse from ringing the bell, used his sleeve microphone to summon another of the team, an expert in lock picking. The simple tumbler lock was opened within seconds and the two men disappeared inside. Two more men casually approached the building and slipped in through the open door to regroup with the others, leaving the remaining two men outside posted nearby.

The Russian team leader, knowing the location of Ban-croft's apartment, pressed the button for the elevator and wasted precious moments for it to open before looking at the indicator panel and realizing that it was stuck on the eighth floor. A tightness gripped his chest as he knew with a terrible certainty where the man in question had gone. The Russian looked down the long hallway to his left and saw the bottom of the emergency stairwell that serviced all of the apartments on the north end of the building. He led his men at an all-out run and upon reaching the stairs, began taking them two at a time.

« 24 »

MIKE SEMKO AND Rachel Sidrane got out of the taxi on the corner of Fifty-seventh Street and Sutton Place South to see a cop in a scooter parked at the curb in front of an elegant brick town house across the street. Semko's attention was immediately drawn to a dark blue Ford sedan with four men in it parked behind the scooter, and then to a black Mercedes with a uniformed driver and a man riding shotgun parked behind the Ford.

"Looks like we might have some action over there."

"That's the residence of the secretary general of the United Nations. It probably has something to do with him."

"Does his security detail always stay posted outside the house?"

"I don't know. On the few occasions when I've seen them the secretary general was either arriving or leaving. I think he has additional security inside the house and the men in the cars are there to escort him back and forth to the UN."

"With the cop on duty outside," Semko said, "the usual procedure for an escort detail would be to return to a layoff site somewhere until he's ready to move again."

"Maybe he's leaving soon."

"Yeah. And maybe it isn't what it looks like."

"I doubt that."

"Let's find out."

"I don't think that's such a good idea."

"I'll handle it. You'd be surprised how much information you can get by acting stupid," Semko said, and started across the street against the traffic.

"You're off to a good start," Rachel said to herself, and waited until the light changed a few moments later before stepping into the crosswalk.

Semko drew the undivided attention of the men in the Ford as he walked up to the small three-wheel vehicle and addressed the cop.

"I called in a suspicious persons report about an hour ago. Your guys see anything?"

"Suspicious people in New York City?" the cop said, with a feigned look of incredulity.

"I noticed a couple of guys hanging around and thought you might want to check them out."

Semko's gaze shifted to his right, fixing on the four men in the dark blue Ford parked behind the scooter. The car windows were down, and they were listening to his conversation with the cop. Their postures stiffened as they stared back, their eyes watching Semko's every move, but concentrating on his hands.

"Who are you?" the cop demanded.

"A concerned citizen, that's all you need to know."

It was the wrong answer in the wrong tone of voice to a man who on a daily basis encountered the largest population of street crazies to be found anywhere in the civilized world, with the possible exception of Teheran. But the intimidating remark was intentional on Semko's part, to gauge the reaction it would bring from the cop and the men in the Ford.

"Back away from the vehicle," the cop ordered in a no-nonsense voice. "Lets see some ID."

"You know, you got an attitude problem."

Rachel reached Semko's side in time to hear the last exchange.

"You'll have to excuse my husband, Officer," she said with a friendly smile. "He watches too many *Kojak* reruns."

Taking Semko by the arm, she pulled him onto the sidewalk and began walking away just as the four men in the Ford got out of the car, their right hands inside their suit coats resting on the Uzi machine pistols in their shoulder holsters.

"Keep him on a leash, will ya, lady," the cop called after her.

"I got your leash," Semko said, loud enough for the cop to hear.

Rachel tugged on Semko's arm, leading him farther away from what was about to become a full-blown confrontation.

"That accomplished a lot."

"It told me what I needed to know. I've seen staged scenes with phony cops and security guards before. Strasser's a master at it. If those guys were some of his people, they would have let it play out a lot longer before they committed to a premature response that would have blown their operation."

"Not bad, Semko. A little crude, but not bad."

Rachel felt Semko's body tense as he slowed his pace and pulled her to the inside of the sidewalk.

"See the guy across the street at two o'clock?"

Rachel looked without turning her head. "Short, heavy build, green jacket?"

"That's him," Semko said, his eyes now moving quickly back and forth across the broad avenue and finally locking on a second man.

"There's another one. This side of the street at eleven o'clock. Tan jacket, gray sweater underneath, standing in front of that small van at the corner of the building."

"I see him," Rachel said, then looked past the man to the

raised inscription on the front of the building. "That's One
Sutton Place South."

"We're in business," Semko said, and still holding Rachel's arm, led her into the cul-de-sac where they sat on a
bench near the entrance ramp that led down to the small park.
From their vantage point, both the man across the street and
the man at the corner of the building were within their line of
sight.

JURGEN STRASSER CARRIED two paintings, a Renoir and a Degas,
wrapped inside the canvas tarp as he came out of Bancroft's
apartment and crossed the vestibule to the service elevator. He
stepped inside and reached for the button to unlock the doors,
when he was startled by a loud bang—the sound of the emergency stairwell door being thrown open and crashing into the
wall.

Strasser laid the paintings on the floor beside Martinez's
body and withdrew the sound-suppressed pistol tucked into his
waistband beneath his sweater. He flattened himself against the
wall at the edge of the open doors and made a rapid bobbing
motion with his head, moving it outside, then immediately
back inside the elevator. He caught a brief glimpse of four
men fifteen feet away at the far end of the vestibule; all were
crouched into a stable shooting platform, their weapons held in
a two-handed grip and sweeping the area ahead of them.

One of the men had seen the quick head movement and
gestured silently to the others to move forward.

Strasser knew he had been seen, but remained motionless,
pressed against the wall. He listened to their labored, shallow
breathing, assessing his situation as they drew near. Were they
cops, or part of Bancroft's personal security force? He guessed
the latter. But what had brought them on the run? And where
had they come from? There was no way they could possibly
know what had taken place inside Bancroft's apartment. But

perhaps the old man had somehow tripped a silent alarm before he killed him. Whatever had caused them to respond, at this point it had to be unclear to them what they were dealing with, and therefore they would be reluctant to shoot first and ask questions later. He was counting on that, on enough hesitation in their reaction to give him the edge he needed.

After taking a deep breath and exhaling slowly, Strasser spun low into the open doorway and began shooting. He fired two shots at each of the men, acquiring his targets with remarkable speed and precision. Two of the Russians fell dead from head wounds; a third was hit twice in the chest, immobilized, and thrown back against the wall of the vestibule, where he slid to the floor to die as his lungs filled with blood. None had gotten off a shot.

The fourth man, young and inexperienced, was frightened into momentary inaction, but had enough presence of mind to drop to one knee, lowering his profile and causing one of Strasser's well-aimed shots to miss and the other to hit wide to the left in his shoulder. The bullet had gone in and out of the muscle without striking bone, and though stunned, the Russian gamely returned fire. He was off balance and in some pain, but one of his five shots came close enough to pass through Strasser's sweater and scrape the side of his rib cage.

Strasser's next, and final, shot creased the Russian's skull, sending him reeling backward, where he fell facedown on the floor, unconscious. The Russian's weapon was not sound suppressed, and the shots had echoed loudly in the high-ceilinged, windowless vestibule. The sharp reports traveled down the elevator shaft, but by the time they reached the bottom all that remained was an insignificant pop that was impossible to distinguish from the sound of the street traffic outside.

Strasser quickly closed the doors and pressed the button for the bottom floor. Unsure of what might await him as he got out

of the elevator, he released the near-empty magazine from the
pistol and replaced it with a full one.

SEMKO AND RACHEL had watched the two Russians grow more
anxious with each passing minute. The man across the street
glanced repeatedly at his watch, while the one closest to them
constantly looked up and down the sidewalk as though he expected disaster at any moment.

"Something's going down inside that building," Semko
said. "Look at those guys, they're as nervous as a chicken at a
voodoo ceremony.

"Stay here," he told Rachel, and got up to move to a spot
that would provide a view of the sidewalk in front of the building and still allow him to keep both men in sight. He began
walking slowly along the cobbled walkway at the far side of
the cul-de-sac when he saw a man come around the corner
from the direction of the entrance to One Sutton Place South.
The slope of the man's shoulders, the sharp, handsome features, and the way he moved told Semko that he had found
Strasser.

The Russian at the corner did a double take as the tall, lanky
man with dark blond hair brushed past him carrying a canvas
tarp folded under his arm. He was the same man who had
spotted Strasser earlier, and this time, after realizing he had
removed the coveralls and bandanna worn into the building, he
recognized him immediately. He spoke into his sleeve microphone, alerting his teammate across the street, who began
moving in his direction.

Semko froze in position behind a tree near the black Mercedes limousine parked at the curb. Earlier, he had seen the
chauffeur sitting at the wheel reading a newspaper, and judged
him to be precisely what he was. His eyes were now hard on
Strasser as he opened the side door of the minivan and placed
the tarp inside.

Semko looked back toward the bench at the entrance to the park and saw Rachel watching him closely. He motioned for her to take cover. She responded at once, moving behind another large tree close to the bench. Unnoticed by Semko, or anyone else, she slipped her hand into one end of her specially designed shoulder bag. The leather bag served as a normal purse carried over the shoulder, with the exception of a hidden compartment in the center that contained a holster for a weapon. The compartments on either side of the bag functioned as one would expect, but the center section was accessible from the outside through a tear-away Velcro closure at one end. The gun could be quickly brought into play by drawing it from inside the hidden section, or in extreme situations, fired directly through the other end of the bag. Rachel had pulled the Velcro strip open and stood calmly with her hand inside the center section, out of sight and wrapped around the grip of the Walther PPKS in the holster.

Semko's attention shifted to the Russian at the corner. He had seen him speaking into his sleeve, but was unsure of the man's affiliation. Were he and his partner part of Strasser's operation, or were they part of the Russian effort Brannigan had told him about? The question was answered by the Russian's body language; he placed his hand inside his jacket and kept it there as he walked cautiously toward the van.

Semko drew the Browning High-Power nine-millimeter pistol from the shoulder holster beneath his Windbreaker and flipped off the safety as he held the weapon down along the seam of his trousers. Out of the corner of his eye, he saw the second Russian cross the street and join his teammate just as Strasser closed the side door of the van and moved forward to climb into the driver's seat. Semko was about to make his move when the Russians preempted him.

Strasser had also seen the Russian speaking into his sleeve, and picked up on his teammate hurrying to join him. He continued to act casually, biding his time until they moved in. When they were within ten feet of the van, he angled his body away from them and withdrew the pistol from beneath his sweater. He opened the driver's side door and, using it as cover, raised the gun and fired.

The Russian closest to him fell to the sidewalk from a bullet that tore through his neck and embedded itself in his spine at the base of his skull, instantly paralyzing and killing him. The second Russian drew his weapon and dropped into a crouch. He got off two shots that missed their target and hit the door of the minivan before Strasser's return fire sent two bullets into the center of his chest and brought him down.

"Strasser!" Semko yelled from across the cul-de-sac, and clearly saw the startled look on the terrorist's face at hearing his name.

Strasser jumped into the van and started the engine as Semko broke from cover behind the tree and ran toward him, firing into the front passenger-side window. In the heat of the moment, obsessed with the hated adversary he had been hunting for three years, Semko had forgotten about shooting to incapacitate, in the event Strasser did not have the file the DDO wanted with him and needed to be questioned later. Instead he had shot to kill, and his three rapid-fire rounds splintered the glass and impacted in the support pillar forward of the steering column, missing Strasser's head by less than an inch.

The volley of gunfire from the Russian and Semko had brought the four UN bodyguards scrambling out of the Ford, their machine pistols held in the shoot-back position, safeties off, their fingers on the triggers. Two of them positioned themselves at the front entrance to the secretary general's residence, their heads swiveling back and forth as they tried to locate and identify the threat. The two remaining bodyguards, followed by the cop from the scooter, ran in the direction of the sound of the gunfire, fearing that the point of attack was at the rear of the official residence through the walled-in garden bordering the cul-de-sac.

The three men sprinted to the corner and swung wide, out into the center of the cul-de-sac, to see Semko fire another three rounds into the cab of the minivan, then dive to the pavement as the man at the wheel fired back—a defective shell casing, crimped at the base, failed to feed properly from the magazine into the chamber and caused Semko's gun to jam, sending him diving out of the line of fire.

At the sight of Semko dropping to the ground, Strasser slid over to the passenger-side window and took careful aim through the hole blown in the glass by the exchange of gunfire. Just as he was about to squeeze the trigger, two shots that he did not hear, fired by someone he could not see, struck the edge of the window, sending him scrambling back behind the steering wheel.

Semko had been desperately trying to clear his jammed weapon, and was also unaware of the timely covering fire that had saved his life. It was Rachel who had fired the shots, from thirty feet away and at a nearly impossible angle. The Walther PPKS she braced against the trunk of the tree to steady her aim was fitted with a highly advanced sound suppressor no larger in length or diameter than a roll of quarters and weighing less than four ounces. Constructed without mesh packing or wipes, its baffles forced the main propellant gas jet away from the bullet and into specially designed liquid environment cells where the gas was cooled at a much faster rate than with a conventional suppressor. The overall effect was to reduce the muzzle blast to little more than a loud hiss. When used in conjunction with subsonic ammunition, the only noise, unidentifiable to the untrained ear as being related to a gunshot, was the click of the Teflon-coated slide as it returned to pick up another round from the magazine.

Neither of the two bodyguards was aware of Rachel's presence at the far end of the cul-de-sac as they raised their machine pistols to take aim at the minivan. Uncertain of what they were dealing with, they assumed that the man behind the steering wheel had killed the two men on the sidewalk and still posed a possible threat to the secretary general. They stood in the direct path of the van, their weapons trained on the windshield. One of them kept a wary eye on Semko as he tried to clear his weapon, while the other shouted for Strasser to get out of the vehicle with his hands where they could see them.

Strasser put the van in gear, floored the accelerator, and headed directly for them. The two men fired sustained bursts into the windshield until one of them was hit head-on and run over, and the other was struck at an angle and thrown twenty feet from where he stood. The hail of bullets from the machine pistols blew out a large portion of the glass above Strasser's head a split second after he ducked low behind the dash. The cop, standing off to the side, tried desperately to get off an accurate shot from his service revolver, but Strasser veered toward him, forcing him to dive to the ground and roll out of the way.

Semko, having cleared the jammed round from his weapon, fired three shots through the rear windows of the fleeing van, but with no effect. "Goddamnit!" he shouted in his frustration at watching Strasser speed away. Then he remembered the limousine parked behind him. He turned and ran back to the far side of the cul-de-sac and pulled open the driver's door of the long, black Mercedes. The chauffeur, lying flat on the seat, cringed at the sight of Semko looming over him, a gun in his hand.

"Don't shoot me! Don't shoot me!" the frightened man cried out.

Semko grabbed him by the collar of his uniform coat and pulled him out of the car, then jumped inside and brought the powerful engine to life. The tires squealed as the heavy vehicle lurched forward, the rear end swaying as it roared out into the intersection.

Two cars, traveling in opposite directions on Sutton Place South, swerved to avoid colliding with the Mercedes as it sped across the avenue to Fifty-seventh Street. The cars smashed into each other, their momentum driving them into a third car and causing a pileup that blocked the street and brought traffic to a standstill.

Semko had the minivan in sight. It was weaving wildly in and out of heavy traffic as it neared the intersection at First Avenue. He relaxed somewhat when he saw the light up ahead change to red.

Strasser cursed aloud at the changing light and cut off a taxi before screeching to a halt. Only three cars prevented him from making a right turn onto First Avenue, but he could advance no farther in the bumper-to-bumper traffic. Cars parked at the curb on his right made it impossible for him to cut onto the sidewalk. A U-turn on the two-way street would have left him nowhere to go but back to the Sutton Place South intersection, and he already heard the wail of police sirens closing on the area. He looked in the side-view mirror and saw the big Mercedes attempting to angle its way through the line of cars idling behind him. He recognized it as Bancroft's car, and a brief glimpse of the face behind the wheel told him it was the man who had fired at him with almost deadly effect back in the cul-de-sac; the same man he had seen in Paris.

Semko considered jumping out of the car and running up to the van, but he realized that the light would probably change before he got there and he would only lose precious ground. He sounded the horn continuously and motioned for a man in a Volkswagen to move off to the side so he could squeeze through, but all he got was a single-digit salute.

The light turned green and the traffic began to creep forward. First Avenue was still crowded with cars that had not made it completely across the intersection when the light changed. Strasser inched his way forward and glanced up the avenue. The cars were moving even slower than they were on Fifty-seventh Street. He decided to continue heading west to Third Avenue, the next intersection allowing northbound traffic that would take him farther uptown. At the first opportunity, he swung into the opposite traffic lane and pulled around a delivery truck partially blocking the intersection, then continued across Fifty-seventh Street, where he cut off two drivers and forced them into cars parked at the curb.

Four of the cars in front of Semko turned right, clearing the way for him to close the gap. He saw Strasser cut hard to the inside lane and force a BMW up onto the sidewalk, then ignore the red light and speed across Second Avenue. Semko had no choice but to follow suit. The oncoming traffic on the eastbound side of the two-way street was stopped by the light, and he pulled into the opposite lanes just as a city bus turned right off Second Avenue and swung wide into his path. He sideswiped the lumbering vehicle and continued on through the intersection where he struck another car and sent it into a spin.

Strasser was less than ten yards from the intersection at Third Avenue when he was again bogged down in the relentless traffic. His eyes swept quickly over the area ahead to a broad patch of sidewalk in front of an office building at the corner. He pressed the accelerator to the floor, rammed a small foreign car in front of him, and drove it into the car ahead of it. He continued to push both vehicles forward, opening a space that allowed him to jump the curb and cut across the sidewalk.

Pedestrians screamed and scattered as he roared up onto the walkway and almost lost control of the van when he smashed into a newspaper kiosk before bouncing down off the curb onto Third Avenue. A cop car responding to the "officer needs assistance'' and ''shots fired'' calls at Sutton Place South was using his siren and lights to get through the intersection when he saw the crazy stunt. He made the connection upon seeing the van's bullet-riddled windshield, and gave pursuit. He had no sooner swung into action than he locked his bumper with the loading platform of a furniture truck he rear-ended when it cut sharply to the left to avoid Strasser.

The broad, five-lane avenue was one-way northbound, and traffic was spread out and moving quickly. Strasser gained two blocks before Semko rounded the corner from Fifty-seventh Street.

A symphony of honking horns, angry drivers screaming obscenities, and screeching brakes followed Semko as he weaved the limousine recklessly in and out of the fast-moving cars, his eyes searching the street ahead for the van. Just when he thought he had lost him, he saw Strasser swerve from the center lane two blocks ahead and broadside a westbound car with a glancing blow as he took the corner at Sixty-first Street.

Semko cut to the inside lane and closed the distance to one block by the time he took the same corner on two wheels. He saw Strasser up ahead, speeding through the intersection at Lexington Avenue, only to come to an abrupt halt as the driver of a Volvo station wagon blocked the narrow street in his attempt to back into a parallel parking space. The man misjudged the angle, and pulled forward to try again, when Strasser simply rammed him out of the way.

Semko reached the Lexington Avenue intersection to see the van roar across Park just as the light turned green. The three cars that remained between them turned onto Lexington, and Semko gained more ground. He raced toward the Park Avenue intersection, now less than one hundred yards behind Strasser as he continued heading west toward Madison Avenue. The light was still green, giving Semko a clear path, until an old

lady walking a meticulously groomed white miniature poodle
with a pink bow on its head stepped into the crosswalk.

It took all of Semko's high-speed driving skills, learned
during his years with Delta Force, to avoid running the old
woman down. His speed was in excess of seventy miles an
hour when he slammed on the brakes and swerved up onto the
sidewalk at the corner. He sheared off a lamppost and tore a
street sign from its foundation before bouncing down off the
curb onto Park Avenue and into an uncontrollable skid that
spun the huge Mercedes across the northbound traffic lanes
and up onto the center island, where it rolled over on its side in
the middle of a bed of tulips.

Uninjured except for a sore shoulder and a welt where his
head had struck the steering wheel, Semko released his seat
belt and shoulder harness, forced open the door, and pulled
himself out of the limousine. He kicked at one of the headlights in a rage of frustration, then remembered Rachel and ran
off the far side of the median strip, where he jumped into a
taxi stopped at the light in the southbound lane.

"Sutton Place South," he told the driver, who had watched
the entire incident.

"You just gonna leave that there?"

"I got a permit to park anywhere I want."

The driver nodded knowingly as he turned on the meter and
pulled away from the light. "It's like I've been tellin' people
for years. In this city, you got the money, you can do whatever.
But if you don't mind my sayin' so, pal, you oughta get a
chauffeur for that thing. 'Cause you ain't exactly no candidate
for driver of the year. Know what I mean?"

« 25 »

Jonathan Westcott handed Strasser the first aid kit he kept in his office desk, then stood nervously by watching him clean and dress the small laceration where the bullet had scraped his rib cage.

"I want those paintings out of here as soon as possible," Strasser said as he pulled on his shirt.

"My assistant is crating them now," Westcott said, gesturing toward the gallery workroom. "He'll have them at the Austrian Airlines air freight section in about an hour; they'll go out on the six-fifteen flight to Vienna."

"Make sure your assistant stays in the workroom and leaves for the airport by the front exit. I don't want him seeing my face."

"He knows nothing about you." Nor does he want to, Westcott thought.

"Keep it that way."

The small television on the table across from the desk caught Strasser's attention, and he turned up the volume. It was tuned to CNN, where he had heard the news bulletin about the shootings at Sutton Place South as he came in the rear door of the gallery after eluding Semko. The initial report had been sketchy, attributing the incident to an attempt on the life of the secretary general of the United Nations. An on-location update was announced, and the scene switched from the studio news room to a reporter in the street.

The reporter was still attributing the incident to ''a well-coordinated, highly professional, but fortunately unsuccessful attempt on the secretary general's life.'' The face of the studio anchor again filled the screen and began speculating about a possible conspiracy.

''Morons,'' Strasser said, and switched off the television.

''Do the police know it was you?''

''Someone does, but I don't think it's the police,'' Strasser said, still bothered by how the man who had called out his name had learned his true identity.

He was even more disturbed at how the man had known Bancroft would be his next victim. Maybe he had gotten lucky and somehow paper-traced him to New York from Paris and put him under surveillance. It was possible the Canadian passport, and the supporting documents he had used at the hotel and car rental agency, were compromised. He would have to change identities before leaving the city.

He closed his eyes to envision the face of the man who had chased him in the limousine. When he had first seen him in Paris, he thought he recognized him, and assumed he was a Mossad operative. But it was an irreconcilable assumption; he had never had any direct confrontations with the Mossad until Paris, and he had seen this man somewhere before that. Strasser switched his train of thought to where the answer was most likely to be found; who could have learned his real name? A counter-terrorist organization? Yes. But which one? CIA? The man dressed like an American. Delta Force? There had been a confrontation with them . . . in Düsseldorf, three years ago.

''Düsseldorf,'' he said aloud, and it all came back to him. The Delta Force assault on the safe house apartment. He had killed two of them and wounded a third, if he remembered correctly. The man he had wounded had fired at him and missed just before he dived out the window, and it was at that moment when he had stared into his eyes. Yes. It was the same man. He was certain of it. But there had been no Delta Force unit in Paris; the man had acted alone. Perhaps the men he had killed in Bancroft's apartment building and on the street were part of a Delta Force team, but he doubted it. Their weapons and less-than-professional tactics suggested otherwise. Too many people seemed to be closing in on him much sooner than he had expected, but at least he was finished in New York and would soon be operating on more familiar ground.

"Call Drussard," Strasser told Westcott. "Tell him you have the last two paintings from the New York list and that I will contact him tonight."

SEMKO GOT OUT of the taxi to see at least a dozen radio patrol cars and numerous unmarked police cars angled into the curb in the immediate area of One Sutton Place South. The service entrance of the apartment building and the cul-de-sac were cordoned off with hastily erected barricades, and three ambulances and two windowless vans from the Mortuary Division blocked the northbound lane of the avenue, causing traffic to be directed through the single lane left open. A throng of reporters and mobile television news crews shoved their way through the crowd of onlookers gathered at the barricades and along the sidewalk, pointing cameras and shouting questions at any cop who looked their way.

With the discovery of Philip Bancroft's death, twenty-five detectives had been brought in from Borough Command to augment the task force investigating what the press had labeled the "Art Murders." The detectives canvassed the area, some taking down the license numbers of all the vehicles parked along both sides of the street and questioning anyone who had witnessed the shootings in the cul-de-sac, while others conducted door-to-door inquiries throughout Bancroft's apartment building and those apartments directly across the street that fronted on Sutton Place South.

Semko crossed the street in the direction of the barricaded cul-de-sac where a crime scene unit was gathering forensic evidence. He saw the cop from the scooter sitting at the rear of an ambulance, his arm in a sling, talking to a plainclothes cop who was surrounded by enough brass to fill a Pentagon corridor.

Rachel was nowhere in sight, and Semko moved through the sidewalk crowd to get a closer look inside the cul-de-sac, being careful to stay out of view of the cop from the scooter. He saw that the bodies of the two men Strasser had shot had been removed; chalk outlines marked where they had fallen. One of the UN bodyguards lay on a stretcher near another of the ambulances, waiting to be taken to the hospital. His partner, the man Semko had seen Strasser hit head-on and run over, was being zipped into a body bag.

Semko was still searching the crowd for Rachel when a loud gasp from a woman behind him caused him to look toward the apartment building. Four attendants from the Mortuary Division, assisted by a host of uniformed cops, emerged from the service entrance to One Sutton Place South. They carried what seemed to be an endless procession of body bags. Semko counted six, and one man on a stretcher with his head bandaged.

He turned his attention back in the direction of the cul-de-sac, and it was then that he saw Rachel. She was sitting in the rear seat of an unmarked police car parked just outside the barricaded area, her hands cuffed behind her back. Two patrolmen stood beside the open door of the car guarding her. Semko began to move toward her, hoping to catch her eye, when a loud voice rose above the constant chatter of the crowd.

"That's him! That's the one who stole Mr. Bancroft's limousine!" It was the chauffeur, standing just inside the police line and pointing directly at him.

Semko stood his ground as four uniformed cops approached. A plainclothes cop who appeared to be in charge broke off a conversation with one of his detectives and the two men immediately came over to where Semko stood surrounded by the uniformed patrol officers.

The cop from the scooter saw the commotion and recognized Semko. "He was with the woman, Lieutenant," he called out from where he sat at the back of the ambulance.

"Mike Semko," Semko said as the lieutenant stopped in front of him. He extended his hand only to have it ignored.

"Lieutenant Kelly," Kelly said, then spoke to one of the uniformed officers. "Pat him down for weapons, cuff him, and read him his rights."

"Before this goes any further, Lieutenant, you might want to call the commanding officer of your Intelligence Division, Deputy Chief Conlon," Semko said, giving the name Brannigan had told him to use if the need arose.

Kelly waved off the patrolman who was about to frisk Semko. "Check it out," he told the detective sergeant next to him.

"You on the job?" Kelly said to Semko, thinking that perhaps someone at the Intelligence Division had assigned undercover officers to his case without telling him.

"No."

"Then what?"

"Maybe we ought to wait until your man makes the call."

"That woman was with you?" Kelly asked, gesturing to Rachel, who was now aware of Semko's presence.

"Yeah. She's with me."

"You were involved in the shootout here?"

Semko confirmed that he was with a simple nod of his head.

"You care to elaborate on that?"

"Guy fired at me. I fired back. I tried to catch him. He got away."

"According to the chauffeur, you fired at him first."

"Could have happened that way."

Kelly's temper flared. "Look, Semko, I want some straight answers, and I want them now! I've got nine dead bodies on my hands; that's a goddamn massacre even in this city."

Semko had a long-standing respect for cops, especially those who served in large metropolitan areas, and he did not want to be any more uncooperative than necessary. He pointed to the chalk outlines on the pavement inside the barricades.

"I saw those two go down from shots fired by the guy in the van. I fired at him; he fired at me. Then he ran over two UN security people, and I grabbed the limo and chased him."

"Who was driving the van?"

"I'm not sure," Semko said, remembering the DDO's admonition about not wanting anyone to get to Strasser before he did.

"You're not sure who the guy was, but you opened fire on him?"

"Seemed like the thing to do."

"You're pissing me off, Semko."

"I've told you what happened, as far as what I saw and did."

"But you're not telling me why, smartass. How was it you found yourself in the middle of all this?"

"Just lucky, I guess."

Kelly reached the limits of his patience just as the detective he had sent to call the commanding officer of the Intelligence Division appeared at his side.

"He and the woman are cleared all the way up to the commissioner," the detective said.

"Cleared for what?" Kelly snapped.

"The deputy chief didn't say. Just that it was 'hands off' unless they're interfering with your investigation."

"They sure as shit aren't helping it any," Kelly said. "Release the woman and tell her I want to talk to her," he told the detective, and then turned back to Semko. "What are you two? FBI?"

"There's no call for insults, Lieutenant."

Kelly allowed a small smile, harboring his own small resentment for an agency he knew to have some of the best and some of the worst people working for it. He seldom saw anything but the latter, who on more than one occasion, when he had been forced to cooperate with them, had run roughshod over his investigations.

"You obviously got some clout behind you, Semko, so there's not much I can do about your uncooperative attitude. But if there's anything else you can tell me about what went down here, I'd appreciate hearing it."

"I've got nothing that's going to help your investigation."

"Why don't you let me be the judge of that?"

"I've told you what I can."

"And how about you?" Kelly said to Rachel, who had reached Semko's side in time to hear part of the conversation. She had said nothing upon being detained by the cop from the scooter when he saw her trying to leave the cul-de-sac after Semko drove away.

"Sorry, Lieutenant, I don't know any more than he does."

"Lieutenant!" a uniformed patrolman called out as he ran up to Kelly. "We just got a report on a fire at Sixty-third and Madison."

"So? What the hell do I care about a fire?"

"It's at an art gallery," the patrolman said. "They pulled a guy out, dead from a gunshot wound to the head. And they found a red-and-white minivan parked in the alley behind the place. Windshield's full of bullet holes.''

"Take over here," Kelly said to the detective sergeant standing beside him, then called to another detective to come with him as he went to his car.

"Mind if we go along?" Semko said.

Kelly looked at Semko, then Rachel, believing they knew a great deal more than they were telling him and hoping to find out as much as he could. "I take it we're on the same side?"

"We're after the same person, just for different reasons," Semko allowed.

"Then maybe a little cooperation might be in order."

"I'll do what I can."

"The two you saw shot down on the sidewalk, and four more inside the building were Russians with diplomatic passports," Kelly said, now strongly suspecting with whom Semko and Rachel were affiliated. "You know anything about that?"

"Only what you just told me."

"Yeah, right. Get in the car."

As Semko opened the rear door for Rachel, he saw the man he had pulled out of the limousine approaching.

"Hey!" the chauffeur shouted. "Where's Mr. Bancroft's car?"

"I left it uptown," Semko called back. "At the corner of Sixty-first and Park Avenue."

"Where are the keys?"

"In the ignition. But don't worry, it's parked where nobody will bother it."

In spite of himself, Kelly had to laugh. He had already received a report that the limousine had been found overturned in the center island on Park Avenue.

"You're a real piece of work, Semko."

"Guy's going to be upset enough when he finds it," Semko said, then slid into the backseat beside Rachel. "You okay?"

"Just fine."

"I told you it was going to get rough."

"And you were right."

"I'm glad you had enough sense to stay out of the way."

"Me too."

A PASSERBY ON Madison Avenue, who had stopped to admire the paintings in the gallery windows, had seen the smoke as it began to curl under Westcott's office door and drift out into the exhibition room. Finding the entrance to the gallery locked, she had rushed into the antiques shop next door and called the fire department in time for them to confine the worst of the damage to the rear of the building.

The captain from the fire department told Kelly that the fire was deliberately set, probably intended to cover up the murder. He further surmised that the propellant had been gasoline, used to saturate the office area; an empty five-gallon can was found in the alley beside the van.

"Looks like whoever did it was trying to get rid of some documents, too," the captain said. "A bunch of papers from the file cabinets, an address book, and some other stuff too charred to recognize were thrown in a pile and doused with gas."

Upon seeing the name of the gallery, Semko had recognized it as being midway down his list of those suspected of dealing in stolen art. While Kelly and the detective with him examined the van parked in the alley, he and Rachel slipped into the office by way of the rear door and moved slowly through the smoky ruins.

Rachel copied down the phone number still visible on the scorched and partially melted base of a telephone separate from the multiline unit that served the gallery.

"It's probably a private line," she said to Semko, who had given her a questioning look. "We can have someone check the telephone company records. See what calls were placed during the past few days."

"Good thinking."

"I have my moments," Rachel said, and followed Semko as he picked his way through the charred debris to the open door of the workroom adjoining the office.

The fire had done only minimal damage to the small room before being extinguished, and Rachel saw a canvas tarp lying on the floor beneath a long work table.

"Isn't that the tarp Strasser put in the back of his van?"

"Looks like it," Semko said.

Rachel examined a small stack of thick wooden slats and heavily padded wrapping paper at one end of a work table.

"What's that stuff?" Semko said.

"Crating material. Used for packaging paintings for shipment."

"Shit!" Semko said. He had no doubts that the gallery owner was Strasser's local contact for the art underground, and his death and the scraps of crating material only confirmed what he already suspected. Strasser had finished his business in the city. "He's gone."

"I was just thinking the same thing," Rachel said as Kelly appeared in the doorway of the workroom.

"The man they pulled out of here died from a single gunshot wound fired into his eye socket," he said to Semko. "The same way Philip Bancroft, one of the victims at One Sutton Place South, was killed. Not your usual MO for an art thief, wouldn't you say?"

"Bancroft was an art collector?" Semko asked.

"Yeah. With more money than God. Why?"

"How did he earn his money?" Rachel interrupted before Semko could answer.

"Bancroft Industries," Kelly said. "Laser-guided weapons, Star Wars–type stuff."

"And Stewart and Cabot?"

"Stewart was just your ordinary run-of-the-mill old man with a couple hundred million; Cabot was a retired diplomat, old money," Kelly said. "Now that I gave you a little, how about something in return?"

Semko pointed out the tarp beneath the work table and told Kelly what he had witnessed when he first saw Strasser. "There were probably paintings wrapped inside it," he added, then indicated the crating material on top of the table. "And by the looks of this, they're already in the pipeline to somewhere."

"Well, this guy you say you're not sure you know finally made a mistake," Kelly said.

"What's that?"

"His prints are all over the van parked out in the alley."

"They won't do you any good."

"And why not? You're telling me there's not a jacket on this guy somewhere in the world?"

"I'm telling you he's a pro who's never cared a damn about leaving prints behind before. Which means nobody's got him on file."

"All right, Semko. Give me a break, will you? Just who, or what, the hell are we dealing with?"

"He's finished here," was all Semko said in response.

"Who's finished here?"

"The man we're both after."

"Come on, I need more than that."

"If he isn't on his way out of the country by now, he will be soon. Your problems with him are over."

"Well, my investigation sure as hell isn't. Including today's bloodbath, I've got thirteen open homicide cases ranging from a grocery store delivery boy to Russians with diplomatic passports, not to mention three high-profile citizens. Throw in the guy they pulled out of here, and that makes fourteen.''

"I've got nothing for you right now, Lieutenant. But you have my word that when, and if, I can, I'll give you what you need to close your cases."

"When and if, huh? My two least favorite words."

"Beats the hell out of can't and won't."

« 26 »

Nikolai Leonov anxiously paced the floor of his office on the eighth floor of the Russian mission as he listened to the report from Boris Voslensky, the man he had sent to Bellevue Hospital to interview the lone survivor of the surveillance unit at One Sutton Place South. The Russian whom Strasser had wounded suffered a concussion from the bullet that creased his skull, but he was awake and lucid enough to reveal a crucial observation that stunned Leonov when Voslensky returned to the mission to brief him on what he had learned.

"For the two years prior to the dissolution of the East German state," Voslensky said, "he was posted to Stasi headquarters in East Berlin as KGB's liaison for the Second Chief Directorate's Section for Extraordinary Matters. It was his first assignment upon completing his training, and, in the course of his duties, he visited the terrorist training camp at Massow. It was there that he met and had brief conversations with Jurgen Strasser on five separate occasions during that two-year period."

"And he's certain that this Strasser is the man who shot him?"

"He is positive."

"Does he know what Strasser's duties were at Massow?"

"He remembers him as being the senior instructor."

"Was there anything else?"

"Nothing other than his sincere apologies for having failed in his duties."

"I want a full written report on my desk within the hour," Leonov said and escorted Voslensky from the office. Just as he was about to close the door, he saw a short, overweight man exit the elevator and rush down the hall toward him.

"Colonel Leonov?" the man gasped as he tried to catch his breath. "I am Viktor Kuzin. I was told to report to you immediately."

"Come in, Kuzin," Leonov said, and directed him to sit in one of the chairs at a small grouping of furniture at one end of the office.

Leonov went to his desk and retrieved a file folder, then returned to sit on the sofa opposite Kuzin. "I am told that you are an expert on art, particularly the art treasures stolen and destroyed throughout Europe during the Great Patriotic War," Leonov said, using the Russian term for World War II.

"I have a graduate degree in fine arts from the Academy of Science," Kuzin said, still breathless and perspiring from the hurried trip uptown from his office at the United Nations.

"It is my understanding that you were at one time involved with our own questionable art collections from that period."

Judging from the urgency of his summons to appear at Leonov's office, and the high authority from which that summons had come, Kuzin had no doubt what agency of his government Leonov represented, and had no intention of holding back any information the man wanted.

"I was in charge of the administration and maintenance of the various repositories that contain the collections you are referring to," Kuzin said, choosing his words carefully.

"You are familiar with the recent art thefts here in the city?"

"Only what I've read in the newspapers."

"I want you to look at this list of paintings," Leonov said, removing a neatly typed document from the folder.

The document contained a listing of the paintings missing since World War II that Leonov knew to be in the possession of the eleven original men in the Goering File. None of their names appeared on the list he had prepared from the master file, only the titles of the paintings and the artists to whom they were attributed. Although he had no verification of any paintings having been stolen from Bancroft that day, he had included in the list of those already stolen the two he knew Bancroft had in his collection.

"Those in the column on the left belonged to the men who were murdered," he told Kuzin. "Those in the column on the right are paintings that have been missing since 1945."

Kuzin examined both columns. He was familiar with most of the paintings. "And what do you wish to know, Colonel?"

"Judging from what has already been stolen, can you determine a pattern of selection, and if so, which of the paintings in the column on the right do you believe would most likely be stolen next, rating them in order of highest probability."

"Using their monetary value as a criterion?" Kuzin asked.

"If that is the most logical procedure."

"It would seem to be one of the considerations, in view of the recent circumstances surrounding those in the column on the left."

Kuzin sat back in his chair, remaining silent for what seemed an eternity to Leonov. When he finally looked up from studying the document and spoke it was with the authority and conviction of a man who knew his subject matter well.

"The eight paintings listed as already stolen are mostly of one school and period, heavily represented by impressionist and postimpressionist. However, I do not believe they were selected on that basis, but rather for their commercial desirability and their similar provenances."

"Provenances?"

"Individual histories," Kuzin explained. "All eight of the paintings, to the best of my knowledge, are not missing from well-known museum collections, which would make it very difficult, if not impossible, to establish legal ownership if they were. They are, I believe, from private collections that would not pose the same legal questions if well-forged documents accompanied them."

"Then apply those principles of selection to the paintings listed in the column on the right."

Leonov watched patiently as Kuzin began numbering all twenty-seven paintings, giving those that fell into both categories (most commercially desirable and those he knew not to have been in museum collections) the highest ratings.

"Please take into consideration, Colonel, that my evaluations for those I selected for their current value on the illegal market are purely subjective," Kuzin said as he handed the list back to Leonov. "But I believe they are a reasonable reflection of their enticement to collectors given the other parameter of the selection process."

"Thank you," Leonov said. He then leaned closer to Kuzin, his voice low and ominous and filled with the full weight and power of his authority. "You will discuss our conversation with no one. Is that understood? No one!"

"Of course, Colonel. I will say nothing."

Kuzin, more than a little distressed by Leonov's intimidating presence, used his handkerchief to mop his damp brow as he got up to leave. The old days were not so distant that he could not recall the terror the KGB had struck in the hearts of his countrymen, and he was astute enough not to underestimate their successors, no matter what they now called themselves.

With Kuzin gone, Leonov immediately went over the art expert's selections. The two paintings Kuzin had given the highest ratings were ones Leonov knew had once belonged to Oliver Cummings of Boston, the remaining American from the original group. Cummings, a man of considerable inherited wealth and a career Foreign Service officer like Cabot, had died nine years ago. Before retiring from the State Department he had managed to recruit three promising replacements: a diplomat currently serving as deputy chief of mission at the American embassy in Syria, a high-level staffer on the Senate Select Committee on Intelligence, and a brilliant analyst who had recently joined the staff of the National Security Council.

Cummings's art collection had been bequeathed to a Boston museum, and his daughters, his sole surviving heirs, were both inconsequential trust-fund dropouts, married and divorced, and held no interest for Leonov and were never approached. With Strasser's apparent interest being solely in stealing paintings for resale on the illegal market, it was safe to assume that if he researched his victims during the selection process, which Leonov strongly suspected he did with some outside help, neither of the women would be likely targets.

It was Kuzin's second- and third-highest selections that drew Leonov's attention. The paintings in the possession of Gianfranco Falcone of Florence, Italy, and Herbert Darcy-Williams of London, England. Both men had paintings that were, according to Kuzin, highly prized by collectors, and had come from private collections.

Of the two men, Falcone was the less important, no longer being of any real value to Leonov's operations. An old man in his early nineties and retired from his position as head of a family-owned international banking concern, Falcone had long ago served his purpose by recruiting four replacements within the Italian government and the banking industry. The murders of Stewart and Cabot, because of the discovery of the stolen art from World War II, had received international press coverage, and although any similar fate befalling Falcone held the possibility of causing those he recruited to panic, that was not a primary concern for Leonov at the moment. The Englishman, however, was an entirely different matter.

A second-generation agent, Herbert Darcy-Williams was one of the most valuable, if not *the* most valuable, operative agents in the Goering File, the only one to have penetrated the upper levels of a Western intelligence agency. His father, a wealthy aristocrat and a former member of Parliament, had died twelve years ago, but not before recruiting his son, his only child, under threat of having the family name disgraced. The son, a somewhat pompous and arrogant man, who took great pride in his title of baronet—a hereditary title ranking next below that of baron—had, at the time of his recruitment fourteen years ago, just received his PPE—Philosophy, Politics, and Economics—degree from Balliol College, Oxford. After much prodding by the illegal who handled him, he joined the British SIS (Secret Intelligence Service, equivalent to the CIA and often mistakenly called MI-6), where he had gone on to hold positions in areas where Leonov could only have dreamed of placing an agent.

Darcy-Williams had been inside Century House (the modern, nineteen-story office tower on Westminster Bridge Road in London that houses SIS headquarters) for most of his career, spending much of his time with the NATO Desk that handled all intelligence liaison with Great Britain's allies (except the CIA, which has a separate desk). Three years ago he was reassigned, as an area specialist, to the staff at the SIS training facility at Fort Monckton near Gosport on the south coast of England. The paramount importance of this reassignment to Leonov was to be found in the fact that there were few, if any, covert operators in British intelligence who, when preparing for top-secret missions, or before being posted to an

SIS station abroad, did not go through training courses at Fort Monckton—or the SIS training center in Lambeth, South London, where Darcy-Williams also taught on a rotating basis—putting him in a position to learn the identities, and assignments, of a large majority of the new recruits and covert field operatives in the SIS.

Darcy-Williams's highly sensitive position and personality quirks, however, posed certain problems for Leonov, and warning him of impending danger from Strasser held its own perils. A nervous and occasionally paranoid type, fully aware of his importance to Leonov and often unresponsive to specific direction, he had always been a problem to handle—periodically missing three or more scheduled checks of his dead drop and staying out of touch for months at a time. With the demise of the Soviet Union, he became increasingly difficult, fearing, although Leonov had gone to great lengths to reassure him those fears were unfounded, that he would be exposed by one or more of the KGB officers who had defected to the British following the failed coup in August of 1991. Leonov could only imagine the psychological state of the man if he was aware of the fate of Strasser's victims in New York City and the common ground he shared with them.

The current Russian illegal intelligence officer servicing Darcy-Williams had never actually met the man. The illegal who had originally handled both the father and the son retired shortly after the old man's death, and Leonov, at Darcy-Williams's insistence, had restricted all contact with his new handler to dead-letter drops; it was a prudent arrangement, given his erratic behavior and extremely sensitive position inside the SIS.

Any attempt to put him under even the most discreet protective surveillance, as had been done with Bancroft, held the possibility of not only compromising him, but if he noticed the surveillance and mistook it as a threat from his own side, there was no way of predicting which way he would turn. Despite the risks, Leonov knew that arrangements had to be made to warn him to find some credible premise for dropping out of sight until Strasser could be eliminated.

There had never been any reason to enact the emergency contact procedures devised to alert him of imminent danger—a call at home by his illegal leaving an innocuous message that would alert him to check his primary dead drop immediately. The message left at the dead drop would then instruct him to call his illegal at a public telephone number to discuss at length the urgent business that had prompted the emergency contact.

Leonov's other problem also weighed heavily. Only the original and one copy of the Goering File were believed to have ever existed: the original found in the truckload of official files and personal papers captured by a Soviet army unit at a roadblock near Karinhall, the reich marshal's estate north of Berlin, and the copy retrieved from Goering's administrative aide, Egon Hofer, at the home of his sister in Salzburg shortly after the end of the war.

But now someone had found a previously unknown copy of the file, and the problem was compounded by that someone's being a former East German intelligence officer who might at any moment realize that what had fallen into his hands was far more valuable, if sold to the highest bidder among the western intelligence agencies, than any amount he could hope to get for all of the paintings on the list combined. It was as potentially disastrous a situation as Leonov could have imagined, but so far there was no reason to believe that Strasser had any idea of the file's true value. At least now, Leonov thought, he knew with whom and what he was dealing, and with a little luck and proper timing, he could get to Strasser before any further damage was done to his operations.

After instructing the secretary assigned to him to book him

on the next available flight to London, using the name from the second of four sets of diplomatic identification documents in his possession, he sent an urgent cable to Yasenevo. The message was "eyes only" for Yevgeny Primakov, head of the External Intelligence Service, requesting any and all information in their files on Jurgen Strasser, formerly of East German State Security. He hoped that Primakov, with his knowledge of the international terrorist community, might know of Strasser, or of someone who did and could provide him with a photograph and in-depth background, and have the information waiting for him when he got to London.

Leonov next drafted a coded message, written on a one-time pad for which only the illegal servicing Darcy-Williams held the key. He cabled the message, using a back channel, to the *rezident* at the Russian embassy in London, along with instructions on how to contact the illegal immediately.

In light of Darcy-Williams's two residences—a house in London, and an ancestral family home in the country not far from the Russian-owned estate at Flimwell in East Sussex used by their ambassador to Great Britain—Leonov included additional instructions to the London *rezident*. He was to have two separate protective surveillance units put on standby: one at a London safe house, and one at the Flimwell estate. They were to await further instructions upon his arrival. Aware that Strasser could not reach London more than a few hours ahead of him, and certain that he would carefully plan his approach to the Englishman, Leonov felt no compulsion to begin the protective surveillance any sooner than was absolutely necessary; bearing in mind that if Darcy-Williams's illegal made immediate contact with him, the surveillance would not be at all necessary.

Returning from the code-and-communications room on the seventh floor, Leonov went to the small apartment provided for him in the mission and packed his personal belongings. The television in the sitting room was on and tuned to CNN, the station where he had heard the first reports on the Sutton Place debacle on the set in his office. A commentator was summing up what had been learned so far and showing film footage of the scene shortly after the police arrived. The press now knew that Philip Bancroft, and not the secretary general of the United Nations, was the target of the killer, and was yet another victim in the Art Murders case.

Leonov's stomach tightened into an uncomfortable knot as he watched the shots of the body bags being carried from the apartment building earlier that afternoon—some he knew contained the remains of the Russian surveillance team. He was about to switch off the set when the commentator went on to report that the police could not, or would not, identify a man and a woman believed to have been involved in a related exchange of gunfire with the killer at the scene prior to the arrival of the police. A brief shot of a limousine lying on its side in the middle of Park Avenue was described as the result of a high-speed chase through the city streets in which the unidentified man had pursued the man believed to be the assailant.

The implications of the report were not lost on Leonov. If the unidentified man and woman who were on the scene before the police were CIA, there was every reason to suspect they knew far more than he had imagined, and it was not illogical to assume that what they were searching for was the copy of the Goering File now in Strasser's possession.

Leonov put a halt to the paranoia, aware that the pressure he was under was causing him to project his own concerns into what could well be a totally unrelated incident. It was possible that the CIA was hunting Jurgen Strasser for any number of reasons, and finding him, had placed him under surveillance before closing in, only to have him lead them to Sutton Place South.

The CIA could have tied Leonov's arrival in New York to a parallel hunt for Strasser, or their surveillance of him when he went to meet Bancroft's illegal could just as well have been due to his unknown status as a diplomat. Whatever the reason, they would certainly have no difficulty learning of his departure regardless of the change of identity, and would pass him on to their London station for continued surveillance upon his arrival there. With no time for elaborate counter-surveillance measures, he dismissed the matter as beyond his control. He had no intentions of making any direct contact with Darcy-Williams's illegal, and once Strasser was found, he would orchestrate his capture or elimination from a distance, so he had no immediate concern of leading the CIA to Strasser before he could find him. As long as they did not have access to information that would enable them to predict where and when Strasser would strike next—and without the Goering File there was no way they could—Leonov felt he still had the upper hand.

As he left the mission by the rear exit and climbed into the car to be driven to the airport, he was feeling much less confident and enthusiastic about his first field assignment. The glow was off the novel and heady experience, and he found himself thinking wistfully of the unhurried pace of his office and the more mundane and analytical methodology of an operation that had, until a few days ago, run smoothly for over forty-five years.

MIKE SEMKO AND Rachel Sidrane had gone to the CIA safe house on West Sixty-eighth Street after leaving the scene of the gallery fire. It was just after six-thirty in the evening when Semko got the return call he was waiting for from Jack Brannigan, the CIA's deputy director for Operations.

"Give your sidekick an 'atta girl' for me," Brannigan said. "The unlisted telephone number from the gallery paid off.

There were nine calls in the last six days to a gallery in Paris, owned by a man by the name of Claude Drussard. Interpol says he's a shady character who's been involved in the illegal art market for the past thirty years.''

"You think that's where Strasser's headed?"

"No. He's most likely on his way to London."

"Why London?"

"The Russian my counterintelligence chief's people have been tailing is just about to board a British Airways flight to Heathrow Airport. Leaves at seven and gets in at six forty-five tomorrow morning."

"And he's the one hunting Strasser?"

"What do you think? Two hours after he showed up in New York the shit hit the fan."

"How does he know Strasser's going to London?"

"Let's just say we have reason to believe he has information we don't and leave it at that," was how Brannigan answered the question.

"You're not hamstringing me on this, are you, Jack?"

"You have my word that you're getting everything you need to complete your mission. Nothing, and I mean absolutely nothing, is being left out that could help you get Strasser."

"What about this Drussard character?"

"I've instructed the Paris station to sit on him until further notice."

"Stevenson and his crew? You've got to be kidding! If Strasser shows up he'll eat them for breakfast."

"We've got a time element to contend with, Mike. We've got to go with the assets we have in place. Stevenson's instructions if Strasser shows are to have his people continue the surveillance until you and your people can get into position."

"How soon can you get me to London?"

"One of our Gulf Stream IV's is inbound for LaGuardia Airport right now," Brannigan said, checking the time on one of the wall clocks inside the twenty-four-hour operations center at Langley. "They'll be waiting for you at the Marine Air Terminal. Should put you in London within an hour of the Russian. And we checked the airline schedules; Strasser can't arrive much sooner no matter which flight he takes out of New York, Boston, or Toronto, which are the most likely points of departure for him."

"You going to have someone watching the London airports?"

"Both Gatwick and Heathrow," Brannigan said. "But your description of him isn't much to go on, plus he's probably disguised himself, and there's no guarantee he's going to take a direct flight."

"I'd rather you pull them. He's more likely to spot them first."

"Consider it done."

"You might want to send some of the guys from my snatch team over," Semko said. "So they'll be in place when I need them."

"My deputy tells me there are some old friends of yours already over there," Brannigan said. "A Delta Force troop at the British SAS base at Hereford. They've been there for the past two weeks on a cross-training exercise. Thought I'd put a team together from them if it's okay with you."

"Perfect."

"They'll be on standby alert. Check in with me when you get to London for any further updates."

"Roger," Semko said, and hung up. "We're off to London," he told Rachel, who had already drawn that conclusion from the side of the conversation she had overheard.

"If Strasser is going to follow the same pattern, he'll be using a local gallery tied to the art underground," Rachel said. "I'll tell my support team to notify our London people to have a list of the most likely suspects waiting for us when we get there.''

''I don't want them anywhere near anyplace Strasser might turn up.''

''You've made that perfectly clear.''

Semko gathered the few things he had unpacked at the safe house and stuffed them into his leather carry-on as Rachel called her Mossad support team across town. Semko's mood changed from one of anger and frustration at losing Strasser to one of eager anticipation at the promise of another chance at him.

The private jet provided by Brannigan was waiting on the tarmac outside the Marine Air Terminal, its engines idling, when Rachel and Semko arrived. They were airborne within ten minutes and headed out over the Atlantic as the last of the evening light faded into night.

JURGEN STRASSER HAD gone directly from the gallery on Madison Avenue to his hotel room, where he quickly packed and once again altered his appearance. He had made the Air Canada flight leaving LaGuardia for Toronto at four o'clock with only minutes to spare.

His hair again dyed brown, and wearing contacts that turned his blue eyes green, he settled into the first-class seat aboard Air Canada flight 856 from Toronto to London. The name on the passenger manifest read Ernst Innauer, in keeping with the Austrian passport he was now using. The ultrathin latex appliqué, a realistic replication of a large wine-stain birthmark, which he had glued on his right cheek, blending in the edges with makeup, completed his physical disguise. It was the first time he had worn the device, with the exception of when the passport photograph was taken at Stasi headquarters three years ago, and he was amazed to find how effective it was. Not only was it the first thing people noticed when they saw him, but it had the subsequent effect of causing them to make polite efforts not to stare at it, and in so doing avoiding looking directly at his face altogether.

As the flight lifted off the runway shortly before 8:00 P.M., Strasser opened his briefcase and removed the photograph and one-page biography that Drussard had sent to him in New York the previous day. He was at first puzzled by the relatively young age of the man who was to be his next victim, then read on to learn that Herbert Darcy-Williams was the son of the man who had originally purchased the Nazi art, and had inherited his father's collection.

He returned the photograph and background notes to his briefcase and took out a map of England and a street plan of London, purchased at the airport bookstore. He began to familiarize himself with the locations of the two homes owned by Darcy-Williams, but finding that he was too tired to concentrate, reclined his seat and closed his eyes. Sleep would not come, however, and he again found himself thinking of the man who had chased him in the limousine, wondering if he would see him again. He still had not reconciled the coincidence of his showing up when he did with any logical sequence of events that might have led up to it, and the American Delta Force was not known to operate in the manner the man he remembered from Düsseldorf had; they would have been far better organized and prepared, and he would have never gotten out of the cul-de-sac alive. And there was still a small voice telling him that the amazingly fast response of the men he believed to be Bancroft's security guards had been far too timely.

Strasser forced the troublesome thoughts to the back of his mind and reminded himself of what he had accomplished to date, and what lay ahead. Another four million dollars were to be had from the Englishman, with an additional seven million from the paintings in the collections of the men in Rome and

Madrid. A total of twenty-nine million dollars when added to what he had already netted from his victims in New York, more than enough to keep him in operational funds for a long time to come. It was with those comforting thoughts that he finally fell asleep after the long, adrenaline-charged day.

« 27 »

Mike Semko sat in the front passenger seat of the gray Ford sedan, his body angled against the door to allow him to watch the road behind. Rachel, seated in the rear, caught his eye and slowly shook her head in dismay at the stupidity and carelessness of the CIA case officer, operating out of the London embassy under cover of a consular affairs officer, who had picked them up at the airport.

It was Rachel who had seen the man across the parking lot taking their photographs with a long telephoto lens as they came out of the customs-and-immigration annex at the Heathrow corporate terminal.

"My guess is they're Russians," Rachel said.

"And my guess is you're right," Semko replied as he again caught sight of the two men in the dark green Audi following four cars behind.

"What the hell were you thinking?" he demanded of the young case officer at the wheel. "Or were you thinking at all? You led the sons of bitches right to us."

"The chief of station was instructed to expedite your arrival. I had no choice in the matter."

"The DDO gave those instructions?"

"I believe they came from the chief of Counterintelligence."

"So you waltz right out of the embassy and pick us up in a goddamn car with diplomatic plates. Why didn't they send someone operating under nonofficial cover?"

"I don't know," the case officer said, his face flushed with embarrassment. "I was told to pick you up at Heathrow and to help you in any way I can."

"If you really want to help, stay the hell away from me. I'll contact the station if and when I need them."

Semko knew that the Russians were better than most at determining their rival's order-of-battle, the internal structure of an intelligence agency's station inside an embassy. Active field officers had to be identified from among the legitimate diplomats, or valuable time and manpower were wasted on surveillance of those chosen at random, which was a hit-and-miss proposition that made efforts to determine an opponent's intelligence targets, or to conduct countermeasures to protect one's own operations, near impossible if they were constantly misled by nonintelligence personnel and decoys deployed to distract them from those engaged in espionage.

The Russians' prior success at identifying CIA case officers was the primary reason the Agency had changed its long-established method of operation, and moved most of its personnel away from embassies, establishing them under NOC (nonofficial cover) by setting up legitimate business enterprises, or hiding them within one of the many American multinational corporations that willingly cooperated with the CIA in such matters throughout the world.

It was the thought of the NOC operatives, and the scrambler-equipped cellular telephone he saw mounted on the center console of the embassy car, that prompted Semko to take matters into his own hands.

"How much longer until we're in the city?" he asked the case officer at the wheel.

"Fifteen minutes. Do you want me to try to lose them?"

"Not yet. Call your operations officer at the station. Tell him I want an NOC in the city to get in a car with a telephone and call you on this phone."

"What do you have in mind?"

"He's to drive around until we get into London, then you find a place where he can intercept the Russians and stall them long enough for us to get away."

Twenty minutes later, the CIA case officer turned onto a quiet residential street in London's South Kensington district. The dark green Audi paused at the intersection until they were almost at the end of the block, then crept slowly onto the same street. The Russians had no sooner turned the corner than an attractive woman driving a tan Opel squeezed past them, slowed to a stop, and cut off the engine, effectively blocking the narrow one-way street. The woman made a helpless gesture with her hands as she feigned having problems restarting the car. The Russians tried to pull around her, but she had stopped at an angle, leaving barely enough room for a bicycle to pass on either side.

By the time she brought the Opel back to life and pulled off to the side to let the Audi through, the case officer was around the far corner and three blocks away, where he paused to let Semko and Rachel out of the car to disappear down an alleyway between two apartment buildings. The Russians came out of the one-way street in time to see the brake lights of the Ford flash as it slowed to make another turn. They hurried to close the distance, unaware that the passengers were no longer in the car.

TWELVE BLOCKS FROM where Semko and Rachel got out of the embassy car, Jurgen Strasser left the art gallery owned by

Matthew Gibbs, Drussard's London contact. The gallery was located in an area south of Hyde Park where Knightsbridge, Chelsea, and South Kensington converge on one another; a quiet backwater where unhurried neighborhoods of low-set row houses and unique shops border tree-lined squares and crescents that spill around corners into a maze of cobblestoned lanes, leading one to believe they were laid out by the Mad Hatter. Strasser, his muscles still stiff from the long transAtlantic flight, decided to walk the short distance to Belgrave Square, and, consulting his street map, set out along the labyrinth of crooked lanes.

Belgravia, the most elegant part of London's West End, with its magnificent early-nineteenth-century houses and sunken gardens, was once the exclusive domain of the city's most prominent and wealthy citizens. Some still remain in residence, but many of the stately homes have been taken over by embassies and institutions. It was just off Belgrave Square, from which the area takes its name, that Strasser found the short, dead-end street called Belgrave Mews South. Darcy-Williams's eighteenth-century Georgian house was halfway down the secluded tree-lined block that Strasser quickly sized up as being impossible to stake out without drawing the attention of the neighbors and the bobbies, who patrolled the area in greater numbers than most other districts due to the high concentration of security-conscious residents.

Strasser made a slow sweep of the block, walking down one side and up the other, reinforcing his initial evaluation and already thinking ahead to Weldon Hall, his target's ancestral country home in East Sussex. About to turn the corner in the direction of Belgrave Square, he heard a door close heavily behind him. He turned to see a man come out of the Georgian house midway down the street; a tall, elegantly dressed man, whom, after a moment, Strasser recognized as Darcy-Williams from the photograph Drussard had supplied.

Partially hidden by a large sycamore tree at the corner, Strasser watched as the Englishman quick-stepped to a freshly waxed and gleaming black Bentley Mulsanne Turbo parked at the curb. He fumbled impatiently with his keys before opening the door and sliding behind the wheel. Strasser stepped out of sight around the corner as Darcy-Williams drove to the head of the dead-end street and turned in his direction, accelerating past him, too preoccupied to notice the man staring at him from the sidewalk.

Strasser continued in the direction of Belgrave Square, then walked west until he reached the area around Harrods department store where he found a public telephone box. Having learned that the direct approach worked well, particularly with servants, he dialed the home number Drussard had listed for the Englishman. The call was answered by an elderly woman with a cheerful voice, who told him what he already knew: Darcy-Williams was not at home.

"How unfortunate," Strasser said, using his best English accent, which might have fooled anyone but an Englishman. "I have some important papers for him. Can you tell me when he might return?"

"He's off to the country," the woman said. "But you should be able to reach him at Weldon Hall within an hour or so, if you must."

"Thank you so much," Strasser said. "I'll ring him there then."

"Who shall I say—"

But Strasser had hung up before the woman could complete her question.

He looked at his watch. It was just past ten o'clock, twenty-five minutes since he had seen Darcy-Williams drive off. It would take him a half hour or so to retrieve the car he had rented and left at a parking garage near Victoria Station, which would put him at Weldon Hall within an hour of the English-man's arrival.

THE FIRST TWO galleries on the list Rachel had picked up by means of a brush contact in front of the Armani store on Sloane Street proved unproductive. The third gallery, owned by Matthew Gibbs, initially got them more of the same blank stares and righteous indignation the others had shown when asked if they had seen a man matching Strasser's description or knew of a man by the name of Claude Drussard who was known to deal in stolen art.

Gibbs, an effete, haughty man with his hair pulled back into a ponytail and dressed in loose-fitting white silk trousers and a black silk shirt worn open at the neck, seemed unusually ner-vous about the line of questioning. He reacted angrily, insist-ing that they leave immediately, when Semko, following his instincts, suggested that Gibbs might be telling less than the truth. With nothing more than a gut feeling to go on, and four more galleries to visit, Semko decided not to press the issue, but rather put Gibbs under surveillance later if the others did not pan out.

As they were about to leave, Rachel noticed something that made her pause: a crumpled, empty pack of Davidoff ciga-rettes that had missed the wastebasket beside the glass-topped desk in the partitioned area in the corner of the gallery that served as an office. She remembered seeing one of the New York detectives use the tip of a pen to remove an identical empty pack from the floor inside the minivan parked in the alley behind Westcott's gallery.

"You wouldn't happen to have a cigarette, would you?" Rachel asked.

"Never touch the awful things," Gibbs replied. "And I do not permit smoking on the premises."

Rachel picked up the crumpled pack and smiled at Gibbs.

His expression and nervous fidgeting told her all she needed to know.

The significance of what Rachel held in her hand was not lost on Semko; he also remembered seeing the detective pick up the empty pack of distinctive German-made cigarettes and place it in an evidence bag.

"We don't want you," Rachel said, before Gibbs completely recovered his composure. "As a matter of fact, if you tell us what we want to know, we'll pretend we never had this conversation."

"Whatever are you talking about?"

The store was empty of customers, and Semko crossed to the entrance and locked the door, returning to take the crumpled pack of cigarettes from Rachel and hold it close to Gibbs's face.

"The last gallery owner who handled stolen paintings for the psychopath who left this here died of a gunshot wound to the head less than twenty-four hours ago in New York. Shot through the eye," Semko said, causing Gibbs to flinch. "When he's finished here, I promise you he'll do the same to you."

Gibbs took a step back from Semko but said nothing.

"We know he's been here," Rachel said in a calm, understanding voice. "What we need to know is where he went."

"I haven't the slightest idea what you are talking about, and I insist that you leave immediately before I summon the police."

"Somehow I don't think that would be in your best interests," Rachel said.

"I want you to leave. Now."

When Gibbs turned to walk toward the front of the gallery, Semko grabbed him by an elbow and spun him around. "There isn't time for any more of your bullshit, pal. This man has killed damn near everyone he's come in contact with. Now where did he go?''

"Unhand me this instant!" Gibbs demanded.

Semko would have laughed at the ridiculous remark had it not been for the anger building inside him. Instead, he lowered his right shoulder and drove a fist deep into Gibbs's stomach, which doubled him over and sent him to the floor, where he curled into a fetal position and began gasping for breath and whining.

"Get up!" Semko shouted, then grabbed Gibbs by his ponytail and pulled him to his feet to prop him against the wall for a second blow.

"For God's sake, Semko!" Rachel said, and stepped between them. She had only half meant the reprimand, concerned that Semko might knock Gibbs unconscious, causing them to waste valuable time waiting for him to come to. But, having seen and participated in an occasional Mossad field interrogation, she knew the value of properly applied force. More than once, she had played the reasonable side of the "good cop/bad cop" act herself, and knew from the glance she exchanged with Semko that that was what he had in mind, although she doubted it was necessary with someone like Gibbs.

"I apologize for my partner," she told the badly shaken Gibbs, who was staring wide-eyed with fear at Semko. "Please, tell us what we need to know and we'll leave."

Gibbs began shaking uncontrollably, and Rachel helped him into the chair behind the desk. "Can I get you a glass of water, Matthew?"

Gibbs shook his head. "I think he damaged something inside. It hurts so much."

"I'll damage your goddamn brain, you lying little shit!"

Gibbs let out a high-pitched squeal as Semko slapped him

across the face and knocked him off the chair before allowing Rachel to hold him back by again stepping between them.

"Please, Matthew," Rachel said, helping the now terrified Gibbs back into the chair. "This man, Strasser, is a murderer; he must be stopped."

"He called himself Dieter," Gibbs finally said, his eyes fixed on Semko as he spoke.

"Where did he go?" Rachel asked gently.

"I don't know. He said he would be back, later this afternoon."

"With the paintings?" Semko asked.

"No. He told me to ring up Drussard and inform him that he was in London and that he would most likely have the paintings tomorrow evening if all goes well. He's coming back to pick up something Drussard has sent to me by overnight delivery to pass on to him."

"Then we'll wait for him here," Rachel said to Gibbs. "If you don't mind."

Gibbs nodded in acquiescence.

"Is there a back room where we can stay out of sight?"

Gibbs pointed to a door leading off the rear of the gallery. "You're not from Scotland Yard, are you?"

"Not exactly," Rachel said. "You go on with your normal routine and forget that we're here."

Not bloody likely, Gibbs thought, his eyes fixed warily on Semko. "You're not going to have me arrested?"

"I told you," Rachel said, "it's not you we're after."

Leaving Gibbs to compose himself, Rachel and Semko entered the small work area at the back of the showroom, keeping the door cracked just enough to see anyone entering the gallery.

"You were a little premature with the rough stuff," Rachel said. "Didn't your mother ever tell you that you can catch more flies with honey than with vinegar?"

"She did. But when I got a little older, I learned that if you pull the wings off the little suckers, they'll pretty much eat whatever you give them."

SEATED OUTSIDE THE country pub on his meticulously maintained 1978 Triumph Bonneville motorcycle, Adam Carter entirely looked the part of the London cabdriver on holiday. Despite the urgency of the message from Leonov, he had taken over two hours to make the one-hour trip early that morning, riding slowly through a number of towns and villages midway between London and Mayfield, scouting for a location with a public telephone where he could return later and wait without drawing attention.

It was just past ten-thirty when Carter pulled on his helmet and kick-started the old Triumph. He rode slowly out of the village and headed west, eventually leaving the main road and pulling to a stop where a rough-timbered bridge spanned a stream. He parked the motorcycle beneath a gnarled old beech tree at the edge of the woods, and taking his knapsack and canteen from the luggage rack at the back of the motorcycle, he followed a sun-dappled path that led deep into one of the larger private country estates in all of Sussex—that of Herbert Darcy-Williams.

Grassy forest spaces gave way to a broad, open meadow broken by hedgerows and a small orchard. In the distance, Weldon Hall, a sprawling masterpiece of Edwardian architecture, sat on top of a knoll with a commanding view of the 123-acre estate. Carter continued on the path, skirting the estate, and staying within the tree line along the fringe of the meadow until he came to a large oak felled by a storm more than twenty years ago. The huge trunk had been trimmed of its branches by one of the estate's caretakers and left where it had fallen at the water's edge, to serve as a place to sit and enjoy the peaceful scene.

Carter knelt at the side of the stream to fill his canteen with cold water, then sat on the broad tree trunk and opened his knapsack and removed his packet of sandwiches. Anyone passing by on the footpath would have seen the not-uncommon sight of someone out for a walk on a fine spring day in the English countryside, stopped for a quiet picnic lunch at a picture-postcard spot.

What they would not have seen was the small metal tube, containing a handwritten message, that he placed inside an obscured fissure caused by the lightning strike that had long ago uprooted the tree.

Having completed the emergency contact procedures, Carter sat back to enjoy his sandwiches and the cool spring day, not wanting to leave too soon in the event that he had been observed entering the woods. He had earlier called Darcy-Williams's London home and the country estate, leaving messages with servants at both places: "I am returning Mr. Darcy-Williams's call regarding his inquiry about a Queen Anne table advertised in the Sunday *Times,*" was what he had told the servants. There had been a number of advertisements for Queen Anne tables in the venerable London paper the previous Sunday, but no such inquiry was made by Darcy-Williams.

All that was left for Carter to do was return to the telephone box in the town square and await the Englishman's call.

« 28 »

A CODED MESSAGE from Darcy-Williams's illegal was waiting for Nikolai Leonov when he arrived at the Russian embassy at number 13, Kensington Palace Gardens. The message acknowledged receipt of Leonov's instructions at 7:10 A.M. that morning and confirmed that emergency contact procedures would be initiated immediately, adding that Darcy-Williams had just returned from holiday on Sardinia's Emerald Coast and had three days remaining before he was due to return to his duties at the SIS training facility at Fort Monckton.

The information Leonov had requested from the External Intelligence Service's headquarters at Yasenevo had arrived by diplomatic pouch shortly before he touched down at Heathrow Airport. He opened the sealed packet and sat staring at a photograph of Strasser, taken six years ago during a ten-day visit to the Soviet Union when he had conducted a seminar on innovative techniques in the field of explosive devices at the KGB's former terrorist training center located forty miles east of Moscow. The file that accompanied the photograph contained a synopsis of Strasser's activities while with the East German Stasi, and concluded with the most current information available—it was believed that Strasser, still calling himself "Dieter," had reorganized and taken over the Red Army

Faction after the collapse of the German Democratic Republic, and had been responsible for at least one terrorist act, at an Amsterdam synagogue. Information received through Arab world contacts indicated that Strasser's former financial backers had cut him off, and he was in dire need of operational funds—the latter confirming what Leonov suspected was the reason for Strasser's stealing the readily marketable paintings, and a positive indication that he might look no further into the significance of the Goering File.

Leonov had come to the same conclusion as Strasser about Darcy-Williams's London home on Belgrave Mews South: It did not lend itself well to prolonged surveillance, nor was it a likely place to attempt a forced entry. He presumed correctly that Strasser would concentrate on the country home in East Sussex. Aware of the dangers of having a protective surveillance team spotted by locals, or by Darcy-Williams, who might mistake them as a personal threat, Leonov decided nonetheless to err on the side of caution, rather than depend on the Englishman to contact his illegal in time to get him safely tucked away.

The *rezident*'s operations officer had spent a considerable amount of time at Seacox Heath House, the ambassador's country home located one hour southeast of London in Flimwell, East Sussex, and was familiar with the area. He was called in to brief Leonov, and after being shown the location of Darcy-Williams's estate on a large-scale map of the countryside around the village of Mayfield (nineteen miles west of the ambassador's residence), he assured Leonov that the heavily wooded terrain surrounding Weldon Hall would provide ideal cover for a surveillance team, allowing them to stay well out of sight, yet within striking distance of anyone approaching the estate.

The twelve men the operations officer had personally selected, some experienced in "wet affairs," the old KGB term for assassinations, were operating under cover as trade inspectors within the Russian trade delegations in London, and as such were not under the constant scrutiny of British counterintelligence. In anticipation of any extraordinary measures that might be required, one man on each of the two six-man teams placed on standby at the ambassador's residence was sniperqualified and equipped with a sound-suppressed rifle capable of killing a man at a thousand yards.

Convinced that immediate action was the prudent course to follow, Leonov used the secure computer link to the Flimwell estate to contact the intelligence officer in charge of the protective surveillance teams. Along with the cable ordering the first team into position at Weldon Hall, he also used the fax machine to send a copy of the photograph of Strasser. Their orders were to abduct him on sight, or to kill him if necessary, but regardless of the method used to eliminate him as a threat, they were to bring him, or his body, and all personal belongings back to the ambassador's country home.

THE STREETWISE OPERATIVES of MI-5 (the British security service whose domain is internal counterintelligence) have few, if any, peers in their ability to keep tabs on suspected espionage agents on their home ground. However, the service is drastically understaffed when it comes to the personal surveillance of the two hundred-plus Russian intelligence officers and agents operating throughout the country.

One of MI-5's more successful operations is conducted by the "watchers" from its K Branch Russian section assigned to observation posts at the choke points at both ends of Kensington Palace Gardens. Their task is to monitor those entering and leaving the complex of Russian buildings (the embassy, the attaché's office, and the consular section). It was a call from the watchers' customs and immigration liaison at Heathrow Airport that alerted them to an unknown Russian diplomat arriving on a British Airways flight from New York. Within the hour a watcher at a third site, midway between the two choke points, observed the man identified as Sergei Petrenko (the name Leonov was traveling under) getting out of a car with diplomatic plates and entering the Russian embassy. His picture was taken with a 1500-millimeter telephoto lens, and he was logged in and marked for further surveillance.

The name *Petrenko* appeared nowhere in MI-5's extensive files, and his appearance was yet another incident in the increased Russian activity that had begun early that morning—a morning when MI-5 watchers found themselves being led all over the city by known Russian intelligence officers, whom they soon realized were acting as decoys to stretch their resources thin and lead them away from whatever it was they had in the works. A host of tradecraft tricks had been used—stepping off trains at the last second, switching taxis three and four times en route to a destination that revealed nothing of their intentions, and stopping to engage complete strangers in conversation, who in turn had to be followed until the diversions were discovered.

K Branch's efforts to maintain surveillance on the thirty-plus intelligence officers operating under Russian diplomatic cover, who were subject to travel restrictions within the country, were well organized and highly successful. However, those operating under Russian commercial covers—news organizations, banks, trade delegations and councils, Aeroflot personnel, and the staffs at various Russian residential buildings (including those at the ambassador's country estate)—whose travel throughout the country was not restricted, were impossible to keep under close supervision. Telephone lines were routinely tapped and a variety of other highly sophisticated electronic surveillance methods were employed, but the measures were never enough to ensure complete coverage of every suspected field operative.

K Branch had no current coverage on Seacox Heath House, and consequently, no one from MI-5 observed the Russian surveillance team as they left the ambassador's residence for Darcy-Williams's estate. Using three cars, in the event a mobile surveillance was required later, they left at fifteen-minute intervals, with each car taking a different, circuitous route, eventually to meet at a remote spot a short distance from Weldon Hall.

DRUSSARD'S INSTRUCTIONS ON how to find Darcy-Williams's country estate left something to be desired, giving only the route number and describing the location as a few miles west of the village of Mayfield. Immediately upon arriving in London, Strasser had removed the birthmark disguise and contact lenses and had washed the rinse from his hair at the safe house apartment he kept on Gunter Road in Chelsea, and not wanting to draw attention to himself by asking directions, he had twice backtracked along the country road before finally spotting the small brass plaque on the ivy-covered stone pillar at the entrance gate to Weldon Hall.

He followed the long sweeping driveway past rolling pastures sprinkled with primrose and wild daffodils to where it ended in a cobbled courtyard at the entrance to an imposing Edwardian mansion. The black Bentley he had seen Darcy-Williams driving in London was parked beside a Jaguar Sovereign off to one side of the courtyard, and Strasser pulled in behind them. He checked the Russian-made Makarov P6 pistol he had taken from its hiding place at the safe house, making certain there was a round in the chamber before slipping it back into its custom-made shoulder holster secured under his left arm. The semiautomatic pistol, designed as an assassin's weapon, was complete with an integral sound suppressor and was smaller and more compact than, but not as accurate or reliable as, the Sig Sauer he would have preferred to bring

with him but had tossed into a trash barrel in Central Park—
reluctant to risk having it found during the thorough inspection
the British, with their strict gun laws, were known to occasionally give the luggage of those passing through customs.

As Strasser got out of the car, he paused briefly to stare at
the magnificent stone mansion. The exterior evoked the atmosphere of what one would expect to find inside: large, high-
ceilinged rooms paneled in a variety of rich, mellow-toned
woods, each with its own fireplace; battered leather armchairs
in a Jacobean library with copies of *Shooting Times;* hats and
gumboots strewn about the hall; the walls hung with rare tapestries and fine paintings, and every room heavy with priceless
antiques. The realm of the ruling class, Strasser thought, a
decadent lot given to perpetuating the arrogant alcoholic lie of
English superiority, as one of his Leipzig University professors had once described them.

The sound of a distant vehicle drew Strasser's attention as
he walked toward the huge double doors at the front entrance.
He stopped to determine the direction of the sound, then continued across the courtyard toward the west wing of the house,
where he found a narrow access lane, bordered on the far side
by a towering hedge that verged on an open meadow. The lane
branched off the courtyard and continued along the west wing
past a terraced garden at the rear of the house. Strasser followed it around to the garage area, where the hedge ended and
a low stone wall provided a view across the open meadow. A
few hundred yards away, he saw a white Range Rover skirt the
edge of an orchard and move slowly through a break in a thick
hedgerow to head in the direction of an open farm gate that led
to the stables beyond the garage. A dozen or so fox hounds
barked in chorus as Strasser walked past the kennel to where
the lane ended at the stable yard. He stood near the open gate
and watched the boxy station wagon bounce and sway across

the uneven ground, finally recognizing Darcy-Williams at the
wheel as he drew closer.

DARCY-WILLIAMS DIDN'T notice the man walking along the stone
wall at the rear of the house; he was too preoccupied with the
message he had just retrieved from the dead drop inside the
fallen tree on the southern boundary of his property. Ex-
hausted from the previous day's tedious change of planes and
long airport waits on his return from Sardinia, he had slept late
that morning and taken his breakfast on the terrace at the rear
of his London house. He had initially dismissed the inexplicable telephone message given him by one of his household
staff, knowing full well that he had made no inquiry concerning an antique table. It had been years since he had gone over
the emergency communication procedures with his Russian
handler, but midway through his breakfast, as he began to read
the morning paper, it came back to him, and he had rushed
from the house, deeply concerned with what might have
prompted the emergency contact. Had the revelation come a
few moments later, he would have discovered the story on the
"Art Murders" in New York City on the second page of the
London. *Times*.

Darcy-Williams was more than a little disturbed by the urgent tone of the message retrieved from the dead drop, having
delivered a list of newly arrived SIS personnel at Fort Monckton to the very same location just two days before leaving for
Sardinia—a scheduled report that he handled as he had countless others over the past fourteen years. Had he made a mistake in using the old signal that told his handler the dead drop
was loaded? The signal was scheduled to be changed months
ago, but he had considered the new arrangement to be incon-
venient and had not complied with his handler's instructions.
Had his recalcitrance been his undoing, leading to his activi-

ties finally being discovered? He always knew that someday it might come to this.

THE RUSSIAN INTELLIGENCE officer in charge of the six-man surveillance team deployed around Darcy-Williams's estate had seen Strasser drive into the courtyard and get out of the car. The field glasses he used to observe him from a stand of birch trees approximately one hundred yards away revealed enough of the man's features for him to make a positive identification after a quick comparison with the photograph sent from the London embassy.

He used a hand-held portable radio to alert the sniper on his team, who was located in the meadow through which Darcy-Williams had just driven—the Range Rover had passed within ten feet of where the sniper and his spotter lay concealed near the opening in the hedgerow. The alert was unnecessary; the spotter had also seen and recognized Strasser as he drove into the courtyard, and had a much better view of him through the powerful tripod-mounted telescope he had been using to watch the area around the house.

Positioned 240 yards away, at an angle that provided an unobstructed view of the front courtyard and the rear of the mansion, he had watched Strasser cross to the west wing and disappear behind the high hedge as he entered the lane. Staying out of sight of the Range Rover, he and the sniper had backed out of the hedgerow and crawled in the direction Strasser had gone, picking him up again as he emerged from behind the hedge and continued along the low stone wall in the direction of the stables. Upon realizing that Strasser was waiting at the open farm gate for the arrival of the Range Rover, they crawled back under cover, inside the dense bramble and blackthorn hedgerow, where they took up a position that gave them a direct line of sight to the area around the gate and the stable yard.

The sniper then settled into a prone position, making certain the barrel of the bolt-action Vaime Mk.2 rifle did not protrude beyond the opposite side of the hedgerow. The Finnish-made 7.62-by-51-millimeter-caliber sniper rifle, popular with antiterrorist units around the world and renowned for its accuracy at distances up to one thousand yards, was equipped with an integral sound suppressor—a state-of-the-art system that, when used with match-grade subsonic ammunition, made no more noise when fired than an air rifle and was impossible to detect at distances over twenty-five yards.

The sniper rolled onto his side, opened the bolt of the rifle, inserted a round into the chamber, and closed and locked the bolt. After removing the gloves he wore to protect against the thorny shrubs, he looped his left wrist through and around the leather sling, then tucked the butt of the weapon just to the inside of his shoulder muscle before again lying flat and shifting his weight until the rifle pointed naturally in the direction of the open gate. He next placed his cheekbone comfortably on the stock, positioned his eye behind the scope, and adjusted the magnification to bring Strasser into sharp relief.

The range-finding telescopic sight was equipped with a scale located in the bottom left of the reticle, calibrated to an average man's height of five feet eight inches. The sniper fixed the scale on Strasser's image and, compensating for his above-average height, judged the distance to be 245 yards. An easy shot for a man with his expert training, given that the target was stationary and required no "hold off"—there was no crosswind with which to contend—and adjustment for elevation was negligible with the rifle being zeroed for a distance within five yards of the target.

Remaining in position, the sniper looked away from the scope to avoid eye fatigue, but his spotter, using the powerful tripod-mounted telescope, continued to watch Strasser, concentrating on his hands for any sign of a weapon. As the white

Range Rover approached the stable yard, the spotter saw Strasser move to the right of the open gate, his upper body still visible above the low stone wall. The sniper again put his eye to the rifle's telescopic sight and found the crosshairs centered on his target's chest.

"I have a shot," he whispered over the radio to the team leader.

The response came back immediately. "Do you see a weapon?"

"No," the sniper replied. "But our surveillance subject is now within range of a handgun."

"Our orders are to take Strasser alive if possible. Shoot to kill if he poses a clearly identifiable threat; otherwise take no action."

The team leader then spoke into the radio to the two men he had posted on the opposite side of the house. He instructed them to return to their car and take up a position at the end of the driveway, where he and the man with him would join them to lie in wait to intercept Strasser when he attempted to leave the estate.

DARCY-WILLIAMS DROVE into the stable yard and stopped the Range Rover to get out and close the farm gate behind him. As he opened the door and slid from behind the wheel, he found himself face-to-face with Jurgen Strasser.

"Yes?" Darcy-Williams said, his condescending tone indicating his annoyance at the intrusion. A second, more appraising look made him stiffen. There was something in the stranger's eyes and his body language that marked him as a player. But on whose side? Is this it? he thought. Have they come for me?

"I've come about the paintings," Strasser said, a crooked grin on his face; he was going to enjoy his time with the arrogant Englishman.

"The paintings?"

"Specifically your Cézanne, Matisse, and Pissarro."

Darcy-Williams stared dumbfounded at Strasser, unable to believe what he was hearing, though he was somewhat relieved upon detecting a trace of an accent, one he mistook for that of a Russian. Certain as always that he knew what everything was about before it was explained to him, he now believed that the man standing before him was the Russian handler he had never met, and that the mention of the paintings was perhaps a long-forgotten recognition code, or one he had never bothered committing to memory when he was first recruited.

"Good lord, are you mad?"

Much to Strasser's surprise, Darcy-Williams took him by the arm and led him to the rear of the Range Rover, out of sight of a gardener, who briefly appeared on the lane, then disappeared in the direction of a vegetable garden on the far side of the stables.

Intrigued by the strange response, Strasser offered no resistance and went along with the Englishman as he continued with his indignant reprimand.

"Your message made it quite clear that I was to contact you by telephone. Have you taken leave of your senses, coming to my home, in broad daylight?"

"I want the paintings," Strasser said, and again fell silent to let the curious scene play out.

"You want the paintings? My God, you Russians are a cheeky lot, aren't you? I've provided you and your puppeteers with information for the past fourteen years, and now you expect me to simply hand over the paintings that got me into this mess in the first place. I should think not."

Strasser's usually unflappable composure was momentarily shaken as it all began to make sense. The curious incidents that had puzzled him over the past few days came back to him: Cabot's remark about his Russian masters, the brush contact in front of Bancroft's apartment building that he'd attributed to an overactive imagination, the unusually fast response time of the men he had assumed were Bancroft's security. They all fit with what the Englishman had just blurted out.

"I've kept my part of the bargain," Darcy-Williams said, "and if you want any further cooperation from me, you will do the same."

"You made no bargains with me," Strasser said, the grin returning to his face. "But you're about to."

It was then that Darcy-Williams realized he had made a terrible mistake. "Just who are you?"

"Someone who's going to kill you, very slowly, if you don't tell me everything I want to know."

"Have you the slightest idea with whom you are dealing?"

"Yes, I do. But you don't."

Darcy-Williams saw from the look on Strasser's face that no amount of bluffing or posturing was going to make the slightest difference. His concern shifted to one of somehow gaining control of the situation and limiting the damage to what had already been done.

"Let's find a quieter place to talk, shall we?" Strasser said, and grabbed the Englishman by his tweed sport coat, shoving him out into the stable yard. Darcy-Williams attempted to pull free, only to find himself pushed through the open door of the tack room, where Strasser kicked his left knee out from under him and sent him sprawling to the floor.

THE SNIPER WAS about to take his shot when, in compliance with his team leader's explicit instructions, he held off, still not certain that the Englishman was in imminent danger. He made a second call on the hand-held radio, reporting that Darcy-Williams was struggling with Strasser as they crossed the stable yard, and received the shoot-to-kill order. He reacquired his target and again applied a slow, steady pressure to the trigger, centering the crosshairs on the middle of Strasser's back as he shoved Darcy-Williams into the tack room. A split second before the rifle fired, Strasser swung the tack room door closed behind him. The hollow-point subsonic bullet struck the heavy oak door at the precise moment it slammed shut. The low-velocity round penetrated only halfway into the two-inch-thick door, the sound of its impact masked by the heavy thud and the clang of the metal latch as it fell into place.

"Move in," the team leader replied to the sniper's frantic report on what had just happened. "Fire only if you are certain of a kill shot," he added, not wanting a wounded Strasser to kill the Englishman in response to their attack, if he had not already done so.

Darcy-Williams lay in a corner of the tack room, bleeding profusely from the broken nose and shattered front teeth Strasser had inflicted on him. It had taken only a few blows before he succumbed to the pain and the threat of the hammer's being cocked on the semiautomatic pistol as it was aimed at his kneecap.

Strasser had already figured out most of what the Englishman told him, and he believed him when he insisted that he did not know the name of the Russian intelligence officer in charge of the Goering File operation—it made sense that he would not know the man's identity, only how to contact his handler.

"Tell your Russian friends that I'll be in touch," Strasser said, amused by the look of immense relief on the Englishman's face upon realizing that he was not going to kill him.

"Whom shall I say the message is from?" Darcy-Williams asked, feeling somewhat proud of himself for only having added minor details to what he had already inadvertently divulged.

"Just tell them that Dieter will contact them through some of his old acquaintances within their organization."

As Strasser opened the door to the tack room and entered the stable yard, Darcy-Williams removed a handkerchief from his pocket and stemmed the flow of blood from his nose. He then used his index finger to probe his battered mouth for damage and winced as a broken front tooth fell into his hand.

So you think you have it all, he thought as he watched Strasser leave. Well, not by half. Bloody Hun.

THE SNIPER AND his spotter had taken a position behind the stone wall enclosing the stable yard, and were about to close in when Strasser came out of the tack room. Through the open door they saw Darcy-Williams rising to his feet as Strasser crossed to the lane and continued in the direction of the house. The sniper immediately reported his observations to the team leader waiting at the foot of the driveway.

"Continue to cover the Englishman," the order came back. "We'll handle Strasser when he tries to leave."

By the time Strasser reached the courtyard, he fully realized the monumental significance of what Darcy-Williams had revealed. The Russians would pay well for the file in his possession, far more than he could hope to realize from the rest of the paintings. And then there were the Americans, and the British, and any number of governments who would pay a small fortune to know whom the Russians had compromised and had been running as agents-in-place for over forty-five years, providing none knew that their opponents or allies had already bought the same information. Or even if they did, Strasser reasoned further, they would still pay handsomely to know what the others knew. The possibilities were endless if he handled it properly. The fortuitous turn of events brought an uncommon genuine smile to his face as he got in his rental car and pulled out of the courtyard.

Moments later the smile disappeared as he rounded a curve and saw two cars pulling into position to block the end of the driveway one hundred yards away. He counted four men as they got out and took cover behind open doors, their machine pistols pointed directly at him.

Strasser's adrenaline surge reached its peak as he considered his options. Off in the distance, he saw that the pastures on both sides were enclosed by low stone walls that continued along the road frontage and joined the pillars at the end of the drive, ruling out any cross-country escape in either direction. Slowing the car almost to a stop, he studied the way the Russians had parked to form their blockade; the smile returned when he saw the mistake they had made.

The front ends of both vehicles were angled together in the center of the drive, in the turnoff area on the far side of the stone pillars. Had they brought the cars only a few yards farther, just inside the pillars, the solid stone columns would have prevented any side impact from forcing either of them far enough out of the way to get through.

Strasser had run roadblocks before, having taught the techniques in training exercises at Massow, and on two occasions had found himself in real-life situations where he had put those very same techniques to use. He began moving slowly forward, calculating the precise angle of impact required to knock the car on his right far enough away from the pillar to allow him to break out. He had no doubt that the men behind the doors would unleash a barrage of automatic fire at him as he came within range, but he had never known anyone stupid enough or insane enough to hold their position and continue firing when faced with an onrushing vehicle.

He was counting on that as he cinched his seat belt and shoulder harness tight. He stayed to the far right of the driveway as he pressed the accelerator to the floor, then ducked low and peered over the top of the dash to align his left fender with the open door of the vehicle on his right. Rapid-fire bursts erupted from all four machine pistols as he roared down the driveway, shattering his windshield and spraying the interior of the car with tiny shards of glass. So intent were the four shooters on killing him that none had thought to concentrate their fire on his tires. A blowout at the speed he was traveling would have caused him to lose control and prevent his striking the target car at the necessary angle, if indeed it would not have sent him careening off into the pasture. Some of the nine-millimeter rounds struck the grille of the car, but they weren't powerful enough to damage the engine and immediately impair its performance.

When Strasser was within ten yards of the blockade, he saw the four men dive for cover behind the stone pillars. With the gunfire ended, he pulled himself upright behind the wheel and, looking through an undamaged part of the windshield, made a final adjustment in his angle of approach as he braced himself for the crash. The Ford sedan he was driving was equal in weight and size to the Russians' cars, and at seventy miles an hour the powerful glancing blow with which he struck the car on the right sent it rolling onto its side, where it lay against the second car.

The force of the impact threw Strasser forward, but the seat belt harness, and his bracing grip on the steering wheel, kept his head from striking the windshield as he cut hard to the right and skidded out onto the roadway. He again ducked low as the two Russians who had taken cover behind the pillar closest to him opened fire and sent a flurry of rounds through the side window. He fought to regain control of the car, but the rear end broke loose and fishtailed wildly, finally regaining traction when it slid off the paved surface into a culvert. Strasser kept the accelerator to the floor, driving half-in and half-out of the shallow ditch until he managed to steer back up onto the road.

He was out of the effective range of the Russians' machine pistols by the time they fired their last desperate bursts. The rounds thudded harmlessly into the trunk of the Ford as Strasser looked in the rearview mirror to see the four men running to the car left standing on all four wheels. He was over a crest out of sight by the time they untangled the two vehicles and backed out onto the road, only to find that the rear end damage to the second car was such that pursuit was impossible.

At the first intersection, Strasser turned off the road to Mayfield and headed south through the quiet countryside of open pastureland and low, wooded hills. He found a secluded spot and made a quick stop to use the jack handle to pry the left front fender away from where it was rubbing the tire, but when he drove away, he discovered that the crumpled fender was not his only problem. The crash had damaged the frame and the front end shimmy made keeping the battered car on the road a constant challenge. He slowed to a manageable speed and continued changing directions, following other secondary routes that led him west and then south again, until a few miles outside the small town of Ringmer the opportunity he was hoping for presented itself.

Peregrine Atkins, an amateur ornithologist from the nearby town (his father was also a bird watcher; raptors were his passion and the genesis of the unusual name he had given his son), had parked his vintage Jaguar at the side of the road and walked partway into a pasture brimming with wildflowers. He sat on a rise overlooking the area, his binoculars to his eyes, engrossed in identifying the variety of birds flitting about the field, and noting them in his journal. The shadow cast by the tall stranger standing just behind him caused him to look over his shoulder.

"There's a lovely kestrel plying the hedgerow on the right," Atkins said with a pleasant smile. "They feed mostly on mice and insects, you know; caterpillars, grasshoppers, beetles, and the like. Contrary to popular belief, they take very few birds.''

Strasser nodded with feigned interest, then scanned the deserted area before reaching inside his leather jacket to remove the Makarov pistol from his shoulder holster.

''Have a look,'' the friendly bird watcher said, and offered his binoculars. His expression turned to one of shock as Strasser's hand came out of his jacket holding the pistol.

The sharp click of the slide returning to pick up another round and the forceful hiss from the end of the barrel of the sound-suppressed pistol did little to disturb the birds nearby, and only a few took flight as Atkins's lifeless body tumbled backward off the rise. The grass in the pasture was knee high, tall enough to conceal the body from anyone passing by on the road, and Strasser left it where it had fallen, one neat, round hole in the center of its forehead.

As Strasser drove away in the vintage Jaguar, heading back to London, he began thinking of how best to exploit the new opportunities provided by the file his father had left behind. He would approach the Russians first. Once they learned what had happened, they would be eager to strike whatever bargain was necessary to save what had to be an extremely valuable operation. His train of thought was interrupted by a momentary flashback to the one unknown remaining in the equation: the man who had chased him in New York. It made no sense that a Delta Force mission could be in any way related to the Russian operation he had stumbled across. It had to be coincidence that their paths had crossed when they did. A piece of information unrelated to the Goering File that had led them to him. Had he lost the American when he left the States, or was he out there somewhere, still hunting him, perhaps for what had happened in Düsseldorf three years ago? He ended the speculation with a shrug; he had dealt with the American counter-terrorist unit before, and he would do so again if necessary.

« 29 »

Semko and Rachel had been sitting in Matthew Gibbs's gallery for over four hours when they saw the young case officer who had picked them up at the airport come through the front door.

"Son of a bitch!" Semko said, and stormed out into the gallery, where he grabbed the case officer by the scruff of his neck and dragged him into the back room. "What the hell is wrong with you?"

The case officer pulled free of Semko's grasp and backed cautiously away. "We got an urgent cable from Langley. You're to leave here immediately and contact the DDO."

"How did you know where to find us?" Rachel asked.

"The operations officer at the station had the same list of galleries your friends gave you. Process of elimination."

"Did it occur to you that in that process you probably led the Russians here?" There was more than anger in Rachel's voice, but she kept the other disturbing thoughts to herself.

"I made certain I wasn't followed."

"Oh, well, that puts my mind at ease," Semko said. "You goddamn moron!"

The case officer's face turned crimson and his temper flared. "Look, Semko, I don't know who or what you are, but I'm not going to take any more of your abuse. I was told to find you ASAP. I'm following the station chief's orders. If you have any complaints, take them up with him.''

Semko turned away to keep from punching the face of the man who stood glaring at him with righteous indignation.

''We have a secure communications setup at a safe house in Chelsea,'' the case officer said, and handed Rachel a slip of paper with an address on Elyston Street just off Brompton Road. ''You can call from there.'' He paused for a moment, then said, ''I was told to stand by in the event you needed transportation.''

The laugh that Semko let out was not one of amusement. ''Just give me the keys to your car, and get out of my sight.''

NIKOLAI LEONOV'S FIRST field operation, once viewed as an exciting and promising opportunity for promotion and praise, now seemed to promise nothing less than the ruination of his career. Within fifteen minutes of Strasser's escape from Weldon Hall, he had heard first from the surveillance team, and then from Darcy-Williams's illegal, whom the Englishman had called to try to explain away his unwitting revelations.

The delayed response to the urgent cable Leonov had sent to Yevgeny Primakov, the chief of the External Intelligence Service at Yasenevo, had him pacing the office in the embassy imagining the worst possible repercussions for his failure. When the reply finally came, it was with both relief and disappointment that Leonov read his instructions. The delay had been due to the arrival of another cable at Yasenevo, shortly after Leonov had sent his. It was from Boris Tumanov, a Russian intelligence officer in Munich. Tumanov had contacted his superiors in the Germany-Austria department at Yasenevo and informed them of his conversation with ''Dieter,'' a man he knew from a KGB assignment four years ago that had brought him in direct contact with the East German's terrorist operations. He reported Dieter's demand for a meeting the follow-

ing day in Munich, with "someone in a position to bargain."
When Tumanov had pressed for the reason for the meeting, he
was told only that "they will know why."

In response to Strasser's demand, Primakov was making
arrangements to bring a team of the External Intelligence Service's paramilitary operatives to Munich from Zossen. Located in eastern Germany, seventeen miles south of Berlin, the
underground command center at Zossen, headquarters of the
German high command during World War II, was taken over
by the Russians at the end of the war and served as the headquarters for the Group of Soviet Forces–Germany until the
collapse of the East German state. The paramilitary unit stationed there were former *Spetsnaz* troops (unconventional warfare forces that are the Russian army equivalent of American
Special Forces) who were now attached to the External Intelligence Service's special operations section. They were posted
to Zossen as a security element until the last of the highly
classified code and communications equipment in the underground command center was dismantled and shipped back to
Russia.

A ten-man team was being selected from the security element and would arrive in Munich that night. Leonov's orders
were to proceed to Munich and make contact with Tumanov.
Once Strasser set the time and place, he was to meet with him
and agree to whatever demands he made, and to stall for
enough time for the special operations team to organize a response to the situation. Command of the operation to eliminate
Strasser would now be in the hands of the leader of the team
from Zossen, and Leonov's sole function, once Strasser was
found, was to identify and secure the file in his possession. To
prevent any further dissemination of the information in the
Goering File, Leonov was instructed to reveal nothing of its
contents to the men from Zossen, and they would be instructed
not to ask.

Leonov understood the reason for bringing in the special operations team. Strasser eventually had to be killed. Even though he had come to them first, there was no guarantee that whatever conditions they met would not be followed by more demands, or that he would not sell copies of the file to other intelligence agencies. Whoever Strasser approached would have ultimately killed him in any event, if not to prevent his marketing copies of the file and breaking his bargain of exclusivity, then simply for the information he carried in his head.

The only positive note for Leonov in an otherwise disastrous day was the identification of the man and woman the surveillance team had photographed at the airport; their arrival in England resonated with the news report Leonov had heard of the mysterious man and woman who were involved in the debacle at Bancroft's apartment. The man had been identified as Michael Semko, a former Delta Force trooper now believed to be part of an elite unit within the CIA's counter-terrorist section. Photographs taken of him in Vienna and Madrid had been found in the files at Yasenevo. The woman was unknown to them, but was assumed to be CIA. The surveillance team that had followed them from the airport, and lost them after their arrival in the city, had continued following the man with whom they were last seen. The fact that the CIA had not shown up at Weldon Hall, and the discovery that they were canvassing London art galleries, convinced Leonov that their efforts to find Strasser were directed at anticipating his next victim; an approach that told him, although they obviously had some method of tracking Strasser's movements, they did not have knowledge of the names in the Goering File or any information that could compromise the operation.

But Primakov was taking no chances. Though the CIA's parallel hunt for Strasser was perceived as unrelated to the Goering File, his orders to the special operations team were to kill Semko and the woman if they showed up again.

In coordination with the operations officer at the embassy, Leonov worked out a plan to get to Munich. He made reservations on a flight from London to Frankfurt, where arrangements were made for a counter-surveillance team to meet him and escort him to Munich, making certain he wasn't followed to Tumanov's apartment.

IT TOOK SEMKO and Rachel more than an hour to elude the Russian surveillance team they spotted immediately upon leaving the gallery. After driving six blocks, they parked the car, took a series of taxis, and finally lost them when they entered Harrods department store to leave by another exit moments later and get into a taxi that had just discharged a passenger. They got out of the taxi four blocks from the safe house in Chelsea and, at Rachel's insistence and direction, walked a "route" until she was satisfied they were no longer being followed.

"What makes you think he's going to Munich?" Semko asked the deputy director for Operations, who had been anxiously awaiting his call at the twenty-four-hour operations center in Langley.

"Because he just made his first big mistake," Brannigan said. "He called a Russian intelligence officer, Boris Tumanov, who used to be part of a KGB logistics support team for the East Germans' terrorist ops. We learned about him through the files we got from Stasi headquarters. He's operating out of Munich now, selling surplus Russian military equipment for hard currency to third world countries and his old terrorist contacts. We've had his phone bugged for the past ten months."

"Why the hell would Strasser make contact with the Russians? I thought they wanted his ass as much as we do."

"I'm not sure why," Brannigan said. "But my best guess is

he's decided to make a deal with them for the file we're after."

"What did he say to the guy in Munich?"

"He identified himself as Dieter, and Tumanov knew who he was immediately. He told him to go to a public telephone and call him at a number in London, but Tumanov wanted to know more before he got involved. Strasser said he was coming to Munich and wanted a meeting tomorrow, and if Tumanov didn't want his superiors in Moscow to feed him feetfirst into a blast furnace, he'd get to a public phone and call him back."

"Where did Strasser call from?"

"Victoria Station. We put someone on it as soon as we could, but Tumanov made the return call from a pay phone only a block from his apartment and it was a brief conversation. By the time we got someone to Victoria Station it was too late."

"Why didn't you call me?"

"The London station chief wasn't sure which gallery you were in and didn't want to waste time calling every place on the list."

"You've got the Russian in Munich under surveillance?"

"As I said, we've been on him for ten months. Our plane's still out at Heathrow, so get your butt to Germany and check in with the Munich base as soon as you get there. Something's about to break. Soon. I can feel it."

"Have the Delta Force team from the SAS base meet me there. Germany is Strasser's home ground, and if he's got any of his Red Army Faction buddies backing him up things could get nasty. I'd like some people with known abilities to work with."

"Sorry. I couldn't put that together on short notice," Brannigan said. "They're on a joint field training exercise and won't be back in until tomorrow. But I'm sending a team of our special ops people from the Frankfurt base to Munich. They'll be waiting for you when you arrive."

Semko was about to launch into a tirade about the incompetence of the London station, but decided against it. "Look, Jack, just promise me a couple of things. If Strasser shows before I get there, give the Munich base explicit orders not to move on him without me. And under no circumstances is anyone to meet me at the airport; I'll initiate contact when I'm ready."

"Were there problems in London?"

"Don't ask."

"All right. I'll inform Munich base to keep their distance."

Rachel had said little since leaving the gallery; she was troubled by what she saw as flagrant, avoidable errors made by people who should have known better.

"Why is Strasser meeting with the Russians?" she asked when they left the safe house in Chelsea. "It makes no sense; they've been trying to kill him."

"I don't know," Semko lied. "I guess we'll find out when we get to Munich."

"Stop at the pay phone at the next corner. I want to check in with my support team and bring them up to date."

"Why didn't you call from the safe house?" Semko asked as he swung into the curb.

Rachel did not answer, and again fell silent after completing the call and getting back in the car.

Semko pulled out onto Brompton Road and immediately swerved back to the left side of the street, narrowly avoiding a head-on collision with an oncoming car. In a momentary lapse, he had forgotten the British rules of the road. "What's bothering you?"

"Right now, your driving."

"Besides that."

"Too many things have been going wrong."

"Yeah, well, I apologize for the idiots they've been sending to help us, but I'm sure the Mossad makes its share of mistakes."

"What if they weren't mistakes?"

"What do you mean?"

"I'm not sure."

Semko held Rachel's gaze for a long moment, then shrugged off what she was suggesting. "Jack Brannigan wants Strasser dead as much as I do. And he's a good friend. There's no way in hell he's leading me down the garden path. We'll get Strasser. I promise you. We'll get him."

"ARE YOU AWARE of any problems Mike Semko had with the London station?" Jack Brannigan asked Alfred Palmer, his counterintelligence chief, when he returned to the secure room in the twenty-four-hour operations center after a short break.

"I wasn't informed of any," Palmer said. "I told them to facilitate things for him; provide any assistance he required. Why? Did something go wrong?"

"He didn't say, specifically. But I know Semko. Somebody screwed up. See if you can find out what happened."

"I'll have someone look into it."

"Is the team from the Frankfurt base en route to Munich?"

"They left half an hour ago."

THE MOSSAD WAS constantly conducting surveillance operations against their Arab neighbors, looking for any hint of activity that might threaten Israel's security. Four months ago they learned of a planned series of meetings between Arab world leaders and high-ranking officials from the new Russian government. The meetings were to be held in England at the Russian ambassador's country residence in Flimwell, and a topnotch electronic surveillance team was sent to London from Tel Aviv. The team's efforts to tap into the secure telephone lines and computer link were unsuccessful, but the latest in laser communications intercept devices, set up at hidden observation points around the Flimwell residence, were used with great success to monitor the conversations at the three meetings that took place over a period of six weeks.

The scientists in Mossad's research and development department in Tel Aviv had also found a way to compromise the Russians' fax machine, allowing them to read every message sent or received by intercepting and unscrambling the transmissions. The ingeniously conceived fax intercept system was effective regardless of the communications protocol, "handshake" signal, speed, or resolution used, and "invisibly" captured all transmissions directly on-line, whether sent by slave machines, wireless transmitters, satellite down links, or multiplexers; and recorded those transmissions onto its own hard drive. Although no current surveillance effort was directed against the Flimwell residence, all fax transmissions were still monitored as a matter of course.

The code and communications clerk at Israel's London embassy first discovered the intercept of Strasser's photograph. With no qualifying text accompanying it, he had placed it aside to wait and see if a later transmission would explain its significance. When checking the intercept's "take" four hours later, he found a message sent from the Russian ambassador's country residence by a man who identified himself as the leader of a protective surveillance team. The message was a brief after-action report to another man by the name of Leonov, informing him that a man by the name of Strasser had managed to escape from the trap they had set for him. The team leader reported the time Strasser had left a place called Weldon Hall, and in which direction he was seen heading. The message concluded with the assurance that the subject of their protective surveillance was safe, and that four men had been left in position at Weldon Hall to provide security for him until further orders were received. A return message instructed the sender to use the secure telephone line to contact Leonov directly, thereby cutting off the code clerk's access to any further information on the incident.

The code clerk, as a matter of routine, informed the Mossad's head of station of the intercepts. The head of station, aware of the hunt for Strasser, immediately realized their significance and put a call in to a Mossad "helper," who was a member of the British press. Within the hour, the journalist called back to inform him that Weldon Hall in East Sussex was owned by Herbert Darcy-Williams, a wealthy aristocrat serving with the Foreign Office (Darcy-Williams's official cover, which concealed his SIS ties). The Mossad head of station then forwarded the photograph and message to Tel Aviv, including the information gained from the journalist.

« 30 »

JURGEN STRASSER DID not like loose ends; in his experience they were responsible for compromising more operations and getting more people killed than any tactical mistake he had ever made. With that thought foremost in his mind, he had used the same disguise and passport with which he had entered England, and took a flight to Paris that allowed him a three-hour layover before his connecting flight to Munich.

After calling his bank in Liechtenstein to confirm that the money owed him for the paintings taken from Bancroft's apartment had been credited to his account, he rented a car and, rather than risk using the one uncompromised safe house still available to him in Paris, took a hotel room near the airport, where he removed his disguise and washed the rinse from his hair before driving to the vicinity of Drussard's gallery on the rue de Seine in the Saint-Germain section of the city. The time available to him before his flight to Munich precluded his usual lengthy counter-surveillance measures, and considering it unlikely that his connection to the Frenchman had been discovered, he parked the car three blocks from his destination and did only a quick sweep of the area before entering the gallery.

The look of surprise on Drussard's face when Strasser entered the small, neatly kept office at the rear of the showroom quickly changed to one of concern.

"Was there trouble in London?"

"Nothing I couldn't handle."

"And the paintings? Gibbs hasn't called confirming their delivery."

"The paintings are no longer of any interest to me."

Drussard's expression turned to one of confusion. He had not yet learned of the death of Westcott in New York City; with the much bigger story of the massacre at Bancroft's apartment, the related report of the fire and the gallery owner's death had not been picked up by the international press. The Frenchman's knowledge of the events was limited to what had occurred at Sutton Place South, and his only concern was that because of what had happened, Strasser might have gotten cold feet and decided to back out of the most lucrative deal Drussard had ever made.

"The reports from New York said the Russians were involved. Have they created problems for you?"

"I want the lists of names and paintings I gave you."

"But we had an agreement."

"The lists," Strasser repeated.

Drussard shrugged in compliance and unlocked the top drawer of the desk. "I wish you would reconsider. I have already found buyers for the remainder of the paintings. I could perhaps increase your percentage if that would convince you to continue with our arrangement."

Strasser looked past Drussard as he handed him the two sheets of paper from the desk drawer, his gaze falling on the personal computer and then on a small office safe in the corner. "Open the safe."

"There is nothing in there related to our dealings, only my personal papers and a small amount of money."

"Open it."

Drussard hesitated. "I assure you there is nothing in the safe that is of any concern to you."

The sight of Strasser reaching inside his jacket and removing the sound-suppressed pistol changed Drussard's expression of innocent disappointment to one of fear. He quickly got up from behind the desk and dialed in the combination of the safe and pulled open the door.

Strasser motioned him aside with the barrel of the gun, and dropped to one knee in front of the safe. He removed the documents he found on the shelves and placed them on the desk after glancing at them to find they contained a duplicate of the original lists, an accounting of the money received and paid out to date, and a record of who had purchased the paintings he had stolen. He then opened a small drawer in the center of the safe and found what he suspected the Frenchman might be keeping there: a three-and-one-half-inch microdisk labeled KOENIG FILE, the cover name he had used when they first met.

"I used the computer to keep track of our transactions and the sales to my clients; I forgot that I made a backup disk," Drussard offered lamely. He was now visibly upset, and became even more so upon seeing the deadly look in Strasser's eyes.

"Turn on the computer."

Drussard sat at the console and did as ordered. The screen came up blank with the exception of a small symbol of a key in the upper left-hand corner, indicating that a code had to be entered before the system could be accessed.

"Enter the code."

Again Drussard complied. "I kept nothing of our dealings on the hard drive. Only on the disk and the printed copies."

"Call up the directories."

Drussard did so without hesitation, and continued to follow Strasser's orders, accessing the only two programs on the computer, one for accounting and another for word processing, and subsequently erasing the contents of the directories and the disk Strasser had taken from the safe.

"And now our business is finished," Drussard said. "I have kept my part of the agreement; all of the money owed you has been deposited in your account as instructed, and you have eliminated any record of our transactions."

"With one exception," Strasser said as he dropped the documents he had taken from the safe into the wastebasket beside Drussard's desk. "The knowledge inside that greedy little head of yours, which I am sure you would eventually give to whomever you might contract to steal the rest of the paintings."

The two shots that tore through Drussard's left eye socket could not be heard outside the office, and Strasser sat calmly on the edge of the desk, curiously watching the pool of blood collecting around the Frenchman's head as he set the contents of the wastebasket on fire with his lighter and waited until they were reduced to ashes.

"WE'RE IN POSITION to take him when he comes out," the case officer from the CIA's Paris station said into the small hand-held radio as he sat in a car near the end of the block.

One of the local agents the CIA had stationed at observation posts in the street had alerted the mobile teams to move in when he saw a man who answered Strasser's description enter the gallery, and there were now four men each covering the front and rear exits of the three-story building.

"Take no action," Palmer Stevenson, the Paris station chief, replied from the code and communications room at the embassy.

"There are only two ways out of the building," the case officer radioed back, anxious to have the capture of an international terrorist among his credits. "There's no access to the upper floors from inside the gallery; he's got to come out the back or the front door on the ground level. We've got them both covered."

"Your orders are to observe and report his activities."

"But, sir—"

"I repeat, take no action."

"Yes, sir," the case officer said, his frustration evident.

Stevenson was equally disappointed and somewhat confused by his explicit orders from the counterintelligence chief at Langley, orders that superseded earlier instructions from the deputy director for Operations. The message had been sent separate and apart from the Agency's normal top-secret traffic and had been transmitted over the "restricted handling" channel, telling Stevenson that it was highly sensitive, and according to the CI chief, sent with the full knowledge and approval of the director.

The station's operations officer, who was sitting next to Stevenson in the code and communications room on the top floor of the embassy, shook his head in dismay at what he had just heard.

"The director's got a full-court press on for this guy, and they want us to let him slip away when we've got him nailed?"

"Ours not to reason why," Stevenson said.

THE BAVARIAN CITY of Munich, founded by monks on the banks of the Isar River in the eighth century, is much older than the German nation established in 1870 of which it became a part. It is a place of contrasts: of Gothic architecture and modern structures; of museums and breweries; of the somber tolling of cathedral bells and the oompah-pah of brass bands; and of elegant restaurants and haute cuisine and noisy beer gardens and pig knuckles.

During World War II, Allied air strikes dropped in excess of sixty thousand bombs on the city; the British raided by night, and the Americans came over in waves by daylight. The powerful explosions and subsequent fires destroyed most of the principal buildings and factories, along with entire neighborhoods. Today, in museums and public buildings throughout Munich, one can find aging, sepia-tone photographs of what the city looked like in the spring of 1945: a barely recognizable place of despair and devastation, where huge sections were reduced to little more than roofless, skeletal structures with tottering walls and twisted girders reaching skyward from charred ruins; where headless statues on pedestals scarred by shrapnel stood as defeated sentinels. When the war ended, twelve million metric tons of debris, the remnants of centuries past, were eventually bulldozed into heaps of Gothic, Renaissance, baroque, and rococo rubble and trucked off to the suburbs, where they were graded into great mounds of rolling hills, covered with topsoil, and then landscaped into parks that still bear silent testimony to the Nazi era.

The people of Munich, rather then creating a new and modern city of glass and steel from the ruins, have, for the past forty-seven years, carried out an obsessive restoration that has rebuilt virtually everything as it was before the war. If anything remained of a structure, it was restored; if nothing remained, it was rebuilt in precise detail—museums, opera houses, churches, every red-tiled roof and painted facade, every baroque tower, every rococo cherub and gargoyle, every fountain, spire, and gable—until the scars were nowhere to be seen, the only wounds within, and the once-elegant capital of Bavaria was itself again.

It was early evening when Semko and Rachel arrived at the Munich airport to find that Brannigan had kept his word; no one was there to meet them at the corporate terminal at the south end of the field. They rented a car and drove to the Marienplatz, the city's medieval square and central crossroad in the heart of the retail district. From there they set out on foot, conducting a countersurveillance effort they had discussed in advance. Semko was familiar with Munich from his army days, when he had spent two years at the 10th Special Forces Group base in nearby Bad Tölz shortly after returning from his final tour in Vietnam. He was fond of the city's food and its atmosphere and mostly its beer, and usually found an excuse for a short visit before returning to the States whenever he finished an operation in Europe.

He and Rachel strolled casually along the Weinstrasse, the main shopping thoroughfare, mixing with the throngs of people who filled the nineteen acres of traffic-free streets set aside as a pedestrian zone. They entered shops only to turn around and leave immediately, watching for anyone caught off guard by their erratic actions. They used store windows to watch for reflections of any too-familiar subjects, and twice stopped in mid-block to turn around and retrace their steps and then cut quickly down a side street. After giving Rachel directions to a nearby beer hall, they split up, with Semko going immediately to the designated meeting place to observe her arrival fifteen minutes later.

Once certain they were not being followed, they left the beer hall for a tiny café in the atrium courtyard of a small indoor shopping mall of exclusive boutiques located halfway down one of the narrow streets leading off the Weinstrasse. It had been Semko's decision to stay away from the CIA's Munich base, an office complex operating under the cover of an import/export firm specializing in laboratory equipment. He had called the base and given the case officer in charge of the special operations team from Frankfurt the telephone number of a pay phone on the wall opposite the café, instructing him to call him back from a public telephone.

The case officer returned his call ten minutes later, and at Semko's request, gave a description of himself and how he was dressed and agreed to meet him at a gift shop on the second level of the three-story indoor mall within the hour. Semko had given no description of himself, and said nothing about Rachel's being with him. The gift shop and the mall's entrance and exit were within view from where he sat at the café table, allowing him to observe the case officer when he arrived and to make certain he was not under surveillance before approaching him.

Semko turned his attention away from the courtyard and the open stairway leading to the upper floors when he noticed that Rachel's mood had again darkened. She sat silently sipping her coffee and staring at the people at nearby tables.

Memories of the things her grandmother had told her began moving in and out of Rachel's conscious thoughts, and, for a reason she did not entirely understand, she felt the need to talk. She told Semko of her grandmother's miraculous survival of Auschwitz, the murder of her grandfather and their five-year-old daughter, her namesake, and of her father's being smuggled to Switzerland. A single tear rolled down her cheek as she told him that for many, as in the case of her grand-mother, there were no photographs or diaries or letters, only oral histories passed on by the survivors to the next generation. She told him of the significance of the painting she had seen in the *New York Times* article on the murder of Edward Winthrop Stewart, and how she had hoped to get it back, and how dis-heartened she was by what the police had told her.

"You have anything that proves she owned it?"

"Nothing. And the chances of getting the courts to return it to her are virtually nonexistent. I guess that's what has me so damn depressed; that, and these people reminding me of what was done to my grandmother. Anyway, I should apologize for unloading this on you. It's not as though we don't have enough problems with that psychopath Strasser still out there."

"I'm glad you told me," Semko said, and leaned over to gently brush away the single tear with the back of his hand.

"And I'm sorry about what happened to your grandmother and her family."

The spontaneous gesture of kindness and sensitivity surprised Rachel, for, until that moment, she believed that the hardened, dispassionate loner sitting beside her was incapable of sincere compassion for others. Rachel squeezed his hand and then the tender moment they had shared ended abruptly when she saw Semko's eyes lock onto a man who had just entered the atrium courtyard.

"That's him," Semko said, after watching the case officer take the open stairwell to the second level. "Wait here and keep an eye out for the bad guys. And by the way, for an art history major, you're catching on to the spook stuff pretty good."

Rachel watched as Semko made contact in the gift shop, then left the mall with the tall, heavyset case officer to return fifteen minutes later and rejoin her at the café table.

"We're on. Strasser's called his old KGB buddy, Tumanov, and set the meeting with the Russians for tomorrow."

"He talked openly on an unsecured line?"

"No. He told Tumanov to go to a public phone and he went to the same one he used this afternoon. Our Munich base was counting on him doing just that and had it bugged."

"Where's the meeting?"

"The big outdoor beer garden in the Englischer Garten. At lunchtime," Semko said, his voice full of the excitement of promised action. "Like I told you. We're going to get him. So cheer up."

MOSHE SIMON, HEAD of the Mossad's research department, entered David Ben-David's office in the Tel Aviv headquarters and lowered himself wearily into a chair opposite the intelligence chief's desk. The old man with the legendary memory sat silently shuffling through a stack of papers in his lap, reviewing his notes before he finally raised his eyes to peer over the top of thick rimless glasses and speak in a soft, frail voice that told nothing of the inner strength of the man who had survived three years in a Nazi death camp.

"Birth records in Erfurt, Germany, confirm that Jurgen Strasser is the son of Heinz Dieter Strasser, the former SS major who died on the Obersalzberg."

"When we first talked you mentioned something about reviewing the transcripts of a debriefing we conducted ten or twelve years ago with a KGB defector the British shared with us. Was there anything more on his allusion to a top-secret section that had something to do with stolen Nazi art?"

"Specifically art looted and confiscated by Reich Marshal Hermann Goering," Simon said. "The Kavalkov debriefing. Yes, I did review the transcripts."

Ben-David, accustomed to the old man's methodical ways, waited patiently, knowing that Simon would divulge his findings in his own good time.

"Kavalkov also made reference to the fact that there were illegals attached to the mysterious section his drunken friend told him about. Seems there was some grumbling about all the best ones being assigned there."

"Which leads you to suspect what?" Ben-David prompted gently.

Simon shrugged and said, "It is my understanding that illegals are best used to service and control highly placed agents recruited within targeted countries."

Ben-David smiled. The old man believed in the Socratic school of teaching, what the Mossad chief thought of as the "figure it out for yourself" school.

"I also contacted an acquaintance at the British Museum," Simon went on. "He told me that the Englishman, Herbert Darcy-Williams, who according to the communication intercepts made by the London station the Russians were protecting from Strasser, had an excellent art collection, inherited from his father, who was of the same generation as the men murdered in New York.''

''So tell me, Moshe, what do you make of all this?''

''An educated guess about what has the Russians so upset about Strasser's activities?''

''That the men who've been murdered for selected paintings in their art collections had some involvement with Hermann Goering, and that because of that involvement they were later blackmailed into acting as agents for the Russians. And Strasser has somehow acquired a list telling him who those men are.''

''There's hope for you yet, Ben-David, my friend,'' the old man said with a rare smile. ''The 'somehow' can logically be attributed to his recently deceased father, in view of the fact that the murders and thefts began shortly after his death. And taking into consideration the father's timely proximity to where the Goering collection was found at the end of the war, I would suggest to you that whatever information the Russians found to incriminate those they blackmailed was also found by the late Major Strasser.''

''And the Russians want desperately to get the duplicate list to protect their agents.''

''Even more so, I would imagine, since the information you have just received about the meeting in Munich indicates that Strasser has come to realize its true value to them.''

''And the Americans?'' Ben-David said.

''You of course recall that the file from the Berlin Documents Center, sent to us from one of our people in Bonn, revealed that the American OSS were hunting for Heinz Strasser shortly after the war ended. It is not unreasonable to assume that the father's death and the son's recent activities would have caught their attention. One could also reasonably assume that their main interest in finding Strasser is to get possession of the list they were looking for forty-six years ago."

Ben-David thought of how the CIA was bungling that effort, according to the information Rachel had related to him through her support team, but said nothing to the old man as he got up to leave.

"Thank you, Moshe, you've been a great help."

"If there is anything else you need, I will be in my office."

With the old man gone, Ben-David swung his desk chair around to the computer terminal and began to type out a message to the support team in Munich. The message was automatically encrypted, and within seconds of pressing the button to transmit it was sent from an antenna on the roof of the headquarters building up to a communications satellite and relayed back down to an identical terminal in a Munich safe house, where it was automatically decoded and appeared in clear text on the computer screen.

SEMKO HAD DECLINED the offer of the safe house apartment made available by the Munich base that night, and he and Rachel checked into adjoining rooms in the Hilton Hotel, chosen because it bordered the southern boundary of the Englischer Garten park. They had dinner in a restaurant off the main lobby and retired to their rooms shortly before ten o'clock, after having agreed to get an early start the next morning and familiarize themselves with the meeting site and the surrounding area.

Rachel luxuriated in a long, hot bath, then slipped into a robe and placed a call to the Munich number given her when she had contacted her support team in London. She began by giving her present location and the time and place of Strasser's meeting with the Russians, but her report was interrupted by one of the team members, who informed her that an urgent

message had just come in from Mossad headquarters: she was
to contact Ben-David immediately.

When calling her support team from an unsecured telephone
in the same area as their safe house, Rachel did not concern
herself with the line's being tapped. The telephones in the
Mossad safe houses were equipped with state-of-the-art security equipment capable of defeating or screening out the entire
array of bugging devices: radio frequency transmitters, tape
recorder activators, direct taps or line interfaces, lineman's
handsets, inductive pickups, infinity devices, hookswitch by-
passes, and internal modifications. The equipment, however,
was not entirely reliable for international calls, such as the one
Rachel was about to make to Tel Aviv.

The self-contained battery-operated portable scrambler she
removed from her carry-on luggage did nothing to detect or
defeat bugs; it was strictly a voice privacy device with acoustic
couplers designed to be attached to the handset of any telephone. Lightweight and compact, with over fifty thousand possible code combinations, it operated over long international
distances, using a digitally controlled speech spectrum inver-
sion process that prevented unauthorized interception by
scrambling the conversation. After being filtered through the
scrambler, a conversation between parties with identically
equipped telephones was heard in clear voice, while anyone
monitoring the call heard only a garbled transmission, barely
recognizable as human speech. Units compatible with Rachel's were coupled to one of the telephones on Ben-David's
desk in his office at Mossad headquarters, and to one on the
same line that rang in his study at home. It was on the office
extension that Rachel reached him at ten forty-five that night.

"The kind of amateur mistakes the Americans are making
get people killed," the Mossad chief told her. "I want you to
keep your support team close by from now on."

"You said the CIA was lying about the focus of their operation. What do you mean, specifically?"

"Eliminating Jurgen Strasser is not their primary objective. They are after some documents he has. Documents the Russians are going to do whatever it takes to get before the CIA does. And make no mistake, your American partner, Mike Semko, has to know about it."

"So that's the reason for the meeting. Strasser wants to make a deal with the Russians for the documents?"

"There won't be any deal, at least not one the Russians will keep. They're going to kill him, one way or another, and anyone who gets in their way."

"Are the documents of any interest to us?"

"Yes, and if you have an opportunity to get your hands on them, by all means do so. We can make copies and give the originals back to the Americans later."

"How will I recognize them?"

"If I'm right, they'll be records of business transactions, probably art sales, made between Hermann Goering, or someone representing him, and the three men Strasser has murdered so far. And probably a number of other non-Germans, including the father of the Englishman he went after in London, Herbert Darcy-Williams. If you see any or all of those names on the documents you'll know you've got the right ones."

"What if he doesn't have them with him and there's a window of opportunity to eliminate him?"

"Carry out your original orders. We can go after the documents later."

"Semko is going to make an attempt to grab Strasser during the meeting tomorrow. I'm certain of it."

"What about his CIA friends at the Munich base?"

"I don't know. He seems to want to stay as far away from them as possible. I don't think he has much confidence in them after what happened in London."

"I'll instruct your support team to be at the meeting site to cover you," Ben-David said. "Look for them and stay close enough that they can back you up if anything goes wrong.

"And Rachel, trust no one but your own people." It was now with a fatherly tone that he spoke, deeply concerned with her personal safety. "Do you understand?"

"Yes. I understand."

Rachel sat on the edge of the bed with the phone in her hand long after the call was completed. She felt personally betrayed by Semko's having lied to her about his true objective. Her first thoughts were to go next door to his room and confront him with what she had learned, but then she rationalized and accepted what he had done as intrinsic to the profession she had chosen; under the rules of the game, given the same objective by Ben-David, she would not have revealed any more than was necessary. Confronting Semko now would accomplish nothing, and would more than likely drive a wedge between them, making it difficult, if not impossible, for her to carry out her orders to eliminate Strasser, or to be in a position to get the documents if the opportunity arose.

She went to the minibar and made herself a drink, then opened the sliding glass door and stepped out onto the small balcony that overlooked the city. Somewhere off in the distance she heard a clock tower tolling the eleventh hour, and her thoughts were again of her grandmother. It was well past midnight when she came back inside and went to sleep, to dream of what she imagined her grandmother's life in Vienna was like before it was torn apart.

« 31 »

BEER GARDENS ARE to Munich what sidewalk cafés are to Paris, and the Chinesischer Turm is one of the largest beer gardens in Munich. Capable of seating seven thousand people at row upon row of long green tables and wooden benches, it is located in a picturesque outdoor setting along the shore of a small lake and throughout a grove of chestnut trees at the southern end of the Englischer Garten park.

Frequented by a more sophisticated crowd than the places favored by tourists, the Chinesischer Turm, which takes its name from the Chinese pagoda at its center, is popular with students and professors from the nearby university, and would-be artists and intellectuals from Schwabing, Munich's version of the Parisian Latin Quarter. An oompah band on a platform in the pagoda plays the traditional drinking songs, but few if any of the patrons sing along or bang their steins on the table as in the old days. The preferred pastimes are reading, conversation with friends, card games, and chess, while downing quart-size steins of beer along with pretzels, radishes, and the inevitable bratwurst and sauerkraut.

By twelve-thirty the Chinesischer Turm had reached its lunchtime peak of a few thousand people, a situation that Jurgen Strasser had counted on to provide the anonymity and

confusion of crowds for his meeting with Nikolai Leonov, the
man Tumanov had told him to expect. He had spent the night
in a safe house apartment in Schwabing, with five members of
his Red Army Faction terrorist group, who, at his orders, had
driven to Munich from his base of operations south of Baden-
Baden. After briefing them on what he had planned, Strasser
gave them a detailed description of Semko, and instructed
them to mix with the crowd, staying close enough to respond
in force to any attack on him by either the American or the
Russians.

The leader of the ten-man special operations team the chief
of the Russian External Intelligence Service had sent from
Zossen had decided not to make any attempt on Strasser at the
beer garden. He had ruled out the possibility that the former
Stasi officer would be foolish enough to bring the documents
with him, and he knew from experience that any effort to
abduct him under such crowded and unpredictable circumstances, where any of his terrorist friends providing security
could not be easily spotted, held the potential for disaster. He
had instead ordered Leonov to make certain that a second
meeting was required to comply with Strasser's demands.

Leonov had arrived at the beer garden shortly after Strasser,
but it took him the better part of thirty minutes before he
spotted him in the huge crowd; he sat drinking a stein of beer
at one end of a long table that was cast in deep shade by
overhanging branches, apart from the dozen or so lunchtime
sun worshipers who sat in the warmth of the dappled light at
the other end. A footpath behind the table led into a densely
wooded section along the shore of a small lake. With the
Marienplatz, the city's central square, less than one-half mile
away through the woods, the path provided an excellent escape
route in the event of trouble.

Mike Semko and Rachel Sidrane had completed their reconnaissance of the beer garden and the surrounding area early

that morning, and not wanting to take the chance of being seen by Strasser if he arrived before the lunchtime patrons, had left to walk through the park until the crowd began to gather. They had not taken into account the number of customers who would arrive early to stake out their favorite tables, and by the time they returned more than a thousand people had already descended on the area.

With the beer garden operating under the self-service rule, hundreds of customers had converged on the *Schenke,* the draft beer counter at the pagoda, while even greater numbers milled about or stood in small groups, holding their steins of beer and talking. The situation made any long-distance views of those seated at the tables scattered throughout the trees an impossibility.

Semko and Rachel stayed together, mixing with the noisy crowd while moving slowly among the tables. Unknown to Semko, four of the Mossad officers from Rachel's support team were doing the same thing, observing her from a distance that allowed them to move in quickly if she required assistance. Intent on Rachel's progress through the crowd, they didn't notice that they themselves were under surveillance by the CIA's team from Frankfurt. Each of the Mossad officers in turn suffered the same fate. Approached from behind, they felt the barrel of a gun, concealed by a magazine or newspaper, pressed firmly in their ribs by men who took them by the arm and told then in a calm but firm voice to come along quietly. Escorted to the outskirts of the park, they were taken out of action and locked in the back of a large van.

The four men and one woman from the Red Army Faction group had seen none of this. Scattered throughout the crowd in positions that gave them a clear view of Strasser, their eyes were constantly appraising all those in his immediate vicinity. One of them, who sat with the group at the sunny end of

Strasser's table, took note of a tall, overweight, and middle-aged man approaching from the direction of the pagoda.

Strasser spotted the man a moment later and slipped his hand inside his leather jacket to rest on the grip of the sound-suppressed pistol secured in the shoulder holster beneath his left arm.

"I believe you are expecting me," the man said when he reached the table. "My name is Nikolai Leonov."

"Sit down," Strasser said, and removed his hand from inside his jacket as the Russian sat across from him and leaned forward to speak in a voice barely audible above the band and the crowd noise.

"Tumanov tells me you have something of interest to me."

Strasser simply grinned and handed Leonov a slip of paper with his numbered account and the name of his bank in Liechtenstein. "I want forty million dollars transferred into this account by this time tomorrow. Considering the damage I could do to your operation, I am certain you will agree it is a bargain price."

"First I must see what we will be paying for," Leonov said.

"No games, please. You are well aware of what I have, and you are not dealing from a position of strength, my Russian friend. So I suggest you do precisely what I tell you to do or I will take my business elsewhere."

"And what assurance do I have that you will not do that in any event?"

"None. But then what choice do you have?"

Leonov bristled at the arrogance of the man sitting opposite him, but kept his composure. "I cannot guarantee to have that amount of money for you within twenty-four hours."

"Your External Intelligence Service, or whatever you call yourselves now, has hard currency accounts far in excess of that amount in at least one bank in Luxembourg and two in

Switzerland that I am familiar with from my days with the Stasi. The transfer of funds will take no more than an hour.''

"I must present your proposal to my superiors and they will have to make the arrangements.''

"Just have it done by noon tomorrow.''

"And when will we receive the file?''

"When you deliver the second part of our bargain.''

"And what might that be?''

"Something I am having a great deal of difficulty obtaining,'' Strasser said, reminded of the inferior substances for which he had been negotiating with the arms dealer in Paris. "Five cases of your chemical warfare mortar shells; specifically those containing sarin, tabun, and soman. If I remember correctly, there are six to a case. And I want two of the small mortar tubes needed to fire them.''

Leonov was taken aback by the demand. Of all the easily transportable chemical weapons, these were the most deadly. Colorless, almost odorless, and extremely lethal, when released in a crowded area any of the three was capable of killing hundreds of people within minutes of exposure. But the unexpected stipulation provided what the leader of the team from Zossen was hoping for: the transfer of the weapons would require that the second meeting be in a remote location far removed from any area where they might be accidentally discovered by the police, a location that could be staked out well in advance of the meeting.

"We no longer have such weapons,'' Leonov lied, not wanting to make Strasser suspicious by agreeing too readily.

"Don't insult my intelligence. You have an underground storage facility full of them at the base you are dismantling in Neuruppin, sixty kilometers north of Berlin. I know for a fact that they have not yet been transported back to Russia.''

Leonov knew that the chief of the External Intelligence Service would never receive permission to place such weapons in the hands of a terrorist; certainly not when they could be traced back to him, but he agreed with the demand as he had been instructed to do.

"I will of course also have to discuss that with my superiors."

"There is nothing to discuss," Strasser said. "I will contact you through Tumanov later today and give you further instructions on where to make delivery. You will have them at the location I give you no later than noon tomorrow. After I have examined them and confirmed that the funds have been transferred into my account, I will turn over the file."

The delivery site Strasser had in mind was his base of operations at a secluded farm in the Black Forest, but he had no intentions of giving Leonov the location until he and the members of his RAF group had returned to secure the site before the Russians could send anyone there ahead of them. Compromising the secret location was of no concern to him; with his newly acquired wealth, he planned on establishing a much more suitable training area when his business with the Russians was completed.

"We must protect our own interests," Leonov said. "I will bring the chemical weapons with me, and once I see the file and I am assured that we are getting what we have bargained for, I will place a call from a portable telephone and give the order to complete the transfer of funds into your account. Within fifteen minutes of my call, you will be able to verify that it has been done."

Strasser nodded in agreement. "You will bring no more than four men with you for your own personal security while transporting the chemical weapons. They will travel in one car and remain out in the open at all times when they reach the meeting site. The weapons are to be in a van with a driver and you as the only passenger."

"I assume that you have not spoken to anyone else about the contents of the file?"

"You assume correctly."

"May I ask how it came into your possession?"

Strasser was about to tell Leonov that it was none of his business when his attention was drawn to a group of men standing near the draft beer counter at the pagoda.

A short, heavyset man with a thick neck was shouting at someone Strasser couldn't see, cursing him for bumping into him and spilling his beer down the front of his shirt. He went after the offender and shoved him as he attempted to move off into the crowd. It was then that Strasser saw the accused man's face as he turned and drove a fist into his pursuer's stomach, sending him to his knees, doubled over in pain.

"What is it?" Leonov asked, at seeing the change in Strasser's expression as he shifted his position on the bench to get a better view of the confrontation.

"My American nemesis," Strasser said, and slipped his hand back inside his leather jacket. "Leave now," he told Leonov. "I will call you this evening."

Leonov got up and disappeared into the crowd. Looking back over his shoulder, he saw Strasser rise to his feet and head toward the footpath behind the table.

One of the Red Army Faction terrorists, a woman, who was positioned nearby and had witnessed the hurried departure, was unsure of the nature of the threat or where it was coming from. She joined the man who had been seated at the far end of Strasser's table, and they stood with a group of people near the path to cover his retreat into the woods. The three remaining members of their group, who stood off in the crowd to the left and right of the table, saw their colleagues' reaction and began moving in their direction, drawing their weapons and concealing them beneath their jackets as they scanned the crowd.

Semko had spotted Strasser and had been moving slowly toward him, skirting the table to approach him from behind, when the man he assumed was a drunk accused him of spilling his beer. He realized that the drunk had compromised his approach when he saw Strasser look in his direction and get up from the table. He was so focused on the hated terrorist that he did not notice the man and the woman who had taken up positions at the entrance to the path, nor did he see the three men moving toward them on his left.

"Stay here," he told Rachel, and began shoving his way through the crowd, abandoning any pretense of his intentions. His actions quickly drew the attention of the three men on his left. Their semiautomatic pistols came out from beneath their jackets at the same moment Semko drew his weapon and broke into a run toward the path.

Strasser was still in sight, and Semko looked for an opening in the crowd that would allow him a clear shot at his legs to bring him down. Shouts and screams broke out as a number of people saw the pistol in Semko's hand. Others saw the weapons carried by the three men now rushing to cut him off. People began shoving those around them to get out of the way and panic spread throughout the immediate area as those who were unaware of what was happening were knocked to the ground by the human stampede that followed.

The man and the woman standing at the entrance to the path left their three colleagues to cover their withdrawal as they ran after Strasser in the event an ambush awaited him up ahead. Semko saw the woman first, then the man, as they broke from the confused group of beer drinkers who began to scatter in all directions in response to the rapidly spreading pandemonium.

The noise of the panicked crowd carried through the woods, and Strasser began running when he heard it. He was again puzzled by how the American had found him, but attributed it to the likelihood that the Russians had inadvertently led him there. He turned to look behind him and almost fired at the man and the woman running toward him until he realized they were his own people. He motioned for them to split up, then left the path and cut through the woods where he knew it was only a short distance to where the park ended near the Marien-platz and a warren of streets that led off in all directions.

Semko had lost sight of Strasser, but with the crowd in front of him dispersed, he closed quickly on the wooded area. As he was about to enter the path, a chorus of shrill screams and shouts made him look to his left where he saw a group of students run away from three men who were crouched into stable shooting stances with their weapons pointed directly at him. At that moment, Semko believed he was going to die. He spun quickly to his left and dropped to one knee, hoping to fire at least a few shots to throw off their aim, but the odds were against him.

What happened next took him by complete surprise: all three men, one after the other, in less than two seconds, fell to the ground, dead from well-placed shots to the head. Semko had heard no gunfire, and quickly looked in the direction from which he determined the shots had come. To his amazement, he saw Rachel standing forty feet away, a small sound-sup-pressed semiautomatic pistol gripped firmly with both hands as she moved cautiously toward the fallen men, her weapon still trained on them.

After recovering from the momentary shock of seeing it was Rachel who had saved his life, Semko jumped to his feet and continued after Strasser. He saw no one up ahead on the path, and slowed his pace to a jog as his eyes searched the deep shadows among the trees, hoping to catch a glimpse of a flee-ing figure. But he saw nothing. He entered the woods to pause and listen, and heard only the distant sounds of traffic from the busy streets less than one hundred yards away outside the park, and the noise of the beer garden behind him. He had no doubt that Strasser was by now out of the park and into the streets. Disgusted with himself for having once again failed, he slipped the pistol back in his shoulder holster and came out onto the path where he found Rachel waiting for him, her right hand inside the hidden gun compartment in her shoulder bag as her eyes moved constantly through the woods and along the path.

"I blew it. The son of a bitch got away."

"We've got to leave," Rachel said. "Every cop in the city is on his way here."

The image of the three men she had shot at the beer garden flashed before his eyes. "Where did you learn to shoot like that?"

"I had a basic firearms course at the academy. Everyone takes it. Even research analysts."

"There's nothing basic about acquiring three targets and dropping them with head shots from forty feet in a second and a half with a small semiauto."

"Beginner's luck," Rachel said, and started down the path away from the beer garden.

"Anyway, thanks," Semko said as he walked along at her side. "I'd probably be dead if you hadn't nailed them when you did."

"Do you think that will be carried over into my next life as good karma or bad karma?"

"If I were you I definitely wouldn't count on getting any brownie points for it.

"Beginner's luck, huh?" Semko added as they reached the landscaped grounds of the Englischer Garten and headed toward the Marienplatz. "So they issue state-of-the-art sound suppressors to everybody in your research department, or what?"

* * *

THIRTY MINUTES AFTER the incident at the beer garden, the head of the CIA's Munich base contacted Jack Brannigan at the twenty-four-hour operations center in Langley, Virginia, and gave him a full account of what had happened.

A few minutes later, a second call only darkened the DDO's mood. It was from the Mossad chief in Tel Aviv. Ben-David was livid over the treatment of his men, who had been released from the van only after it was established that Strasser had escaped. Although Brannigan did not admit as much to Ben-David, he had not given the order to forcibly abduct the Israelis, and attempted to pass it off as a case of mistaken identity; but the Mossad chief would have none of it. After the call was completed Brannigan was about to launch into his own tirade with Alfred Palmer, his counterintelligence chief, and the man he suspected was responsible, when George Sinclair, the CIA director, spoke up.

"I want you to pull Semko," Sinclair told Brannigan.

"Why?" the DDO said. "There were no documents transferred. The Russians will have to set up another meeting, and they'll more than likely use the same pay phone. And if they don't, we now have Leonov under surveillance. So either way, we're back in the game."

"The game has changed. And I don't want your man Semko screwing it up. Pull him and the Mossad woman."

"What's changed? We haven't gotten the file, and Strasser is still walking around. And as far as screwing things up goes," he said, directing his remarks to his counterintelligence chief, "we blew a surveillance in New York that could have ended this then and there, we compromised Semko in London, and we lost a perfect opportunity to grab Strasser in Paris. Hell, Semko may have come up short, but he's the only one who's done anything right."

Brannigan was still angry over learning that his CI chief had countermanded his original orders to the Paris station—orders that had instructed them to put Drussard under surveillance, and to take no action if Strasser showed up and Semko was in position to grab him. But Semko had not been there, and there had been an opportunity to get Strasser when he came out of the gallery, and because of his CI chief, they had lost it. Palmer had explained, none too convincingly, that since they knew Strasser was on his way to Munich, he thought they could make a much more concerted effort there, given the experience of the special operations team they had access to in Frankfurt.

"We're talking about another day or two at most until the Russians get back to Strasser," the DDO argued. "Let Semko run with it; if we keep him apprised of their movements and leave him alone, I guarantee you he'll complete the mission."

"It's over, Jack," Sinclair said.

"What the hell is going on here? Either you've forgotten the objectives of this operation, or I'm missing something. We can still get the file."

"It's over," the DCI repeated.

The director exchanged looks with Palmer, whose expression gave away more than intended. It was at that moment that Brannigan came to a realization that both stunned him and sent his Irish temper soaring. It all began to make sense. The clumsy tradecraft, the purposely missed opportunities, and the nagging thoughts from the beginning that the director was being less than forthcoming with his reasons for some of his operational decisions.

"You've had the file all along, haven't you?"

Palmer looked away, and Sinclair remained silent at the accusation.

"Answer me, goddamnit! You've had that fucking file from day one, haven't you?"

The director hesitated, then decided that the time had come to do what he had hoped would not be necessary when he brought Brannigan in to orchestrate the hunt for Strasser. Had Semko not gotten as close as he did, and had things gone as planned, the operation could have been written off as a failure without ever arousing the DDO's suspicions. But that opportunity was lost.

"BACKLASH has a few more wrinkles than I first told you," Sinclair finally said. "And yes, it's been ongoing since October of 1945, when a museum scholar with the OSS Art Looting Investigation Unit got lucky. He was working at the central collecting point in Munich, where all of the stolen art and related documents were being stored until their rightful owners could be determined. Thanks to the Germans' anal-retentive penchant for redundancy in their recordkeeping, he came across a complete duplicate set of Goering's files."

"And the short version is, we've been running every agent the Russians believe they've recruited ever since."

"Precisely. Including the second generation the originals recruited at our instructions. Jim Angleton put BACKLASH together and ran it from its inception until his retirement in 1974. He played the Russians like a five-string guitar for almost thirty years. It was a thing of beauty. Probably his best operation. Since then it's been handed over to the succeeding counterintelligence chiefs, and the same strict compartmentalization has been maintained. The only people who know so much as the BACKLASH code word have been each president, their national security advisers, directors of Central Intelligence, and the CI chiefs. And now you. It was set up that way for obvious reasons."

"From what I've heard of the way Angleton operated, you're lucky he told anyone."

"He was a strange duck, but he had his moments; I didn't realize how grand some of them were until BACKLASH was passed on to me and I reviewed its history," the director said. "Hell, Jack, even you could only begin to imagine what it's accomplished in the past forty-five years. In some instances we've caused the Russians to change the direction of entire research and development projects that cost them millions of man-hours of work and billions of dollars before they finally realized they were on the wrong track. Sure we had to give them some gems every now and then, but even that was done with masterpieces of misdirection.''

"When you first briefed me on BACKLASH, you said there were wealthy and influential Brits and Europeans among those who had bought Goering's art. Have you been running them, too? Without the knowledge of their own governments?''

"Every last one of them, including their recruits.''

The expression on Brannigan's face was one of grudging admiration.

"And without a hitch, I might add,'' the director said. "We'd have the people they thought they owned at State or on the Hill feed them information on shifts in policy or our secret agendas for disarmament talks, things they'd eventually learn anyway, but couldn't do us any real harm. When we had one of their people working for us and we knew it was only a matter of time before they caught up with him, we blew his cover. We even blew some of our own operations when we knew they were destined for failure; like the Bay of Pigs and some of our ops in Vietnam, and our supply routes into Afghanistan when it became clear the Russians were getting sucked dry and were on their way out.

"If we knew that a new missile or aircraft we had in development had serious design flaws, we made sure they got the most current information, then we'd wait six months before leaking it to the press, to give them time to incorporate the same flaws into their programs. That way they believed the information wasn't tainted, they had simply stolen what was a flawed project for us as well. They got just enough genuine technical intelligence information, like current weapons systems that were about to undergo major modifications or were going to be scrapped within the year for the next generation, so that the things we fed them that did real damage weren't suspected as deliberate attempts to mislead them. Even the good stuff we gave up—the guidance systems and improvements in radar technology—had its down side for them; we knew how to defend against them, and we knew their weaknesses. We let them steal computer technology with bandit microcodes that we could activate remotely designed into the central processing units. Remember the Paris Air Show, the year they tried to show off their new supersonic transport, the 'Concordski'? It crashed on its final approach to the airport. Made them look like a bunch of incompetent morons who couldn't even duplicate what they'd stolen. They eventually chalked it up to pilot error; but that sure as hell wasn't the cause.

"The list is endless, Jack. Just knowing what the Russians had on their shopping lists told us what they knew and what they didn't know, and where they were concentrating their efforts, and how far they had gotten. But the bottom line on BACKLASH is that it was one of the major contributors to the bankruptcy and eventual collapse of the Soviet Union."

There was a part of Brannigan that appreciated the irony of what he was hearing, and its far-reaching implications. But that did nothing to calm his anger at being excluded from the true purpose of the hunt for Strasser, once he was brought in to run the operation. And then, as his mind went back over the events of the past few days, the full force of what had happened, or rather what had been allowed to happen, struck him.

"You could have prevented Philip Bancroft's death," he said to Sinclair. "You had to know he would be one of Strasser's targets."

"And just how could we have done that, without compromising what has been one of the most important counterintelligence operations this agency's ever run? Think it through, Jack. We were forced to put this operation together on very short notice. Losing a few people to Strasser was one thing; trying to save them and having the Russians discover that we turned them forty-six years ago would have destroyed decades of work.''

''If you were running Bancroft you had to have established ways to communicate with him clandestinely. You could have arranged something that appeared perfectly ordinary to keep him out of Strasser's reach.''

''When it became obvious that Strasser was only after the paintings, we knew that the damage he could do would be limited. Any attempt on our part to prevent him from carrying out his plans could very easily have backfired and led the Russians to suspect that we had information that could have come from only one source. They knew we were on to the file at the end of World War II, and over the years we made occasional efforts to convince them that we were still looking for it. After the second murder in New York we realized what was happening, and decided that if we ignored it, it would make the Russians wonder why we hadn't put it together. Our objectives were to make them believe we suspected that a copy of the file had finally surfaced and that we were going after it, but in the end to let them get to it first, and we've done that.''

''Then why in the name of God did you have me bring Semko in?''

''You said yourself that he was the best man for the job. I wanted the Russians to believe we were serious about this, and if they had any information on Semko in their files, which there is every reason to suspect they do, his presence is very convincing.''

''You took one hell of a chance,'' Brannigan said. ''You had no guarantee that he wouldn't get the file and blow the whole operation.''

"I thought it would be much easier to control the information he was getting. I wanted him kept at a safe distance, just far enough behind Strasser to convince the Russians that we were in the game. I had no way of foreseeing that the Mossad would learn about the Russian surveillance of Bancroft in New York and put Semko a lot closer than I ever intended him to get. I have to admit, that gave us a good scare."

"And the meeting at the beer garden today?"

"We had people there to compromise any attempt he made on Strasser."

"Well, you've got another uncontrollable factor on your hands now. After the stunt you pulled with the Israeli support team, we should have known that the joint operation to get Strasser is nothing more than a charade."

"What they do doesn't matter now. After the Englishman Strasser went after contacted his Agency control and told him what happened, we knew that Strasser would be dealing directly with the Russians. I decided to make one last pretense in Munich and then let things take their course. All we have to do now is make certain the Israelis don't get close enough to get the file before the Russians do, and I've got that under control."

"Then let me enlighten you about something you don't have under control: Mike Semko."

"Just tell him to back off, that the Frankfurt base will handle it from here on out. I've ordered them to go through the motions and nothing else."

"We may have a slight problem with that. Semko isn't going to be that easy to call off without a damn good reason."

"Are you telling me you can't control one of your own people? That he doesn't follow orders?"

"It's not that simple. He'll stand down from the mission to get the file without question, but calling him off Strasser when he thinks he has a chance at him is another matter entirely. I know the man, he's a friend, and one of the most loyal people I've ever known. One of the Delta Force troopers Strasser killed in Dusseldorf saved Semko's life in Vietnam; he's been helping to support his kids ever since, even helped put them through college. For Semko, death ends a life, but not a relationship; he doesn't forget his friends, and he won't rest until he gets Strasser. It's the only reason he agreed to sign on with the Agency in the first place."

"If he's your friend, then make him understand, without telling him about BACKLASH, that it is not in his best interests to disobey orders."

"Without telling him how important it is to let the Russians get to Strasser first, I can't guarantee anything."

"I'll say it again, he's to know nothing about BACKLASH, or even that we want the Russians to succeed. And if you don't get him out of the picture, I will."

Brannigan's temper flared again. "You do anything that places his life in jeopardy and you've got me to deal with."

"I was only thinking of putting him under surveillance," the director quickly backtracked, not wanting to antagonize his DDO any more than he already had. "We can simply make certain that he doesn't get anywhere near Strasser until the Russians get the file. They'll kill the son of a bitch anyway, so Semko won't need to be involved any further."

"He's due to check in with me anytime now," Brannigan said. "I'll do what I can."

When Sinclair left the operations center, Palmer, who had sat quietly by to let the director do the talking, offered his apology for the initial subterfuge. Brannigan cut him short with a less than sincere acceptance of his excuse that he was only following orders.

The DDO's thoughts were elsewhere, on an operation Semko had run for the Agency near the end of the Vietnam War. On the second day of a mission into North Vietnam to kidnap a North Vietnamese Army general, Semko had missed two of his scheduled radio transmissions. After three more days of no radio contact, the consensus was that he and the five Nung mercenaries who had parachuted in with him had been compromised. Given up for dead, eleven days later Semko, after miraculously evading an NVA battalion that had been tracking him, walked out of the jungle along the DMZ, with his team intact, marching the North Vietnamese general in front of him, a pistol to the back of his head.

Brannigan smiled at the memory. Sinclair had never been in the arena. He had come to the Agency from a desk job at the Office of Naval Intelligence, to spend the next twenty years behind another desk on the analytical side of the Agency, until his promotion to DCI. He had no frame of reference for understanding the passions of a man like Mike Semko, a man who was not to be taken lightly, and one never to be counted out.

It was with a profound feeling of betrayal that Brannigan took the call that came in to the operations center from a pay phone somewhere in Munich.

"WHAT ARE YOU talking about, back off?" Semko said. "You put somebody on the Russian who showed up at the beer garden, didn't you? They hadn't finished their business. There's got to be another meeting. Just let me know when it's going down; or tell me where I can find the Russian and I'll take over the surveillance myself."

"You've got to back off, Mike."

"Come on, Jack. What? You lose confidence in me? I can still nail this bastard. You know I can. If some slob hadn't accused me of spilling a beer all over him when I was making my move, I'd have him for you right now, alive."

Brannigan considered telling him that the beer-spilling incident probably wasn't an accident, but knew it would lead to other questions he was not at liberty to answer.

"I'm sorry, Mike. The situation has changed. That's all I can tell you."

"That's bullshit. You're not telling me anything."

"I'll do everything in my power to get you back onto Strasser later, but for now you've got to let it go."

"He'll disappear and won't surface again until he kills some more innocent people."

"You'll get another chance at him; I give you my word. But not now. You know how it works, Mike. We've been through it before. Remember the mission into Laos, Mu Gia Pass."

"Yeah, I remember. I lost three damn good men from my team on that chickenshit operation. And for what? Nothing. We found the truck park and a whole regiment of NVA and then they wouldn't send the air strike I called in because in the four days it took me to find the goddamn place Washington called a bombing halt."

"Well, it's sort of the same situation now."

"Not good enough, Jack. I've got promises to keep."

"For Christ's sake listen to me, will you? They'll take measures to keep you out of it if they have to, and I can't stop them. It's that important."

"They! Who the fuck are they? Never mind. I get the picture. You got the props kicked out from under you, right?"

Brannigan said nothing.

"Look, I'll make this easy for you. I'm resigning as of this phone call. As far as the original mission objective is concerned, I'm out. But I'm not backing off on Strasser. I've been after that scumbag too long to pass up the best shot I've had yet. No hard feelings, Jack. Like you said, I know how it works. See ya."

"Damnit, Mike, you can't—" But the other end of the line went dead.

* * *

RACHEL HAD HEARD nothing of the heated conversation from where she sat in the lobby of the Hilton Hotel, but the look on Semko's face when he came out of the telephone booth told her that things had not gone well.

"I want you to level with me about something," Semko said as he sat down beside her on the sofa in the main lobby.

"The way you've been leveling with me?" Rachel said, almost without thinking.

"You figured that out, huh?"

"That and a lot more," Rachel said, but stopped short of telling him what she had learned about the World War II documents from Ben-David.

"Well, it looks like you were right about something else, too, what you said in London, about too many mistakes."

"I wasn't absolutely certain until I saw that man spill his beer down the front of his shirt and blame you. That incident was staged. After you knocked him to the ground, he got up and motioned with his head to another man near the pagoda, and they both disappeared into the crowd."

"Figures. Look, I don't know what they're up to. And at this point I don't give a shit. I gave up trying to figure out the suits a long time ago. I admit, I didn't level with you on the mission objectives. I still can't. But I give you my word, what I didn't tell you never put you in any more danger than you were already in. But that's history now. I'm out of it. I was always after Strasser, and I still am. Same as you. And now I could use your help to get him."

Rachel believed, in light of what Ben-David had told her, that Semko was telling the truth, but her loyalties were to the Mossad; and although Semko's remark suggested that he was abandoning the effort to get the documents, that had no bearing on Israeli interests. She still had questions about why the CIA would intentionally place stumbling blocks in the way of the man they had sent to carry out their own mission, and suspected that there was yet another hidden agenda of which even Semko was not aware. But she still wanted very much to carry out her orders to eliminate Jurgen Strasser, and if possible to get the documents, and she saw a continued partnership with Semko as beneficial toward that goal.

"What do you have in mind?"

"Do your people have anybody working the Russian who showed up at the meeting today?"

"I don't know, but I can assure you they aren't going to be overly enthusiastic about cooperating with you after what happened to them at the beer garden."

"So does that mean you're in or out?"

Rachel hesitated and then said, "I'm in. My objective has always been to get Jurgen Strasser. I haven't received any orders to the contrary."

"Then let me talk to your support team."

"I doubt that it's going to do much good."

"Can't hurt to try. Besides, it's all I've got going for me now."

"That, and me," Rachel said with a whimsical smile.

"I'd still like a straight answer about where the hell you learned to shoot."

"Maybe someday I'll tell you."

"Art history major, my ass," Semko said as they left the hotel lobby.

« 32 »

IT WAS A nasty part of Munich, very un-German in its dirtiness. Inhabited by prostitutes, drug dealers, addicts, drunks, and migrant workers, its streets and alleys and tenements and honky-tonk bars were the seamy side of the prosperous city, far removed from the glamour and glitter of the showcase avenues with shops full of the best that money could buy.

It was late afternoon when the attractive young woman got out of the taxi two blocks from her intended destination and walked along the grimy street. She was dressed in jeans and an expensive suede jacket, and looked out of place and vulnerable. But anyone judging her solely by her appearance would have made a terrible and costly mistake, for she was far more dangerous than most who would prey upon her. Her name was Erica Hohner, or Inge Wendel, or Gretchen Zimmerman, or Marlene Steiner, or any number of aliases by which she had come to be known to the German police and international counter-terrorist organizations during the past eight years. But she was born Erica Hohner, twenty-nine years ago, to a respectable upper-middle-class German family in Stuttgart. It was at the age of fifteen, filled with an inexplicable wild hatred and poisoned ideals, that she became infatuated with her border-line-lunatic terrorist idols, Baader and Meinhof, who had declared war on the Establishment and founded what would eventually become the Red Army Faction.

Her current idol and mentor was Jurgen Strasser, whom she had met shortly after graduating from college when she was sent, by the leader of the RAF cell she had joined, to the secret terrorist base in East Germany for her training and indoctrination. She was following Strasser's orders as she turned the corner and headed toward the designated rally point, a small immigrant-owned Pakistani restaurant in the middle of the block.

Erica and her four colleagues were to split up and take counter-surveillance measures after leaving the beer garden, then rendezvous at the restaurant before driving back to their base of operations south of Baden-Baden, where they would be met by Strasser. She had not yet learned of the three men Rachel Sidrane had shot, nor was she aware of the car that pulled in to the curb one block behind the taxi that had stopped to let her out.

Two of the men from Rachel's support team had gone unnoticed by the CIA officers who had locked their colleagues in the back of the van earlier that day. Their assignment, along with four local agents, had been to watch the outer perimeter of the beer garden. They had heard the screams and shouts of the crowd and begun moving in that direction, when one of them saw and recognized Erica Hohner as she exited the wooded path to merge with the strollers in the landscaped grounds of the Englischer Garten. The Mossad's objective was not only to eliminate Jurgen Strasser, but also anyone else in his organization who had taken part in the bombing of the Amsterdam synagogue, as Erica Hohner had. The man who spotted her began following at a distance as she left the park. He stayed with her until she stopped for coffee at an outdoor café on the Marienplatz, then he reestablished contact with those who had been released from the van and called them in to assist him with the surveillance.

A second car carrying four men, and in radio contact with the first, was close behind when the taxi stopped. When the first car reported that Erica Hohner had turned the corner onto a side street, they sped toward the intersection and arrived just as she approached the entrance to the restaurant. A jukebox blaring through the open door of a bar across the street masked the sound of the car pulling up, and Erica's back was to the two men who jumped out and caught her by complete surprise. They quickly pinned her arms to her sides, picked her up off her feet, and carried her to the curb where they threw her onto the floor in the back of the car and dived in on top of her as the driver sped away.

One man knocked her unconscious with a blow to the base of her skull with the knife-edge of his hand, while the other searched her for weapons and removed a nine-millimeter semi-automatic pistol from her shoulder bag and a small revolver from an ankle holster wrapped around her left leg. The broad-daylight abduction had taken less than ten seconds and had drawn no more than insouciant stares from a few drugged-out addicts slumped in nearby doorways, and prompted a hurried retreat by two hookers standing near the corner. It was a neighborhood where random violence, drunken brawls, and muggings were daily events, and where no one ever called the police for any reason.

THE THREE-STORY BRICK house in the Munich suburbs was on a large corner lot, thickly screened with tall evergreen trees. It belonged to a Mossad helper, a local building contractor who kept it available as a safe house. Semko parked the rented car in the driveway and followed Rachel through a garden gate and around to the back door. They were met by Rubin Weissman, a

short, wiry man with intense dark eyes, who gave Rachel a
stern look of disapproval as he stepped aside to let them enter.

"Why did you bring him here?"

"Because I asked her to," Semko said.

"Hear him out," Rachel said.

"I'm not interested in anything he has to say."

"You want Strasser, don't you?" Semko said.

"And we'll get him. Without your help."

"I had nothing to do with what happened to you at the beer
garden."

"Is that right."

"The Agency compromised me, too, then pulled me off the
operation. But I'm still going after Strasser."

Weissman's attention turned to another member of the Mossad team, who had gone out the front door as Semko and
Rachel came in the back. He was carrying a small, hand-held
wireless transmitter detector/locator and nodded to Weissman
as he entered the kitchen.

"He's led someone here," Weissman said to Rachel.

"No one followed us," Semko protested. "I made sure of
that."

"There's a tracking device on your car. You can be followed
from as far as four miles back."

"They're probably my own people," Semko said. "Doesn't
that tell you something?"

"It tells me that I want nothing to do with you."

Rachel pulled Weissman aside and took him into an adjoining room for a private conversation.

"After what happened to you at the beer garden, I'd say it's
pretty obvious that they've had you under surveillance since
you got here. And they're following him to keep him from
getting to Strasser. Which means we've all got the same problem, and regardless of your suspicions, I believe Semko can be
trusted."

"I don't."

"I want you to break us out."

"Without any backup?"

"The CIA has far more personnel available to them than we do. We can't all shake their surveillance; but with your help, Semko and I can."

"I'm not going to place you in jeopardy again, not with a loose cannon like him."

"You're forgetting that this is my call. Until Ben-David says otherwise, I make the operational decisions and you are to provide support for me. And I say that we can still get Strasser, and, with a little luck, the documents."

"I was told that you didn't participate in any operations directed against the United States."

"I don't, and I'm not. This isn't against them, it's against Strasser. The CIA brought us in to help, so I'm going to help. If I get the documents, we share them. If I get Strasser, then we've accomplished the original objective. As far as I'm concerned this is still a joint operation."

"For the record, I'm against it."

"Fine, you've made your point. Now, do we have any local agents or helpers watching the Russian Strasser met at the beer garden?"

"No. We have something much better. Erica Hohner."

Rachel's surprise was genuine. "Where?"

"In the basement."

"What has she told you?"

"Nothing yet. We just started interrogating her about an hour ago."

"If she knows anything that can lead us to Strasser, he's going to change his plans when she doesn't turn up."

Weissman smiled. "We thought of that. We have a number of highly placed friends with the press and the police in the city. They agreed to report that she was shot and killed while

trying to escape from the park. The story's already been on the
television news. We made sure she saw it.''

Rachel thought for a moment, recalling the biographical
data and psychological profile she had read on Erica Hohner
during her research of the current members of the Red Army
Faction.

''How's she holding up?''

''We don't have the time for drugs, so we've decided on the
rough stuff. The problem is, she keeps passing out.''

''Most of what I've read about her indicates she's not very
bright, but the psychological work-up we have on her suggests
she's a situational psychotic with a low tolerance for pain. If
you get too physical with her and she snaps you're not going
to be able to trust anything she tells you.''

''You have a better idea?''

''As a matter of fact, I do.''

Rachel returned to the kitchen and told Semko about Erica
Hohner, a name with which he was more than familiar, having
made it a point to read every scrap of information Delta Force
and the CIA's counter-terrorist section had gathered on the
members of the RAF since his run-in with them in Dusseldorf
three years ago.

''How would you like to play good cop, bad cop with her?''

''Do I get to be the bad cop?''

''No. I do,'' Rachel said, and spent the next twenty minutes
telling Semko what she had in mind.

Weissman reluctantly agreed to Rachel's plan, and instructed the two men conducting the interrogation to leave the
basement room when Semko entered.

Erica Hohner sat on a bare wooden chair in the center of the
damp, windowless room. A single light bulb hung from the
ceiling, its harsh light glaring off the whitewashed walls.
Erica's ankles were bound to the lower legs of the chair, and
her hands were tied to the arms. She was naked except for her

high-cut bikini-style panties, and despite the cool temperature, she was drenched in perspiration. A blindfold covered her eyes, preventing her from seeing her tormentors, and she cocked her head to the left and then to the right, listening to determine if they had left her alone. She stiffened at the sound of someone approaching and sensed that they had stopped to stand directly over her.

Semko glanced at the video camera mounted on the wall in a corner of the room, then his eyes fell on a small hand-cranked field telephone off to the side of the chair. The instrument was rigged to send electric current through a pair of wires with alligator clips on the ends that were attached to the nipples of Erica's breasts. Blood caked at the sides of her mouth, the result of her biting her tongue from the jolt of the electric shocks. She had involuntarily relieved herself from the excruciating pain that had racked her body, and the smell of urine permeated the stuffy air from a puddle that had collected beneath her.

Semko reached down and removed the blindfold. The eyes that looked up at him were filled with a mixture of fear and loathing. He felt a brief moment of pity for her, until he reminded himself of what Rachel had told him: this was the woman who, among other atrocities, had personally placed the bomb in the Amsterdam synagogue and slaughtered eighteen people.

"They stripped you to your panties to add a sexual dimension," Semko said in a friendly, almost apologetic voice. "It adds to the humiliation and the sense of being violated. The blindfold adds to the element of fear; people are more terrified when they can't anticipate or prepare themselves for what's coming next."

"Who are you?" Her voice was weak, but still defiant.

"This is going to hurt a little," Semko said, and winced as he removed the alligator clips from her nipples.

"You're not one of them. You sound like an American."

"I am. My name's Mike Semko. I'm with the Central Intelligence Agency. And I'm sorry you had to go through this."

"What do you want?" There were signs of relief in her expression, but none of gratitude.

"I want Jurgen Strasser."

"I told the Jews, I don't know anyone by that name." Until only an hour ago, when the Mossad began interrogating her, she would have been telling the truth; she had known Strasser only as Dieter.

"I'm not your enemy," Semko said. "I can get you out of this, but you've got to cooperate."

"I don't know anything."

The timing for what Semko did next was a result of Rachel's earlier instructions. He crossed to where the clothes that had been stripped from Erica at the beginning of the interrogation lay on a table against the wall. He picked up her blouse and draped it around her shoulders to cover her bare breasts.

"Do you have any idea what these people are going to do to you if you don't give them what they want? Or for that matter, even if you do."

"I don't care."

"You will. Believe me. And regardless of how strong you might think you are, in the end you'll tell them what they want to know. They're very good at this. And they have all the time in the world."

Erica averted her eyes and said nothing, but the small reflexive shudder that shook her body told of the psychological effect of his words.

"Look, if you stonewall me, my orders are to turn you over to them. And if I don't get Strasser, they will. He's a dead man no matter how you look at it. And as far as he and the rest of your organization know, you're already dead. So what do you have to lose? You tell me where to find him; I'll get you out of here and make sure you're set up somewhere you can start over again with a new identity. Like I said, you're eventually going to tell them anyway, and you can't be foolish enough to believe for one second that they're going to let you live when they finish with you.''

Erica again made eye contact with Semko, and Rachel, watching on the video monitor at the console outside the room, read her expression as an indication that in her desperation she was beginning to accept Semko as someone she might trust. Taking her cue from the terrorist's first sign of weakening, she burst into the room.

''Get out!'' she screamed at Semko.

''I'm not finished talking to her.''

''Get out! Now!'' Rachel crossed to the field telephone and picked up the alligator clips Semko had removed, then pulled the blouse from around Erica's shoulders and threw it on the floor.

Erica cringed at Rachel's touch. It was another new face, another unknown element for her to contend with, and Rachel played her part well, glaring into the terrorist's eyes with all the fanaticism she could affect.

Semko grabbed the alligator clips from Rachel's hand and stood between her and Erica. ''This is my prisoner. We told you where to find her, and we were supposed to conduct the interrogation.''

''You've had your chance. Now we'll handle it our way.''

''You want to go to war with the CIA over this? I make one phone call to my boss, he calls your boss, and your bull-dyke ass will be on its way back to Israel tonight. Now you get the hell out and let me finish.''

''Ten minutes. That's it. If she hasn't told you where Strasser is by then, she's mine.'' Rachel stormed from the room and slammed the door behind her.

''We don't have much time,'' Semko said, donning an expression of deep concern as he picked up the blouse and again draped it over Erica's shoulders. "My government's got no beef with you; the Israelis, on the other hand, have their own way of looking at things. They think you killed a bunch of their people. They kind of take a dim view of stuff like that. So what's it going to be? Me or them?"

Erica's shoulders slumped and her head dropped to her chest. The change in her defiant posture and the confused and frightened expression on her face told Semko that she had weakened further with the threat of renewed torture.

"I need an answer."

"They'll let me leave with you?" Erica finally said, and Semko knew he had her.

"They've got no choice. It's our operation. Now where's Strasser?"

"What time is it?"

Semko looked at his watch. "A few minutes past six."

"I don't know where he is now, but I know where he will be in a few hours. At our base of operations."

"And where's that?"

"Are you familiar with the Black Forest region of our country?"

"Vaguely," Semko said, then untied the ropes that bound her hands and feet and removed a map of Germany from the inside pocket of his Windbreaker. "Show me."

Her legs were wobbly, and he helped her over to the table where he spread out the map. She flexed her fingers, stiff and cramped from the impeded circulation, then pointed to a location in the southwest corner of Germany.

"It is in the central Black Forest region, fifty-five kilometers south of Baden-Baden. Precisely two and one-half kilometers south of Baiersbronn, on autoroute four sixty-two, you will see an unmarked gravel road on your right. The road leads through the forest into the foothills. After you have gone another three-point-six kilometers you will see another unpaved road on your left. Follow it to where it branches left and right. Take the road to your left. Exactly two-point-seven kilometers from the fork, the road ends at a small farm. That is our base of operations.''

''What's the terrain like?''

''It is in its own valley, surrounded by high hills. There are a few small open fields that were once grazing land, but they are fallow and overgrown. The rest of the land is wooded.''

''How many buildings?''

''The house, a barn, and two small outbuildings that were used as equipment sheds when the place was a working farm.''

''Any neighbors?''

''None close enough to be seen or to be disturbed by the gunfire when we are shooting targets. It is an isolated area. Much of the surrounding land is government protected, what you call in America a national forest. That is why Dieter chose it.''

''How many of your people are there?''

Erica hesitated. ''I've told you where to find him.''

''I need to know what I'm going to be up against when I go after him. How many people?''

''Eleven . . . no, eight,'' she said, remembering the newscast footage of her three dead colleagues in the beer garden. ''There will be eight, and Dieter.''

''What kind of weapons do they have?''

Erica hesitated again, but after taking a deep breath of resignation continued. ''Automatic assault rifles, two or three shoulder-fired rocket launchers, and an assortment of small arms.''

''Grenades?''

''No. There are plastic explosives and detonators and timers in a room in the barn where we construct the bombs, but nothing that could be used to defend against an attack.''

"What are Strasser's plans once he gets there?"

"To complete his business with the Russians. They are to bring him the chemical weapons that are part of the deal he is making with them. He has something they want very badly; he didn't tell us what it is."

"When are the Russians making the delivery?"

"Tomorrow. Before noon."

"Good," Semko said, "I appreciate your help."

With that, the door opened and the two men who had been interrogating her entered. They grabbed her and dragged her back to the chair, shoving her down hard and holding her there.

"What are you doing?" she screamed, her eyes beseeching Semko, who stood by watching as one of the men again threw her blouse to the floor. "You promised to take me out of here if I cooperated."

"I lied," Semko said.

Erica screamed and struggled in vain against the strong hands that held her down on the chair. She leaned forward and spat at Semko as he turned to leave. "You bastard! You lying bastard!"

"I've been called worse," Semko said, and shut the door as he left the room.

He joined Rachel at the video console and watched as one of the men stuck a hypodermic needle in Erica's upper arm. She was quiet and docile within seconds.

"They've got time to use drugs now," Rachel said. "Before they're through with her she'll tell them everything she knows about the RAF and their supporters."

"Then what happens?"

"She'll be taken to Israel to stand trial for the Amsterdam bombing. If she's found guilty, she'll be executed."

"I done good, huh?"

"You were very good, very convincing," Rachel said, and

looked directly into Semko's eyes with an amused expression. "My bull-dyke ass?"

"I've always had a flair for the dramatic."

THE ELECTRONIC SURVEILLANCE experts from the technical support team at the CIA's Munich base had not trusted to luck that the Russians would continue to use the public telephone one block from Tumanov's apartment. While the meeting at the beer garden was taking place, they had tapped into the lines of the five public phones within a four-block area. Their foresight payed off that evening when Leonov used one of the five phones to return Strasser's call.

Parked in a panel truck crammed with electronic equipment a few blocks from Tumanov's apartment, the Americans recorded Strasser's directions to his base of operations, and the time for the meeting: between eleven and noon the next day. They also received an unexpected bonus when they listened in on a call placed from another of the five telephones by the leader of the Russian special operations team. He had ordered six more of his men from Zossen to bring a van with them and to meet him that night at a rendezvous point he had selected in the vicinity of Baiersbronn.

The chief of the Munich base was pleased with the information. It meant that rather than having to follow Leonov to the meeting site, he could go there directly. Upon reporting what he had learned to the twenty-four-hour operations center in Langley, he was more than a little confused by his instructions from the deputy director for Operations. But as a field operative with more than fifteen years' experience, he had more than once received orders that appeared on the surface to contradict the stated goals of the mission, and he did not question them now.

He and two of his men were to proceed to the vicinity of Strasser's base of operations and communicate directly with

Brannigan at the twenty-four-hour operations center, by means of a portable satellite radio. They were to observe the meeting site at a distance and report what was happening, as it was happening. And under no circumstances were they to take any direct action or interfere in any way with what transpired between the Russians and Strasser.

The Munich base chief was also ordered to have the team assigned to him from the Frankfurt base maintain their surveillance of Mike Semko and the Mossad woman with him. They were to be considered "unfriendly" to the operation, and at the first indication that they had learned of the meeting site and were headed in that direction, they were to be taken into custody and held until further notice.

Those orders had come directly from the director, and when the Munich base chief asked what measures were to be taken if Semko and the woman offered resistance, he was told simply that he was to instruct the Frankfurt team to respond in kind.

« 33 »

THE LOCAL CIA agent watching the Mossad's suburban safe house saw Semko and Rachel pull out of the driveway shortly after dark in the silver-gray Audi sedan they had rented at the Munich airport. He radioed the information to the two special operations officers from the Agency's Frankfurt base parked three blocks away, who immediately resumed their mobile surveillance. They tracked the Audi to a sporting goods store, and then to the Hilton International, where they watched Semko and Rachel go inside, only to reappear twenty minutes later and drive out of the hotel parking lot to leave the city and head west on the E 11 autobahn toward Salzburg.

The magnetically mounted transmitter attached to the underside of Semko's car had been placed there in a matter of seconds, while he was completing the paperwork at the rental agency's desk. The low-profile beacon transmitter, with a range of five miles under optimum conditions, was not much larger than a bar of soap and emitted a pulsed radio frequency signal back to the direction-finding receiver mounted beneath the dash of the surveillance vehicle, where it was monitored by the man acting as the tracker.

"I wonder where they're going?" the tracker said.

"Strasser's meeting with the Russians is in the Black Forest area, right?"

"Right. And our orders are to interdict Semko and the woman only if it looks like they're heading that way," the driver said. "So I don't care where they're going as long as it's in the opposite direction."

A few moments later a change in the readout on the receiver caught the tracker's attention. "Slow down. I think he's stopped."

The compass display on the backlit LCD monitor, which gave bearing and direction-of-travel information on the target vehicle, showed it to be dead ahead, approximately two miles away. The motion sensor indicated that Semko's car had indeed stopped, and the bar graph on the signal-strength meter moved toward the top of the register as the beep tone rose in pitch and intensity, telling them that they were closing fast on the transmitter.

"Maybe he pulled off to get gas," the driver said, and slowed to fifty miles an hour to watch for an exit sign.

"No. It's at least ten miles to the next service plaza."

Four more members of the Frankfurt team were in a backup car a mile behind the tracking vehicle, in radio contact and ready to assist in the event Semko and Rachel had to be stopped and taken into custody. The tracker informed them of the situation and told them to reduce their speed and hold their position behind them.

The beep tone became a steady screech as the lead car came out of a long sweeping curve to see the Audi stopped at the side of the road one hundred yards ahead.

"They must have car trouble. Drive past them."

"Ah, shit!" the driver shouted, then slammed his fist on the dash as he looked across the median strip to the eastbound lanes just as the headlight of a passing motorcycle flashed briefly on two people getting into a car parked at the side of the road.

"What?" the tracker said, then followed his partner's gaze to see a car pull out from the shoulder on the eastbound lanes. He immediately grasped what had happened. "Jesus. They really set us up."

"How far to the next crossover?"

"About eight miles. At the service plaza."

"Goddamnit!" the driver said, as he stared at the aluminum-post-and-rail barrier running down the middle of the median strip.

"We can radio back to the base, have someone try to pick up the surveillance before they get too far away. Did you get a good look at the car?"

"No. Dark color and small. That's all I could see."

"Maybe they can get some surveillance cars into the area around Strasser's hideout, grab them before they get too close."

"There are any number of ways into that place. We can't cover them all. And besides, our orders are to keep a low profile. Face it. We blew it. Give the Munich base a call and tell them."

SEMKO HAD ASKED Weissman to have his local helper provide a car that was fast and could also handle the back roads into the meeting site. What he found waiting for him exceeded his expectations. The Porsche Carrera 4 was equipped with all-wheel drive and capable of speeds in excess of 140 miles an hour. Quick and nimble, there were few cars that could stay with it for any distance.

The eastbound traffic was light, and Semko pulled into the outside lane and took the powerful sports car up to 130 miles an hour before backing off to cruise along comfortably at 120.

Rachel had calculated the distance to Strasser's base of op-

erations to be 215 miles from where they were told they would
find the Porsche. They planned to take the autobahn to Stuttgart, then south to Herrenberg before heading west on the
secondary roads that led into the Black Forest. At the speed
they were traveling, she estimated they would reach the area
before midnight, allowing them to get into position under the
cover of darkness, long before Strasser took whatever security
precautions he had planned for the meeting with the Russians.

Semko and Rachel had stopped at the hotel to change
clothes, and both were dressed in jeans and hiking boots and
wore heavy sweaters under dark green parkas, all purchased at
the sporting goods store in anticipation of spending a chilly
night in the woods.

"Check the back," Semko said, as he flashed his high
beams and roared past a slower-moving car. "See if they managed to get all the goodies."

Rachel looked in the backseat and found two fitted weapon
cases and two small knapsacks. She brought them forward,
one at a time, and examined the contents. The fitted cases each
held an H&K MP-5-SD submachine gun equipped with an
integral sound suppressor and a Pulse Beam laser sight.
Weighing less than eight pounds and just over twenty inches in
length, they were capable of firing eight hundred rounds per
minute in the full automatic mode.

"Nice," Semko said, as Rachel held one of the weapons up
for him to see. "Can you handle a submachine gun?"

"I think I can manage."

"Learned that in art school, too, huh?"

"It was a tough school," Rachel said, as she opened the
knapsacks and looked inside.

Weissman had gotten everything Semko asked for, including five additional thirty-round magazines for each of the submachine guns, a pair of night-vision goggles, a pair of field

glasses, a set of small, hand-held radios in the event they were separated, and a state-of-the-art infrared thermal imager.

"It's all here," Rachel said.

"Are the magazines loaded?"

"Yes," Rachel confirmed after checking.

"See if you can find something on the radio. Anything but rap."

Rachel tuned to a classical music station and reclined her seat. She closed her eyes and was asleep within a matter of minutes, much to Semko's surprise.

A light rain began to fall as the Porsche sped past the Augsburg exits, but it changed to little more than a fine mist as they approached Stuttgart, and stopped altogether by the time Rachel awoke from her hour-long nap and sat quietly listening to a Mozart symphony as they headed south to Herrenberg and then west into the central Black Forest region.

When they left the autobahn, Semko cut his speed in half as the terrain and the scenery changed dramatically. The winding two-lane roads were pitch black with the exception of an occasional passing car and the faint glow from secluded towns and little cuckoo-clock villages with tall, thin church spires off in the distance. Groves of birchwood and beech trees intermingled with dense stands of spruce and pine and silver fir, now and then giving way to small fields and open pastureland. The gravel road they took just south of Baiersbronn was rough and narrow and cut into the sides of a series of hills. Semko stayed well to the inside, away from the steep drop-off on his left, and slowed to thirty miles an hour as the road began a steady climb into the higher elevations.

The low scudding clouds were soon swept away by a frontal system moving across the mountains, and a full moon shone brightly on the endless forests of dark evergreens from which the region got its name. Gloomy and forbidding on the outside, the forest derived an inner luminescence, almost a mystical

glow, from the moonlight, and Rachel was reminded of a
course she had taken on the Holocaust at Tel Aviv University.
Part of the course had dealt with the history of the German
people, and she recalled something the Roman historian and
orator Tacitus had written about the Germanic tribes more than
eighteen centuries ago, when the Roman legions had found the
mountain crags and canyons of the Black Forest impregnable
and unconquerable: "The woods and groves are the holy
places of barbarians, giving shelter to their free and unbridled
spirits." So much of the German soul, she recalled the professor who taught the course telling her, was nurtured and shaped
by their love of nature and the cruelties and myths that went
with it. To understand that mystical side of the Germans, he
had said, was to understand how a nation that had given so
much that was good and beautiful to literature and music could
have subscribed to the madness of Hitler's Third Reich.

"You okay?" Semko said as he noticed the same distant
look in her eyes he had seen at the café in Munich.

"I'm fine."

"We're getting close."

As they descended into a deep mountain valley, Semko saw
a break in the trees ahead. He checked the odometer, and
found the left turn precisely at the point Erica Hohner told him
he would. He switched off the radio and the headlights, using
only the parking lights as he slowed the Porsche to ten miles
an hour on what was now an uneven dirt road barely wide
enough for one car. Just before he reached the spot where the
road branched to the left and right, with the farm less than two
miles away, he spotted what he had hoped to find and pulled
off the road onto a narrow farm track that cut into the woods
on his left. The soft needles of the evergreen branches that
crowded the track brushed against the sides of the car and all
but obscured the way. He bounced in and out of deep ruts,
scraping the undercarriage several times and almost bottoming

out before making a sharp turn to the right where the track became impassable. He got out of the car and looked back in the direction he had come; the Porsche was well off the road and screened from sight by a thick stand of pines.

"We'll hike in from here," he told Rachel, who had already gotten out of the car and pulled on her knapsack.

The way Rachel handled the small submachine gun was not lost on Semko, who watched as she smoothly and quickly inserted a magazine, engaged the safety, and pulled back the bolt to put a round in the chamber.

"You're taking your purse?" he said as he saw her slip the strap over her head and secure it under her right arm.

"It's a shoulder bag. And I don't go anywhere without it."

"Suit yourself," Semko said, deciding it was one of those "girl things" that he had never understood the logic of on the few occasions when he had made the mistake of asking for an explanation.

The Mossad helper had provided a large-scale topographical map of the immediate area that showed the location of the old farm, and using a small, shielded penlight, Semko spread it open on the roof of the Porsche and got his bearings before he and Rachel set off into the forest.

In the pale glow of the moonlight that filtered down through the trees, the night-vision goggles proved unnecessary for the trek through the woods. They started down a steep slope, grabbing on to branches to slow their descent, and digging in the edges of their boots to keep from slipping on the thick carpet of pine needles and leaves on the forest floor. At the bottom of the slope Semko checked his compass, then led the way through a narrow gorge, following the course of a mountain stream in the direction of the farm.

It was rough country, and they moved even slower now, carefully placing each step as they worked their way through the low brush and thickets along the bank of the fast-flowing

stream. They continued in the same cautious manner for another hour, pausing every ten minutes to watch and listen, until
they reached an area where the floor of the valley broadened
and the woods began to thin. Just ahead, Semko could make
out the edge of an overgrown field of waist-high grass, and he
moved toward it and dropped to one knee just inside the tree
line, signaling Rachel to come alongside and do the same.

Two hundred yards ahead of them, at the far end of the field,
they saw the dark outline of an old stucco-and-timber farmhouse with a steeply pitched roof. A large barn could be seen
off to the right, along with one of the outbuildings that Semko
guessed was an equipment shed. Lights were on inside the
house, and a thin column of smoke rose from a single chim-
ney; Rachel thought briefly of the warmth of the fireplace as
she zipped up her parka against the cold mountain air.

They remained within the deep shadows at the edge of the
field as Semko took the night-vision goggles from Rachel's
knapsack and adjusted the head strap until they fit snugly over
his eyes. He switched them on, and the dark recesses of the
high ground approximately one hundred yards off to his left
became visible in the eerie green light. He moved his head in a
slow arc, scanning back and forth, until just below the crest of
a hill he noticed a rock ledge that was partially hidden by
overhanging branches and appeared to have a commanding
view of the house and most of the farm.

He checked the house again, this time noticing the three
cars parked near the barn, then returned the night-vision goggles to Rachel's knapsack and motioned for her to follow as he
got up and moved off in the direction of the ledge. They stayed
well inside the tree line as they climbed the steep grade leading to the top of the hill, moving quickly and deliberately
across a few small open spaces until they were again under
cover of the forest. As Semko had suspected, the location
proved to be a perfect observation site, a military crest less

than sixty yards from the house that overlooked most of the surrounding area. Behind them, the ground rose almost vertically to another ledge that jutted out to form a partial roof over their heads, concealing them from view of anyone moving along the actual crest of the hill. Stands of evergreens to their left and right screened their flanks, and in front of them, a thinly wooded slope of deciduous trees and low pines fell quickly away to the clearing around the house.

It was one forty-five in the morning when they settled into position on the ledge, and Rachel, forgetting none of her training, observed the rules of noise discipline as she leaned toward Semko and whispered mouth to ear.

"I've had a nap. I'll take the first watch."

Semko held up two fingers. Rachel nodded that she understood; he wanted to sleep no more than two hours.

Semko sat cross-legged with his back to the rock wall behind him, cradling the submachine gun in his lap as he lowered his chin to his chest and closed his eyes. Below them, at the bottom of the slope, the lights in the farmhouse had gone out, and Rachel took the night-vision goggles from her knapsack and began slowly searching the nearby woods and the immediate area around the house for any sign of movement. Her eyes adjusted to the green-tinted world seen through the goggles, and soon she was able to pick out the small night creatures that scurried along the forest floor, and even locate an owl perched in a nearby tree whose plaintive calling had drawn her attention.

Alert and feeling no need for sleep, she let Semko rest longer than the two hours he had asked for. During her third hour of the watch, she began to believe that her senses were playing tricks on her. The moon was no longer overhead, and the light in the forest had diminished significantly. She thought she heard the sound of someone moving through the woods above the ledge and to her right, but the night-vision goggles revealed nothing, not even a mouse or other nocturnal forager that might have explained what she had heard. She continued to focus on the area and thought she saw a brief shadowy movement, but attributed it to the night breeze gently swaying the branches of the evergreens that drooped to the floor of the forest.

A ground fog that had risen from the valley drifted slowly through the trees and played further tricks on her eyes. And when she heard the soft, shuffling noise again, this time louder and more distinct, she decided to wake Semko. His eyes snapped open at the touch of her index finger pressed to his lips, telling him to remain silent. After the few moments it took until he was fully awake, she removed her finger from his lips and pointed to their right flank.

Semko turned his head slowly in the direction indicated and cupped his hands around his ears to help capture any distant sounds. He heard nothing but the soft sway of the pines and the rustle of the leaves in the breeze. He took the night-vision goggles that Rachel held out to him and focused on a section of low pines and scrub below and to their right. He thought he saw something move, then stop and move again, but he couldn't be certain. The ground fog drastically reduced the range and effectiveness of the goggles, and he set them aside and silently slipped off his knapsack to remove the thermal imager.

The unique, hand-held surveillance device resembled a compact video camera in size and shape, but served an entirely different purpose. The infrared images it produced were thermal pictures of heat radiation patterns invisible to the naked eye, but which all objects and living things emit in relation to the area around them. Highly sensitive to temperature differences as small as 0.9 degrees Fahrenheit, the imager could detect and delineate objects or persons in complete darkness or under natural cover from as far away as fifteen hundred feet, and could easily distinguish between an animal and a human being.

The remarkable instrument was capable of detecting even residual heat, from the organic decomposing of a recently buried body in a shallow grave, or from the engine, tires, and brakes of a recently operated vehicle. Living, breathing human images appeared as ghostly specters in shades of black, gray, and white, with the areas of the body emitting the most heat—the head and chest area—appearing the brightest.

Fog had no effect on the thermal imager—the cold dampness actually enhanced its performance—and where the night-vision goggles could not detect anyone concealed in the trees or thickets, the imager easily delineated their heat signature from within the natural foliage. It was while training the device on a thick patch of fog that enveloped the woods thirty yards below and to the right of the ledge that Semko caught his first glimpse of what had drawn Rachel's attention earlier.

He counted ten of them, moving through the fog like phantoms, appearing all the more like ghostly aberrations when viewed through the thermal imager. Their line of march indicated they had come over the ridge behind the ledge, and Semko watched as they descended even lower. They held their weapons in the shoot-back position and moved expertly from cover to cover, eventually to gather in a tight group approximately eighty yards below and to the right of the ledge where the ground leveled off and the trees gave way to an open field in front of the house. One of them, obviously the leader, used hand signals to direct the others into concealed positions, and they quickly settled within arm's reach of each other facing the farmhouse and the road leading up to it.

The way they had moved through the woods and conducted themselves suggested they were no strangers to operating in a tactical environment, and Semko wanted to know with what, or whom, he was dealing. He focused the imager on the two persons closest to him, and pressed a small button on the side of the device that allowed him to freeze the images and study them in detail. Although their body heat clearly defined each man, he could not determine what weapons they carried, or if they were wearing any sort of uniform that might tell him if they were there in any official capacity.

He handed the thermal imager to Rachel and indicated where she should look, then flashed the fingers of his right hand twice to tell her there were ten of them. She held the device to her eyes, moving it slowly back and forth until she located each of them, then leaned toward Semko and whispered softly in his ear.

"Who are they?"

Semko shrugged.

Rachel observed them for a few minutes longer, then handed the imager back to Semko. "What do we do now?"

Semko put his mouth to Rachel's ear and said, "We wait. See how this shakes out."

Within the hour, the first trace of dawn appeared as a grayish white ribbon of light along the rim of the mountains on the eastern horizon. The ground fog began to thin and lift, and Semko went back to using the night-vision goggles in an attempt to see more details. He increased the magnification and zoomed in on the figure closest to him. The man was lying prone among some low scrub brush behind an old horse-drawn plow overgrown with weeds, his weapon to his shoulder, the barrel resting on top of the rusted and long-discarded piece of machinery and pointed toward the house. Semko focused on the outline of what he immediately recognized as an assault rifle, and after studying its configuration and seeing that the stock pressed into the man's shoulder was the open metal frame folding type, identified it as Russian-made—an AKR, also known as a Krinkov—a cut-down, submachine-gun-sized version of their AKS-74 infantry assault rifle that was currently issued to their special operations units.

"Looks like the Russians have arrived," he whispered to Rachel. "And this time they sent in the first string."

« 34 »

THE DEEP SHADOWS of the woods were left untouched by the gray dawn light, and Semko and Rachel continued to observe the Russians through the night-vision goggles, making certain they did not move unnoticed from their present positions. When the first golden rays of the morning sun slanted through the trees and dappled the forest floor, Semko switched to the field glasses and saw that the Russians were dressed in civilian hiking clothes much like those he and Rachel wore, and all carried small, military-issue rucksacks. His initial assessment of their weapons was confirmed, with one exception that became evident in the light of day: the man farthest from the ledge had an SVD Dragunov sniper rifle with a telescopic sight as his primary weapon.

Shortly after the sun rose full above the horizon, faint sounds from below the ledge began drifting up through the woods: the sounds of people stirring in the farmhouse. Semko heard a door slam at the rear of the house, and saw three men come out and stand together near an old stone well. They were smoking and talking in loud voices, and were soon joined by three more of their colleagues. Five of them were armed with American-made M-16 assault rifles, one with an M-203 grenade launcher mounted beneath the barrel—a weapon Semko remembered well from his Vietnam days, and one that Erica Hohner had lied about, or had forgotten to mention.

The sixth man had an even more worrisome weapon slung over his shoulder: a Russian-made RPG-7. The shoulder-fired rocket-propelled grenade launcher, developed as a tank killer, was also an effective antipersonnel weapon with a range in excess of eight hundred yards. Semko noted that the RPG-7 was loaded, with the distinctive aluminum cap and safety pin still in place on the tip of the projectile that protruded from the front of the launcher. He also saw that the man with the grenade launcher mounted to his M-16 wore a bandolier of at least ten of the deadly forty-millimeter rounds for the weapon across his chest, while the man with the RPG-7 carried a canvas satchel with four additional rocket-propelled grenades.

If Erica Hohner had told the truth about how many of her colleagues would be at the farm, there were still two of the RAF terrorists inside the house with Strasser. Semko had been surprised that Strasser had not put out perimeter guards for the night, at least in the immediate vicinity of the house, and even now, the six men gathered around the old well seemed totally unconcerned with any security precautions as they stood out in the open in the bright morning light.

Semko and Rachel were well camouflaged from anyone looking in their direction from the house, their position screened by the saplings and brush growing out of the rock outcroppings just below the ledge. Semko crawled to his left, to where the ledge ended and the ground fell sharply away to a heavily wooded section that led down to where the men were gathered. Ten yards into the trees, a shallow gully ran down the slope through dense brush to where the ground leveled off, providing excellent cover from the Russians on the right and from the terrorists below for anyone staying low in the depression.

He continued to study the lay of the land and the available

cover leading to the rear of the house, then crawled back to the center of the ledge and again used the field glasses to observe the Russians. A slight shift in the direction they had been looking revealed that the voices of the terrorists had reached them, but they were at least eighty yards away, facing the front of the house, and their angle of view precluded their seeing where the men had gathered at the well. Semko felt Rachel tap him on the shoulder and turned to look in the direction she was pointing.

Strasser's men had finished their cigarettes and were dispersing. Sixty yards below, three of them came around the side of the house facing the ledge. One stopped at the corner and dropped into a prone position to cover the section where the road ended at a parking area near the front entrance. Another moved farther to the right, a few yards into the woods behind a thick clump of brush to cover the same area, while the third took a position behind a boulder ten yards away from the second man and faced in the same direction.

It was now obvious to Semko that they were concerned only with covering the front of the house. He lost track of the three other men, who had moved off in the direction of the barn, but he assumed they would take up identical positions on the opposite side of the house to cover the same area from a different angle.

Semko again checked the Russians. They had not moved, and Strasser's men were unaware of their presence. Though only sixty yards from the three terrorists who had taken cover below the ledge, the Russians were well inside the tree line and concealed from view by low scrub brush and boulders.

Semko's initial plan had been to wait until Strasser put out his security element for the meeting with the Russians; then, once they were settled into position, he would work his way around them to wherever Strasser was. He and Rachel could easily have eliminated the three men directly below them, but

that course of action now risked drawing the attention of the
Russians. Their presence required a different approach to the
problem, and he once again checked their positions. What he
saw next complicated matters even further.

The leader of the Russian team used hand signals to tell
three of his men to take out the terrorist they had seen appear
from the rear of the house and take cover on their left flank.
Semko watched as the three Russians backed out of their positions and begin crawling deeper into the woods to approach
their targets from behind. Semko then saw the team leader take
a hand-held portable radio from his parka and hold it to his
mouth, and he immediately understood what was happening:
whoever was due to meet with Strasser was probably waiting
nearby for the signal to come ahead. Believing that the three
terrorists on his left were the full extent of Strasser's security
element, the Russian team leader was telling them that he had
things under control and was giving the all-clear.

Semko realized that the Russians were completely unaware
of the three terrorists who had moved off to the far side of the
house, two of them in possession of the grenade launcher and
the rocket launcher. Any mistake the Russians made in going
after the three they had spotted would bring the others into
play and alert Strasser to the ambush. It was the man with the
rocket launcher who worried Semko most. If he knew how to
handle the weapon, and it had to be assumed that he did, he
could take all ten of the Russians out with a single round from
the powerful weapon.

Semko knew he had to act now, before things got out of
hand and caused him to lose yet another opportunity to get
Strasser. He turned to face Rachel and motioned for her to
move back against the rock wall of the ledge with him.

"We can't take on both the Russians and Strasser's people," he whispered. "I'm going to get closer to the house to
get a shot at Strasser when he comes out, or if I can, go inside

after him. If I play this right the rest of them will end up killing each other and never know we were here.''

Rachel was about to protest when Semko raised his hand to silence her.

"I need someone on the high ground to let me know what's going on around me down there," he told her. "If all hell breaks loose, forget about me and haul ass out of here through the woods on the other side of the hill. They'll be too concerned with their own problems to chase you down even if they do see you."

Semko removed his knapsack and took out the two palm-sized portable radios the Mossad helper had supplied. He handed one to Rachel and clipped the other one to his belt, then ran the wire for the plug-in earpiece up the back of his parka and out the collar. With the earpiece in place he could receive transmissions without giving away his position.

"If the Russians move, or if any of Strasser's people look like they've seen or heard me, break squelch twice and I'll come up voice as soon as I can. Understand?"

Rachel nodded that she did, then leaned forward to whisper in Semko's ear, but changed her mind. She put her radio earpiece in place and used the field glasses to watch the area below as Semko crawled off the ledge to the left and disappeared from sight.

NIKOLAI LEONOV SAT in the front passenger seat of the panel truck, bracing himself as it bounced and swayed in and out of the deep ruts of the dirt road leading to the farmhouse. The windowless rear area of the panel truck did not contain the crates of chemical weapons Strasser had demanded; it held the six additional men brought in from Zossen that evening, who suffered the same uncomfortable ride as Leonov and the driver. With their AKR assault rifles slung tightly across their chests, they sat on the floor and held on to the cargo tie-downs to keep from being tossed about. The four men in the Mercedes sedan following the truck fared better on the rough road, and closed the distance between the two vehicles when the trees gave way to open fields and they saw the farmhouse in the distance.

The driver of the panel truck had slowed when the house came into view, and Leonov slid back the partition separating the passenger compartment from the cargo area.

"Remember," he told the men in the back, "you are to stay inside until I come around to open the rear doors. At that point your teammates who are already in position will open fire on Strasser and anyone with him. When you come out you will take positions on the opposite side of the road from them and direct your fire at any of Strasser's people left standing. You are then to proceed with the others to search the house and the barn until the area is secured."

The men nodded their understanding, and Leonov closed the partition concealing them from view of anyone outside as the truck slowed to a stop in front of the old farmhouse.

Jurgen Strasser looked out the living room window to see Leonov climb out of the panel truck carrying a portable telephone in a field case. He continued to watch as the driver of the truck and the four men in the Mercedes got out and stood in the open on either side of the tall, heavyset Russian. Satisfied that they were not armed with anything more than pistols they might have concealed beneath their jackets, Strasser then turned to the two men with him, both armed with M-16 assault rifles.

"If the men with Leonov reach for anything, even a cigarette without asking, shoot them."

With that, Strasser tucked a pistol into his waistband at the small of his back and picked up the leather portfolio containing one of the copies he had made of the Goering File. The two men with him led the way out the front door and stood to his left and right when he stopped a few yards from Leonov. They immediately trained their weapons on the four men from the Mercedes and the driver of the panel truck.

"Are you ready to complete our business?" Strasser said, and held up the leather portfolio for Leonov to see.

"May I first examine the contents?"

"Of course," Strasser said, and tossed the portfolio to him. "Then you can place the telephone call while I examine the cargo."

Semko had heard the panel truck arrive, and rather than follow the gully to the bottom of the slope, he had stopped halfway down and cut through the woods to a point where he could observe the front of the house. He froze in position at the sight of Strasser walking out to meet the man he had seen with him at the beer garden, then quickly looked in the direction he had seen the three terrorists take cover below the ledge.

Two of them lay dead, their throats cut, with the Russians who had killed them lying under cover beside their bodies. The third Russian was working his way around a thicket of briars and had not yet reached the terrorist closest to the house. He was still ten yards away and crawling toward him through a dangerously open grassy area.

From his vantage point, Semko had a clear shot at Strasser as he stood out in the open facing Leonov. The suppressor on his submachine gun would reduce the sound of his shot to no more than a forceful rush of air that could not be heard more than twenty feet away, and the subsonic ammunition assured there would be no sonic crack when the round left the barrel. There was nothing to give away his position. He could kill Strasser and then disappear into the woods in the heat of the ensuing firefight between the Russians and the terrorists.

With his eyes fixed on Strasser, Semko lay flat on the ground and angled his body to compensate for the sloping terrain, then settled into a stable shooting platform and carefully parted a clump of scrub brush directly in front of him. He next extended the retractable stock of his weapon and changed the fire selector switch from three-round-burst to single-shot, then tucked the stock into his shoulder and squeezed the pressure switch attached to the front of the pistol-style grip and activated the Pulse Beam laser sight. The advanced laser optic, effective to one hundred yards with the naked eye, provided rapid target acquisition, allowing accurate point-and-shoot capability with both eyes open holding the weapon at hip, waist, or shoulder level.

The sun was still low on the horizon, casting the front of the house where Strasser stood in shadow and providing perfect operating conditions for the laser sight. Fifty yards from where Semko lay on the wooded slope, an intense, pulsating red dot, the size of a nickel, was immediately projected onto the base of Strasser's skull, marking the point of impact for the bullet.

Semko took a deep breath, exhaled slowly, and squeezed the trigger. A loud warning cry rose from the woods in front of him, and he released the pressure on the trigger to look up and see the terrorist under cover at the side of the house turn and fire a burst from his M-16 into the face of the Russian, who had gotten within five yards of him before the weight of his body snapped a piece of deadwood that had gone unnoticed in the high grass and given away his position.

The scene in front of Semko erupted into one of confusion and chaos. The two men standing beside Strasser opened up on the driver of the van and the four men who had gotten out of the Mercedes, killing them instantly. Bursts of automatic fire came from the Russians in the ambush positions along the edge of the woods, killing the two men with Strasser. The rear doors of the panel truck were thrown open, and the *whoosh* of a rocket-propelled grenade, fired from the side of the barn forty yards away, filled the air. Only two of the six men inside the truck managed to get out before the rocket tore into the side of the cargo area, blowing it apart in a blinding orange-white flash that killed the four men still inside and ignited the gas tank into a secondary explosion that turned the vehicle into a burning, smoking hulk within seconds.

The terrorist with the grenade launcher had seen the Russians inside the tree line at the edge of the field when they opened fire, and in the next instant, the blooping sound of the weapon was heard, followed by a powerful explosion from the forty-millimeter grenade as it landed just inside the woods. Semko saw two of the Russians killed outright by the blast, and two others writhed in pain on the ground, bleeding from shrapnel wounds to the chest and stomach that would soon take their lives.

Just before the rocket struck, Semko had seen Leonov run behind the Mercedes and take cover with the two men who had escaped from the truck. A moment later, he caught a quick glimpse of Strasser running back toward the house, then lost sight of him.

The *whoosh* of another rocket reached Semko as he turned and began crawling toward the rear of the house. He looked back to see the fiery tail of the deadly projectile stream across the field and explode inside the tree line. But the three remaining Russians, who had been positioned just inside the woods, were already up and moving toward the house, and safely away from where the rocket impacted. It was the last round the man with the RPG-7 would fire; this time the back blast from the launcher had given away his position. Forty yards away, the Russian with the sniper rifle dropped to one knee, took careful aim, and killed him with one shot.

Joined by the two men who had succeeded in taking out the two terrorists assigned to them, the leader of the Russian team regrouped with his four remaining men. At his orders, three of them, including the sniper, immediately began running past the front of the house in the direction of the barn, intent on eliminating the terrorist with the grenade launcher and the man with him, who was now firing his M-16 on full automatic at Leonov and the two men behind the Mercedes, effectively pinning them down.

The terrorist closest to the house had rolled away from where he had killed the Russian crawling toward him, and stayed undercover as the battle raged. He rose to a crouch and began to back away from his position when he saw the Russians regroup only ten yards from where he was concealed in the brush. He was unaware that Semko had seen him move, and equally unaware of the red dot flickering on the side of his head just above his ear as he turned toward the rear of the house. Semko fired and killed him; the only recognizable sound was that of the man's body hitting the ground.

The Russian team leader, in his peripheral vision, saw the terrorist fall, but had no idea where the shot had come from. Seeing no apparent threat, and attributing the man's death to a stray round, the team leader immediately focused his attention back on the three men advancing toward the barn and, along with the man with him, provided a withering barrage of covering fire. But the terrorist with the grenade launcher was experienced and well trained. The antipersonnel round he fired landed at the feet of the three men rushing his position, killing two of them and mortally wounding the third. The Russian team leader shouted to the two men behind the Mercedes to provide covering fire as he and the man with him ran toward the barn to continue the assault. The terrorist beside the grenadier fired a short burst from his M-16, then disappeared around the side of the barn in a hail of fire from the men behind the Mercedes.

The grenadier cursed the cowardice of his colleague who had fled, but held his position. When the two men running toward him were twenty yards away, he hastily fired from the hip as bullets tore into the side of the barn and the ground around him. The grenade went wide of its mark, exploding harmlessly off to the side of the onrushing men. Before the grenadier could fire the M-16 as an assault rifle, a three-round burst from one of the men behind the Mercedes tore through his chest and killed him. The team leader signaled for the men behind the Mercedes to join him, and all four, with Leonov following, moved slowly forward, the barrels of their weapons sweeping the area before them as they searched for the terrorist they had seen run around the side of the barn.

Rachel had been using the field glasses to watch Semko's progress when she saw him leave the gully and veer across the slope when the panel truck arrived. She was observing the area around the rear of the house to make certain no one approached him from behind, when she noticed the open door of the equipment shed across the yard from the stone well. She focused on the darkened interior of the shed and saw something that she had missed earlier. She was about to radio Semko when the firefight erupted; then, following a strong hunch, she decided to take action. With everyone's attention directed toward the battle at the front of the house, she left the ledge and moved quickly down the slope. She stayed in the gully until she reached the open area near the stone well, then quickly crossed to the shed and hid near the open door, behind a stack of empty fifty-gallon fuel oil drums that had obviously been used for target practice.

Strasser had run back into the house to the small room off the kitchen he used as a study. He gathered up the original of the Goering File, and the four other copies he had made, and placed them inside an aluminum briefcase full of money. He then ran back into the living room to peer outside just as the three Russians advancing on the barn were killed by the grenade blast. He saw no possibility of getting to any of the three cars parked nearby, and raced to the kitchen and out the rear door.

He ran across the yard and entered the equipment shed, where he quickly strapped the briefcase to the rack over the rear fender of the motorcycle parked inside. The powerful trail bike, with its knobby off-road tires, was perfect for negotiating the narrow hiking paths that ran into the hills behind the house. He mounted the bike, then switched on the fuel tank and the ignition, and attempted to kick-start the engine. He saw something move just outside the door, and looked up to see Rachel standing in front of the shed, her submachine gun pointed at him. His eyes followed the beam of light from the laser sight to where it ended in a flickering red dot in the center of his chest.

"You're not going to shoot an unarmed man," Strasser said, his voice icy cold. He had not seen Rachel before, and was unsure of who she was.

"That's exactly what I'm going to do, and I'll tell you why," Rachel said, and moved just inside the shed to avoid being seen by any of the Russians.

For a split second, Strasser's eyes glanced to the left, then back to Rachel as a peculiar smile turned up a corner of his mouth.

The terrorist who had fled around the side of the barn was approaching Rachel from behind, his eyes searching the immediate area in front of him to see if anyone else was with her. Convinced that she was alone, he raised his M-16 to his shoulder and took aim, only to shudder and stare dumbfounded at Strasser as the weapon fell from his hands. The convulsions that shook the terrorist's body as he dropped to the ground at first startled and confused Strasser, until he saw Semko appear from behind the well, the sound-suppressed submachine gun at his hip.

Rachel heard the man fall, and she spun quickly around and

dropped to one knee. She was about to fire at another man in the distance near the edge of the woods when she saw it was Semko. He was aiming over her head when the submachine gun spit and hissed again, and Rachel dived flat on the ground, turning to see Strasser, a pistol in his hand, thrown from the motorcycle by the two three-round bursts that riddled his chest.

Semko approached cautiously, then reached for Rachel's arm and pulled her to her feet. "You okay?"

"Yes," Rachel said, and followed him into the shed as he kept the laser sight centered on Strasser's chest where he lay on the dirt floor, arms and legs askew, his shirt and jacket soaked with blood. Semko kicked the pistol away from Strasser's side and knelt to place his fingertips on his neck to feel for a pulse.

"Is he dead?"

Semko nodded, then said, "It was too quick. I wanted him to know who and why."

"There were a lot of reasons why," Rachel said, and removed the aluminum briefcase from the rack at the back of the motorcycle. She placed it on the seat and snapped it open, and was about to pick up the documents lying on top of the neatly bound stacks of money when a sound near the open door made her and Semko look behind them.

"Drop your weapons!" Leonov ordered.

Semko made a swift appraisal of the four men standing beside the man he had seen with Strasser in the beer garden, and knew that any attempt to turn and fire would be futile. The four Russians held their assault rifles ready to fire, their fingers on the triggers. Semko dropped his weapon, followed immediately by Rachel.

"And now, young lady," Leonov said, "if you would please hand the briefcase to me."

Rachel moved forward and did as Leonov asked, then stepped back to stand beside Semko.

Leonov opened the briefcase and carefully examined the documents, then again looked at Semko and Rachel.

"Unfortunately even if you both swore to me that you have not read the documents inside, I could not possibly take the risk that you have and allow you to live."

Leonov closed the briefcase and spoke to three of the men with him. "You will escort me back to the car."

He then turned to face the Russian team leader and simply nodded his head as he left with his three-man security detail, their eyes constantly moving over the surrounding area for any terrorists they might have missed.

The Russian team leader's name was Anatoli Mikoyan; he was thirty-eight years old, and he, as well as six of the men he had lost that day, was a highly decorated veteran of the Afghan War. And despite his years of bloody combat, he had never shot an unarmed, defenseless person in his life. He stared hard at the beautiful young woman and the man with her, then took a deep breath and resigned himself to his duties.

Rachel read the man well, and took her cue from the reluctant look about him.

"Please," she pleaded. "Don't kill me. I didn't look inside the briefcase, I promise you I didn't."

Mikoyan's eyes softened, but not his resolve. "I'm sorry," he said, and slowly raised the barrel of his weapon. "Please forgive me."

"No! Don't! Please," Rachel said, and grabbed Semko's arm and pressed against his side. "Semko, do something."

Semko felt completely helpless for the first time in his life, and put his arm around Rachel to comfort her. "At least we got rid of Strasser."

Rachel lifted her head to kiss Semko on the cheek, a gesture that made Mikoyan hesitate before he squeezed the trigger.

The hesitation cost him his life as three silent, rapid-fire shots tore into his neck and head.

Semko stared in disbelief as he saw the Russian topple backward to the ground. He looked down at Rachel and saw her right hand was inside the center section of her shoulder bag; the tip of the integral sound suppressor on the Walther PPKS inside the hidden compartment was flush with the opening at one end of the bag and pointed in the direction where the Russian had been standing.

"Damn!" Semko said with genuine admiration and astonishment. "You're somethin' else. Remind me never again to question a woman when she wants to bring her purse."

He then rushed to the front of the shed and peered around the corner. Leonov and the three men had reached the front of the house and were out of sight. Semko quickly pulled Mikoyan's body inside, then picked up his weapon.

The distinctive report of the two short bursts he fired into the air from the AKR resounded loudly off the surrounding hills.

"That should buy us some time," he told Rachel. "And we're out of here."

"What about the documents in the briefcase?"

"What documents?" But Semko had never been very good at lying, and the fact that he knew precisely what Rachel meant showed in his expression.

"You know what I'm talking about."

"Forget them. Your mission was to get Strasser. It's over. It makes no sense to press our luck; three of them are still out there armed with submachine guns, and they know how to use them."

"I want to get the documents that were in the briefcase."

"I can't let you do that. I gave my word to a friend that I was out of it. My only objective was to get Strasser."

"And how are you going to stop me?"

"I won't. But I won't help you either."

"Your friend lied to you; you know that."

"I think they lied to him," Semko said, then cast an anxious glance in the direction of the house. "Look, they're going to come looking for the guy you just shot anytime now. We've got to get out of here."

Rachel considered her options, and had no desire to face the remaining Russians alone. She believed Semko meant what he had said, and reconciled herself to forgoing the documents and considering her original mission accomplished.

"Are you coming?" Semko said, and stepped outside the shed to watch for the Russians.

Rachel came out and stood at his side. "You disappoint me, Semko."

"Don't let it bother you too much, I do it to myself all the time," Semko said, and led the way as they sprinted across the yard to disappear into the cover of the woods beyond the well.

The man Leonov sent to expedite Mikoyan's return came running back to where the undamaged car they had appropriated from the dead terrorists was idling in front of the house.

"Anatoli is dead," he shouted to Leonov. "The Americans are gone."

"Get in," Leonov said, and ordered the man at the wheel to drive off. He cared nothing about the Americans, or anything else, now that he had what he believed to be the last copies of the Goering File in his possession.

"What about Mikoyan's body, and the others?"

"What about them?" Leonov said, with the knowledge that they had carried no identification. "We can't take them with us. They died a hero's death. Remember them for that."

The driver pulled the car into a tight turn and sped away from the house. Leonov looked back over his shoulder, clutching the briefcase in his lap. Semko and Rachel were nowhere in sight. A costly and near-disastrous operation, he thought, but it was over. Before the day ended he would be back in his office at Yasenevo, an office he vowed never to leave again if he could help it.

« 35 »

IN THE DIRECTOR'S private dining room on the seventh floor of CIA headquarters in Langley, Virginia, George Sinclair poured himself a glass of scotch, and one for Alfred Palmer. The real-time report Sinclair had received from the Munich base chief, who had observed at a distance most of what occurred at Strasser's farm, and relayed it back to the twenty-four-hour operations center over the satellite radio as it was happening, did not conclusively establish that the Russians had succeeded in getting the copy of the Goering File in Strasser's possession. Leonov had been seen leaving with a briefcase, but there was no way of knowing what was in it. Six hours later, Jack Brannigan's call from Semko confirmed that the Russians had indeed gotten what they were after, and the DCI was in a mood to celebrate.

Brannigan's pointed absence from the quiet celebration dinner was felt all the more for the resignation he had submitted to the DCI little more than one hour ago. But then all operations had their casualties, Sinclair thought as he and Palmer raised their glasses to the continued success of BACKLASH, and despite the occasional setbacks, the game always went on as before.

*   *   *

FOUR THOUSAND SIX hundred miles east of where the director of the Central Intelligence Agency and his counterintelligence chief sat toasting each other, Nikolai Leonov walked across the parking area inside the high-security compound at Yasenevo. It was just past 2:00 A.M., and he had spent the past three hours with the chief of the Russian External Intelligence Service, briefing him in depth on the events of the past five days. When he finished, there had been praise for his handling of the operation and promises of a promotion to full colonel.

Leonov should have been in high spirits after the meeting, but he could not help thinking about the small inconsistencies that had crept into his thoughts as he made his detailed report to his superior. If pressed, he could not have delineated exactly what was troubling him; it was more a sense of things being slightly out of kilter, things that had perhaps come to him too easily, or had been handled in a way that seemed far from the level of professionalism he had expected from the CIA. But there was nothing concrete, nothing to fix on with any degree of certainty, and he forced the troublesome thoughts from his mind as he drove out of the compound. It had ended well. The Goering File was secure. What more could he ask?

ON THE DRIVE back to Munich, Semko had stopped at a service plaza on the autobahn and placed an anonymous call to the police station in Baiersbronn to give them directions to Strasser's base of operations, and a brief description of what they would find there. It was then that he learned that a forest service employee and a distant neighbor had heard the explosions from the grenades and the rockets and called the police, who were now on the scene. The policeman Semko spoke with was more interested in who he was and how he knew so much about what had happened, a line of questioning that immediately prompted him to hang up the phone and leave the service plaza in the event the call was being traced.

He and Rachel arrived back in Munich late that afternoon and had an early dinner at a small Bavarian restaurant off the Marienplatz before returning to the hotel for a long, and much needed, night's sleep. They were lost in their own private thoughts, and feeling the unsettling effects of what Semko referred to as coming down from a combat high (the ebbing of the sustained adrenaline flow that had coursed through their bodies that morning). Their conversations on the drive to Munich and during dinner had been strained, with long silences, and did not become any less so when they drove to the airport the next morning.

It had been only five days since they first met in New York City, but the intensity of the time they had spent together, and the need to rely on each other in the life-and-death situations they had faced and survived, had formed a bond that would last for the rest of their lives, even if their paths were never to cross again.

Semko's flight to Frankfurt with a connection to New York did not leave for another hour, and he waited with Rachel in the boarding lounge until her El Al flight from Munich to Tel Aviv was announced. Semko had never been very good at partings, in fact he dreaded them, as well as any situations that involved outward displays of emotion.

They walked together to the gate, and as Rachel put her carry-on bags down and turned to say good-bye, their eyes met and held. Semko stood silently before her, hoping the right words would come. He was about to reach out and shake her hand when Rachel bridged the awkward moment by moving closer and giving him a quick embrace.

"We were a good team," she said.

"Yeah. We had our moments, didn't we?"

"Are you going to make amends with the CIA?"

"No. I called the DDO last night; briefed him on how it came out. He said all was forgiven, but I've had enough."

"Getting too old to walk the edge?"

"Something like that. I read somewhere that when you look into the abyss, the abyss also looks into you. I think I saw something looking back this time."

"That's from *Thus Spake Zarathustra,*" Rachel said. "And I'm impressed. You've read Nietzsche."

"Yeah. I like his poems."

Rachel smiled and picked up her bags. "Be well, Semko," she said, then turned and started down the boarding ramp.

"Hey!" Semko called after her. "You said your parents live in New York?"

"Yes, they do."

"Well, I'll probably be in Washington for a while. When you come to visit them, give me a call. I'll come up; we could have dinner or something."

"That would be nice," Rachel said, then continued down the ramp, knowing that it was probably the last time she would ever see him, and denying the strong, conflicting emotions she was feeling at that moment. There was so much about him that was right, but the same instincts that had set off warning lights when she first saw him standing at the sea lion pool in Central Park again reminded her that the attraction was for all the wrong reasons. There was no denying his basic nature. He was a man who would always keep himself to himself, and seek out the action wherever it was; and miss it if he ever tried to convince himself that he no longer needed it.

She looked back as she neared the end of the ramp, and saw him still standing at the gate. He waved as she turned and entered the plane, a little-boy-lost look on his face that was completely out of character.

SEMKO ENTERED THE small Upper East Side bar just off Lexington Avenue shortly after six o'clock to find Lt. Mike Kelly waiting for him in a darkened corner booth. He looked every inch the New York cop as his eyes flicked around the room, sizing up every customer at the bar and anyone who came in the door.

Although the "Art Murders" had stopped as Semko told him they would, Kelly still had fourteen open homicide cases and was under increasing pressure to solve them from City Hall and the brass at One Police Plaza, who were being battered by the news media. His investigation had gone nowhere since he last saw Semko five days ago, and it was with eager anticipation that he left the task force office and drove uptown to meet him when he called from the airport.

"To tell you the truth," Kelly said as Semko slipped into the booth, "I didn't expect to hear from you again."

"I gave you my word."

"That you did. So tell me you've got good news."

"Okay. I've got good news." Semko motioned to the bartender to draw him a beer, then waited until he brought it to the booth before continuing.

"Well, you going to tell me what it is, or am I supposed to guess?" Kelly said as Semko took a long drink from the frosted glass.

"By this time tomorrow, the police in Baiersbronn, Germany, should have a complete work-up done on the bodies they pulled out of an old farm in the mountains yesterday. Send them the prints you lifted from the minivan in the alley behind that art gallery. Ask them to check them against the guys they got in their morgue. I guarantee they'll have a match for you, and in all probability a photograph of the guy the way they found him at the scene. His face wasn't shot up, so the cop from the scooter over at Sutton Place should be able to make a positive identification from the photo; he saw him drive off in the van."

"You said bodies? The Germans have more than one?"

"Oh, yeah. But only one of them had anything to do with

what happened here. And you can count on the German cops having as many questions for you as you have for them, because they won't be able to ID your man from his fingerprints, and they're going to want to know who the hell he is.''

''Do you know who he is?''

Semko took another drink of his beer and peered over the top of the glass at Kelly. ''Yeah, I know.''

''So, who is he?''

''You didn't get it from me, understood?''

''No problem.''

Semko gave him Strasser's name and told him of his past affiliation with the Stasi and of his terrorist activities after the collapse of East Germany.

''So this Strasser was stealing art to raise money for his terrorist operations?''

''Right.''

''And what about the paintings he stole?''

''Follow the trail from the art gallery.''

''We've been doing that, but his partner skipped, and we haven't been able to find him or any records.''

''Get a list of the phone calls made from the gallery for the three days prior to the fire. You'll find what you're looking for.''

''I have somebody on it, but so far we haven't come up with anything. He made a lot of calls.''

''Check out an art dealer by the name of Drussard in Paris.''

''And how does the CIA tie into all this?'' Kelly said, scribbling in his notebook as he spoke.

''CIA? What CIA?''

''Okay, forget I asked that one. What about the Russians?''

''Can't tell you that either. Correct me if I'm wrong, but what I already gave you should be enough to close out the homicide cases here in the city and get the press off your back.''

"If it all checks out and I get a certificate of death for Strasser from the Germans, it's definitely enough." Kelly extended his hand and Semko shook it. "I know you've stuck your neck out for me, and I appreciate it. Maybe I can return the favor sometime."

"You want a beer?" Semko said.

Kelly glanced at his watch. "Sure, I'm off duty."

Semko signaled to the bartender, then waited until he brought the two beers to the booth before leaning across the table to speak in a low, conspiratorial voice to Kelly.

"Listen, what you just said about maybe returning the favor sometime. You mean that?"

"Yeah. I meant it. And why do I have this feeling I'm going to live to regret it?"

EPILOGUE

THE FIRST THING that struck Semko about Tel Aviv was how modern it was; the second was the number of soldiers. They were everywhere, strolling along the streets, shopping, relaxing on benches on the promenade overlooking the ocean, simply going about their daily business. Some wore civilian clothes, but all openly carried Uzi submachine guns slung over their shoulders as casually as the English carried umbrellas against the possibility of rain.

Before leaving New York, Semko had called an old friend from his Delta Force days, now working as a civilian with State Department security at the American embassy in Tel Aviv. With only sketchy background information, a last name, and unsure of exactly where in Israel the person lived, Semko was prepared to hear that the task was impossible. But the name was not as common as he had feared it might be, and six hours later his friend, after enlisting the aid of an Israeli colleague, called him back with the full name and address of the person he believed Semko was looking for.

Forty-five minutes after leaving Ben Gurion Airport Semko's taxi pulled up in front of a stone walkway that led through well-landscaped grounds to a one-story modern home on a small estate in the exclusive Tel Aviv suburb of Savian.

When the cab had stopped, Semko opened the suitcase he had insisted on keeping with him, and removed his clothes from inside and placed them on the backseat. As the curious driver watched through the rearview mirror, Semko pulled four Velcro strips loose at the inside corners of the oversized suitcase, and exposed the false bottom to remove a flat package wrapped in plain brown paper and measuring twenty-four inches by eighteen inches in size. Semko told the driver to wait for him, then got out of the cab, taking the package with him.

The old woman who answered the door had the most haunting eyes Semko had ever seen. Her face was deeply lined and she was small and frail, but Semko immediately saw the family resemblance and recognized the familiar inner strength and self-confidence that emanated from her.

"Mrs. Sidrane?" Semko said. "Esther Sidrane?"

"Yes. I am Esther Sidrane."

"My name is Mike Semko, and I have something for you; actually it's from your granddaughter, Rachel."

"From Rachel?" The old woman smiled at the thought of her granddaughter. "You are an American?"

"Yes."

"A friend of Rachel's from the university?"

"A friend of Rachel's."

"Please, come in," she said, and stepped aside as Semko entered the marble foyer of what he could see was a remarkably beautiful house.

"Why didn't Rachel bring it herself?"

"It's sort of a surprise, for both of you," Semko said, and handed her the package.

"Is it for an occasion, or am I to open it now?"

"Whenever you wish."

Esther placed the package on a table in the foyer and began removing the wrapping paper. As she pulled aside the folds and saw what was inside, she let out a soft cry and then stood

motionless except for a slight trembling in her hands. Semko
saw her waver and list to one side, and caught her before she
fell. He swept her up in his arms and carried her to a sofa in a
bright and airy room off the foyer where he laid her down
gently and placed a pillow beneath her feet.

"Are you all right, Mrs. Sidrane? Do you want me to call a
doctor?"

It was then, when the old woman looked up at him and
smiled, that Semko saw the tears in her eyes, and the expression on her face that was a strange mixture of joy and sorrow.

"Please, bring it to me."

Semko brought the package to her and stood silently by as
she raised herself to a sitting position and held it in her lap to
carefully remove the rest of the paper.

"Are you sure you're feeling all right?"

"Yes. I'm fine. It was just the shock of seeing it again.
Please, Mr. Semko, you must stay and have some tea and fruit,
and we will talk."

"I'd like that very much, but I'm afraid I have to be going."

She stared deep into Semko's eyes and smiled in a way he
had never seen anyone smile. A calmness, a sense of great
relief seemed to have descended on her, as though a tremendous burden had been swept away.

"Thank you so much for coming," she said, and then
paused to look again at the painting. "I'm sorry, I don't know
what else to say. I can't began to tell you how much this means
to me."

"I think I know," Semko said, then bent down to kiss her
softly on the cheek. "It was very nice meeting you, Mrs.
Sidrane, and please give Rachel my regards."

Esther Sidrane did not see Semko leave the house. She sat
immobile, mesmerized by the painting, her thoughts filled with
bittersweet memories and the image of her husband on that

day in Vienna so long ago when she brought their newborn daughter home from the hospital, and he had given her the treasured gift.

"Oh, Eugen," she murmured as she caressed the frame with her fingertips, and then in a soft, plaintive voice began to recite the mourner's Kaddish.

SEMKO HAD TWO hours before his return flight to New York, and as he sat drinking a cup of coffee in the airport café, he thought of calling Rachel. He got as far as looking up her number in the telephone directory, but then changed his mind. He had done what he had promised himself he would do, and it was time to move on. Not the most intuitive of men when it came to the opposite sex, he did, however, recognize an impossible relationship when he saw one. Rachel was beautiful and intelligent and had a sense of herself that he greatly admired, but he knew he had nothing to offer her, nor did he deceive himself with the notion that she would ever get involved with someone like him. He had long ago resigned himself to the fact that he would, in all probability, spend the rest of his life in a series of meaningless relationships, and had accepted that as his fate after the mess he had made of his marriage to Janet.

He sat in the café until it was near the boarding time for his flight, then left the main terminal area and went to stand in line to go through the security checkpoint at the concourse leading to his departure gate. The young woman who thoroughly examined his carry-on bag smiled flirtatiously as she zipped it closed, and was about to hand it back when her eyes widened as she looked past him to see two airport security guards carrying Uzi submachine guns hurrying in her direction. Semko turned to see what had startled her just as the two men stopped on either side of him, each grabbing one of his arms.

"You will come with us, Mr. Semko. Immediately."

"What for?" Semko said. "What's this about?" and then

his stomach tightened into a knot when it occurred to him what might have happened: they had somehow found out he had smuggled the painting into the country. Then Semko remembered the taxi driver; he must have reported what he had seen.

The two men led him into a small room off the concourse, obviously used for interrogating suspicious passengers. The room was bare except for a small table and two chairs in the center.

"You will wait here," one of the men said. Then they both left and locked the door behind them.

Semko cursed and kicked one of the chairs across the room. One of the few times in my life I try to do something good and decent, he thought, and I screw it up. He pulled the upended chair upright and turned it around to straddle it, resting his chin on the back and staring at the stark white walls of the room.

It was well over an hour before he heard someone placing a key in the door, and looked up to see Rachel enter the room.

"Ah, damn," Semko said, and got up from the chair.

"And it's nice to see you again, too."

"Hey, look, I'm really sorry I put you and your grandmother in the middle of this. I'll make sure they understand you had nothing to do with it."

Rachel walked over to him and reached up to place her hands gently on his face. She stood on her toes and kissed him, long and passionately, then stepped back and smiled.

"That was a beautiful and wonderful thing you did, Mike Semko. And I'll love you for it as long as I live."

"Wait a minute," Semko said, upon regaining his composure from Rachel's kiss. "You're responsible for this? You had them lock me up in here?"

"I have friends in high places."

"Nice. Real nice. I've been sitting here wondering what it

was going to be like rotting in an Israeli jail for the next ten years.''

''By the time my grandmother told me about your visit, I realized your plane would be gone before I could get here. I wanted to thank you.''

''You don't have telephones in Israel?''

''How on earth did you get the painting?''

''You sure you want to know?''

''Yes, I do.''

''Remember the New York cop? Kelly?''

''The one from Sutton Place?''

''Yeah,'' Semko said. ''I did him a favor; he offered to reciprocate. I took him up on it. Once he heard the story, he was more than willing to help. Anyway, your grandmother's painting, along with some of the others they found in the secret room in that guy Stewart's house, were locked up in the property room in the nineteenth precinct station house. They were holding them until the courts could decide who got them. Kelly found out that they were about to honor the Metropolitan Museum of Art's claim on your grandmother's painting under the conditions of Stewart's will, since they couldn't prove it was stolen art. So, to make a long story short, we came up with a plan.''

''Sooner or later they're going to find out it's missing, Semko. And they're also going to find out that I was making inquiries about it when I was in New York.''

Semko flashed a Cheshire cat grin. ''No, they won't.''

''What aren't you telling me?''

''I'm sure it won't come as any great surprise to you that the city you were born and raised in has the largest concentration of crooks and con men in the world, not to mention weirdos. And the cops know every one of them. Would you believe that there are even people there who will paint anything you want: van Goghs, Monets, Rembrandts, even sign them with the real guy's name. Takes an expert to tell the difference."

"The Metropolitan Museum of Art is going to spot it as a fake the minute they lay eyes on it."

"So? Stewart had a fake painting in his secret room? What can I tell you."

Rachel smiled and slowly shook her head. "As I've said before, Semko, you're more than just a pretty face."

"Ain't it the truth. Sometimes I even surprise myself."

"And me. In a way I never expected."

"That's better than disappointing you, huh?"

"Much better," Rachel said. "So, you were going to leave without even calling to say hello?"

"A little bit of me goes a long way."

"You missed your plane."

"I think there's a couple more flights to New York today. I'm sure I can get on one of them."

"How would you like to spend a few lazy days in a comfortable apartment overlooking the Mediterranean? I can show you the sights. Israel is a beautiful country; it grows on you."

"Whose apartment?"

"Mine."

"I think I'd like that. You're not going to seduce me, are you?"

"Not in your wildest dreams, Semko."

"Hell, Sidrane, in my wildest dreams you'd take a number."

It was the first time Semko had heard her laugh, and he laughed with her as she slipped her arm through his and they left the room.

"You're a real charmer, you know that?" Rachel said, and squeezed his arm affectionately as they walked along the concourse.

"So I've been told. Listen, I'd pretty much sell my soul for another one of those kisses before I leave."

"It could happen," Rachel said, then looked up at him with a smile and a wink. "I'll tell you what I will do, if you're a real good boy."

"What's that?"

"I'll teach you how to hit what you shoot at."

J.C. POLLOCK
IS THE MASTER
OF NON-STOP ACTION

From the bamboo jungles of Southeast Asia to the Iron Curtain of Eastern Europe, J.C. Pollock's bestselling action thrillers are taut, hard-hitting adventures featuring the most advanced special-warfare techniques and weaponry. Read them all—if your heart can stand the action.

- ❏ **CENTRIFUGE**   11156-0 $4.99
- ❏ **CROSSFIRE**   11602-3 $5.99
- ❏ **THE DENNECKER CODE**   20086-5 $4.99
- ❏ **MISSION M.I.A.**   15819-2 $5.99
- ❏ **PAYBACK**   20518-2 $5.99